#2
A West Siblings Novel

Running OUT OF Road

Emily Tudor

Copyright © 2026 by Emily Tudor

All rights reserved.

No part of this publication may be reproduced, distributed, or transmitted in any form or by any means, including photocopying, recording, or other electronic or mechanical methods, without the prior written permission of the publisher, except as permitted by U.S. copyright law. For permission requests, contact@authoremilytudor.com

The story, all names, characters, and incidents portrayed in this production are fictitious. No identification with actual persons (living or deceased), places, buildings, and products is intended or should be inferred.

No part of this work may be used for generative artificial intelligence (AI) training. No AI was used in the creation of this book.

Book Cover by Hannah Nguyen

Illustrations by Hannah Nguyen

Edited by Kristen Hamilton

DaisyTheo art by @raozify on Instagram

DomTeags art by @petrichorpeacee on Instagram

VinceBree art by @misunderart on Instagram

TristanLivvy art by @summerrgrove on Instagram

1st edition 2026

For anyone wondering why they can't reach into their body and fix themselves. I promise it won't be like this forever. Here's to learning another way to climb the tree.

And for my younger self who always wondered why she was so much more sensitive and emotional than everyone else. This was all for you.

Recommended Reading Order

Hi! The book you're about to read is *technically* a spin-off from the other duet I have published. Now, it's not necessary to read *The Hart Sisters* duet prior to this one, but there are a few spoilers for those two books in this novel since it takes place after the events of that duet. However, if you do want to read it in the proper order, it can be found below!

Reading Order:
The Road Not Taken (Hart Sisters #1)
The Road Less Traveled By (Hart Sisters #2)
On the Road to Ruin (West Siblings #1)
Running Out of Road (West Siblings #2)

Content Warnings

This book features alcoholism/drinking on page, descriptions of grief, accidental overdose on-page, verbal abuse (mentioned on-page but not explicitly shown, not between main couple), depression, mentions of suicide, thoughts of low self-esteem, body image struggles, physical altercation not shown on page. Please proceed cautiously.

Below are some resources if you need them.
988 you can text and call in English and Spanish. The crisis text line—text 741741 in English and Spanish.
https://allianceofhope.org/ is a support resource specifically for people who have lost loved ones to suicide—they have community forums, support groups, and general information.
https://findahelpline.com/ is a huge resource of support hotlines, especially for anyone outside of the US or want support in a language other than English or Spanish.

Dicktionary

For those who want to skip to the spicy parts, or those who want to skip straight to them.

Chapter 21
Chapter 26
Chapter 27
Chapter 29
Chapter 42

Playlist

Franklin House — Brenn!
Call Your Mom — Noah Kahan
chaotic — Tate McRae
Looking For — Brenn!
To Be Loved — Adele
MACHINE GHOST — Erin LeCount
We Grew Old — Yuat
The House I Grew Up In — Sydney Rose
Camden — Gracie Abrams
Let Down — Radiohead
The Yawning Grave — Lord Huron
Look After You — The Fray
I THINK I'M LOST AGAIN — Chase Atlantic
Girl Of Constant Sorrow — Avery Anna
Pieces — The Band CAMINO
The Smallest Man Who Ever Lived — Taylor Swift
Robin — Taylor Swift
[there is still time] — Searows
The Garden — Devon Gabriella
Visiting Hours — Ed Sheeran
Stubborn Love — The Lumineers
Save Me — Noah Kahan
Who We Are — Hozier

So Long, Honey — Caamp
Let It Happen — Gracie Abrams
In The Wind — Lord Huron
Headlights — In Color
colorful — asiris
How To Live — Del Water Gap
Obsessive — Chase Atlantic
No I'm not in love — Tate McRae
Pool — Samia
Lovesick — Paige Fish
Nettles — Ethel Cain
Carry You — Novo Amor
Bad Omens — 5 Seconds of Summer
Something, Somehow, Someday — ROLE MODEL
In the Light — The Lumineers
chemtrails — Lizzy McAlpine
Penthouse — Kelsea Ballerini
Words — Gregory Alan Isakov
White Winter Hymnal — Fleet Foxes
hope ur ok — Olivia Rodrigo
Packing It Up — Gracie Abrams
I've Seen It — Olivia Dean
Every Side Of You — Vance Joy
Dog Days Are Over — Florence + the Machine

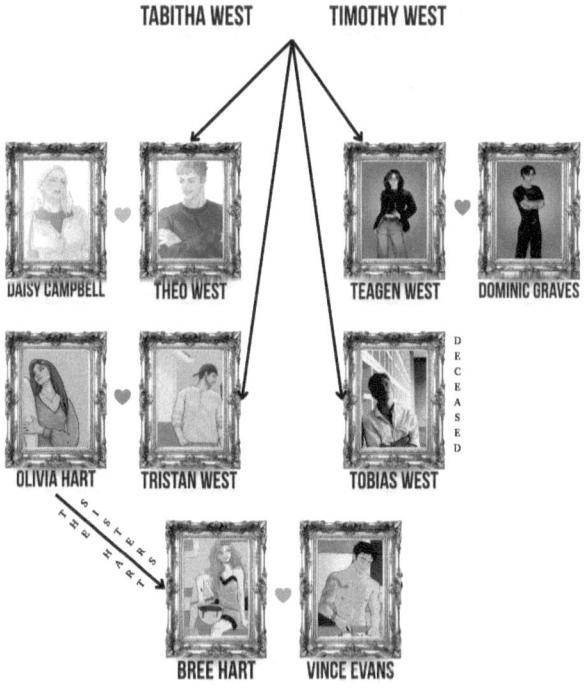

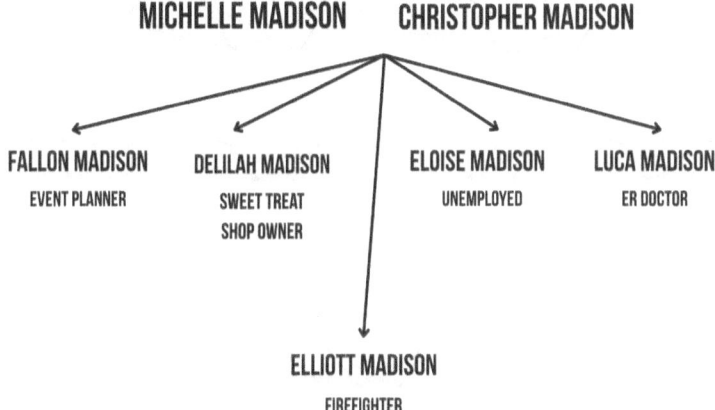

"Some people care too much. I think it's called love."

— A.A. Milne, *Winnie the Pooh*

"It's not your fault."

— Sean Maguire, *Good Will Hunting*

Prologue

The Funeral

— FRANKLIN HOUSE BY BRENN!

Numb.

It's all I am lately and it's all I'll ever be because my brother is dead. Today is the day we lay him to rest, six feet in the fucking ground, never to be seen or heard from again.

Today is the worst day of my life.

I take another sip from my flask, wanting to stop my mind from feeling anything. Every time I catch a glimpse of the casket, I'm reminded I couldn't save Tobias. He was struggling—barely holding on because of the weight of his own mind—and I couldn't protect him.

The ghost of who my brother once was is going to haunt me forever. I could have helped, could have reminded him how loved he was even if his mind tricked him and said otherwise.

I'll survive this. I know the ache will go away. As time goes on, it will hurt less and less that my brother no longer exists, and I'm supposed to mourn him with all of these strangers beside me. Strangers who barely knew him, at least not like we all did as his siblings.

Tristan, Teags, and I are going to have a hole in our family forever. First our dad and now Tobias. Two family members I loved—one who created me and one who grew up with me—are both gone, and there's nothing I can do to bring either of them back.

I take another sip from my flask, hating the emotions spreading through my body. I don't want to feel like this. I want it to go away. I want it to stop because the weight of it will crush me. I know it will. I've never been good at standing on my own two feet. I'm not as strong as Tristan is. I'm not as resilient as Teags is. The two of them were always better equipped at handling things like this—the big emotions.

I'm the weak link. I can't handle all of this. I can't fake a sad smile and thank people for their condolences during this tough time.

It's not a tough time. It's *the* toughest and nothing anyone says will bring him back.

My siblings know it. If my mom were coherent today, she would know it too. Tristan laid both of our outfits out this morning, no doubt knowing simply getting out of bed would be too much. He's fallen right back into caretaker mode, just like always. It's what he did when our dad died, and I should have known it's what he would do again. He rushed back here from California, uprooting his life to come back and take care of us all.

I was away when I got the call from Teagen. I have lots of regrets, but one of the biggest ones is calling my sister a liar when she told me the news about our brother. She was sobbing on the phone, and I called her a liar. I told her she was mistaken, and once it really hit me, I checked his location and it was off. I knew then and there that what Teags had told me was true.

I immediately went to a bar and got drunk because I didn't want to feel the unbearable weight that flooded my body as soon as the words sunk into my brain. I don't even know how I got onto the plane back to Pennsylvania. These past few weeks have all blurred together into one long nightmare I can't wake up from.

It's been two weeks since my brother died, and every time I feel like punching something, I take a sip. Part of me knows I'm not going to drink my brother back to life, but I don't want to feel this pain if I don't have to. I'm not even sure how the human body is cut out for feelings as big as the ones I've felt recently.

My eyes can barely move off of the final resting place of Tobias. Ever since we got in here, I keep wishing he would come out of it. It also doesn't help that we're all in the front row. I have a direct line to the place where my brother rests, and it's all I can focus on.

I take another sip as Tristan and his buddies get over to where our family is sitting, and the funeral director steps out as everyone takes a seat. He might say a few things, but I barely hear anything as my mom heads for the podium. I take another drink as Tristan moves from beside me.

This is too much. It's all too fucking much. This place, these people, they all serve as a reminder of my dead brother.

I'm sure I'll survive this, but I'll never recover from hearing those three words across the line that day. I'll always be stuck in that phone call, the words telling me he was dead echoing through my brain.

I had talked to him two days before that. I called him because I was struggling down in South Carolina. Work had been keeping me in one place, which stressed me out. Stagnant is not a word used to describe me, and being on the same assignment for longer than planned started to make my bones ache. I called Tobias and talked about my issues for two hours before he had to go do something, and I thanked him for always listening to me. The last thing I ever heard him say was that.

"Any time, brother. You know that's what I'm here for."

Then I got the news.

Why didn't I press him more when he brushed me off when I asked him how he was doing? Why didn't I try a *little* fucking harder for him to tell me the truth about how he was feeling? Why did he put my shit before his? I didn't know he was struggling, and I keep replaying the call we had, wondering if I missed something.

I'm pissed off—mostly at myself, but also at him. I haven't admitted that out loud yet. I've been too afraid to because I know how much of an asshole I sound like if I do. I might be the worst brother in the world for being angry at him, but why didn't he reach out? We could have helped. We could have tried to.

At the end of the day, I'm left here feeling like a failure, the worst brother on the planet, and a fucking idiot.

He needed saving, and nobody could save him because we didn't know. Hindsight is the worst thing in the world, and I have to live with this feeling forever. I have to live with knowing I couldn't save my brother from what he was struggling with.

Like I said, I'll probably survive this. I'll survive these feelings, this hatred, this ghostly feeling where I don't actually want to exist, all of it. I will survive because I have to—because Tobias didn't.

But I can't think of any moment in the future where I'll ever recover from this. I don't see how that's possible, and I don't know if I'll ever recover from my brother no longer being on this planet. I'll never see him smile again. I'll never look at the scratches of our heights on the wall at our childhood home the same again. He'll no longer grow old with the rest of us.

Tristan sits next to me, and I didn't hear a single word of what he said. I throw my arm around him because he looks like he could use something to lean on, someone to hold him up straight because he no longer can—or maybe I'm the one who needs it.

"You did good," I say as I hand him my flask.

He takes it, finishing it off, but little does he know I have two more in the car waiting for me. "Thanks."

After the funeral, Tobias is buried. As the group of us throw dirt on the casket where it will rest forever, I can feel myself breaking a little bit more.

By the time I get home and back to the room I grew up in, I black out, not wanting the excruciating pain to swallow me whole, and knowing it will anyway, sober or not. I'm not going to be able to outrun it, but as soon as it catches me, I want to be as numb as I can.

I'm empty, and going forward, that's all I want to be.

Chapter One

Two Years Later

— CALL YOUR MOM BY NOAH KAHAN

"Another," I signal to the bartender, my legs feeling like they're no longer attached to my body.

"Here you go." He slides the drink over to me. "Anything else? A coffee or something?"

I nod. "Coffee. Can you split it into two cups?"

He looks at me a beat too long before walking toward the pot. I know it's an odd request, but I'm not about to explain myself to him. I'm a frequent flyer at this bar—when I'm home, at least—but I don't know his name or anything about him. Pretty much all he knows about me is my drink order. Just how I like it—no attachments and no small talk while I'm drowning in my sorrows.

I've stopped understanding myself and everything about my life for the last couple years. Ever since my brother died, I've been adrift, unable to put my feet back on the ground. After doing that for so long, it feels like the only thing I know how to do well.

I take the shot of bourbon, still staring at the two coffee cups in front of me. I was trying to take it slow, knowing I have places to be in the next few days, but I think that's why I'm here in the first place.

I'm about to reach the last stop. The final destination on the road trip Tobias set me on after he died. I'm still not sure why he's sent me around the country, but I'm honoring his last wishes.

I have all of the envelopes from the previous destinations, but according to the instructions in the first letter, I can't open them yet. I can't open them until I have *all* of them, and I can already tell when I get to Vermont it's going to fuck with my head. Tobias and I loved our vacation house in Vermont. We used to beg our mom to go back every summer, but we never did after our father died. In a few days, I'll be back in Nettles for the first time since I was a child.

This will be my first time back without Tobias. Back to the place we used to love. Back to a home that hasn't been ours in a long time even though my mom refuses to sell it. I don't know why she never wanted to get rid of it, but when I asked her about it when I got back here the other day, she told me there were still boxes of our stuff up there.

She always meant to go back and sort through them, but it seems by some twist of fate, Tobias is sending me to do what our mom never could.

I take the shot, wanting to numb the pain I'm feeling about missing my brother, before the bartender comes over with another one.

"Coffee okay?"

"It's fine." I haven't touched it. "I'll do another bourbon and close out my tab."

The part I don't understand is why he planned all of this for me before he passed. He left letters and sent me on this goose chase, but he had to have planned it all before he died. He took the time to map this all out for me and the worst part is I have no fucking idea as to why.

There were so many sides to my brother that I never knew about, and now I'll never discover anything new about him again. Because he's dead.

He's gone, and all I have left of him is this bucket list and all the pieces he scattered around the country. I don't know if he's trying to show me something. I don't know what his end goal with this was, but the sooner I get up to Vermont, the sooner I'll find out.

I down the last shot the bartender gave me, throw a few bills down, and thank the version of myself a few years ago that got the perfect job to be able to complete the bucket list Tobias left for me.

I work as a photojournalist for a magazine in Pennsylvania. I've always loved traveling, especially lately when home doesn't really feel as such. Don't get me wrong, I miss my mom and my siblings while I'm gone, but part of me has always felt drawn to other places. I like discovering new towns, places, and faces. I love seeing other people's lives through the lens of my camera. My favorite thing in the world as I travel all over is realizing I'm a guest in someone's hometown. Here I am passing through this place I've never been, but for someone else, it's home. For someone else, they know every twist and turn of the road, but I have to use my map to get around.

It's also the perfect job for me because it allows me to never stay in one place, and I can pick the places I want to go and photograph, unless they require me to be somewhere specific. I've never gone out of the country for work, but after my small stint in Vermont, maybe that's where I'll head next.

I haven't thought too much about it yet, knowing Vermont could be my toughest and most emotional search yet. All of the other places he sent me were quicker trips, but I can already feel in my bones that this one is going to take me by surprise. I'm not sure why I feel this way—the alcohol probably isn't helping—but I'm equally terrified and curious as to what my future holds.

The only thing I'm certain of is that the future no longer holds one of my brothers, and I'll have to live with that until I meet him wherever he is. I'm sure he'll be standing at whatever door waits for me, ushering me in with a smile on his face.

For now, I have to get through my life without him, and I haven't figured out how to do that yet.

"Knock, knock," my mother says as she enters the room. "I brought you some breakfast before your long drive."

Forcing my eyes open after a night like yesterday is difficult, but I do it because I don't want my mom worrying about me. She's been through enough.

When I see what's on the tray next to my bed, I smile. She made me my favorite breakfast from when I was young—chocolate chip pancakes with strawberries.

"I thought while I had you here, I'd savor it." She sits on my bed, her hand finding my cheek. My mother, Tabitha West, might be the strongest person I know. She lost my father—her husband and other-half—and her child.

When all of us kids were growing up, I think we all idolized how in love my parents were. Except maybe my sister because she's always gagged at the thought of being in love. But me? I knew I wanted a love like theirs someday. Life hasn't driven me down that path in the last twenty-six years, and all hope for the future has been lost. Love is in the backseat for me. I don't want to know what comes next; thinking about the years ahead is hopeless too. I don't want to know what comes after the last letter I'll ever get from my brother. I have more than my siblings and my mom got, but no amount of anything will feel like enough. Everyone got one, but I get one every time I get to a place on this list. He leaves them for me, small clues of where to start to find whatever breadcrumbs he's left for me.

Vermont is the last stop, and I'm determined to run this road out as long as I can. Work doesn't mind, especially since I've been sending them pictures for different articles at every stop. I'm technically a freelance photographer for the magazine, and I have no desire to settle down and get a desk job.

"Theo?"

My mom's voice shakes me out of my hungover haze.

"Are you alright?" She touches my face, her palm against my forehead. "You feel a bit warm."

"I'm fine." I sluggishly sit up in bed, taking in the room around me that hasn't changed a bit. "Just tired."

"I remember those days." She smiles to herself. "I don't miss them one bit."

"I was celebrating the Fourth of July."

She tilts her head at me. "It's July 10th, darling."

Shit. Is it really? Am I really losing track of time that fucking easily now? "I'm kidding."

She just nods and smiles. I don't think she's buying a word I'm saying. "Eat up before you go. I know Tristan's coming over to help mow the lawn and weed today, so we can help you pack up your car. I assume you haven't packed yet?"

"Of course I haven't." I smirk as I grab the tray, taking a huge bite of the pancakes she made me. It tastes like childhood. Like warm summer mornings when school started and the four of us would all walk to the bus stop together.

"Thank you, Mom. This is perfect before my long drive."

She waves me off. "You know no matter how old you kids get, I'll still take care of you." Her face freezes, no doubt a thought of Tobias floating through her mind as it does mine. "I'll be downstairs if you need me."

"I love you."

"I love you, too, sweetie." She shuts my door with a soft click, and I'm alone again.

I already feel the need to reach for a drink as soon as my thoughts filter in, but I can't. I'm not getting behind the wheel for eight hours drunk. I might be an idiot, and I might not know how to cope with any part of my life right now, but I'm not dangerous.

I try not to think about anything as I eat a few more bites of my breakfast. Once I'm full, I grab my clothes out of the clean bins I folded them in yesterday before I got so drunk I barely remember getting home. Since I don't really have a place of my own, I've been traveling pretty light while completing Tobias's bucket list. One day, I'll find a place where I belong, but for now, I remain a guy whose life can be packed into four large suitcases.

I come back in between every travel stint, so I'm technically still living in my childhood home. The ghost of what my family once was haunts the halls of this place; I still see the younger version of me who felt so full here.

Now I'm empty. Broken. A shell of what I once was.

"Come on, Tobias!" I hear the echo of my younger self as I look out at the tree in the front yard. *"I bet I can beat you to the top."*

"Don't get too cocky," he says. *"I've practically memorized your path up."*

"That's not true," I remember saying to him. *"Come on."*

He beat me climbing the tree that day, and practically every other time before we grew up and the only thing we were climbing was the stairs up to our bedrooms.

I wish I could hold the younger version of myself and shield him from every bad thing headed his way, but I can't. It's going to happen to him, and I can't stop it, I can only watch it happen. I can only feel it happen and remember every sharp pain of grief, hurt, and sadness rip through my bones until there's nothing left.

I try to stop thinking of all this, and as I organize my clothes and zip my suitcases shut, I try to put my thoughts in between my clothes, deodorant, and all the letters that remain unopened.

I drag them all downstairs, taking one final look at my bedroom in case I forgot anything before I open the front door and run straight into my brother. My only remaining brother I can still feel with my two hands, not worried he's going to disappear into thin air. He's the oldest, then it was Tobias when he was still here, then me. My only sister, Teags, is the baby of the family, and boy did she have it rough growing up with three older brothers who annoyed the hell out of her all the time.

Tristan always was the one who wanted to get the hell out of here. From a young age, he had his sights set on any place but Pennsylvania where we all grew up. How ironic it is that we've now switched roles? He's the one who came back, stayed, and built a life here. I'm the one who's running all over the place staying anywhere but here.

"Hey, man," he says, pulling me in for a hug.

"Hey," I say into his ear. "Mom told me you came over to help her weed the yard."

"I'm just trying to help her out since she's been so busy with other things lately. Did she tell you she joined some sort of book club?"

I shake my head. "No. She neglected to tell me that. I really don't know how she manages all of these groups or whatever."

Our mother has decided to try and get out of the house more and put herself back out there. I'm proud of her, but all of this sounds like a lot of work to manage along with her actual job. She works in sales and is able to work from home, so I understand her need to get out of the house since she's always here. Last I heard, she had joined a baking class, knitting for beginners even though she's been knitting for our entire lives, and now she's in a book club.

"She asked Liv to do a talk with the club after she recommended her book," Tristan smiles, no doubt thinking about the love of his life. Olivia

Hart was the best thing to happen to him, and her and her sister Bree's presence in our lives has made everything feel so much richer. I feel lucky to know them both, even in the small bursts I get to see them with how busy we all are.

No matter what, we all carve out time around the holidays to get together. Liv and Bree don't talk to their parents anymore on account of them being horrible people, so we're lucky to have them around our table for every special occasion.

"Mom should be Liv's publicist at this point," I joke, grabbing a suitcase in my hand.

"I'll help you," Tristan says as he grabs two of them, carrying them to my car—a silver 4Runner. I place my stuff in the trunk, the space filling up quickly with all of the other shit I have in here—snacks, pillows, blankets, a snow brush, and all of my camera equipment to be specific. My entire life is in this car, and though that's pretty sad, it's how I prefer it.

"You boys forgot one."

"Mom—"

I cut Tristan off. "Let me get that. It is mine after all."

She just waves her hand at us. "Oh, stop fussing. You both worry too much about me."

"Can you blame us?" Tristan says. "You have a bad back. If you so much as bend to the ground and pull one weed today, I might have to call Vince on you."

"Don't you dare call your soon to be brother-in-law," she points at him. "I am *fine*."

The two of us look at one another, not believing her for a second. Our mother is a stubborn woman, and that's absolutely where Tristan and Teags get it from. I'm more akin to how my dad was—nonchalant and go with the flow. I'll get where I need to go eventually, and whatever road I head down is the right one for me.

"Give your mother a hug before you leave again." She pulls me in before I can open my arms. "You be safe up there, and feel free to call me and ask what things you're not sure to get rid of. Whatever you want to keep you can, but if you get through it all, I'm going to sell it."

"What? You're finally going to sell the house?" Tristan's eyes are bulging out of his head. I thought she had told him and Teags about this, but if he doesn't know, then she doesn't either. To be fair, she hasn't been back to Pennsylvania since Thanksgiving last year, and this does seem like a more in-person conversation. I hope she's doing well in Arizona. I miss my sister and all the cold stares she used to give me when I did something stupid—which was a lot. I honestly don't know how she grew up with the three of us boys and still managed to turn out okay. She might be the most headstrong of all of us, and I'm proud of her every day.

She would probably punch me for saying that because that's just who she is. Though, I feel like all of us are to blame for that. She had to be strong growing up with us three idiots. We were fucking rascals as kids.

"It's time," my mom says. "I've held on long enough."

"I'll send pictures," I tell her. "And I promise I'll call. I'm not really sure how long I'll be up there."

"You never are," Tristan reminds me. "You were in New York City for all of two days, but you were in Charleston for almost a month. That would drive me insane."

"Then it's a good thing you're not the one doing it," I say as I shut the trunk to my car. "I'll see you both soon, and I'll keep in touch like I always do."

"You fucking better," Tristan says as he brings me in for another hug.

"Language," our mom says under her breath.

"Sorry," we say at the same time. She takes one last look at the two of us before disappearing to the backyard, no doubt secretly pulling weeds before Tristan gets back there and starts doing all the dirty work.

"Can I ask you something?" he says, staring at the front of our childhood home for a beat longer than normal.

"Sure."

"What exactly is it that you're looking for on these trips?"

"Why do you ask?" I wonder why this is coming up now.

"Is it a physical thing? Are you looking for him? His ghost? What are you looking for, Theo? Because I can't imagine living your life between suitcases is doing anything fulfilling for you."

I stare at the ground, a small smile coming to my face as I open my car door. He's right. It's not doing anything for me, but that's exactly why I'm doing it. I'm not locked down or tied anywhere, just how I like it.

It's a good question, really, and I do have an answer for him, though he isn't going to like it.

"A reason."

With that, I shut the door, and when I back out of my driveway I take one last look at my childhood home, my only older remaining brother standing in front of it waving at me as I drive out of sight.

Chapter Two

— **CHAOTIC BY TATE MCRAE**

THE WORST PART ABOUT being recently divorced is how easily annoyed you get at the thought of people in love.

"The proposal was perfect," Jamie says as she shoves her ring in my face.

Well, I guess that answers my question of if she's changed since high school. That's the weirdest part of coming back to your hometown. The people you once knew are either gone, have completely changed, or stayed the same. It looks like Jamie hasn't changed a bit, but her soon-to-be-husband, Brooks, is sitting next to her and looks like he'd rather be anywhere else but here.

Ever since high school graduation, he's had this same look on his face that hasn't gone away yet, if ever. I was stupid to think a few years away from here would have drastically changed things. Brooks and I have known one another since we were kids. He's like the brother I never had. I knew him when he still had that blinding smile across his face no matter what time of day it was, but now, this grumpy version of him is all that we get. And you never ask Brooks about what changed with him to make him like this. He never wants to talk about it, and all of Nettles knows not to ask.

A few different things could be causing my cynicism over Jamie and the story of their proposal falling out of her mouth. For one, my divorce was officially finalized after months of fighting with my ex-husband over our assets. Another thing being the look on my friend's face as his fiancé flashes her ring into my face for the thirtieth time.

The ink is finally dry on my divorce papers, yet here I am back in the game doing makeup consultations for brides in Nettles, Vermont—my hometown and the place I ran back to when I fled Boston at the beginning of the year.

Brooks is unhappy. It's easy for me to tell because I'm unhappy, too, just in a different way. He's miserable in this predicament, and I'm upset with the state of my life and how it's unfolded in the past year.

Brooks has been unhappy for years, and he's getting *married* soon. This should be the best time of his life, but I can tell his heart isn't in it. When news spread of their engagement, we were all shocked. Sure, they had been together for a long time—another thing we're all shocked about according to my best friend, Delilah—but this was not the route anyone thought they would take. I guess this is the natural unfolding of things. One minute you're in school, the next you're out in the world dating someone you think is perfect for you, getting married, and talking about kids. Then you're back home, divorced, and your life looks nothing like you thought it would.

His bride-to-be continues talking and I do my best to pretend like I'm actively listening to her, but she's so blinded by the rock on her hand that she doesn't notice the looks I'm giving Brooks, only to be met with his indifferent stare.

I originally told him I wasn't going to work at his wedding, but Jamie wouldn't stop talking about me and how much she wanted me to do her makeup. Apparently, she looked at my portfolio and saw some of the makeup looks I did for higher end clients back in Boston, and wouldn't settle for anything less.

I'm flattered, really I am, but it's hard for me to see the silver lining when I remember my wedding day so clearly. It was supposed to be the best day of my life, and I thought it was. It was all a lie. It was a smoke screen covering up everything else and I can't bear to think about how stupid I was. How young and naive I was to believe my husband was going to love me with everything he had like I had promised to do to him.

I meant the words I vowed, but he didn't, and now I'm back in my hometown, running my own boutique and freelance makeup artist business while I deal with the fallout from my divorce.

"Oh my goodness, I could talk for hours," she says as she takes a sip of the water I brought her at the beginning of the consultation. "But let me pull up the color palette of our wedding so you can start to create some eye looks from that."

"Oh, well, this is the first consult—"

"Yes!" she squeals as she scrolls on her phone. "The first of many meetings between us! I want to do at least a few trials to make sure it's perfect for our wedding."

"Oh, um, that's not—"

She cuts me off again. "I'm sure you can make an exception for me. I want everything to be *perfect*." She squeezes Brooks's face before her phone starts buzzing. "Oh, shoot! I'm going to have to cut this short. Apparently, my bridesmaid dresses are on backorder or something. Honey, do you mind showing her the colors and finishing up here?"

Brooks nods at her, still having said nothing the entire appointment.

"I'll see you at home, darling." The bell above my door dings as she leaves.

The two of us sit for a moment with the small hum of the music I put on each morning at the store in the background.

"So, can I see the palette, *honey*?" He practically flinches as I say it and his eyes pinch together. I can't help but laugh a little as he throws his head back in the chair.

"She's handling all of the plans," he says. "Can she email everything to you?"

I nod. "For someone who's getting married soon, you sure seem like you'd rather be doing anything else."

"For someone who has been back here for seven months, you sure haven't said much about why you're living in your parents house again."

Fuck, he's got me there. "I said it first."

"Really? That's what you're going with?"

I shrug.

He sighs as he stands and peruses around my shop. "This place has really come together."

Ah, there's the subject change I expected.

"Thanks to you and Delilah," I remind him. Brooks Turner is not only a member of one of the two founding families of Nettles, but he's also very good with a hammer. He helped build the shelves and the checkout counter in my store, and I'm forever thankful he wanted to help me make this a store of my own.

I had something of my own once, and then it got ripped away from me. The lease for my boutique in Nettles is in my name and the store is all mine.

"How is Delilah these days?"

"You would know if your families stopped this stupid feud you all have going on."

That earns me an eye roll. Nettles has two founding families from way back when—the Madisons and the Turners. Brooks and his sister are from the latter family. Delilah and her four other siblings are from the

Madison family. I don't even know why they hate one another, but I already know it's probably a stupid reason if it's been going on for this long.

"She's fine. You know Delilah," I add.

"That girl carries the sunshine in her pocket," he whispers loud enough for me to hear.

"That she does. Which place are you headed to after you leave?"

"Wherever my parents aren't today." He picks up a mascara wand and pokes it. "Just like every other day."

Most of the businesses in Nettles are run by a Madison sibling—the ones still in town—or Brooks's family. Then there's mine, stuck between them all like the knot in the middle of a rope two people are trying to pull.

"So, the bar, I assume?"

"Probably. I have to get ready for the inspection coming up, and that place needs the most work."

"Understood." I nod as I head for the door, flipping the sign on the door to officially open for the day. I always close the store for event consults, but since this one was basically a dud, I guess I didn't really have to. "Are you ever going to tell me why you're doing this to yourself?"

I know there's a reason. I know there's something he's not telling me about this arrangement between him and Jamie.

"I'm fine, Daisy."

"You're not. You're slowly dying inside."

"Yeah?" He stares at me. "And how would you know?"

Because I've been there before. I recognize the look on your face as the one that would stare back at me in the mirror like it did this morning, like it does every morning. "Personal experience."

"Are you going to elaborate this time?"

"Not if you aren't going to," I challenge him.

He takes another look at me before he turns around and leaves.

"That's what I thought," I say to myself as I press skip on the song that just started playing.

As I gear up for another slow day at my store, part of me isn't excited for another night of insomnia about what the state of my life currently looks like after the day is over.

But I did figure out my dinner for later, and I might be the only twenty-five year old on the planet excited to eat a chicken caesar salad.

This might not be how I saw my life turning out when I thought about the future, but at least I have some things to look forward to, even if it's something as simple as dinner.

Chapter Three

— LOOKING FOR BY BRENN!

I FORGOT HOW PEACEFUL driving feels to me. Not only has my car felt like my home for a while—all of my belongings coming with me everywhere I go—but it's also a time where I can remember all the memories of my siblings and I in the car together.

"*Are we there yet?*" I can hear my younger self asking my parents in the front seat.

"*Not yet, honey.*" *My mom turns around and grabs my hand.* "*Almost.*"

"*You're so impatient.*" *Tobias jabs at my arm.*

"*Be nice,*" *Tristan tells us.* "*I'd hate to break up a fight between you two in a moving car.*"

I've been on the road for a few hours, and I've only thought about turning back a few hundred times. Maybe if I never do this and the list is never finished, I can still have a piece of my brother that will never leave.

Back when there were still four West siblings, we would all talk about the future. All of us besides Tobias went to Summit University, the school basically around the corner from us. Tristan always wanted to leave, but that was when he was sure we were all old enough. When he graduated, he went to California, fulfilling his lifelong wish.

I was never really sure what I wanted to do with my life, so I chose Summit because it was close to home and I could save money commuting. Plus, the photography program was amazing, and even when I didn't know what to do with my life, I knew a camera was going to be a part of it. My mom bought me my first one when I was young—a small blue Polaroid camera. Since then, I've always loved capturing the moments around me, some of my favorite memories from my childhood pasted in a scrapbook my mom and I made.

Teags went because of the business program, and I can only assume she wanted to stay close because she was the last one left. By the time she entered college, I was about to leave and embark on my new job as a photojournalist, Tobias was all over the place, and Tristan was in California.

She was the last of us left, and when Tobias died, she and my mother were all alone in Pennsylvania waiting for us to come back home. She had to shoulder that all on her own, and the guilt of what I said to her on the phone haunts me at every turn.

I thought drinking would help to numb the pain of our brother dying. I thought it would make it less real, or maybe that would wake me up from the nightmare I was living in where he was gone. The only thing I do remember about that day we were all in the same place again is the white envelope our mom handed to us.

I remember not wanting to open it. It would be the last things he would ever say to me except he wasn't physically saying them. It felt like one of those stupid vacation mugs: my brother is dead and all I have left is this letter. No simple piece of paper could replace any atom of him. It wasn't good enough. Not even fucking close. It took me a week to be able to open it, and when I did, I was so drunk I could barely read it.

I fell asleep with it against my chest, and when I woke up the next afternoon sober enough to understand what it said, I got even angrier.

I all but memorized that first one he sent me, the words floating in and out of my mind as I turn up the music I'm listening to.

```
Theo.
I know you're confused, but it will all make
sense soon. I promise.
Pittsburgh.
New York City.
Summit University.
The basement of our childhood home.
Charleston.
The old house in Vermont.
All of these places have a piece of us, and
I trust you to find them when you visit each
of these spots. You must go in order, top to
bottom. You're smart, Theo. You always were the
one who understood my brain better than most.
I trust that you'll know why I'm sending you
to these places. It will all make sense when
you find the envelopes, but don't open them.
Not until you have them all, okay? And don't
open them without the rest of the family. That
part is important.
   I love you, brother. Don't put this all on
yourself. You couldn't have changed anything.
And even though I'm gone, you can still lean
on me, okay?
   Tobias
```

That last paragraph always makes me mad because maybe I could have changed something about this. Maybe if I had noticed he wasn't himself, he'd still be here. Maybe if I had been able to reach inside of his mind, I could have fixed him. I know he didn't want to hurt us, but he did. I know I can't blame him because he was obviously in a hard place, but part of me does. How dare he do this to us? How dare he not come to any of us and talk about it?

I'll never understand it. I'll never understand why he left me this wild goose chase to go on after he was gone, and I know wherever he is, he probably sees me and is disappointed in how I've turned out. I know every time I pick up a bottle, he's somewhere sighing heavily because he thinks it's his fault that I drink so much.

Sometimes I see him when I'm drunk. Other times, I can't. I think every time I reach for a drink, I hope he's on the other end of the bottle.

The welcome sign for Vermont stops me in my tracks. I can almost see my younger self poking my head out of the window to get a really good look at it. I can almost see Teags with her headphones on in the seat behind me, rolling her eyes because I've disturbed her music. I see Tobias with stars in his eyes watching me be a fucking idiot, and I see Tristan dragging me back into the car, worried I'm going to hit my head on something.

I miss those days when everything felt easier, where everything was whole.

I can barely see my father laughing as he drives, his arm around my mom's seat as he takes a look at all us in the back, his smile lighting up the car. My mom of course has her video camera out. I think that's where I got my love of the camera from—she was always recording anything she could.

I remember when driving up here felt like the happiest time in my life, and now it feels like a death sentence, but I'm not sure whose it is. Tobias is already gone, so that burden is mine to bear. This was always our favorite place—him and I—and when we stopped coming up here after our dad died, the two of us took it the hardest. We had friends up here. We had shared a room because we were the two middle children, and Tristan never liked anyone else in his space. Teags is our only sister, so she got her own room too. Him and I inhabited the same space in this house, often staying up late with our handheld game consoles hidden under our pillows so our parents wouldn't see them when they came to check in on us.

I knew this was going to be difficult, but I'm not sure how I'm going to do this. I'm not strong enough. I'm not *good* enough to have been sent on this journey. I'm all alone, with nothing but this letter to guide me.

I shake my head, not wanting to think of this any longer and instead, turn my attention to the scenery on the drive. Vermont is a beautiful place. I always loved how quiet everything seemed to be up here. The air felt cleaner. The sun felt brighter, more vibrant. Colors looked different up here, the grass greener, the flowers dazzling.

I let the wind run through my fingers as my arm dangles out of the window, the air against my skin reminding me that I'm still here, still alive somehow.

It only takes me another hour to get to the house, and when I pull into the driveway, it's exactly how I remember it.

I remember whipping open the car doors and running around the yard while our parents grabbed all of our things, Tristan helping to bring everything inside. Teags would always go right to her room, needing some time away from all of us after being in the car for that long. But Tobias and I would always run around the yard, and I remember even knocking on neighbors doors to see if any of our friends wanted to come out and play even though we had just gotten there.

I wonder if any of them are still here. I guess I'll find out in the coming days.

Tears fill my eyes as all of the memories rush into my mind, flashes of my brother's face as a kid smiling at me ripping my chest open. He was always so happy, so full of life.

I wonder when everything changed. I wonder if those dark thoughts were always in his head or if they came on all of a sudden and he didn't know what to do with them. I remember his laughter as we ran around the yard, switching between the tire swing and the swings dad built for us. I might forget that laughter one day. One day, I'll probably forget what his voice sounded like. Another day, I'll forget the exact way he smiled at all of us as we sat around the kitchen table.

I need a drink.

No, actually, first I need to get out of this car. I can't sit here and reminisce. I need to rip this bandage off and get it over with. This is the easy part. Coming back here was easy, but the rest of this search is going to be hard. It's going to kill me leaving this place once I find everything I need, but maybe once Mom sells the house, that thread will snap and I won't feel anything anymore.

Maybe this is exactly how Tobias put it together in his head before he died. He was sad and hurting. He didn't know what to do but he knew he wanted to feel better. He knew the only way to stop feeling like this was to stop feeling at all. Then he died by his own hand.

I hope he feels better wherever he is. I just wish it didn't have to happen how it did.

I take a deep breath before I open the door. Every time I've gone to a place on this list, there's been a familiarity that seeps into my bones, and then another white envelope shows up.

I wonder where he's hidden it this time.

My first instinct is to check the mailbox, so I head on down to the street, and sure enough, as soon as I open it, I see it. A small, white envelope with my name on it.

My eyes catch on the house across the street, a familiar flash of light hair infiltrating my memories.

"Hold still," she said to me as she brushed something pink across my eyes. *"I don't want to poke your eyeball out!"*

"Okay, flower girl," I remember saying back to her. *"Are you going to make me pretty like you?"*

I remember her laugh like no time has even passed. *"Sure, Theo. If you think I'm pretty, then I'll make you as pretty as me."*

Tears start to form again not only because this is the last stop, but because the memories are coming back now that I'm here.

This will be one of the last envelopes I receive from my brother and sure it's more than my siblings got, but still. I wish they would keep coming. I wish I could keep receiving these pieces of my brother.

I'm running out of the road in front of me where my brother still exists to talk to me, to send me things, to show me the way, and I don't know how I'm going to let go of that once I reach the end of it.

I sigh heavily again as I tuck the envelope into my pocket, grab my things from the car, and walk into the house.

Chapter Four

— TO BE LOVED BY ADELE

"Knock, knock!" my best friend says as she walks through the door to my shop.

I smile, her presence already lifting my spirits. That's just who Delilah is. If she glowed like an angel, she would be yellow. Bright, confident, joyful are all words that have been used to describe her, from more than just me. I've known her my entire life, and the two of us are inseparable. Even when I moved away from Nettles to pursue my dreams, she was still on the other side of my phone every single day.

When I came back for good, she was the one who picked me up from the airport with arms wide open, a bouquet of flowers in one of her hands and chocolate in the other. She was also the one who convinced me to sell my wedding ring. When I told her how bad I felt doing that, she reiterated every bad thing my ex did, and I was convinced. I made a pretty penny off of it and that's how I funded the first few months of lease for the boutique.

I hold my hands out and she sets the coffee in them—there's a pink sleeve from her shop on it just like there is every morning when she brings me sweet treats from her place.

"I swear you've got secret cameras in here." I take a sip. "You always know what I need."

"Oh, babe." She smirks at me. "That comes from all the years we've spent together. Our brains have almost fused into one."

I can't help but laugh as she brings me in for a hug, and her long, blonde hair hits me in the face. Her silver rings—made from an old spoon—graze against my outfit and get caught in the threads of my shirt. Her big, round cheeks always make her smile seem ten times bigger than it is, and the dimples on her face only amplify her sunny disposition.

The mornings with her before we both open our stores are my favorite moments of the day. It often reminds me how there's still one person on the planet whose face lights up when they see mine—something I'm not used to after cringing in a conference room when my ex-husband used to look at me and call me whatever name he was throwing around in the end.

There's this saying in Nettles that you could throw a rock and hit a member of the Madison family, which is 100 percent true. The Madisons run most of the town, and Brooks's family also has an array of businesses in and around town. Brooks's sister owns the hotel on Main Street, and normally Brooks is at the bar a few blocks down from her.

Delilah owns and runs the coffee shop that also sells ice cream and a variety of other pastries and mouth-watering treats. Her brother, Luca, is an emergency doctor at the hospital. Fallon, her sister, is the event planner in town, and it's been years since I've seen Eloise, but her twin brother, Elliott, is a firefighter in town.

Not to mention, their father is the mayor and is currently in his final term for Nettles.

"How are your parents doing? Is their year-long adventure off to a good start?" She makes herself comfortable in one of the chairs I use for consults.

"I talked to them this morning. They're *very* excited. They were about to board the plane to get to the boat. From there, they'll be on the cruise for a bit and then they'll get off and spend some time traveling some more til they feel like coming back."

"Is it weird being home all by yourself? I don't think I could live at my parents' house without getting the creeps." She shakes her head at me.

"Well, you've convinced yourself that your parents' house is haunted, so that probably doesn't help," I remind her. "And your brothers are also to blame for that with the amount of times they terrified us as kids. Do you remember how many times they locked us in the basement when we were playing dress up?"

"Luca was such an asshole when we were kids. Elliott too," she scoffs thinking of her brothers. "But you forget that if my parents left, this town would fall apart or the Turners would say they were abandoning the town and are unfit to keep running it."

I sigh heavily, hating that there's so much animosity between the families. The worst part is that nobody really knows why they don't like one another. This feud has been going on for generations, but something in the past decade seemed to have made it worse. I guess I'll just have to understand there are some things in life that will always remain a mystery. Most of the kids are all friends, but their parents are still cold with each other.

"Brooks was in here the other day with Jamie," I say, and her eyes grow wider. There is truly nothing better than gossiping with your best friend. Especially about all of the drama in this small town. I swear the wind carries gossip in it, the low murmur of it infiltrating everyone's ears.

"Shut up." She spins dramatically in the chair and leans closer to me. "Tell me everything."

"He's miserable."

"Anyone with eyes can see that. Did he say anything?"

"Nothing he hasn't before and he refused to elaborate when I asked him about the wedding."

"Typical Brooks Turner." She takes a long sip of her drink. "I just got my invite in the mail. Did you?"

I shake my head.

"It'll probably be in your mailbox today."

"I told him I didn't even need an invite since Jamie hired me. I'm going to it despite knowing Brooks isn't happy about this."

"Fallon got one, too, and she's planning the entire thing." Delilah rolls her eyes. "I assume they just want a proper headcount. Practically the entire town is going to be there."

Wonderful. Though, I'd expect nothing less from Jamie. She was always one to love being the center of attention, which isn't necessarily a bad thing. She's also just a pretentious asshole who used to make fun of anyone who wasn't in her little posse in high school.

Including me and Delilah, and the other Madison girls—Fallon and Eloise. Though, Eloise moved away for college and hasn't come back since. So, I doubt she'll be coming back for this.

"Is Eloise coming back? God, it's been years since I've seen her." I was never as close with her as I was with Delilah, but all of the Madison siblings felt like my family. They always welcomed me into their home with open arms, and both Luca and Elliott have told me I'm their honorary sister. I always assumed that was an excuse they came up with as kids to be able to make fun of me like they did their sisters, but nevertheless, I wore that title proudly.

I'm an only child, and I love my parents, but the Madisons were like the siblings I never had, and I often find myself missing the closeness we all shared when we were young.

"She is." Delilah smiles. "I can't wait to see her. It's been way too long since all of us have been together. With Luca working endless hours at the hospital, and Elliott working himself to death at the fire department, family dinners on Sundays have been lonely."

I'm about to say something, but the bell dinging above my door and a few people walking in makes me pause.

"I'll get out of your hair, babe. I probably have a line down the street waiting for me to open officially." Delilah pulls me in for a hug. "If you need a top off, you know where I am."

"I love you."

"Love you, too, girl." She smiles as she walks out of the door, stopping where my customers are browsing. "This mascara is my favorite. Oh! And that palette is always part of my every day rotation."

I hear them murmur a few things back to her as I laugh, and get ready for another day at the store that belongs to me and only me.

Just how it should be.

My head falls against the seat of my car as I try to unwind the day I had.

It was busier than I thought it was going to be when I walked into the boutique this morning. I got a few new shipments of newly released makeup I had ordered, and spent most of the afternoon sorting through it all in my storeroom—even swiping a few new shades of concealer for the kit I use for my clients.

Since I'm a licensed esthetician, I get most of the things I order at a discount, which helps since my ex-husband took basically all of my money in the settlement. It's bad that I don't even care about that. The one thing I cared more about in the entire world he stole out from under me, and I'll never forgive him for that—for any of it, really.

But I have the one thing he needs, and I'm just waiting for the day he realizes I can take things from him too.

Not wanting to spiral too much about this after the decent day I had, I finally get out of my car, heading right to my mailbox for the invitation Delilah said was waiting for me, and the cream colored envelope sits right on top of the pile.

I glance at the house across the street—the one that's normally empty and vacant—and I notice a car in the driveway. I'd go over and check it out, but I assume one of the neighbors is using it. That house has been vacant for more years than I can count, and everyone in the neighborhood knows it, but the house never went up for sale.

It was always weird, though. The owners never let the grass get too tall, and they always had someone keeping up with the maintenance on the outside. My parents said even while I was gone people would still come over and mow, water the grass, and make sure everything wasn't too overgrown. I wonder why.

I always thought the West family would come back. Every summer as a kid, I waited for my friends from Pennsylvania to come back up here, but they never did. One summer they were here and I was playing on the swing set in their backyard, and the next, nothing. My parents explained to me that they were going through a lot and maybe didn't have time to come up here for vacations anymore, and I didn't understand that—at least not when I was a kid.

All I remembered was missing my friends I barely got to see. There were four of them, if I remember.

I shake my thoughts out of my childhood memories and carry all of my bags and mail into the house. The alarm my parents have beeps at me as I open the door, and I drop all of my things in a messy pile and punch the code in.

The one thing I've started to understand about adult life is that having a full-time job is really just bringing the same two or three bags back and forth from your place of work and your house.

I used to love the idea of growing up. But all my life has brought me in the past few years is sadness. I went from feeling like everything was on track for me to being divorced and living in my parents' house again.

Life really has a funny way of not working out the way you want it to, and then laughing in your face when you thought you were doing okay. Oh, you think your marriage is perfect and your husband loves you? Wrong. Oh, the business you've dreamed of having since you were a young makeup artist? Yeah, that won't work out either, and it will all be because you made the wrong decision about who to love for the rest of your life—or however long the love lasts for your partner. You thought the love would last forever, but he got bored with you and cheated.

He *promised* to love me forever, but forever apparently has a different meaning to him and I. Forever as in the rest of my life, but for him that clock was dwindling the minute he slid that ring onto my finger.

I sigh heavily, feeling the tears come how they do every night when I sit at home alone thinking about everything that has gone wrong. There's a lot of things I hate about myself, but one of the main things I loathe is how deeply emotional I can get about things. I've always been like this. Most of my life I've been called dramatic for crying at things that most people would frown at and move on.

I'm trying to take some deep breaths, not wanting to spend another night crying to myself in the shower while avoiding the mirror in my bathroom, when I finally pull myself together. I grab the mail I threw on the floor, and open the messy mail drawer I've been putting everything in for my parents for when they get back, when an envelope with my name on it catches my eye.

What the hell is this?

It looks beat up, some minor scrapes and scratches against the envelope. I don't recognize the handwriting so I have no idea who could have sent it or how long it's been sitting here. Why didn't my parents tell me about this before they left for their cruise?

I grab my phone, immediately swiping to our family group chat.

> Daisy: I found this in the mail drawer. What is this?

I hope my parents have some answers for me, but since it might take a bit for them to respond, I grab it and open it, wondering if what's inside will provide some clarity for me. Most people besides the ones closest to me don't know I'm back in Vermont. I barely even gave my parents proper notice before coming back here after months of fighting with my ex-husband in small conference rooms.

There's no return address. No name besides mine on the envelope.

Dear Daisy, or whomever is reading this,

I know you're probably very confused, especially if you're holding this and your name isn't Daisy, but if it is you, I'm happy this letter got into your hands.

You see, there are things I can't really explain, but if you're still in Nettles then this might work better than I thought. I know it's been a long time since you've seen us all, and things have changed immensely since we were last up here, but Theo and I always wanted to come back. In a way, I guess this letter coming to you is my way of coming back to a place I once loved.

My brother will be back soon, or maybe you've already seen him? I'm not sure when you'll be reading this, so maybe you've already reconnected with Theo and I sound insane, but if you haven't seen him yet, then I'd love to ask for a favor.

I know you and Theo were close when we were young, and he'll be back in Nettles. Take care of him up in Vermont for me, okay? He'll need someone for this part of his journey. He always needed someone to lean on, someone to hold on to when things got to be too much. That used to be me, but I can't anymore. So, forgive him for anything stupid he does. He's just sad and confused about some of the things that have happened since you last saw us. But if you could look out for him for me, I'd really appreciate it.

Theo talked about you a lot as kids. He always called you 'the flower girl' because of your name, often asking our mom if we could go visit the meadows again soon, but we never did, of course. I'm sure you know that. Well, thank you is all I can say, really. If it's you, Dais, thank you. If your name is not Daisy Campbell then please get this letter to her, or if she's not in town anymore, just shred it up as if it never existed.

Tobias West

I read it a few times, confused as to how vague it is, no answers popping into my head as I read it for the fourth time. I remember Tobias and Theo, of course. There was another boy named Tristan, I think, and Teagen was their sister. She and I always liked to throw water balloons at her brothers, most of the time the teams were girls versus boys. We lost every time, but she always fired those things with a fervor I never had.

The memories flash through my head as I stare at the piece of paper in my hand. I open the curtains slightly, staring at the house across the way where I notice a small light that wasn't there before.

There's someone in the house.

I wonder if it's Theo. Or maybe it's Tobias, but from this letter it made it seem like he wasn't coming back here.

I sigh heavily, the curtain drifting closed as I turn to my own empty house, confusion spreading through my head as I decide to finally take a shower. I leave the letter on top of the small table by the door, and as I head up the stairs my phone buzzes.

> **Mom: Oh, I totally forgot about that.**

> **Daisy: Why didn't you tell me this was in here?**

> **Dad: It's been in that drawer for years, darling. We figured it was spam mail so we threw it in there and held it in case you came for a holiday and we could give it to you.**

> **Mom:** You can throw it away if you want. Thank you for keeping the house intact while we're gone! Can we call you tomorrow morning before you go to work? I miss you bunches already.

> **Dad:** I second that.

> **Daisy:** I'd love to talk to you. I'll call you tomorrow, okay?

> **Mom:** Have a good night, Lovebug.

> **Daisy:** You too.

Even after talking to them, I'm still confused about what this letter means. I can't believe they kept it for that long. I was still in Boston when it arrived, but I don't want to think about that part of my life at the moment. Instead I drag myself up to the bathroom and turn on my music, needing the noise to drown out my tears like I have every night since I've been alone.

Chapter Five

— MACHINE GHOST BY ERIN LECOUNT

I WAKE AGAINST THE floor, a small beam of light shining on the hardwoods in front of me.

Fuck.

Where am I? Why is it so cold in here? I turned the heat up before I—

Oh. I forgot. I'm not in Pennsylvania anymore. Yesterday slowly starts to come back to me as I remember driving up to Vermont and finding the letter Tobias left for me. The last one. The one with the final clue to wherever this thing he wants me to find is.

I somehow peel myself off of the floor, the discarded vodka bottle next to me clattering against the floor as I push it away from me. I can't bear to look at it. I can't bear to face my biggest enemy besides myself as I look around the cold and stale house that used to feel lively and colorful.

I thought it would be more dust-ridden. Sure, I need to open the windows, but seeing all of my childhood's best moments in boxes is making me want to scream. This house is a time capsule for me, and for some reason, Tobias has sent me back here to experience all my happiest moments despite knowing his absence would kill me in more ways than one.

"*It's as big as I remember it,*" I hear my younger self saying as I watch the ghosts of my childhood dance through the house.

"*Be careful up the stairs. Remember the second last step is slippery,*" a young Tristan says.

Teags runs up the stairs, skipping that step and heading right for her room, her headphones still on as she shuts her door. My parents' laughter echoes around the living room.

"*Nobody bother her for a little bit.*" *My mom plays with my hair.* "*That means you and Tobias.*"

"*He's the troublemaker,*" *my younger self points a finger at him, and his face is blurry as I try to remember what he said to me.*

The memory fades and my head is pounding, my chest gets tighter and tighter the longer my childhood happiness wraps around my body and doesn't let go. It's almost as if the dust is infiltrating my lungs, reminding me of a time when it felt easier to breathe when nothing bad had ever happened to me.

This is cruel. He's a cruel person. Why would he send me back here? He knew what it meant to me—to us. Why the fuck would he do this to me? I don't know what I'm doing here. I don't know what he wants me to do here besides reminisce about the good old days and cry myself to sleep. I've been at this list for ages and I haven't gained a single ounce of clarity about all this, about why he decided to do what he did. I've been stuck in this same limbo since I read his first letter and I'm still in the same place now than I was back then. It's been years and I have nothing to help dull the ache of Tobias being gone. All I have is a bunch of unopened envelopes and unanswered questions about why he left.

I can't handle all of this. I can't seem to make myself stand up and start rummaging through these boxes looking for something I may never find. It was pure luck that I found everything else he left me, but I can't see myself finding whatever he wants me to look for here, or maybe I just don't want to. Hell, I've barely been here for twenty-four hours and I've already drank myself to sleep to avoid all my emotions.

Everything he knew about me and who I was died when he did. I'm not the same brother he knew. I'm not the same kid who shared a room with him in this house when our family was together. I'm not the same Theo he knew. I'm cold. I'm meaner than I used to be. I can't seem to stand up straight. I hide my sadness by drinking and joking about anything I can. There's a lingering cloud that follows me and I've become really good at hiding the pain from my family. I have maybe one true friend on the planet, and it just so happens I work with him, so maybe he doesn't even like me.

I barely like who I am most days. I can barely stand to be in the same room as myself, all of my thoughts about how stupid and sad I am feel louder when I'm alone. Everything always feels like that, and Tobias knew that. So why did he send me on this list all alone knowing I probably wasn't going to be able to handle it?

You're a sad drunk, Theo. The thoughts won't stop. *Tobias would hate who you've become.* I hate who I've become. *You're not strong enough.* I know. *You're going to fail your brother's last dying wish. How could you?*

I can't do this. Not here. Not now.

Before I change my mind, I grab my keys, the letter, and one of my bags, heading for my car as I drive into the heart of the town, knowing I can't stay here for another second or I'll repeat what happened last night.

As I park outside of the small hotel on Main Street, I can already feel my mind start to come back to me. It felt as if all the ghosts of my childhood were haunting me in that house, and I can't face them. Not like this. Not yet.

I look around the strip of shops and things that are on this street. This is the main hub of Nettles, and it looks familiar, but I swear when I was a kid this all looked a lot bigger. The amount of shops has grown since I was last here, but there's still something so different about this place.

Or maybe it's me. Maybe I'm the thing that has changed after all these years. I can't deny that I'm a much different person than I was the last time I was here. I'm over a decade older than I was. I finally figured out how to grow a mustache. I can drive. I'm completely different, yet this town I used to come to has stayed the same, seemingly untouched by time.

So much of my life has shifted and become disoriented and I'm practically a stranger to this town I once knew. I always loved it in Nettles. The people were always friendly, the food tasted better here than at home, and maybe hindsight is a bitch but my family would always be whole here. I would always have two parents and three siblings in Vermont.

Ever since I've grown up, I feel like I've been chasing myself down. When I was a kid, I didn't really know who I was. I just listened to my parents and liked whatever I liked. Now that I'm older and am developing my own style and taste for things, it's become incredibly difficult to figure out who I want to be. I've been on this planet for twenty-six years and I barely feel like I've scratched the surface of who I am or who I'm supposed to be.

God, I need a drink. I don't care that it's early in the morning and I'm still hungover. I don't really care about anything right now. I have no purpose, no focus, nothing here. Part of me still feels like the little kid in a body that doesn't feel right. My legs don't feel like they exist. My arms feel too long, and my head doesn't feel attached to my body anymore.

I have nothing to hold me upright. I don't know how I'm not constantly falling over myself because nothing feels right.

I take a deep breath and force myself out of the car and into the hotel, needing to lay down and hope something kills me before I grab another bottle to numb myself. Maybe then I'll see Tobias and he can tell me what to do. Maybe then, he'll come back to me and explain everything.

I head to the front desk and the girl behind it rolls her eyes at someone before she looks at me, her eyes widening as I walk up.

I probably look as well as I feel—fucking horrible. I can smell the vodka coming off of my breath, and I really wish I had grabbed my tooth brush before I sprinted out of the house.

This hotel will work for however long I need it to. It has to because I can barely exist in that house without wanting to drink myself into a coma from all the memories that filter into my mind. It hurts even standing in there. The ache spreads from my feet on the hardwoods to my brain hearing the laughter from my younger self and my family that once was all together, not spread all over the country how we are now. Tristan is the only one back home with our mom. Teags is in Arizona, and I've been all over the country for the past two years.

"Hi. How can I help you today?"

"I'm hoping you have a room available."

"We have plenty." She types something on her computer. "Are you looking for one bed or two?"

"Just one is fine. I don't have much." I try to laugh off the pain I'm feeling, and it works because she laughs too.

"You're not from around here are you?"

"Am I that obvious?"

She nods. "How long will you be staying?"

"Uh." I shrug. "I'm not really sure. Can I book the room for the week and then rebook if I need to stay longer?" I'm not sure how long this funk is going to last, but maybe the more time I spend here surrounded by memories, the less it will hurt walking back into that haunted house.

"That's fine. We're not even close to being fully booked." She smiles at me. "Autumn is the busy season."

"I can understand that." The drive up here was already scenic and beautiful. I can't imagine what it looks like when autumn is in full swing and the leaves are turning.

"Name?"

"Theo West." I grab my credit card out of my wallet. I'm sure nobody remembers me up here, but saying my full name makes me shiver. Her short blonde hair swishes with every motion she does as she enters my information into the system. She seems about my age, maybe a little older, but I'm not too good with guessing people's ages, and the small scar near her eye catches mine immediately. I wonder what the story is behind it, but I'm not going to ask. "And you are?"

"Amara Turner." She reaches for my hand. "I own this place."

"Oh, wow," I say as I return her handshake. "Impressive."

"Thank you," she says as she gets my keys ready for me. "Breakfast is included and if you need to do laundry, there are machines on each floor that take quarters. Anything else you need, you can call the front desk. Someone will always be here to answer the phone."

"Sounds good." I nod as I pick up the one bag I grabbed before I bolted. "Got any recommendations for good places to eat around here?"

"My brother runs the sports bar down on Main Street. I'm biased of course, but he's got a great cook that makes a mean burger. Good drinks too. There's also Delilah's, if you're looking for coffee, pastries, or ice cream. If you go any way down this street, you can find something."

"Thank you," I say as I head for the elevator.

"Enjoy your stay."

I'VE BEEN AT THIS hotel for three days, and I still can't seem to find the strength to open the letter that stares back at me, taunting my every move. The crumpled white envelope sits in my hands, my fingers shaking from how fucking nervous I am. It would be so easy to open it, so easy to tear it and find out what hint Tobias has left for me.

All I've done the past three days is watch crappy movies that fill my head with any thoughts besides the ones I want to feel and drink. I walked around Main Street a few times, once because I needed more alcohol, but the other times I needed to get out of the room. It's a beautiful area—Amara was right about this part of town—and my bones have started to settle into my body the longer I spend here.

I fiddle with the eggs on my plate, my bacon and toast already gone, and I'm hoping that will help to soak up whatever is still in my stomach that I didn't throw up this morning. I'm a fucking mess, and I can pretend to have my shit together all I want, but behind closed doors, I'm falling apart.

This is all that looked appetizing to me when I came down here, and part of me wishes I drank a little more because I didn't see my brother at all the past three days.

"Why can't I see you when I'm sober, Tobias?" I whisper to the empty chair in front of me. "Why won't you just give me any answers? Why the treasure hunt? Why am I here when I could be traveling around the world and doing my job?"

So many questions that will never be answered float through my mind, and maybe opening the letter will bring me answers, but part of me knows it will only bring more questions, so I continue to eat, not listening to the nagging feeling in my gut.

I've heard more from my brother after he died than my siblings have. My mom, Tristan, and Teags got one letter each. Somehow, he chose me to get a string of puzzles and hints, and to find whatever he left behind. I know I should feel grateful, but I don't. Not even fucking close. I resent him dangling a bunch of fucking carrots in front of me only to stop them once I finished the list. If it was one and done, I would probably feel better about all this. Maybe I would have come back here with no strings attached and felt better about it. Maybe somehow I would have found my way back without Tobias leading me here.

But he led me here for something. For some reason he wants me in Vermont, and this letter might give me that answer.

I bring my finger up to the small flap, but just as I'm about to rip it open, I choke. I get up, clear my plate, and head back for my room, when a flash of ice blonde hair makes me pause before I press the door to the elevator.

I shuffle back a bit, and my eyes meet ones I'm familiar with. If I close them, I can almost see the same blue eyes looking back at me while I sit on the swings in my backyard. Her eyes are like a painting I've looked at for far too long.

I can almost see her younger face peering back at me after I opened the door, her two rings on the bell at our house my cue to answer it. Two rings because that's how I knew she was behind it. It was like our own secret code because before the first bell was finished dinging, she would ring it again.

"Higher, Theo!" she yells as she pumps her legs.

"I'm trying," I say as my swing starts to pick up momentum. I look over at her, our faces meeting as she smiles, the stream of sunlight illuminating her freckles.

"We're in sync." She giggles, my eyes still trained on her as we go back and forth.

God, she hasn't changed a bit.

"Is that you, Daisy girl?"

Her lips twitch as I say that, and I can tell she remembers me too. God, I can't fucking believe she's still here. I thought she would be long gone by now.

My heart skips a beat because she remembers me how I remember her. I didn't just fade into the depths of her mind to never be heard of again.

And for the first time in a while, I feel a glimmer of something other than sadness spread through my body. Dramatic, maybe, but even when I was younger and the two of us were laughing on the swing set, I knew she was someone that would be hard for me to forget. Part of me was hoping I might run into her, but I thought it was a longshot because of how many years it has been.

But she's still here, and now she's standing in front of me.

"Theo?"

Chapter Six

— WE GREW OLD BY YUAT

After a decently slow week at the boutique, I'm off to my second job helping out Amara, Brooks's sister, at the hotel while she gets some rest. That girl works herself to the bone in more ways than one, and this way, I can pick up a little extra money while I save for my own place.

Luckily, I have time to bulk up my savings account since my parents will be gone for a whole year, and they've been kind enough to let me move back in while I get my life back on track.

I could cry thinking about how they welcomed me back home so easily. I thought after leaving and trying to make a life of my own they would be disappointed in me coming back to Nettles with nothing to show for it, but that wasn't the case. I have the best parents in the world, and I'm glad I got to spend a little time with them before they left.

I update them whenever I can, but I didn't tell them what the letter said because I doubt it will go anywhere. I woke up the other day and the car in the driveway across the street was gone, so I assume whoever that was got what they were looking for. Or maybe it was a realtor taking measurements of the house to be able to sell it. Regardless of what it was, it's gone now and I don't have to worry about it.

But still, the letter I read has me wondering about the house across the street. Could it have been Theo inside the other day? Could that have been his car? I haven't seen him in over a decade, but what if that was him? What if he's back in town? I haven't heard any whispers of someone new coming to Nettles how I normally would, but maybe he's been flying under the radar?

Though, that letter sat in the drawer for years, so my best bet is that it's not the boy I used to know when I was younger who I would only see once a year in the summertime. I doubt it's Theo, the boy who used to push me on the swing set so I could reach the clouds in the sky. I'm sure wherever he is, he's living his life far away from this small town he hasn't been to since he was a kid.

I slide into the front desk and shove my tote bag in the small cubby before I grab my phone and text Amara.

> **Daisy: Things are all good here. Please do not call me a thousand times like last weekend and actually take the day off like you promised.**

> **Amara: No promises!**

> **Daisy: Amara...**

> **Amara: Yeah, yeah, I know I'm being a total helicopter boss, but you know I trust you, right?**

> **Daisy:** I do. I know it's your parents that you worry about, but I can stand my ground if they try and come in. I might cry a little, but that's normal!

> **Amara:** They won't come in. I just worry sometimes.

> **Daisy:** I know, but everything will be fine and if it's not, I'll call you.

> **Amara:** You're the best.

> **Daisy liked one message.**

I smile at my phone as I punch in for my shift, fully prepared to have a nice and slow day here where I can help people with towels or whatever else they may need, before a voice I vaguely recognize says my name.

"Is that you, Daisy girl?"

Daisy girl. There was only one person who used to call me that and I haven't seen him in over a decade. I turn around, and as soon as his eyes are on me, a few hundred memories float through my head about the boy I used to know across the street.

The man who stands in front of me is nothing like the boy I once knew. He's way taller than I am—just how it used to be. I guess that hasn't really changed, but everything else has. His hair is a little lighter than it used to be, and it's a lot more messy. Longer too. He even has a mustache taking over his top lip. He's grown up quite nicely over the years, and I can't even begin to wonder how he remembers me. I feel so different from the girl I used to be, but somehow, he recognized me.

"Theo?" I somehow mumble as a faint smell of vodka hits my nostrils.

"Holy crap." He breaks out of his haze and smiles brightly at me. "Can I give you a hug? Shit, it's been so long."

"Yeah, yes, of course," I blabber as I get out from behind the desk and he wraps his arms around me, the vodka smell stronger than it was before. "God, it's been years."

"Too fucking long if you ask me," he says into my ear. "I can't believe you're still here."

"Well, I haven't been here the entire time," I say as I pull back, his eyes tracing down my body. I cross my arms in front of me as I feel my cheeks get red. God, why am I so awkward? "I left for a bit and then came back."

"It's been a while since I've been back," he reminds me. "How have you been?"

"Oh, just awesome," I say as convincingly as I can. I really don't want to get into what's been going on with me with the boy that used to be my neighbor, so I throw the question to him. "How have you been? What brings you back here?"

I sort of know the answer to my question because my mind flashes to the letter currently sitting on the top of my mail pile. This has to be what Tobias was talking about, and I wonder if he knows I got a letter from his brother. I assume he's keeping in touch with his family while he's in Vermont, and since it looks like it's just him up here, that seems like a fair assumption. Did Tobias tell him about the letter before Theo came back?

I have a feeling I'll be finding out the answers to these questions the longer he's here.

"Oh, you know…" he trails off as if he can't find the words.

"Your eyes look so blue."

He laughs to himself. "My eyes have always been brown, Dais. In fact, your eyes are the bluest ones I've ever seen. They're hard to forget."

The first time he met me when we were ten years old, that was one of the first things he told me. He said he liked my eyes. He said they reminded him of the sky.

"I wasn't talking about the color."

His mask slips, but he throws a smile back on as if it never dropped in the first place. There's something so different about him. Back when we were kids, he looked so carefree, at least from the vague memories I have, but now he's leaning against the counter as if it's the only thing keeping him upright.

Maybe I recognize whatever I see in him because it's the same way I feel. Maybe that's just what happens when you grow up—the air becomes heavier and it's harder to hold yourself up after life keeps knocking you down.

"Well, I have somewhere to be, but we should get dinner and catch up. Are you free tonight?"

I shake my head. "I'm here all weekend."

"Oh, well I'm staying here for a little bit, and—"

"Maybe before you leave we can catch up?" I'm way too nervous right now, and I'm not even sure why. It's not like it's a date. It's just dinner with a boy I used to know, but the thought of that makes my legs turn to jelly and spots start to take over my vision.

My divorce was *just* finalized, and even though we've been separated for over a year, I'm not ready for anything that even resembles a relationship. It is way too early for me to be putting myself out there again.

"Um, I'm not actually sure when I'm leaving."

"Is that so? And you're staying at Amara's hotel for however long?"

He smirks to himself. "Yes and no. I have to head over to my old house and clean it out. My mom wants to sell it, and I wanted to come back here and go through all the things we left behind."

"That's nice of you," I say. I have a feeling there's something else he's not telling me, but I'm also keeping something from him.

"It's the least I could do."

I wonder what he means by that.

"Well, you know where I'll be if you change your mind about dinner. Room 403," he throws me a wink. "And if it helps, I really hope you change your mind. I want to hear all about how life has been treating you. It's been too long."

I can't help the smile that comes off of my face. "I'll think about it."

"Please do," he says as he pushes off of the front desk.

I try to stop the swarm of butterflies that attack my stomach at seeing how nicely Theo grew up, but they continue to flutter around for the rest of my shift, and I know it's probably going to get worse.

It was nice seeing him again, and the letter burning a hole on the table by my front door floats through my mind as he walks out of the front door and turns out of sight.

Chapter Seven

— THE HOUSE I GREW UP IN BY SYDNEY ROSE

God, she's beautiful.

The last time I saw her I promised her I would come back the following summer. I thought I would be back, but as a child, you're really at the will of your parents. Before we could come back, my father died suddenly. That was the first time I was in the front row at a funeral with nowhere to put my sadness. I was at the age where I knew what was going on, but I didn't know why all of my feelings were so huge, so steep and unnerving, and I didn't know what to do with them.

After that, we never went back to Vermont. This is the first time I've been back since I was young, and seeing a familiar face—especially hers—was something I never imagined. My life was so different back then, and part of me wants to keep whoever she thought I was when I was a child intact because if she got to know who I am now, I think she'd run screaming.

I'm a fucking mess, and time has not been kind to me.

But maybe she recognized that? The comment she made about my eyes has been swirling inside of my head since it came from her lips. Could she see the sadness in my eyes even though I thought I hid it well?

Maybe. Or maybe that was something she meant to keep inside of her head that accidentally slipped out. That always did happen with her, even when we were kids. Teags liked her a lot, too, even though she was a pretty closed off kid, but the first time Daisy and I met, we clicked. It's not hard to do that as a child. If you like the same color, you basically become best friends.

The first time I met her, the first thing I remember was hearing the doorbell. I opened it while my parents were unpacking everything, and she asked if she could swing on the tire hanging from the tree in our yard.

I asked my parents if it was okay, they said she was welcome to our yard any time.

From then on, we were inseparable.

"My name's Daisy, like the flower."

"My name's Theo, not like the flower."

I remember making her laugh as she swung from the tire. I spent the rest of that day trying to make her laugh again.

The memories floating into my head hit me in the chest, reminding me of the easier times, reminding me when my family was still whole and together. Happy. We were all happy back then, and I'm not sure if my Dad dying was the beginning of whatever downfall we had, but it surely didn't help. That day feels like a chain reaction into the rest of our lives as a family because no matter what, nothing could make us whole again.

We would always be one short, and now, two. Two of my family members are dead and there's nothing I can do to bring them back. I just have to keep moving, right? The world has continued spinning somehow despite me feeling like it shouldn't be. My world has stopped since the day my father died, and just when I felt like it was beginning to spin again, Tobias left too.

It doesn't feel fair, and I know life will never be as such no matter how much I want it to be. I'll never be able to wrap my mind around all of the things I've been through—and am still going through because it never stops. I'll always be in it. I don't think there is such a thing as getting through the death of two family members, especially someone like Tobias.

My foot starts to feel wet, and when I look down I realize I'm partially in the small pond. I take a look around. I'm not sure how I got here, and I wonder if that's the brain fog seeping in or if the alcohol is altering my brain. I'm sure it's a combination of both.

I shake my foot out of the water and continue my walk, loving the light bustle of people all around town. I smile at a few passersby as I take in the sights, before my phone starts to ring. I've done this walk just about every day, but I'm surprised I made it all the way to the pond without detouring into Delilah's to get a pastry. Amara was right. Her treats are delicious. I've never tasted anything like it.

"Hello?" I say as I don't bother looking at who it is.

"Hey, dude," Tristan says across the line. "I told you to keep me updated. I've been worried sick for days since you never told us when you got to Vermont safely."

Shit. I *knew* I forgot to do something. "Sorry. It's been a weird few days up here."

"Weird how? Are you okay? Do you want me to come up there?"

Oh, Tristan. Always worrying about everyone but himself. Thank fuck for Livvy. She really keeps him centered these days and reminds him to chill the fuck out when he's being overbearing like this. "I'm fine, Tris. I'm wandering around town right now, and my shoe is wet."

"Why is your shoe wet?"

"I almost walked into a pond."

I can practically see his face right now. "You did what?"

"I am *fine*."

"Clearly not if you were so distracted you almost walked into a body of water unknowingly," he chuckles across the line. "What's distracting you? Is it weird being in the old house or is Lucas up your ass about getting him some photos?"

"I haven't talked to Lucas since I left, but I'm expecting a passive aggressive email any day now," I laugh. Lucas is not only my friend, but he's also the guy at the magazine who handles all of the negatives I send him. I only shoot on thirty-five millimeter film for work, and I have all of my stuff with me so I can get some shots of Vermont for a spread that work wants to do about Tobias and this trip he has sent me on. Though, I haven't told my family about this yet. I'm keeping that close to my chest how I'm harboring whatever is in the small envelopes Tobias has hidden for me.

"How are you doing? Are you handling things okay up there?"

Translation: Are you still drinking to an unhealthy degree?

Yes, but I'm not going to worry Tristan with it.

"Stop worrying about me."

"I'll always worry about you."

I know. I know his fears about all of us because they mimic my own. Never again do I want to pick up the phone to one of my family members sobbing because one of us is gone. I can't do it again, but it's inevitable. I can't stop it because it is coming, it's just a matter of when.

"I'm okay, and I'll keep you in the loop, alright?"

"Thank you," he whispers, and as soon as I see a flash of ice blonde hair, I cut off whatever my brother was about to say next.

"I have to go."

"Theo—"

I end the call before he gives me the third degree, and I jog to catch up to the girl I used to know. That's the one good and bad thing about small towns—you really can't avoid anyone.

"Daisy?" I stroll up to her, her head whipping around just in time for me to slide in next to where she's walking. "If you're sick of seeing my face, you can just push me into the pond. I myself almost walked right into it earlier."

And there's that laugh I haven't heard in over a decade that sounds just as sweet as the first time I heard it.

"I have a feeling there's a story there."

I shake my head. "You had to be there."

"Ah, understandable." She smiles at me. "Did you want to walk with me?"

"I would love nothing more," I say as I adjust my camera bag on my shoulder. "Sorry if I bombarded you at the hotel."

She shrugs. "I was just a little caught off guard. It's not every day someone from your childhood comes back and is staying at the hotel you're working at."

"Is that what you do here? From what I remember, your dream job when we were kids was a makeup artist."

"If I remember, you were my very first client."

The memory floats into my mind as we walk. She had gotten this huge makeup kit for her end of the school year gift—her parents got her one thing she wanted at the end of every school year—and one summer, it was a makeup kit. It had eyeshadow, and all of this lip gloss or whatever in it. She had brought it over to our house when we had just settled in.

"Would you be my first customer, Theo not like the flower?"

I remember her smile as she unlatched the box her kit came in, and she started blabbering about what each thing was as she gently brushed it all onto my face. My siblings made fun of me for weeks after we got home, but I didn't care. If she was happy, then I was too. If she was smiling, that was basically all I needed to see.

"I guess I was," I poke her with my elbow as we pass by a small bench by the pond we've been walking around. "Do you want to sit?"

She looks hesitant at first, but after a few seconds, she agrees. "I don't have much time before I have to get back. Amara lets us have two thirty minute breaks when we work all day, and I needed a little fresh air, so I went on my walk early since everyone was checked out already."

"Oh, that's nice. Amara seems like a great boss."

"She is."

"God, I can't believe I'm sitting next to you right now." I turn to look at her. "Daisy fucking Campbell."

"Theo fucking West," she jokes. "I always wondered where you went after you left."

"Are you still across the street from me?"

She nods. "I guess I saw your car there the other night? Was that you?"

"It was."

"How did you end up at the hotel?"

I sigh heavily as I look in front of us. There's a few people walking around, even a few kids biking and laughing to one another. I miss being that carefree and full of life. Now I feel like a walking body with no place to land. "It's a long story."

"You seem to like those."

I can't help the laugh that slips out. "Well, that's why I suggested dinner. There's a little too much to catch you up on."

"Ah." She reaches to pull her hair back, and two pieces of her ice blonde hair fall out of the ponytail and frame her face nicely. I can't get over how little she's changed. Her blue eyes still pierce my face every time she looks in my direction, she's still shorter than me but only by a little bit now—maybe a few inches, and she still has one dimple on the right side of her face. Her hair was a lot longer when we were kids, but it's to her shoulders now. I wonder when she made that change. And the freckles. So many freckles. "Well, same here."

"Over a decade is a long time."

"We were kids when we met. Unless you forgot."

"I had a hard time forgetting about you."

She turns to look at me, her face full of shock. "I find that hard to believe. I'm a pretty forgettable person."

I mimic the expression she just gave me. "I thought about you every fucking summer, Dais. I begged my mom to come back here any chance I had, but she never wanted to."

"Why?" she asks me before finishing the sentence about to come out of my mouth. "It's a long story?"

"Exactly."

She laughs to herself. "Then maybe we need to have dinner or something."

"Or maybe I'll just keep running into you."

She stands up from the bench, laughing as she pulls down the sleeves of her shirt. No wonder she's warm and had to put her hair up. She's wearing long sleeves in the middle of summer. "Run into me whenever you'd like. We are neighbors after all."

"I'll be back at the house sometime this week. I have to start going through all of the boxes we left up here."

"If you need any help, I'm available most nights after I shut the store down."

"Store?" I wonder as she starts to walk away.

"Next time, Theo. That's a conversation for next time."

I can't help the stupid grin on my face at the thought of a next time with her, but as she turns back and throws me a wave, I suddenly find myself not feeling so shitty being back here. Because even though there are a lot of memories that make me want to curl into a ball, there are also memories of laughing with her and my siblings as we ran around the yard.

The good and the bad are fighting a war in my head, but I know I'm going to have to confront that house at some point.

It's just a house, I remind myself. And that may be true, but that isn't what I'm afraid of. It's the wallpaper that holds all of the past conversations I had with my family before we broke apart. It's the furniture my siblings and I used to coexist on. It's the table we all once sat around, Teags getting first dibs at all of the food on it because us boys were bulldozers and ate everything our parents cooked for us before she was able to get something on her plate.

I'll never have days like those again. All I'll have is two empty chairs and place settings at the table, and that has to be enough.

Chapter Eight

— CAMDEN BY GRACIE ABRAMS

"Theo West is back? Is it just him or the whole family?" Delilah asks as she flips the open sign on my door. "Wait. Does he have a mustache?"

I nod.

"Oh my gosh, I've seen him!" her eyes widen as she leans against the counter. "He's been in my store every morning for a week."

"God, it's crazy seeing him again."

"Didn't you have a huge crush on him when we were kids? If I remember, you used to draw hearts with your first initials on them. I think there's still one carved onto one of the trees in my backyard."

I grab one of the test makeup sponges and throw it at her, she lets it hit her.

"What? Am I wrong or am I thinking of one of my sisters?"

I can't even say anything because she's right. Shit.

"Even if you were, it doesn't matter."

She raises her eyebrows. "Why not?"

"You know why, Del."

She sighs heavily before bringing me in for a hug. "That piece of shit didn't deserve any ounce of the love you showed him, and he can quote me on that."

I laugh as a tear falls from my eyes. "I still loved him. Even now, I think part of me will always love him, and I know he doesn't deserve that from me, but that's who I am. It's who I've always been. I'm the girl who feels fucking everything and gets way too attached too quickly, and—"

"Dais." Delilah grabs my face in her hands. "Don't do that."

"What?"

"Don't make excuses for his behavior. You loved him with everything you had, just how you always have. He's the one who weaponized that and took advantage of your beautiful soul. He cheated on you—multiple times, might I add. There's no corner of this planet where that is your fault. You did everything right. He didn't."

I take a deep breath as I let her words soak into my brain.

Derek—my ex-husband—was the first person I ever loved romantically. Sure, I had crushes every now and then, and maybe I would daydream and imagine marriage and kids and a white picket fence with these relationships that never existed past the things in my head, but Derek was the one for me. I was *so* sure of it. I was so sure that he was going to be the one to make me coffee in the mornings. I was so sure he would be the one to write love notes in the fog on the bathroom mirror just to make me smile. Or leave notes in my lunch pail for me to find while I was at work.

But he wasn't even close to being that for me. At first, he would do all of the normal boyfriend things—flowers, random calls throughout the day, forehead kisses when I had just woken up. At first, it was beautiful. He would always talk about marrying me one day, and what our kids would look like.

Then he proposed, and I thought that was the happiest I would ever be. I felt like I was floating off of the ground when he was on one knee in front of me.

Then we got married, another day filled with light. My parents even flew in and my dad got to walk me down the aisle how he always imagined he would. Derek and I danced to the song that was playing in the bar where we first met. It was so full-circle. It was perfect.

And then all the red flags started showing up.

He would stay out later on the weekends. I'd be waiting for him to come home and he wouldn't call when he was late. Then things would get better. He'd bring flowers and take me on surprise vacations when I didn't have any events or clients. It was like I was on a seesaw. There were some days where I felt he was keeping secrets from me, and then he would do something nice and I'd forget all about it. I thought my fears were just that—trepidation about getting married so young. Everyone told us we were too young to make such a commitment, but we loved one another. I thought that was all I needed—his love engulfing me, protecting me from anything bad.

It turns out love can't protect you when the person in the bubble with you is the one trying to destroy it.

I feel more tears coming, and Delilah's hands are the ones wiping them from my eyes this time. It's not just me sitting in the bathroom on the floor, Derek's hands banging against the door as his mistress scurried out of our place.

Oh wait, it was multiple mistresses. And the worst part was they were all clients of mine I had worked on photoshoots with. If the event I was doing hadn't gotten canceled that day, I might still be in Boston with him. I think that's what scares me the most. If I hadn't found out, I would still be with him, loving him with everything I had while he was screwing around with other women behind my back.

"Let it out, Dais."

I start sobbing into her shoulder. "Why did I trust him?"

"Because you loved him."

Yeah, and look where that got me. I'm twenty-six years old, divorced, living in my parents' house again, and I once thought I would become a makeup mogul because Derek said he could make my dreams a reality. We had only just started creating plans for the company when I found him fucking a bunch of models in our bed, and I thank my lucky stars that we didn't create anything huge before his infidelity came to light.

Though, he got all of the rights to everything we had created in the divorce. Everything except the one thing he needs to get the company off of the ground—the recipes to the makeup I wanted to create. I still have them, and he'll never find them. It's not like he'll ever need them. Makeup was always my thing, not his.

"I'm tired of crying over him," I say as I pull back from my best friend's embrace. "I hate that I still feel so much for him."

"Stop," she says as she pushes my hair behind my shoulders. "I love how soft you are. I love that you feel everything down to your bones, and you used to as well. No matter how many times my brothers made fun of us, you always snapped back at them and told them that your feelings were a gift. What happened to that beautiful and strong girl? I can tell she's still with you."

"I don't know, Del. I don't know where she went." I wipe a few more tears from my eyes as she hands me the tissue box. I'm lying to her, yet she doesn't know it. Any version of me died when my ex-husband cheated on me and started telling me I was the problem.

The fight we had after I found him was eye-opening to say the least. He blamed me for all of it. He said I was too busy. He complained I was always too tired to have sex with him. He said he had to cheat because I had been getting bigger and he missed when I was "thinner" and "more attractive." He missed when I didn't have to wear makeup every time I stepped out of the house. He hated how long it took me to get ready because it always made him late to events with his business partners, which was never true. But the way he said it, I believed it. I believed everything he said to me because I loved him, but his love was a black hole, sucking every good thing out of me until I had nothing left to give.

And then I booked it back here and only told Delilah and my parents I was coming home. For the first few weeks, they didn't press me on why I was back. I just hid in my bedroom, starving myself until Delilah kept coming over and demanding to know what was going on.

I told her everything one night when she brought over a bottle of wine, and then we sold my ring.

And that's how I got the store we're both crying in now.

I had a weird relationship with makeup for the first part of this year. It always felt like I was hiding instead of showcasing my love for it how it used to. This thing I used to love and see as art became a mask, and I hated that. I had never felt that way about this thing I loved until my ex-husband mentioned it.

This store saved my life in a few ways. Not only did it get me out of the house and have something to look forward to every day, but it brought back the sense of community I had been missing when I was in Boston. I had no friends in Boston besides the people I worked with on the regular. All I had was Derek and I hate that I didn't see that as a bad sign before it was too late.

"Delilah, are you okay?"

She shakes her head. "I hate seeing you like this, and you know when you cry, I do too. I can't help it."

"Tears of solidarity," I joke with her, and she laughs, the two of us smiling as the tears fall. "I didn't mean to make this conversation sad."

"Don't." She points her finger at me. "I think we both needed a good cry."

"I have a good cry at least once a day where nobody can see me through glass windows."

"Crying on your own is no fun," Delilah throws her arm around me as she grabs my bags for me. "Now, I have two ice cream cones in the shop calling our names. What do you say to a treat while we walk home?"

I can't help but smile at my best friend. I truly don't know how I survived a few years without her within driving distance of me. "I want sprinkles on mine."

"That's my girl."

Chapter Nine

— **LET DOWN BY RADIOHEAD**

I'M ALREADY DRUNK. I knew walking back into this house was going to bring too much shit up, so I came prepared. I stopped by the liquor store after I checked out of the hotel, Amara waved goodbye to me and wished me luck on whatever I was doing in Nettles, and I promised I would see her around.

It's not entirely false. I'm sure I'll run into her again, although according to her, she works a little too much to be able to have any fun.

I'm swaying on my feet as I clutch the letter in one hand and the bottle in the other. I take large swigs of lukewarm whiskey as I try to stop my feelings. It doesn't work. Just like last time, the memories still manage to overwhelm me.

I miss my brother. I miss every single thing about him. His voice. His laughter. His willingness to hold me up when I was feeling too much. Tristan may have become the man of the family, but Tobias was always the one that held me up when things felt too heavy. He was always the one to calm those feelings down by pulling out a puzzle to distract my mind.

God, I fucking miss him.

I somehow make it up the stairs, my balance already fucked as I grab the railing to steady myself. I head down the familiar hallway straight for the door at the end of it. I kick it open, drops of whiskey falling to the floor as I trip into the room I used to inhabit with Tobias when we were children.

I can almost see the ghosts of who we once were still in here, still floating around untouched by time.

"I wish we could stay here forever," I remember saying that to him more than once.

"Nothing lasts forever. That's what makes this place so special. We only exist in it for a little while, and we always leave wanting just a bit more."

God, he was always so goddamn philosophical, even at a young age. Always more well read than the rest of us besides Teags.

"Can you see me? Can you see what you've done to me?"

One day, maybe I'll get myself out of this anger, pain, guilt, and sadness, but today is not that day.

I don't mean what I said—not really. I know he was hurting and he thought it was the only way out. I know it's not his fault he felt how he did. I just wish I could talk to him about it. I wish he could answer all of the questions I still have for him. I wish I could sit at the table and do a puzzle with him one last time.

This house will always be the place I remember my brother the most. Even in Pennsylvania he's not as clear to me as he is up here.

"Come back, Tobias," I say as I take another drink, falling to my knees onto the carpet. "I miss you. I don't want these fucking notes."

I throw the envelope in front of me. It barely makes a sound as it falls to the floor. I take another drink from the bottle I'm barely holding, and I suddenly can't remember if this is the first one I bought or if I opened the second one.

Fuck, I can't breathe.

"I need you," I yell to the room. "I still need you even though you're gone."

If I die in this house in Vermont, then at least I'll die with the last memories being of my brother. If I die here, maybe the first thing I'll see when I wake up is Tobias pulling a chair out for me, a puzzle box sitting in front of him as if he had been waiting for me the entire time.

I feel so alone up here. I could call Tristan. I could call Teags or my mom, but I can't keep leaning on them when they have their own shit to sort through. Plus, they're both moving in the right direction—forward—and I've been stuck in the same place I've been since I got the phone call about what happened. Time has frozen me to that spot, and maybe if I keep drinking, I'll stop feeling.

Maybe then I'll feel better.

"Fuck it," I say to myself as I throw the bottle onto one of the beds, reaching for the envelope that taunts me. I tear it open, finally seeing the last riddle or whatever the fuck he wrote in this that he didn't feel he could say to my face.

```
Theo,
I am neither secret nor treasure, yet I wait
for discovery,
  Guarded by earth and overseen by silvered
night's glory.
  Time's hands have lost me, stories may
surround—
  What am I, silent and sealed, in darkness
profound?
  This is the last one, and remember, don't
open them until you have them all. I promise
it will all make sense soon. Trust me one last
time, brother.
```

`Tobias`

I reread it. I reread it ten times over, none of the words in front of me making any fucking sense, and then I get angry. Every time I read it, I get angrier because I should be able to understand this. I should know what he's trying to tell me because he's my fucking brother. I once knew what toppings he took on his cheeseburgers. I once made fun of him for merely getting a twist ice cream in a cone because of how plain it was. I called him boring. I regret that now, but if he was still here, I'd do it again in a heartbeat just to hear him laugh at how ridiculous I sounded.

I can't figure this out.

I can't breathe.

I can't hold myself up.

How do I stay standing when my body wants to fall to the floor? The floor is comforting. Laying on it means I have nowhere else to fall to. It's the end. I can't fall any further unless the earth opens up and swallows me whole, and I take comfort in that.

God, I'm fucking freezing. I can feel myself start to shiver as I read the letter one more time. I try to grab a blanket, but it won't budge, so I pick myself up and head down the stairs. I miss a few steps and trip, but I somehow catch myself.

Or maybe I don't because all of the sudden, my cheek is cold against the floor.

Fuck, what is happening?

I blink my eyes, the weight too heavy to try and keep them open, but I swear I see the outline of Tobias standing by the front door.

"What are you doing here?"

"Looking out for you."

"Fuck," I carry myself to his silhouette. "Maybe you should have thought about that before you left instead of taking the time to hide all this shit for me. How long did you have this all planned out? Because

I thought this was some spur of the moment decision you made, but it turned out not to be. So you're telling me that not once while you were doing all this did you think you could talk to any of us about what you were feeling? Not mom, or me, or Tristan? What the fuck is wrong with you? You could have come to any of us," I say as I reach out to touch the figure before me, only to smack my hands against the door.

Does he think he's going to get away from me that easily?

I'm panting as I throw the door open, my body still shivering from how cold it's become, and as my knees meet the grass of the front yard, I finally see him again.

"Tobias? Is that you?"

And I don't even get to hear his answer as I slip into the darkness.

Chapter Ten

— **THE YAWNING GRAVE BY LORD HURON**

I'M IN THE MIDDLE of crocheting some small coasters for Delilah's place when a loud bang makes me pause. I don't think it was on my door, but when I hear someone yelling, I get up and head for my front door.

I cautiously open it, wondering why someone could be making all this noise so late at night, but the only thing I see is Theo kneeling in his front yard.

"Theo?" I yell across the street as I tuck my cardigan into me. It's still pretty warm out tonight but cardigans have always been my favorite thing to lounge in, and I don't want the entire neighborhood to see me in my pajamas. "Theo? Is that you?"

He doesn't answer either time I call his name, but I see his lips moving from here. The minute he falls over, I barely think as I sprint across the lawn towards his house. There's a bad feeling in my gut, my stomach swirling as I run to his yard. By the time I get over to him, his entire face is pale, his lips are a light shade of blue, and his body is cold.

It feels like I'm holding a dead man in my hands.

"Theo?" I slap his face lightly a few times. "It's Daisy. Are you okay? Can you hear me?"

When I think he's not going to answer me, his eyes open slightly, and I somehow turn him over as he gags and then throws up in the lawn.

"Shit," is all I can say as I wipe his mouth when he's done. "What did you do? Did you eat something?" I can smell alcohol on his breath, and I guess that answers my question, but now I have about a thousand more.

"Tobias, is that you?"

Tobias? "It's Daisy. I'm here, okay? What do you need?"

God, he's still so pale. It's like he's not even here with me. Gone is the boy I used to know. Gone is the man I met again while we walked around the pond in town. In front of me is someone that smells of alcohol while sadness seeps from his bones.

"I need you, man."

"I'm here," is all I say as he turns to throw up again, only this time he goes limp in my arms. His eyes are no longer staring back at me, and his body is freezing cold. "Oh, fuck."

I slap him a few more times, but as his lips get darker and his face gets paler, I don't even think before I throw his arms around my shoulders and drag him into the passenger seat of my car. I sprint into my house, grab my keys, purse, and phone, and when I get back into the car, I dial Luca.

He answers on the second ring. "Why are you calling my work phone?"

"Are you at the hospital?"

He must sense the panic in my voice because his voice gets deeper. "What's going on?"

"I'm headed to you. Can I pull up in the emergency lane?"

"What are you bringing to me?"

"I—" I can barely speak. I have no fucking idea what happened to Theo to make him like this. "I-I don't know."

"Is it my mom? Is it Delilah?"

"No," I stop his panic before it sets in. "It's my neighbor. I found him unconscious but breathing in his front yard. H-He wasn't making any fucking sense, and he threw up a few times."

"Does he have a pulse?"

"I don't know, Luca!"

"Get him here, but drive safe, okay? I'll be waiting outside for you," he starts yelling to his team about what I told him before he speaks again. "Does he smell like alcohol?"

"A little, yeah."

"Do you know how much he had to drink?"

"No," I say as I wipe a stream of tears from my eyes. As I look over at the man in my passenger seat, I can't see the rise and fall of his chest. "He's not breathing."

"How far out are you?"

"I-I don't know. Maybe fifteen minutes." *If I drive like a maniac like I am now.*

"Check his pulse for me," he tells me and I grab Theo's wrist. I fumble around a little, trying to keep myself steady on the empty road as I search for any sign that he's alive.

"Luca—"

"You're doing fine. Just feel around for it."

I fumble with his arm before I feel a soft thrum under his skin. "I found it. It's weak, but it's there."

"We'll be ready when you get here. Just calm down and focus on driving, okay?"

I nod and mumble before he hangs up the call.

"Theo, if you can hear me, please fucking stay with me," I yell at him. I don't know what else to do. I'm fucking terrified. One of my hands is still wrapped around his wrist because if I let go, he might stop breathing.

It's only a little further to the hospital, but if I get there and he doesn't have a pulse, then this was all for nothing, but if I had waited for an ambulance, he could already be dead.

My heart is beating out of my chest, and I swear dots are covering my vision, but I will not freak out while I'm driving. That's for after Luca has him. Then I can crash and cry and get this adrenaline out of my body.

I'm scared. Terrified that he did this to himself on purpose. He barely said anything about why he was back here. I don't know who his emergency contact is. I don't have his family's phone numbers, and I barely know anything about him. I'm not going to be of any help at the hospital, especially if he dies. I don't know who to call. I don't know what to tell them. I have no answers.

"Stay with me, fuck, please stay with me," I say as I hightail into the emergency room. I can already see Luca waiting for me with a bunch of other people. I barely have time to put my car in park before they're opening my door and dragging Theo out of my passenger seat.

They're all speaking, but I can't hear anything besides the buzzing in my ears as I follow them inside the emergency room. I've never heard chaos feel this silent. The only thing I can seem to focus on is Theo as they wheel the gurney into a room, the doctors cutting his shirt off so they can hear if he's still breathing.

I feel a hand against my arm, and when I look up and see Luca staring back at me, offering me a hoodie to cover up with, I take it before he jumps in to help.

"Go sit in the waiting room. I've got this."

"He has nobody else," I somehow speak through my closed throat.

"Daisy, go," he says as Theo's body starts to shake. "Turn him on his side!" I hear Luca shout as my breathing picks up. All I feel are tears falling down my face, before someone guides me to a chair in the packed waiting room.

I'm sure I look like a mess, but I don't care. All I can do is reach for my phone, and call my best friend. I need her voice to steady me as I come down from this adrenaline rush.

"Dais? What the hell are you doing up this late?"

I can't even say one word before I burst into tears.

— LOOK AFTER YOU BY THE FRAY

ALL I CAN HEAR is the steady beep of the machines around me as my leg shakes.

I told Delilah everything, and she kept asking if I needed her to keep me company at the hospital, but I told her no. All I needed was her to listen to me get it all out. I must have cried in the waiting room for hours before Luca came to bring me to Theo's room. Last he told me, Theo was stable.

They had to pump his stomach, give him a ton of fluids, and monitor him overnight. He may even have to stay a few days, but I haven't heard anything in a few hours.

I look at the man lying in the bed. He looks a lot better than he did earlier. He has some color back in his face, but I wish he would wake up. I'm not going to feel better until I see his eyes open and hear him say something.

The door opens and in walks Luca, still in his same scrubs as earlier as he looks over Theo's chart. I will say, it is nice seeing a familiar face here. Luca is one of the best emergency doctors at this hospital, and having him looking out for Theo gives me a lot of hope.

The familiar Madison blond hair is still perfectly styled even through his twelve hour shift. I thought he was supposed to leave a few hours ago, but it looks like he's still here. Luca always seems to be here—according to Delilah.

"Should we call someone for him?"

"I don't know who to call," I tell him. "Is he going to be okay?"

"He better be." He always was a little too straightforward. "I hope I didn't pump his stomach for nothing."

"Luca," is all I can say. "I'm glad you're here, but aren't you supposed to be home? I'm sure Amelie is waiting for you."

His eyes cast down at Theo's chart, his wedding ring twisting in his finger before he answers me. "Amelie knows what's going on. She's the one who told me to stay."

"Oh."

"He should wake up anytime now. We kept him sedated with some meds so his body could rest, but it's all up to him when he wants to wake up."

"Thank you for all your help."

"It's my job, Dais," he reminds me. "Do you want some food?"

I shake my head. "I'm not hungry."

"You should eat something."

"Luca—"

"Fuck," someone mutters as I turn to see Theo's eyes start to open. "My stomach hurts."

Luca and I rush to opposite sides of Theo's bed, him grabbing his stethoscope to hear his breathing while I grab his hand, feeling for his pulse in his wrist so I can make sure this is really happening.

He's awake. Thank fucking god he's awake.

"How are you feeling?" Luca asks him as he hooks up another bag of fluids.

"Shitty," he says.

"Well, a blood alcohol content of .35 tends to do that."

Holy shit. "What?"

Luca merely raises his brows at me as he takes a seat in the rolly chair. "Dais, I'm going to need you to step out for a few minutes while I talk with him."

"Of course," I say as I head for the door. I'm almost out of here until Theo speaks up.

"She can stay," he mumbles. "It's fine. She can hear whatever you have to say to me."

My eyes move to Luca, and he nods as I head back for the chair I was sitting in. I don't feel like I should be in here for this, but if he wants me to stay, then I will.

"Am I going to be the one to tell you to stay away from the alcohol, or do we have to have another conversation?" Theo says nothing. "I'm a mandatory reporter, now, if you're struggling with something or if you drank that much to try and end—"

"I didn't," Theo cuts him off, his face still as weighted as the day I saw him again for the first time. There's something I'm missing, I'm sure of it. I'm betting that it has to do with the letter I got from Tobias telling me to watch out for Theo while he was here. "I wouldn't."

Luca merely sighs, and I'm sure he doesn't believe him, but I do. I don't think he would try and drink himself to death, at least not on purpose.

"Look, I'm a doctor. I see people just like you come through my emergency room every single day. Everyone that I see is in some sort of pain. Now, it's mostly physical pain, sometimes it's mental, sometimes emotional. Especially the family members I see after I tell them the worst news of their lives. Most of the patients I see are constantly living in pain, whether it be for days, weeks, months, years. I've come to realize that most of the people on this planet are in pain, some are just better at hiding it. Or maybe it only manifests when the pain can no longer hold in one place. I haven't figured that out quite yet, but what I do know is that *everyone* is in pain. So"—Luca rolls closer to his bed and takes a seat—"What kind of pain are you living with, Theo?"

I look at the man in the hospital bed, the beeping of the machines still permeating my ears as he speaks.

"My brother died by suicide. He did it in our family cabin, and he left us all letters before he did it."

My chest caves in more than I thought it could.

"Tobias is dead?" I mutter, and he looks over at me and nods.

"How long ago?" Luca asks him, his tone slightly softer than it was before.

"Two years."

"I know a crutch sometimes seems easier, but in the long run, it will cause more problems. Do you often almost drink yourself to death or is this a first?" He sighs, his voice softer and less demanding than it was before.

"This is a first."

"You can't keep doing this to yourself," he tells him. "If things get tough, you talk to someone. Now, I have some connections with—"

"No. I don't need any of that bullshit," Theo says. "I can handle it. I just overestimated myself."

"If you don't want to go that route, then you can talk to me," I say before I can think. "We are neighbors, after all."

I don't know why I said that. Here he is sitting in a hospital bed after almost dying last night and I think I can magically fix all of this just by being here for him. I know it's not going to be so easy, and I don't even know how long Theo plans to stay in Vermont, but while he's here, maybe I can help lessen the pain. Maybe I can help him through it so something like tonight doesn't happen again.

I can only hope what I offer will help, but I'm sure it's not that easy. What he's going through—even though I don't know all of it—is some heavy shit. He's clearly still grieving and using alcohol as his crutch. I'm no expert on this, but maybe if I help him, he'll change his mind about getting professional help.

"I trust Daisy here to keep an eye on you, but I'm going to put a packet together with resources and things that might be helpful for you in the future," Luca says before he stands up. "You can leave after this entire bag is gone."

"Thanks, doc."

"No need to thank me," he tells Theo before he looks at me. "I better not see you in here again."

"You won't," I promise him as I toss his hoodie back to him. "Tell Amelie I say hello."

"I will," he says as he leaves.

My hand is still in Theo's as Luca leaves, and I can feel myself start to get emotional as the dust swirling in my mind begins to settle.

"Are you okay, Daisy girl?"

"I should be asking you that," I say as I get myself together. "You scared the crap out of me."

"I'm sorry. I didn't mean to scare you."

"I know," I say as I squeeze his hand in mine. "Are you hungry? I can grab something for you."

"I just want to go home," he tells me.

"Soon," I tell him as I take a seat. "You heard Luca."

"Do I have any personal items with me?"

"Uh, yeah," I reach for the blue bag, feeling nothing in it. I can't even remember what he had on him when I dragged him to my car. "Here."

"Thanks," he says, a familiar white envelope coming into view as stares at it for a beat too long before unfolding it. "This is the last thing I'll ever get from my brother."

"I'm so sorry," I tell him. "I know how close you all were." Anyone around the West family could tell how close of a family they were. It's how the Madisons are too. I can't imagine how it felt losing part of your family how Theo has.

It's all starting to make sense now—why he's back, the letter I got, all of it. The pieces are slowly falling into place, but I still feel like I'm missing something.

"I would say it's okay, but I don't think you would believe me."

"I wouldn't," I tell him. "But if I'm going to look after you, then we need to have a talk."

"Geez, Dais, at least invite a guy for dinner first," he jokes, his other hand coming to his stomach. "Ow."

"Even in pain, you're still cracking jokes." I lightly hit his arm. "I'll take you home and you can rest and then we'll talk, okay?"

"You don't have to—"

"Don't argue with me. It's been a very long night and I made a promise to look after you."

"I'm not roping you into my mess," he says, his eyes drooping as he looks over at me. "Because I am a fucking mess, Dais."

"No offense, but I roped myself into your mess the minute I saw you on your lawn. Let me help you, Theo. Let me look after you."

His face twists, and I can tell he feels horrible for the events of the last twelve hours. "Okay, but just know, I'm saying yes to this for extremely selfish reasons."

"Is that so?"

He nods. "I'm just really excited to spend time with you how we used to. Maybe we can even dust off the old swingset in the backyard."

"I'd like that very much," I tell him. "But only when you're well enough."

He throws his head back and groans, and I can tell this next chapter of whatever is going on is going to be exciting or terrifying—maybe even a combination of both. We're headed into the unknown, and I'm way too nervous to unearth whatever seems to be headed our direction.

Chapter Eleven

— I THINK I'M LOST AGAIN BY CHASE ATLANTIC

My head starts pounding the moment I wake up and my memories are hazy as a small stream of light enters the room.

The last thing I remember is the hospital room, Daisy holding my hand and that doctor walking out the door. I'm not even sure I remember how I got back here—all tucked into bed and a glass of water on the table next to me. I never took the sheets off of the furniture. I never got the house ready for me to actually live in it, so how did I end up back here?

A noise from downstairs makes me pause, and I think I already know who it is as I drag myself out of bed. I'm about to open the door when I see myself in the mirror, and fuck, do I look like I've been dragged through the dirt. The bags under my eyes are more prominent than ever, my hair is a mess, my mustache isn't neatly combed how it usually is, and I look way paler and skinnier than I used to.

I cringe at myself as I open the door, softly padding down the stairs as I take them slower than I usually do.

As I get to the bottom of them, the house already looks and feels different. The air is less stale than it was—she must have opened the windows—and this place actually looks like it's been lived in. It's a stark difference from how I remember it last, the ghost of my brother haunting me before disappearing again.

I don't see any bottles either. I must have left more than a few scattered around this place, but they're all gone. If I didn't know any better, I'd think I was still dreaming, especially when Daisy's beautiful face comes into view.

"Good morning, sunshine." She smiles at me. "Are you feeling okay?"

"Better than I was," I tell her as I look around the kitchen. "It smells great in here."

"I hope you don't mind, but I went to the store this morning and grabbed some food for you. The fridge was empty when we got back last night." She almost looks shy about all this. Her face and mindset are saying one thing, but her body language is saying another. She's curled in on herself, practically clutching her cardigan in her fists as she pushes the eggs around the pan, the bacon crackling in another.

I have to say, it's been a long time since I've had someone cook anything for me—besides my mom—and I missed waking up to someone in the space I'm inhabiting.

"I don't mind," I tell her. "It's nice, actually."

"What?"

"Your company," I take a seat at the table, now clean and dust-free.

I swear her cheeks turn a different shade of pink than they were before she plates the eggs and fiddles with the other stuff she's cooking.

"Eat up." She sets the plate in front of me. "Your body needs sustenance."

"Did you sleep here?" I wonder, noticing the green blankets on the couch I've never seen before.

She nods, her voice a mere whisper from what it just was. "I told Luca I was going to look out for you and I meant it."

I ball my hands into fists as I think about how much I hate myself for dragging her into the mess I call my life. I fucked up. I don't want to use her as a crutch. I can't. I'd never forgive myself if I got closer to her only to disappoint her in the future when she realizes I'll always pick a bottle over everything else. I don't want to do that to her, and it's inevitable.

"Dais, look, I'm really glad you're a familiar face up here, but I don't want to tangle you up in the mess that my life is. Fuck." I run a hand through my messy hair. "I hate that you had to see me how you did. I hate that you were so worried about me at the hospital, and I'm sorry for everything I've already put you through, so you don't need to—"

"I'm gonna stop you before you tell me I don't have to do all this for you." She grabs her plate and sits across from me. "I appreciate your apology. I was terrified when I saw you facedown on the lawn, but I'm glad I was here. I made the decision to run over to you and help because I knew something was wrong. You forget how I once knew everything about you, even if we were young and only saw each other a few weeks every summer."

God, I wish we could go back to what we once were. Everything always felt so simple when we were kids. Now, all I do is fuck up. All I do is make a thousand mistakes and not bother to fix them because I know I'm going to make a thousand more.

"I scared you, though."

She nods again and that hits me in the stomach. "I thought you were dead."

I can feel tears start to funnel into my eyes as I think about what I put her through. Normally, I've been all by myself in these places Tobias wanted me to go—well, the ones that required me to travel. Nobody had ever seen me so bad before. It has always been me by myself in hotel rooms, drowning my sorrows and falling over myself.

Vermont holds the most memories of me and my family—especially Tobias and I. I knew there was a reason he put this place last on the list, but what I didn't expect was her. The girl-next-door that took one look at me and decided I was good enough to be her friend. She saw something in me all those years ago, and I bet when she looks at me now, all of that is gone.

"I'm sorry," I tell her, and I'm sure that won't be the last time those two words are uttered from my lips in her direction. "Life hasn't been kind to me since the last time you saw me, which isn't an excuse, I know that. It's been hard, I guess is what I'm trying to say."

"I can understand that." She takes a bite of her eggs. "Life has a way of doing that to you."

"What?"

"Well, I don't know. Growing up you always think it's easier as an adult. Everyone always looks like they have it all together, but when you grow up, all of the things you thought you would be get smaller and smaller. Responsibilities tend to take over, and one day, you look around and nothing is how you thought it would be, but the worst part is, when you look around, it seems like you're the only one who can't seem to figure things out."

Wow. She somehow said every single thought I've been having coherently enough. I was never great at that—getting my thoughts into words. That's more of a Liv or Tobias kind of thing.

"How did you know it was Tobias?" the question slips out of my mouth. I had been wondering ever since his name fell out of her mouth.

She stops chewing her eggs, and before she says anything, she heads for her bag on the couch and pulls out an envelope. My heart stops beating for a second at the sight of it. There's no way that's what I think it is. Did she read the letter I finally opened the other night? It wouldn't make any sense to her, but I can see why she knew it was Tobias.

"This showed up in my mailbox two years ago." She slaps it in front of me, so I grab it, slipping the familiar paper out of the envelope. "I'll admit, it confused me at first, but now it's all starting to make sense."

I read it over a few times. It's addressed to her and it's from Tobias. He really planned all of this out in advance, and that kills me. My brother knew he wasn't going to be here for me, but he's still looking out for me even when he's gone.

I've never felt so confused in my entire life. In a way, I want to punch him, yet I also want to thank him. He always did know what was best for me when I couldn't see it for myself. And that's why he'll always be my big brother.

"So, I guess Tobias wanted us to reconnect."

"I guess," she says, running a hand through her platinum hair. "But why? He didn't even know if I was still here. In fact, the letter came while I was still living in Boston."

"Boston?"

"Mhm," she smiles, but it's not her real one. It looks like she's remembering something she'd rather forget. "I only recently came back to Nettles."

"Huh." I lean back in my chair. "I guess I have some explaining to do."

"Only if you want to." She reaches for my hand. "If it's too hard, you can open up gradually."

"The full story is the least I could give you, Dais." And then it all sort of pours out of me. Everything from my father dying and why we never came back to Nettles to Tobias dying and leaving me this bucket list full of places to go and search for whatever he has hidden for me. I also talk about the investigation that was done after they found his body. I tell her how my sister and mother had to go identify him because Tristan and I weren't there, and how I was so drunk I barely remember getting on the flight home.

I tell her about how my brother only exists in the stories my family will tell of him, and in a small evidence box tucked in the back of a police station in Pennsylvania, if there's anything even left inside of it. That's all that will ever be left of him ever again.

It's actually easier to talk about than she might think. Not just because it's her, but because I'm always looking for ways to mention the two of them in any conversation I can.

That's the hardest thing about all of this. At the beginning, everyone is always asking you about them, but as time goes on, people don't want to hear about it over and over again even though it's the only thing I can think about sometimes.

I just wish people would ask me about them more. I wish more people would listen about how great my father and brother were.

"Wow," is all she can say by the time I've explained it all.

I'm waiting for her to say it's too much. I'm waiting for her to stand up and walk out of this house because she can't handle it all. My grief has always been too much for me to handle, so much so that it spills out into other parts of my life, and I wouldn't blame her for walking out of the door. In fact, I wish she would because I'd rather keep her far away from the tornado my life is at the moment.

"Does that happen often?" she asks me.

"What?"

"Last night."

I shake my head. "I've never been that bad before. I even scared myself waking up in that hospital room." I thought I had done something stupid. I thought I was in another dream, and at first, I thought Tobias was the one grabbing onto my hand, but when I heard her voice, I knew it was real and not another apparition scaring me in the dark.

"Why do you drink so much, if I can be blunt?"

I stifle a laugh. "You can be anything you want in front of me, Daisy girl."

Her lips turn up for the smallest second before she gets serious again.

"When I first heard about Tobias, all I wanted to do was stop feeling. I was young when my father died, and of course, I was upset. It was sudden, and it shook our entire family up." I feel more tears start to come, and I let them. I'm not afraid to cry in front of her. Hell, I've done it a thousand times with how clumsy I was as a child. One time I fell when were were on our bikes riding around town, and I remember it really fucking hurt.

Until the girl I was biking with came over and kissed the red spot on my knee, pulling out Band-Aids and ointment from her backpack and she patched me right up on the sidewalk.

"My mom does that when I'm hurt and it helps me feel better."

"I already feel better, flower girl."

I'd lie and say all of the memories of the girl across from me have only started bubbling up since I've been here, but the truth is, I never really forgot about her. Tobias was right in that letter. I talked about her all of the time.

"But?" she coaxes me to continue.

"But when Tobias died, I felt like my entire world had come crashing down on top of me. When my sister called me and told me, I screamed at her. I called her a liar as she sobbed through the phone at me." A few tears fall onto the wooden table. "I didn't want to believe her, but I also didn't want to feel it if it was true. I don't think I could ever replicate the emotions I had that day again if I tried. I never want to feel that way again, but sometimes, I feel it creeping up on me."

"Like the other night," she whispers. "I'm guessing being back in this house is making that worse."

I nod. "I finally opened the last letter he sent me, and I don't understand the clue he left. I'm a failure. I'm failing him, myself, everything. So, I picked up a bottle and tried to drown my feelings with something else. Obviously, it didn't help, and the guilt won't stop pouring in because I woke up this morning feeling shittier than before."

I put my hands over my face, not wanting her to see how pathetic I am as I wait for her to say something, anything.

— GIRL OF CONSTANT SORROW BY AVERY ANNA

I'm trying my hardest to not burst into tears in front of him. My sadness won't help him right now, no matter how big of a rock is currently sitting in my throat. Here is this person I used to know falling apart in front of me, and here I am trying my best to not cry and have him console me.

This isn't about me. It's about Theo and the grief he's experiencing over his brother, and even if he doesn't want me here wrapped up in all of this, Tobias does, and that's a good enough reason for me to stay.

"I can't help you through this if you're drunk."

"Dais, you don't—"

I put my hand up and he stops. "I want to help. I want to be here for you through this. Not just because we're neighbors and we used to know each other, but because if the roles were reversed, you would be doing the same for me."

"I'm not sure that's true." His head falls forward, and I grab his chin and make him look at me.

"You might not be sure who you are, Theo West, but I know you." I stare at him. "The next time you feel like drinking, come and find me. If I'm not home, I'm either at the store or the hotel. Or with Delilah.

I guess there are a few places I could be, but I'll give you my cell phone number and you can call me if you can't find me."

"You'll be my someone to lean on?" He smirks as my hand still grips his chin, and I can't help but smile back at him.

"You're damn right." I let go of his face and the two of us return to breakfast. "Last night cannot happen again. It's not healthy, and I know I have no right saying this, but—"

"You have every right. You have every right to scream at me, but I know that's not you," he says. "You're Daisy. Soft, sweet, Daisy like the flower."

Hearing him call me that makes my heart skip a beat. I'm not sure I'm the same girl I was when we were kids. I'm sure I've changed way too much. Younger Daisy was as sensitive and emotional as I am now, but I never took that to be anything bad. I didn't think there was anything wrong with me.

But then you grow up, and here come all of the social media posts about how you're not doing enough, how you should be traveling all over the world by the time you're twenty-five, and here comes eighty different articles on every social media platform you're on about five new tricks you can use to lose weight! Because nobody wants to see your hip dips—whatever those are—and stretch marks aren't cute. And hey, your husband wishes you looked how you used to when he met you, and he'll cheat on you with multiple different models because they looked better underneath him than you ever did. Then you'll have to sit through multiple divorce settlement meetings because he tricked you into signing a pre-nuptial agreement he swore you would never need because he loved you.

You'll listen to him say all of these things about you, and you still love him because emotions never just go away for you, they sit and linger in the deepest parts of your body until they burst open and you're crying while your attorney is handing you one-ply tissues.

Then you're back home, divorced, and nowhere you thought you would be when you were fifteen with stars in your eyes about what your life would look like in your twenties when people would finally take you seriously.

Makeup was once an artistry I possessed. It was my escape when the world got too heavy and I could dip into the creative side of my brain. It was comforting when everything else felt like chaos. I miss when I used to sit at my vanity just to create something on the blank canvas of my face. Now the only time I pick up a brush is for someone else because no amount of coverage will erase all of the comments I think about myself when I look in the mirror.

I scribble down my number on a napkin because I don't know where his phone is before I start to clean up breakfast. I'm at the sink when I feel him behind me, his hands on my waist before he spins me around.

"Go home, Dais. I can clean this up."

"You're supposed to be resting. Luca said no heavy-lifting and you're supposed to hydrate."

"I will," he says. "I promise. You can even come back over later after you're done at the store and check on me."

His hands are still on my waist, and it's all I can think about as I stare into the same eyes I once saw every summer. Gone is that familiar boy from the swing set and in his place is someone who has felt the effects of time and growing up, same as me. I'm not the same girl who had stars in her eyes when she looked at the world around her.

Derek killed that part inside of me, and now all I see when I look in the mirror is someone who will never be perfect. Someone who will never look like everyone else does. Someone who isn't pretty. Someone who can't love someone into staying loyal. Love is not enough. It will never be enough, yet I still find myself believing that maybe it can be—one day, love will be enough. Despite all of the shit, and the outside noise, it will survive, blocking all of that out because it's strong enough to.

"Fine," is all I say as I turn the sink off, his hands falling from my hips and immediately latching onto the counter. "There's water in the fridge, and if you need me, call me."

"Okay."

I'm halfway to grabbing my purse before I turn back to him. "Promise me."

"If I need you, I'll call you."

"And don't bother looking for a bottle," I whisper. "I dumped all of the ones I found."

"Thank you," he says, his hands turning white from how hard he's gripping the counter.

"There are puzzles in a box over there." I point to one in the corner of the room. I may have cleaned the necessary stuff I needed to, but I didn't touch anything in the boxes.

"You remembered my fondness for puzzles."

"Of course I did." I laugh at him. "You and I once spent two days on the floor of your room putting one together, and I remember how mad you got at Tobias when he accidentally stepped on it and ruined our finished masterpiece."

I can tell he knows what I'm referencing because his face lights up in a way I haven't seen since he's been back in my orbit.

"I bit his head off for doing that and it wasn't even on purpose," he whispers under his breath. "I'll see you later?"

"Sounds like a plan," I say as I open the door, turning back to him before I leave. "I hope today is better than yesterday."

He doesn't say a word, but he does throw a smile in my direction before I'm headed to my car, exhausted from how little I slept, but somehow, a little more pep in my step than before.

Chapter Twelve

— PIECES BY THE BAND CAMINO

It's been a few days since the incident—that's what I'm calling it now—and Daisy has stayed over for the last few nights. I keep telling her she can sleep in her own bed, but all she does is stare at me for a few seconds before she gets comfortable on my couch.

Last night, she pulled out a puzzle and the two of us started it only for her to fall asleep on me halfway through. She's been trying to make sure I fall asleep before she does, but last night, her exhaustion must have caught up to her.

I'll admit, I feel selfish as fuck while she's around.

On one hand, I hate that she's fussing over me this much and putting her life on hold to watch over me while I'm up here. On the other hand, I fucking love having her in my space. This house feels more alive when I see her floating around, making my breakfast and inhabiting the space.

No matter how many times I tell her to go home, part of me is elated every time she fights me on it.

I spend every day alone while she's at the store, but today, the one task I want to start is finally sorting through some of these boxes. I know my mom told me to take my time up here, but I have to start sometime. She wants to sell this place, so I need to hold my end of the bargain up and actually make myself useful.

My phone rings as I'm about to open the first box.

"I didn't disturb you, did I?"

"You're never a disturbance," I tell my sister. Though, I am confused. She hasn't called me in a while and it's the middle of the day. The last time this happened Tobias was dead. "What's up? It's the middle of the day, aren't you supposed to be at work?"

"I took a few days off. I was feeling a little under the weather."

"Are you okay?" Teags has been very quiet while she's been in Arizona, and I know Tristan and I have been worried about her—him more than me, but that's how he's wired. I'm surprised he hasn't been bugging me more since I've been up here.

"Yup. Fine. Just wanted to call and check in. It's been a while since we talked."

She misses me. I'm sure of it, but Teags is never one to say her emotions outright. She'll dance around them until they burst out of her.

"Well, Vermont has proven to be the hardest search ever. I swear our brother was some sort of psychopath in another life. Good thing he didn't become a serial killer or something. He'd be way too good at it."

"Still hunting for his reason for sending you back to where we spent our childhood? Come on, Theo, I thought you were better at this."

I scoff at her. Doesn't she remember how into mystery novels I was as a child? How dare she insult me like this. "Oh, I've found some clues here, don't you worry. And there's a reason he gave this to me and not you. You're terrible at solving things like this."

"It's not how my brain works, and Tobias knew that."

I pause, feeling tears ready to fall out of my eyes. "Yeah, he did."

That's the one thing about all of us that I love. Separately, we're our own people, but we all have these things that connect us all to each other. Teags and Tobias always loved music, but they would always share their records with us so we could play it while Mom was making dinner with Tristan. Tobias and I loved puzzles, but we always left two sides of the table open in case Teags and Tristan wanted to join. Sometimes they did, other times, they didn't.

"So, what else has been going on?"

"I'm slowly going through all of these boxes. If I find anything you might want, I'll send you a picture. I'm going to start a donation pile, a garbage pile, and stuff we want to keep. I figure that would make it a lot easier for Mom when she eventually sells this place." I leave out the part about being in the hospital and almost drinking myself to death because the last thing I want is to worry my family over something that will never happen again.

Plus, I'm ashamed. If I could only handle things easier, then maybe I wouldn't have this problem I can't seem to get control of. If only I was more stable, more equipped to stand on my own two feet, then my crutch of choice wouldn't drown me every time I take a sip. I'm pathetic. A loser. I can't handle real life without needing something to lean on and hold me through the pain. It's just like Luca said—everyone is in pain. I seem to be someone who can't handle it. Not like most people. I need to be numb. To not feel. To push it to the side.

I'm weak.

"That sounds nice, Theo. I'm excited for you."

"Me too," I say as I set my phone down, ripping the tape off of the box in front of me. "But I have to go. I'm, uh, meeting a friend for lunch."

I pull one of Tobias's old journals out from the box as I rattle off some excuse to her.

"See you soon, hopefully?"

"I'll be back home at some point, but you're in Arizona, so—"

She cuts me off. "Right. Maybe I'll venture back up to Penn. Just tell me when you're coming back, okay?"

Why is she using that voice? "Got it. I love you, Teags."

"Yup. Love you too." I'm surprised to hear her say it back, but ever since Tobias died, she's been a little more vocal with telling us she loves us. Pulling emotions out of her always was a feat, especially when we were kids. She was always the one of us who needed her own time to process everything, that's why Tristan and I were so shocked when she told us she was moving across the country.

I set the journal in front of me as I dust off the cover. Tobias always did prefer composition notebooks for his journals over smaller ones. I carefully open it, flipping through the filled pages as I take in some of the things he wrote down. Most of it seems to be memories between all of us that he wanted to remember, but as soon as I get to some of the feelings, I close it.

I know he's gone, but it still feels like I'm invading his privacy looking through it.

Instead of continuing to snoop, I grab the clue he left me and read it again. I still have no idea what it could mean. This one is the hardest one I've had to deal with and I guess I should have known he would have saved the most complex clue for last.

Part of me is thinking it has something to do with time, like a clock or a watch, but we don't have a standing clock in this house. And all of the rest of them are digital, so there's no way he hid something in them.

I could tear the house apart and look for it in every crevice and corner, but what if he didn't even hide it in the house? What if it's somewhere else?

Fuck, I feel like drinking again.

Part of me longs to reach for my phone and call Daisy, but she needs a break from me during the day, so instead of that, I grab my keys, phone, and camera, and head out of the house towards Main Street. It's a beautiful day out—Vermont in the summer is always beautiful. I can almost feel the ghost of my younger self walking in my footsteps on the same route I used to ride my bike on.

I pass by a bunch of houses, a whole bunch of trees, and trails that people are riding bikes on before I get onto Main Street. It's not too far of a walk because of how small Nettles is.

I take a few snapshots on my walk. I love hearing the soft click of my camera, but one of my favorite parts of photography is seeing the stillness of the photos I take. I can capture so much with just one click, one picture. My life sometimes mimics the photos I take. That stillness, the singularity of one picture, that's what my grief feels like. Here is this photo I took, one moment of the billions we experience every day, yet this single picture captured is what I'll remember. My life feels like that. It has become so still, so stagnant.

I wish things were getting easier for me. I wish every day I didn't have to force myself out of bed and keep on living. I wish I willingly got up every day with a smile, ready to face whatever the world has to offer. That hasn't been my reality for a while now, and I long for the day in the future I get to feel that way again.

I also haven't even started taking any photos for the magazine, so I'm hoping inspiration will strike and I'll see something worth photographing on this walk I've decided to take. I'm surprised Lucas hasn't emailed me yet asking for me to send any negatives I have to him so he can start developing them.

I continue down the street, stopping when I see the mountains in the background matching up with the way the buildings are, so I take a few from different angles from this spot. I bet this would be gorgeous at sunset. Maybe I'll stay down here and bug Daisy when she's done. Maybe she'll finally agree to have that dinner with me—eating together at my place doesn't count. No matter how many times she'll try to convince me that it does.

My stomach starts to growl half an hour into my impromptu photoshoot, so I head into the place Amara told me about. I'm pretty sure she mentioned her brother owning this when I talked to her, but maybe I was wrong.

I take a seat at the bar—it's not too packed in here since it's the middle of the day—and a guy around my age comes over to me.

"What can I get for you?"

"I'll take a coffee, but can you split it into two cups?"

He looks at me the same way everyone does when I ask that. "I guess that's not the weirdest thing I've had someone ask me to do."

I laugh a little as he walks away, fiddling around with a few cups as he makes it and sets it in front of me.

"What brings you into town?"

My eyebrows shoot up as soon as he asks me that. "How'd you know I'm new around here?"

"I know everybody in Nettles, perks of being a bartender," he says, and I'm fairly certain he's being sarcastic. "People tend to spill their guts after a few drinks."

"That sounds about right," I say, knowing I've done that a few too many times. "What's the craziest thing someone has ever told you?"

"Well, one time I had a guy come in looking for someone specific, and they started fighting before I broke it up."

"Oh, come on that's typical shit," I say as I sip from one of my mugs. "I'm talking about something that still keeps you up at night." He sighs in front of me as he searches his mind. "I'm Theo, by the way."

"Brooks," he says as something pops into his mind. "Oh, the worst one was actually a time where this guy came in, got super hammered, and started telling me all about the greatest hookup he had ever had."

"That's not too bad," I tell him, taking another sip.

"He was hooking up with my sister and explaining it in detail."

I spit what was in my mouth back into my mug, a few coughs coming from me as I try to breathe properly again.

"Oh, wow."

He nods at me, eyebrows shooting up as he wipes up some of the residue that came from my impromptu spit take.

"That's horrifying, actually," I cough a few more times before the coffee lodged in my throat finally goes down. "If someone had done that to me about my sister, I think I would figure out some way to erase my memories."

"Exactly," he agrees. "Is yours younger or older?"

"Younger. You?"

"Older."

"Amara, right?"

"Fucking hell, please don't—"

I shoot my hand up so he stops talking. "I stayed at her hotel. She told me about this place when I asked for recommendations around town."

"Thank god," he tells me. "I hope she didn't tell you much about me. She has a habit of doing that and everything she says is incorrect."

"Sounds like a typical sister to me." I shrug as I finish one of the cups. I don't reach for the next one and I can tell he wants to ask me about it. "Are you wondering about the two cups or what?"

"It's only driving me a little insane since you sat down and asked me for it."

I laugh. I can't help it. Normally, I'd throw some money down and leave, not bothering to explain myself, but Brooks seems like a decent guy, and I've enjoyed talking with him, so why the hell not, right?

"When my brother and I used to live in the same house, neither of us liked drinking a full cup of coffee, so we would always split it into two cups, one for each of us. It actually started with our father. He always did that in the mornings. He would make a cup of coffee, leave half of his cup in the fridge for my mom so when she woke up, she would have an iced coffee ready to go. Nobody besides my other brother and sister liked drinking a full cup. For some reason, the rest of us only need a little boost every morning, so the split cup thing kind of trickled down from our parents to Tobias and I."

He nods his head along with my story, and I can see a weight behind his eyes, but I don't ask him about it.

"Now, I do it to remember him."

"Where's your brother now?" he asks me.

"He's dead."

I can tell he wasn't expecting that response, and he starts to weigh his next words in his head. That always happens when you tell someone about someone that's gone. Next are the apologies and the pity. It's like fucking clockwork.

"What was your favorite thing about him?"

It takes me a minute to realize none of the usual shit people say didn't come from his mouth. I'm shocked. I almost wonder if he's ever lost someone to have that question ready so quickly.

"I don't think I could pinpoint just one thing, but there was this one time he called me when I was on my way home from my part-time job in high school." I stifle a laugh at this memory. "He told me there was a surprise waiting for me on the porch, and I could barely hear him through all of his laughter, but I understood it when I got home."

"What happened?" he asks me.

"He had gotten us a new puzzle to work on, but instead of ordering just one, he accidentally ordered one hundred of them."

Brooks and I both laugh—him because he's imagining one hundred puzzle boxes on my porch, and me because I remember the look on Tobias's face as I pulled into the driveway. He could barely breathe as I came up to the front door, and the two of us laughed until Tristan, Teags, and our mom came to see what all the fuss was about.

It was probably the hardest I've ever laughed in my entire life.

"So, what did you guys do with them?"

"We kept one of them, obviously, but we went around to different donation centers and schools and dropped them off. Tobias didn't want to return them even though he had spent so much money on them, so we donated all of them. Honestly, I think there's still about ten of them in my basement at home."

"That's hilarious," he says to me.

"Have you ever lost someone?" I ask. "I don't mean to pry or anything, but you asking me about him isn't something I get asked often after people find out about Tobias."

He braces himself against the bar, his head falling in front of him, a look I've emulated far too many times.

"Not in the same sense that you've lost someone," he tells me. "But yeah, I've lost someone close to me."

"Are they gone for good?"

He shakes his head.

"Then what's stopping you from getting them back?"

"If I were her, I'd stay far away from me. Especially after what I did."

Her? Well, color me intrigued. "I'm probably an expert in fucking things up, but what I've learned is that an apology goes a long way."

"It's not that simple," he tells me. "Nothing was ever that simple with us."

"Is it over completely between you two?"

He only raises his left hand to me, and I spot the ring on his finger.

"So, she's your wife? Ex?"

"She's nothing to me," he tells me. "If it were up to me, she would be my wife already."

That causes my brows to furrow. "Why isn't it up to you, Brooks?"

He's about to start telling me, but instead his phone buzzes in his back pocket, and he sighs heavily as he picks it up. He barely gets one word in before he's looking at me, rolling his eyes as he looks at another guy working with him.

"Can you watch this place for a few minutes?" The guy nods before Brooks turns back to me, the phone not in his ear but whoever's speaking is still talking. "It was nice talking with you. I'll see you around?"

"You bet," I tell him as I take a few bills out of my wallet and leave them on the counter. I guess that was my cue to leave as well. I will admit, that small boost of caffeine did help me a little, and I head straight ahead for the pond, hoping the coffee will somehow help my creativity.

Because along with my body being drained, my mind has been, too, and I miss when being behind the camera was easy. I miss when I wouldn't take a picture because I wanted to soak a moment in for myself.

Sometimes life is all about the pictures you didn't take. Sometimes, the memory is all you need to take you back to the place you were where something was so beautiful you couldn't bear to move your head away and see it through a smaller lens.

Chapter Thirteen

— THE SMALLEST MAN WHO EVER LIVED BY TAYLOR SWIFT

I'M AT THE STORE thinking about a thousand different things when Brooks bursts in and doesn't bother saying hello before shuffling through the new foundation bottles we just got in.

"Uh, hi?" He's not sparing a glance at me as he continues to rifle through the products. "Can I help you find something?"

"A beauty blender?"

I can't help but laugh, but a small twinge of pity twists through my bones. I bet Jamie sent him here for this.

"Come here," I say as I walk around the counter, headed to the section where all the brushes are. I pick up the small sponge and hold it out to him.

"You're telling me this isn't a marshmallow?"

"It's for complexion products," I tell him. "Usually foundation."

"Dais, you know the only type of foundation I know is the one underneath my house."

I laugh as he looks at me like I'm crazy.

"Is there just one size, or do I need eight different ones that all do the same thing?"

"Just the one size is all I have here," I say as I snatch it from his hands, leading us to the register. "Did she ask you to pick this up? Normally, she calls and barks what she needs from me to have ready for her to pick up."

I don't even take online orders for the store, but what Jamie says goes. Everyone in town knows it's best not to mess with her family. Not only do they know powerful people in powerful places, but they *are* powerful people in those same places. You don't cross them. It's basically an unwritten town rule.

Brooks sighs heavily as he leans his head against the checkout counter.

"Why are you doing this to yourself?" I ask him for the umpteenth time. He's miserable. Men should not look this miserable when they're weeks away from getting married to the supposed love of their life.

"Because I have to," he tells me, not elaborating any further like always.

"You don't *have* to do anything, Brooks." I ring up his purchase as he taps his credit card. "You especially don't have to tie yourself into a marriage that you'll be unhappy in just for political gain or whatever your family is telling you this will do."

"Your boy came into my bar today."

I immediately forget what we were just talking about as he switches the conversation. "What?"

"I met him."

I swear my heart stops beating. "Brooks, I swear if you served him anything, I will—"

He throws his hands up. "I remembered what you told me, and he didn't even ask for any alcohol. Just coffee split into two cups. I thought it was odd until he explained it."

I always noticed he did that in the mornings, but I never pressed. I assumed it was some quirk, but it looks like there's a reason for it. "Why did you think it was odd?"

"Because he only drank one of them."

Huh. Interesting.

"Did he say anything to you?"

"You know my rule, Dais," he reminds me. "What's said at the bar, stays at the bar."

I can only roll my eyes at him. "Did he seem okay?"

"He looked fine," he tells me. "Just a little depressed is all."

If you knew what he had been through, you'd be just as sad. I can't imagine still standing after all Theo's family has been through. Though, I wonder why he didn't call me if he felt like drinking. I told him to call, but my phone has been silent this entire morning. Well, except for the morning wake up messages Delilah always sends me.

"Don't we all eventually look the same when we get older?" He looks at me, brows pinched together. "Doesn't everyone look depressed about the way their life seems to be turning out?"

"I think that's just an us thing," he tells me. "Or a Nettles thing."

It's not like my life is depressing or anything. I have a family who loves me. I have beautiful friends who know me better than I know myself. I have a roof over my head and my life could be so much worse.

But there is an absence of romantic love in my life—something I will always long for—and I'm not sure when I'll get that back. It's not like I'm looking for it right now, not actively at least, but I see it everywhere. I see it in the ducks that float in the pond I walk by all the time, careful not to get too far apart from one another. I see it in the ice cream shop Delilah owns when someone grabs two dishes of ice cream instead of one. It still exists—there was never a doubt in my mind otherwise.

But I miss it. I miss knowing someone so completely that I could know when they're going to sneeze before they do. I miss hearing a knock at the door and knowing he was standing on the other side of it, waiting to see me open it. I miss planning meals, and all of the other little things that come with giving your life to someone.

"Yeah, maybe," is all I say as my phone starts to ring. The moment I look down, my entire body freezes to the floor. It's been so long since I've heard from him, so long since his name popped up on my phone that now all I feel in my gut is nausea. It used to be love. I used to have butterflies whenever his name showed up. Now all I feel is fear.

"Dais? Are you going to answer that?" Brooks asks me, but I can barely hear anything over the ringing in my ears. I have to pick it up. If I don't, it will just make him angrier.

"H-Hello?"

"Daisy!" he shouts my name into the phone as if we're two old friends who haven't spoken in a while. "How are you doing, babe?"

"Please don't call me that," I whisper as I turn around, not wanting Brooks to see the look on my face. He would know immediately that something was wrong, and I won't worry him with all of my drama. He has enough going on. "What do you want?"

"Speak up, I can barely hear you."

Those words make my body shake. I always hated hearing that. It's not that I wanted to whisper or talk quietly all of the time. I just get so damn scared of crying whenever I try to speak my mind, so I try not to speak it at all.

"What do you want?" I somehow manage to get out.

"I'm calling to see if you want to meet up somewhere and talk," he pauses. I can hear his dress shoes clicking on the floor he's pacing around. "You basically split after the proceedings, and my lawyer got your papers, but I know you're not still in Boston."

"Of course not."

"Well, where are you? I can fly wherever and we can—"

"I have nothing to say to you," I remind him. "I told you everything you needed to know in that stuffy conference room in Boston."

"Look, all I want to do is talk, Daisy. Don't you owe me that after you decided to divorce me?"

I scoff, unable to hold it back. He acts like it was a spur of the moment thing—our divorce—but all of the red flags from before came crashing down on me the moment I walked in on him fucking someone else in the bed we shared every night.

"No, I don't. You can talk to my lawyer, but when it comes to seeing me, that's not going to happen. I never want to see you again."

"God, always so fucking high and mighty, Dais. You're still mad I cheated on you? Grow up. Everyone cheats in relationships. You're just too soft to fucking handle that fact. You always have been. Now, tell me where the fuck you are, or I will get my lawyer involved."

I sigh heavily, wanting this next sentence to come out in one piece. "Then do it, Derek. I'm not afraid of you."

I end the call before he can spout another word. My breathing gets heavier as soon as I'm off, and I barely have time to think of something else to say before I turn around and grab my purse.

"What was that, Dais? Are you okay?"

I nod. That was the first time I've spoken to him since I signed the papers. I thought he would never speak to me again after he made out with everything he wanted, but apparently, I was wrong. He wants to talk, and something tells me he will stop at nothing to find out where I am.

He sure has the fucking money to do it.

"Daisy, what was that phone call about?"

"Nothing," I say as I head for the door. "Is that all you needed?"

"Did that have something to do with why you're back?" He doesn't bother answering my question, his voice behind me echoing around the store. "Why did you come back to Nettles?"

I grab the handle of the door, the bell ringing as I open it.

"Can you turn the lights off and lock the door for me? The key is by the register." I swipe the sign on the door from open to closed. "Please?"

"Yes, but—"

"Thanks," is all I say before I head out, needing fresh air but unsure of how I'm going to actually breathe it.

Chapter Fourteen

— ROBIN BY TAYLOR SWIFT

I walked around for a little bit after having that coffee, and I somehow found myself on the same bench, watching the ducks and the birds swim around. I don't really know where to go or what to do with myself. I could be making myself useful and clean out the boxes and bins of things at the house, but I'm not sure I want to continue doing that today.

I want to hold onto this place as long as I can. I spent so many years trying to get back here and I don't want to rush through this. I want to savor as many of these memory flashes I keep getting from being back here.

It's strange how a place can hold so many memories you've forgotten over the years. When I was young, this place felt like a whole new land I could explore. If I'm honest, I think coming up here as much as we did made me realize my love for traveling.

Discovering a new place is a feeling unlike no other. Discovering different views of the planet, whether it be from the top of a mountain photographing wolves and bears to a crystal clear lake where it's so silent you could hear a pebble skipping across the water, is something I'll always love.

I always knew there was more to the world than the small suburb I grew up in, and growing up knowing that was all waiting for me to come and discover felt like a race I couldn't wait to complete.

Now that I'm on this journey, I realize maybe the beauty isn't so much in discovering a new place. It's finding out who you are and what your place in the world is.

A flash of familiar hair brings me out of my head, and she doesn't even register that I'm sitting here as she passes by. I swear I see fresh tears on her face and I have the urge to wipe them away and hurt anyone who dared to make her cry.

"Dais?"

She stops in her tracks before turning around.

"Come sit with me," I offer.

She shakes her head. "I really need to get home."

"Just sit and pretend with me for a while."

"Pretend about what?"

"Oh, I don't know." I shrug. "Let's pretend that the world isn't terrifying and out to get us all."

She cracks a small smile as she pulls her sleeves down her arms. "Okay. I could definitely use some of that."

I pat the empty space next to me and she sits. We're looking at the same thing ahead of us, but I know our brains are wandering in different directions. I don't know what she's thinking about, but I wish I could crawl into her mind and figure out how to make her smile instead of cry.

She knows so much about me and my life, but I don't really know anything about hers. Obviously, I don't want to push her to talk about something, but her facial expressions mirror my own sometimes, and I want to ask her about it.

What's making you hurt? Is there a way I can fix it? How can I help to ease your pain like you've done for me?

If only it were that easy. If only I knew this version of her better, maybe I could actually ask and know I'll get a truthful answer. I ask anyway.

"Who's making you cry, Daisy girl?"

"My ex-husband." She sniffles as she pulls a small container of tissues out of her bag. "Well, not even him, really. I'm more disappointed in myself this time."

My eyes widen. I don't know what I was expecting her to say, but it wasn't that. "You were married?"

She nods. "Once upon a time."

I don't know whoever it was, but what a fucking idiot for letting someone like her go. God, look how much of each other's lives we've missed. I can almost feel the younger versions of ourselves sitting in our places. How would I explain all we've been through to my younger self? Would I tell him straight or would I protect his heart from the pain it's going to go through? I guess that's the question, isn't it?

"Sorry, I didn't mean to make things uncomfortable."

"You didn't," I say as I turn to face her. "What happened? Is he here in Nettles? What did he do and do I need to—"

"He's not here. And it's okay, all he did was call me."

"But he made you cry."

"A lot of things make me cry." She sighs. "I can be a little too emotional sometimes."

"Why do you say that like it's a bad thing?"

She shrugs and her bag slips off of her shoulder.

"Did you want to talk about what he said or do you want to sit here and pretend with me?"

"I'm tired of pretending. I think I've reached my limit."

"Then tell me," I say as she finally faces me. "I remember once upon a time telling you I would be your knight in shining armor when people made fun of you at the park. Do you remember that?"

She nods, a smile overtaking her face.

"I don't believe there's a statute of limitations on that, Dais," I chuckle as I grab one of her tissues and wipe the tears still falling. "You've listened to me talk about my brother. Now, it's my turn to listen. I'm all ears, and I've been told my shoulders are perfect to cry on."

"Is that so?"

"Mhm."

She sighs before speaking. "I don't know. I guess you see your life one way but when you grow up it becomes completely different. One day, you're the girl swinging on the swing set, the only thing you're thinking about is how to get higher, and then you blink and you're staring at the same swings with a broken heart and you can barely get your legs to move."

The way she speaks makes my chest hurt. My legs are frozen to the bench and I don't want my movements to stop her beautiful voice.

"I regret the entire last chapter of my life. I wasted it. I spent it with someone who I loved with every fiber of my being and he didn't feel the same way. Growing up, I read all of these stories about how love is enough, how it will always be enough to destroy every dragon, every bad thing the world has to offer, but that's not true, yet I still hope it is. I couldn't force him to love me. I thought he just would because that's what you do when you're in love—you just do. You *are* in love. You're not next to it or near it, you're *in* it. Fully immersed and infatuated with this person you never knew even existed when you were young."

God, I wish I had a fraction of the hope she does inside of her head.

"He fit so perfectly into *everything* about my life and I mistook it for something it wasn't. I thought it was something it wasn't, and he took advantage of that. Our entire relationship was like a game to him, and while he was figuring out how to take everything from me, I was trying to find out how I could give him the world." She stops to catch her breaths. "I sound pathetic but I just wanted him to love me."

"That's not pathetic. Not even fucking close," I say as I scooch closer to her, offering my shoulder; she rests her head on it. "Dais, when it comes down to it, everyone wants to be loved. It's what we're all searching for on this giant rock in space."

"I thought I had it, but all I had were lies, and you know what the worst part is?" She lifts her head quickly and stares at me.

"What?"

"I still think part of me will always love him, despite the fact that he cheated on me."

Cheated? What kind of person would do that to this beautiful woman in front of me? Matter of fact, why would anyone? I always saw love as this sacred bond—my parents and their relationship affirmed that for me. I still see it in my mother even though my father has been gone for so many years. She keeps his memory alive with the stories she's always telling, the jokes she stole from him that he used to tell. She still sleeps on her side of the bed, leaving space for him because that was always their bed, not hers.

"Nobody deserves that," I tell her. "Do you want me to kick his ass?"

She laughs, and the sound grips the broken heart in my chest.

"No, it's okay. I just wish I wasn't such an idiot."

"Don't blame yourself for what he chose to do. That has absolutely nothing to do with you and everything to do with who he is, which to me is a little insecure bitch who didn't see he already had the best thing in front of him that he would ever get in the form of a partner."

Her cheeks turn a light shade of pink before she turns away from me. "I know you don't mean that, but thank you."

"Why wouldn't I mean that?"

"I'm nothing special. That was solidified the moment I found out he was cheating on me. I'm replaceable. I'm the stepping stone most people walk all over before they find what they've always wanted. That's all Derek saw me as, and maybe that's all I'll ever be."

"No," I say as soon as she's done. "Dais, why do you think of yourself like this? What did he fucking do to the girl I used to know who lit up every room just by being in it?"

"I don't know," she sniffles. "Part of her died through millions of conference room meetings where he took everything from me and I sat by and watched. Like I said, everything was easier when I was a child."

"I feel the same way," I tell her. I wrap my arm around her shoulders and pull her close; she rests her head on my shoulder again and I bring my hand up to run my fingers lightly through her hair. "Sometimes, I wish I could go back to the version of myself where my biggest worry was when the porch light would start to flash or the sun setting in the middle of playing."

She laughs against my shoulder. "You always did hate going home after spending all day outside."

No, I hated going home because then I wasn't with you. I only got to see her for a few weeks a year, but Daisy wasn't just a childhood friend. She was the sun that came out on a gloomy day. She was the reason I looked forward to going to Nettles every year.

I had no way to articulate what she meant to me when we were kids, but now that we're older and in the same place again, the words are spilling into my head.

You'll never have the same friends that you do when you're young—only if you're really lucky—and it's a privilege to know her from two different points of our lives. Maybe we didn't really need one another when we were kids, but I think I need her now and maybe she needs me too.

When you're a kid, you're loud and you're never worried about anyone else around you thinking you're stupid or cringey or ridiculous. As you get older, you become all too aware of all the eyes on you, and that's what kills a lot of things, I've learned. That awareness is what ruins everything. I think people would be a lot happier if they leaned into that joy that's so often lost as you age.

But growing up doesn't bring anything easy. It brings death, newfound fears, scary situations, and you have to handle it because you're the adult, even if you still feel like a scared child looking for your parents.

"Why did you decide to come back now? After all these years away?"

"Why do you think, Daisy?"

"For your brother. I assume that's the only reason, though."

Yeah, let's go with that. I didn't know she was still here. I didn't think that was in the realm of possibility when I saw that Tobias was sending me back to Nettles, but now that she's next to me, I'm thanking everything I can that she's staring back at me.

"I'm sorry he didn't love you how you deserve."

"I'm sorry about your brother." She sniffles again and I wipe her alligator tears with my shirt.

"Someone should have stopped us from growing up," I joke. "It's not at all how I thought it would be."

"Do you feel like drinking right now?" she asks me.

"No." I'd give anything to numb myself from the memories spreading through my mind, but I promised her I would stop. I regret the way she saw me that night. I'll never forget it no matter how hard I try. "You're here with me, Dais. Why would I want to be anywhere else?"

I feel her cheeks lift against my shoulder. "Can you walk me home?"

"Only if you promise to come over later and finish the puzzle we started," I tell her. "It being incomplete is driving me insane. I used to be so much better at them."

"I don't think being good at puzzles is a thing." She grabs her bag and stands, holding her hand out to me. I take it, not letting go of her just yet because I love the way her skin feels against mine.

"Oh, you have no idea," I say as we start to walk. "Let me tell you a story about my brother while we walk."

And the rest of the way home is filled with stories of Tobias, laughter, and I even convince her to sit on the swings with me and we talk until the sun goes down. It's just how I remembered it—my childhood here. Every conversation with the girl across the street makes me smile like it used to when we weren't worried about saying the wrong thing, and I savor every moment I can, knowing I'll have to leave this place behind in the future, but not wanting to just yet.

Chapter Fifteen

— [THERE IS STILL TIME] BY SEAROWS

I SLAP MY EYESHADOW brush down on my vanity as I struggle to execute the idea I had in my mind when I sat down. I hate when I'm like this. I hate when I'm too in my head and can't even do the one thing I love that used to calm my racing thoughts.

I've been experimenting with makeup ever since my parents got me my first makeup kit when I was young. Granted, those things were horrible, but as soon as I swiped the brush over my eyelids and created something so colorful it felt like my personality was spread all over my face, I fell in love.

Now, whenever I get stressed, sad, pretty much any emotion I can feel, I sit down and play around with different looks I've seen online or created in my head. It's the routine of it that helps to calm me down. I've been doing makeup for so long that whenever there's a brush in my hand it feels like second nature.

Except for right now. I was trying to do a bold smokey eye, complete with the sharpest winged liner I could imagine.

I know exactly why this isn't working. My ex-husband's voice from the other day keeps filtering into my head. I can't unhear the way he tried to act as if he didn't ruin my life with what he did. I hate that all he did was minimize my feelings and act like I should be over what he did to me.

I don't know where this man got any of his audacity from, but it's undeserving. He fucking cheated on me, and I'm tired of pretending like I should be over it by now. I don't think this kind of thing is something you can just brush off—at least not for me. Sure, I'm a more sensitive person than most, but shit, I was in love with Derek. I was in love with him and he cheated on me with multiple women and made it seem like it was some nonchalant thing.

Fuck that. I loved him. I trusted him. I wanted him forever or as long as I was able to love him, and this is what he does to me? My consequence for loving him and putting him first above everything else in my entire life was betrayal? Infidelity? That was the *best* he could give me?

I know I'm better off without him, but I was so convinced he was the one for me that this fall back down to earth from the clouds has hurt more than I ever thought anything could. But maybe that's why loving him was never going to work out—he had me up in the air where I couldn't see anyone or anything besides him. He was my entire world, and he still fucking broke my heart and then some.

I know he wants the fucking formulas I have. Towards the end, I started to realize there was nothing Derek wouldn't do to make as much money as he could, and I'm glad he handled the business side of all of the future company stuff and I handled the makeup and product side of things. He'll never get the formulas, the product ideas I had, none of it. Not if I have something to say about it.

He only wants them for the money. I wanted to start a business because I loved it, and I think people can tell when someone is just in a certain field for the money aspect. Makeup is my version of art. My face and the clients I work on are my canvases, and the reason I'm in this job is to share that love with the people who come and shop at my store and the private events I do for anything people want to hire me for.

I hope people can tell I love what I do. Whereas with Derek, he just looks at it and sees dollar signs.

Makeup was the very first thing I fell wholly in love with, and even though I've fallen in love with a lot of other things, it will always be what I come back to when everything falls apart.

I sigh as I stare at myself in the mirror, hating everything about how I look. "God, Daisy, what the hell are you doing?"

I grab a makeup wipe off of my vanity before I head down my stairs, needing a cup of tea if I'm going to sleep any time soon. I haven't been sleeping well lately, and I blame it all on my inability to shut my brain off.

As I put my kettle on and head back up the stairs, I glance across the street, my eyes locking on the man in the window going through some boxes. I cried in front of him the other day, and I practically laid myself bare to him. Nobody else really knows about Derek besides Delilah, my parents, and now Theo. I don't know why I even told him about it—or why I sat down. There's something so safe to me about the boy I used to see every summer when we were little. Familiar. Comfortable. Terrifying. All of those words float through my mind as I continue to stare, probably a little creepily at him.

I could always tell what kind of person he was—especially when we were kids. If I scraped my knee, he would help me up. If I was scared, he never forced me to overcome my fears. He never pushed me, except when I asked him to on the swings in his backyard. He always offered the last popsicle even though I could tell he wanted it most times.

He was always the boy I saw in the summer, and I always wished for the summer to come quicker than it did. Time goes slower when you're a child, though. Everything feels like eternity, and you're always wishing for it to hurry up because you want to be an adult, someone people take seriously.

Now, the roles are reversed. I wish time would slow down so I can catch up. For the last year, I've been running to catch a train that's not waiting for me. It never stops. It only keeps moving as if it's taunting me.

My tea kettle whistling breaks me out of my spiral, and I wrap my cardigan around myself as I head for the kitchen. I move the kettle off of the stove, pouring it into a cup and heading back up the stairs to my room, my mind wandering to the boy next door and wondering if he'll need me tonight.

I stay up by my phone, and before I fully drift off, I turn my volume all the way up, just in case.

I'M FINALLY MAKING A dent in some of these boxes, but I'm also making even more of a mess. I've gone through most of Tristan's old baseball equipment he left here, and I even found some cassette tapes that Teags would probably appreciate.

It's been a few days since Daisy and I talked and part of me has wanted to walk over to her door, knock on it, and sit with her for a while. I haven't though. I've seen her in passing, usually before she goes to work and I go on my morning walk, but we haven't spoken since she told me about her ex-husband.

I haven't stopped thinking about our conversation. I had no idea I missed so much in her life. I guess I should have assumed something like this would happen—it's been over a decade since I saw her last—but a divorce was something I never imagined, at least not for her.

Daisy always felt like the flower anyone would want to pick. She always shined the brightest, always smiled the biggest. I'm shocked whoever this guy was didn't realize that. Maybe he's just a fucking idiot, but I am too.

I haven't made any progress on the clue.

> *I am neither secret nor treasure, yet I wait for discovery,*
> *Guarded by earth and overseen by silvered night's glory.*
> *Time's hands have lost me, stories may surround—*
> *What am I, silent and sealed, in darkness profound?*

It still doesn't make any sense to me, and maybe the amount of alcohol I've consumed in the past few years has clogged my brain, but I'd like to think I'm smarter than this. I'd like to think I knew Tobias better and should be able to decipher the only things he left for me.

I'm digging through an old box of Tobias's—with the amount of puzzles in here it's definitely his—when I find one of his old journals. I grab it, the handwriting from when we were kids on the front making me pause, unsure if I want to open it or leave it alone.

I toss it to the side, hoping my search through these things will yield something other than me wanting to drink my feelings away. A small paper slides out of the journal when I throw it to the side, and a familiar white envelope catches my eye.

God, he really thinks of fucking everything doesn't he?

I grab it, ripping it open a lot easier than the last one.

```
Theo,
None of this was your fault.
Page 76. I dog-eared it for you.
Forever,
```

`Tobias`

Those six words at the beginning really trip me up. Of course he knew I would blame myself. How couldn't I? I swear I turned my back for one single moment and he had fallen apart. I grab the journal and flip it to the page, his handwriting more grown up as I see a recent addition to it at the bottom. This is different from my stops before. Normally, it was the one clue and when I figured it out and found the envelopes he left, that was it. There was never all of this other fluff that seems to be in Vermont.

I can't say I'm upset by it because I get a few more pieces of Tobias, but I am fucking confused. How will I know if there are more notes he left for me to find?

`The sky will always be a friend I can depend on. It will always be there, ready to hear all the thoughts that are too scary to write down. Until it falls down too, realizing there is nowhere else to go. The ground is the final place to fall. Find where we fell all those years ago. Find me where you last saw me, or, one of the places you last saw me where we rested.`

Is this a hint to where he left the last envelope? Did he know how difficult it would be for me up here so he stowed some extra hints for me?

I feel some tears start to fall down my face, the newer handwriting driving me crazy. The weight of his absence is crushing me. It's heavier like it normally is when everything feels like it's toppling over, and part of me wants to give in—to drink this all away and hope I might catch another glimpse of him.

Call Daisy, you idiot.

No. I won't come undone in front of her again. I won't put her through all of my shit. She has enough to deal with in her personal life. I don't want to be someone for her to fix all of the time—she deserves better than that.

This is just who I am right now—everything hurts. I knew it would be like this for a while, but I never imagined it would still hurt this much seeing his handwriting against the paper.

Part of me has an idea as to what he might mean, though. The final place we fell before I never saw him again was my father's grave. He had come home from some trip he was on—maybe he was here—and he asked me if I wanted to go visit Dad, and I agreed. It's hard going to the cemetery every year on his birthday with all of us, even harder going alone when I need guidance, so going with Tobias felt okay. It felt safe. It wasn't as difficult sitting there and talking to my father who I couldn't really picture as well as I used to.

This house feels loud, even in the silence. I didn't put any music or a show on in the background to help, because even in the quiet, I can hear the echoes of our laughter when we were kids. I can hear Teags yelling at us to get out of her room after we all tried to annoy her for the third time that day. I can hear the knocks on the door, knowing Daisy is on the other side of it wanting to play outside on the swings or hopscotch.

God, I want a drink. I want to forget. I want to not remember for a few hours that everything in my life hasn't turned out the way I wanted it to.

Would he have left something where our father is buried? Would he really have gone that far to bury something knowing he would end up right next to him?

I could go back home and see. I could without anyone knowing I was even back. I'd just sneak by the cemetery, see if anything was buried, and come back here with or without whatever Tobias has me searching for.

I don't feel ready to do that. I don't want to leave Vermont, so instead of continuing my search into these boxes, I grab a pillow and blanket off of the couch, and make myself comfortable on the floor, knowing I can't fall any further than this before I drift off to sleep.

Chapter Sixteen

— THE GARDEN BY DEVON GABRIELLA

I FLIP THE LIGHT on to the store, and as soon as Delilah's figure comes into view staring back at me, I yelp.

"What the hell are you doing in here?"

"I was waiting for you." She smiles at me. "You're late."

"So, you just sat in here with the lights off?"

She nods. "You might have to reheat your coffee."

"I do that at least three times a day, Del." I set my bags down behind the counter. "I was talking to my parents this morning. They kept me on for a little longer than I thought they would."

"And how are they on the never-ending vacation they're on?"

"They're having a blast." I smile at her. I'm thrilled my parents didn't cancel their trip when I surprised them by coming home. They almost did, but after I told them about what happened, they agreed the alone time would bode well for me.

In Boston, I was always surrounded by people. The city was always bustling and traffic was always insane, but I still found things to love about it. I always thought I was a city girl, especially when I only knew about small town life in Nettles where everyone knows everything about each other.

It was *really* nice to head to a place where nobody knew me. I got to figure out who I was. I got to change and become an entirely new version of myself. I got to introduce myself and not have someone tell me they knew my parents. It was the best thing for me at the time. My college years were filled with meeting new people, trying new things, stepping way too far outside of my comfort zone, and all throughout that time I had Derek and I got to love him through all of the changes and big steps.

Then it all crashed around me. Looking back on all that makes me feel like I was living in an unrealistic bubble where everyone outside of it was screaming at me to escape.

"That's good. They deserve a break from Nettles," she tells me. "Everyone needs one every once in a while."

"Oh, everyone besides you?"

"Exactly." She spins around as she peruses the racks of makeup. "I love it here, Dais. Always will. Why would I want a break from that?"

"Because there is so much of the world to see," I remind her. "Maybe you would want to do that someday with someone you don't even know yet."

She rolls her eyes at me, and I can already tell what's coming. "Well, maybe I'll do that when you accept my offer of setting you up with my brother."

"Del, the ink on my divorce papers is barely dry," I say as I turn the music on. "And I told you, I am *not* going to date one of your brothers."

"Well, Luca is already married, so it's just Elliott left," she reminds me. "He's super sweet, and he's a firefighter! You might be the only woman in town that isn't falling at his feet and coming into my shop to ask about him."

"Do people really do that?" I ask her.

"More often than not."

"Gross."

"I wouldn't have this problem if you dated him." She wiggles her brows at me. "And if you two got married, we would be sisters. Wouldn't that be awesome?"

"It would be awesome," I agree as I grab her hands. "But no."

"Ugh." She fake pouts how she does every time we have this conversation. Ever since I've been back, she's been trying to set me up with someone, whether it be for a one night stand or an actual date.

I've only dated one person in high school, and he moved away, and then Derek. I'm zero for two, and I'm also terrible at dating. I'm a zero to 100 kind of girl, and I fall *way* too easily. I could see someone on the street and by my entire walk to work have convinced myself that they were the one for me just from a glance.

I have to stop doing that. I *need* a little time to focus on myself. The divorce fucked me up more than I'd care to admit, but I made a promise to myself the last time I walked out of the conference room in Boston. I promised I would put myself first, and that's what I'm doing now, and what I'll continue to do until I feel ready again—if I ever do.

"Wouldn't it be good to get back out there? Even if just for sex? I know you mentioned not being a casual sex kind of girl, but you've never tried it."

"I'm not looking for anything of that sort right now," I tell her as I shut my mouth, the bell jingling above the door as a customer walks in. "Welcome in."

"Thanks, Daisy girl," I hear as Theo walks in, his head turning around as he takes in the space. "I can't believe I've been in town so long and this is the first time I've been here."

"Theo West," Delilah says before I can jump in. "Delilah Madison. I've heard *so* much about you."

"Yikes," is all he says as he smooths out his mustache. "That can't be good."

"I'm surprised you don't remember me from when we were kids." She smirks, her eyes locking with mine as Theo peruses the store, his back to us as she raises her brows at me.

"No," I mouth to her.

"Why not?" she mouths back as he turns around.

"Oh, come on." He tilts his head at her. "It's hard not to remember the Madisons, especially in a town like this."

"Yeah, we've got quite the reputation."

"One of the last times I was here, I saw your father's face on every damn street corner.

"Ah, yes," she recalls. "That was his first campaign he ran." Her face falls as she remembers the day after her dad won the race. It was the weirdest forty eight hours of our lives. One minute, we were all celebrating her father becoming mayor. Next, she was in the waiting room of the hospital awaiting news that changed her life.

Delilah's family has been through hell and back, and despite the struggles, she still remains the biggest beam of light in the family.

"He's still the mayor isn't he?" Theo asks her, making himself comfortable against the counter.

"It's his last term. No more campaigns for him," she says. "But I should get back to the store." She grabs her bag. "Dais, seriously think about my offer. It would be good to get back out there."

"Del, I am *fine*," I reassure her. "I'm not looking for anything, remember?"

"I know." She throws her arms around me so her mouth is against my ear. "Just keep yourself open to the idea, okay?"

"Fine," I whisper to her, knowing I'm lying. I can't do it yet. It's too soon. "I'll swing by for lunch later."

"Good. We can go harass Brooks at the bar."

"Sounds good to me."

"Theo, you're welcome to come too," Delilah offers as he throws his hands up.

"I'd never intrude on girl time."

"You can be an honorary member of the girls. We would love to have you gossiping with us."

"I'll think about it," he says as she leaves. There's a few beats of silence before either of us speaks.

"Did you need help finding something?"

"No." He shakes his head. "I came looking for you."

"For me?" I wonder before it hits me. "Did you drink?"

"Wanted to," he tells me as he fiddles with some lipsticks. "But I didn't."

"Good." I nod at him, my arm finding his bicep as he turns to face me. "I'm proud of you."

There's a flash of something across his face before it disappears. "Thanks, but if you want me to stop leaning on you because you've got a lot going on, too, I can. I don't ever want to put my baggage onto you because I know it's a lot, so if it ever gets to be too much, or if it already is, let me know. I'll find a better way of coping that doesn't involve a bottle. Never was good at that."

"What?"

"Coping with the terrible shit that's happened to me."

Same here, I want to say, but I don't. The only thing that came of my divorce was a crippling fear I'm not enough as I am, and some minor body image issues because I truly believed it was my fault he cheated on me.

"Well, you're doing better already," I remind him. "And I practically threw my divorce onto you the other day, and I'm—"

"If you're about to apologize to me, I'm going to walk out of here," he tells me, a finger against my mouth. "Don't do that, Dais. Not to me."

"Well, if we're doing this, then you can't apologize to me either. You didn't push any of this onto me. I chose to run over to you in the lawn that night, and I'm fucking glad I did."

"Tobias sort of pushed it onto you, though."

He's talking about the letter I got. I bet he's thinking I wouldn't be doing all of this without it, but I know he knows me better than that. I think he's scared, or maybe he's trying to push me away because he knows he won't be here for much longer. Whatever it is, I don't like it.

"No, he didn't," I tell him, heading to the back of the storeroom to grab products. As we walk around the store, I notice some gaps I forgot to fill in yesterday. "Do you mind?"

"Do I add these in the back?" he asks, taking the box of lipstick from my hand.

"Yes."

"I don't mind at all," he tells me. "It's a good distraction."

That's why I like it too. It's easy, and stocking the shelves helps me to not think about how I could have been holding my own line of makeup. Instead, it reminds me of why I am who I am. It's the memory of holding the first lipstick I ever held—the one I stole from my mom's purse when I was way too young to be wearing it.

"Why did you feel like drinking?" I ask him.

"I woke up on the floor of the living room wanting to punch something. I was still hurting," he tells me, grabbing a few more boxes and loading them onto the shelves. "I don't know why I expect it to be easier in the morning after getting some sleep. It never is. It always hurts the same as it did the day before, only worse because there's always that split-second where I can't remember anything. That split-second was longer on the mornings I woke up still drunk off my ass from the night before."

"I can understand that," I tell him. "The first few weeks after I found out Derek was cheating on me, I still woke up thinking his body would be next to mine in bed, but it never was, and then I would spend five minutes seeing his infidelity on the playback screen in my mind."

"Fuck, Dais." He accidentally crinkles one of the boxes and then tries to smooth it out. "Sorry."

"It's okay." I grab it from him, our hands lingering in one another's for a beat too long before I toss it back in the box. "You know what has stuck with me all of these years since we were little?"

"What?"

"There was this time I was climbing on one of the trees in my backyard with you. Do you remember when we used to do that?"

He nods, a smile overtaking his face. "I remember trying to race you to the top and always beating you, and if my memory suits me well, there were also some initials carved into the tree."

"You're not wrong." I lightly smack his arm. *How the hell did he remember that?* "That's not what I was talking about."

"Oh, so you're still competitive? Noted."

"Shut up," I chuckle at him. "I always went the same exact way because it was the easiest way I could climb up, and I always used to get annoyed if you beat me. Do you remember what you said to me one day?"

He shakes his head.

"You know, Dais," I echo what he said to me that day. "There's more than one way to climb a tree."

He snickers to himself. "I remember that."

"It reminded me of that one children's book with the tree," I tell him. "Sometimes, I feel like that tree from the book."

"What do you mean?"

"It's how I felt with Derek. I just kept giving him pieces of myself until he swallowed me whole. I wanted him to love me, so I gave and gave until I had nothing left. And he knew that. He knew who I was and he used me the entire time we were together, and I still gave him everything I had. He basically stole my dreams in the divorce and I let him. I didn't fight back. I just sat in that conference room and gave him what he wanted because a small piece of me thought he might come back." I look over at him, his head down and eyes dropping at me. "I'm pathetic, I know."

"No, you're not."

"Ever since you've been back, that sentence has floated through my mind. Since my divorce was finalized, I've felt stagnant, and I guess I still kind of do."

"That's understandable," he tells me. "It's how I feel every fucking morning. I'm not moving forward, I'm just stuck."

"Yeah," I agree. "But maybe there's more than one way for us both to get out of this feeling, right? Because in case you forgot, there's more than one way to climb a tree." I throw his young words back at him and he laughs to himself.

"There is indeed."

"So, maybe we can help each other out and figure out how to climb the tree differently than we have been?" I toss the offer out there, unsure of what it would look like, but offering anyway.

"It seems like Delilah is already trying to do that for you. Is she setting you up or something?"

"Trying to. She means well, but I'm not ready."

"Well, what would get you ready?"

"Better self-esteem," comes out before I can stop it. "I'm kidding. I don't even know why I said that."

I can tell he doesn't believe me, but he doesn't ask me about it any further. I don't know why words seem to just spill out of me around him, but it needs to stop.

"Well, if you ever want to practice going on a date or something, I'm always free for you. I can't even tell you the last time I was on a date, so you'd be helping me out too."

"What would that even look like? A practice date? That sounds ridiculous," I scoff, grabbing the empty box of lipsticks and breaking it down, tossing it into my recycling bin.

"It would be easy. We're friends so it wouldn't be awkward, and we'd go out to dinner and fake a date to make you more comfortable for when you're on an actual one. It's foolproof. One of my best friends did it for his friend in college."

"And how did that work out?"

"Well, they dated for a few years, but that's irrelevant."

"That is totally not irrelevant," I joke with him, taking a sip of my now cold coffee.

"I'm just throwing out the option." He smirks at me, leaning against the counter again. "We're friends and it would never cross that line because I'm a mess and you deserve someone who can give you their entire heart. I don't mind helping you out if you're nervous to get back out there."

"I can't believe we're even talking about this. This is a total hypothetical. I'm focusing on myself for the time being."

"Good for you." He smiles at me. "Maybe I should take a page out of your book."

I ignore the goosebumps spreading down my body as he looks at me, and I change the subject. "Have you made any progress on the clue Tobias left you?"

He shakes his head. "That's another reason I felt like drinking. I'm a fucking failure if I can't even figure out the last clue he'll ever leave me."

"Well," I say as I grab my cold coffee cup. "Let's head for Delilah's and get some breakfast. I doubt I'll be much help, but it can't hurt, right?"

He only smiles at me as he opens the door to the store, flips the sign, and waves me forward. "That sounds perfect to me."

Chapter Seventeen

— VISITING HOURS BY ED SHEERAN

"Here," my brother says as he hands me a cup of coffee. "Want to go on a walk with me?"

"Sure," I say, already knowing where we're headed. "There's less in here than normal."

He holds up another mug—our father's favorite—and I see some liquid slosh around in it, and another stab hits my chest as I'm reminded of what we've lost.

The two of us start out of the house, since our mother is already at work. We always try to have breakfast together on the day my father died, but this year is as incomplete as the last one because Tristan isn't here and the time difference makes it so he's not even awake. He's been different lately. I know the split with Liv really fucked his head up, and I know getting out of Pennsylvania has been what he's wanted his entire life, but with how incomplete our family is, I wish he would have at least called this morning.

Breakfast this morning is tradition, and even Teags and Tobias managed to be here. Teags is in school with a huge test today, and Tobias came all the way from wherever his work has taken him. I know California is far—farthest he could get—but I miss my big brother.

Tobias and I take the short walk to the cemetery, each of us quiet as we take in the sounds of the neighborhood. It used to freak me out when I was younger that we lived so close to a few cemeteries, but I think I was really scared that our father was so close to us but I couldn't go and talk to him like I used to.

By the time we get to his headstone and the empty spaces next to it, the two of us sit in the damp grass, and Tobias sets the mug on top of the headstone.

"Hey, Dad," he starts off. "The two of us have started splitting coffee like you used to when we were kids, but we thought this year we could all share a cup."

"We miss you," I somehow choke out.

"Yeah, we really do," he echoes as we raise our mugs. "Love you, Dad."

I take a deep breath, trying not to let my emotions overwhelm me; Tobias's hand pats my back, letting me know he's here with me. He always is the stronger one of us two. My emotions often overtake me, swallowing me whole until I get them under control somehow, but he is always the more level-headed one.

"Do you think he can see us sitting here or are we just two losers talking to a rock sticking out of the ground?"

My brother laughs, and some of his coffee spills from his mug and drops onto the grass. "Don't call us losers."

"Well, I'm just saying. I know we do this every year, but sometimes I think it's pointless."

"You don't think he knows we're here?"

"Just because we might believe it, doesn't mean it's true."

"If you're saying that, then I can tell you don't really believe it." He takes a small sip of coffee. "Belief is acceptance that something is true, Theo. You don't think Dad can see us or hear us even though he's gone?"

"I don't know, dude." I shake my head. "I just wish he was here instead of us having to come talk with him like this."

"I miss him too." He puts his hand on my shoulder, eyes like mine staring back at me as I look at him. "But you don't need something tangible to believe that he can see us even though he's gone. He'll always be with you. In your memories, in the home videos Mom has, and in the way you laugh. You sound a lot like him sometimes."

I shrug. "I barely remember him."

"It'll come in waves. A scent, a gust of wind, a certain word can even bring you back to who Dad was to you."

"Are you sure?"

"I'm sure, baby brother." His fist nuzzles my hair. "Even when you can't feel him, he's with you, hell, even in those moments you can't, that's especially when he's there with you. He's just trying to let you figure it out."

I nod, his words really infiltrating my mind as I look at the headstone in front of me. He's with me, even when I can't feel him.

"You ready to go back?" I ask him, needing to escape this place where my grief feels heavier. "I have to go to work soon."

"You go ahead," he tells me. "I want to spend a few more minutes here."

"Okay," I tell him. "I'll meet you at home?"

"I'll always meet you at home, you know that."

I WAKE IN A cold sweat, my body barely remembering how to breathe as my brother's face floats out of my mind. I don't know what time it is. I barely remember what day it is as the vivid memory freaks me out. I swear I can still feel the wet grass beneath my touch, but all I see is my comforter as I grab ahold of it. I try to close my eyes again to get it back, but it doesn't come.

"Fuck," is all I whisper to myself as I whip out of bed, not sparing a single glance at anything but grabbing my car keys, phone, and throwing some random clothes in a bag.

I have to go back home, but I know I'm not done here yet. This whole puzzle thing has turned out to be a lot fucking harder than I thought it would be, but I'm not giving up.

The entire drive back to Pennsylvania is filled with dread and short stops when I pull over because my body feels shaky. I probably should eat something, but I need to get back home to see if I'm headed in the right direction.

My phone buzzes a few thousand times on the way back, but I don't bother looking at them until I pull into the cemetery.

> **Tristan: Our sister is missing, according to Dom.**

> **Tristan: Can you keep an eye out at the Vermont house? I doubt she would go up there, but you never know.**

> **Tristan: Vince and Nico are looking for her, but no luck so far.**

> **Tristan: We're all at Dom's house. I'll keep you updated if we find her. He's freaking out and so am I.**

> **Tristan: And please don't ask me why Dom is freaking out. That's another can of worms I really don't want to open at the moment.**

> **Tristan: Miss you, brother. Hope Vermont is going well.**

Teags is missing? I take a deep breath, trying to think of places she could have gone. Maybe after I see if the letter Tobias left for me is here, I can meet up at Dom's house. I'll have to ask Tristan for the address, and obviously I'm worried about Teags, but she can handle herself.

But wait, why would the letter be here? Why would he leave that clue for me in Vermont and have me come back home? Fuck. None if this makes sense. My brain is so scrambled, I didn't think this through.

"Oh, fuck," is all I say as I get out of my car, headed over to my father's headstone. It must have rained earlier because my shoes get wet immediately. By the time I get over to his grave, a familiar figure is curled up in front of it, and part of me is glad she's alive. I know Tristan and I went straight to a different, more terrifying place when he said she was missing, but I'm glad to see she's at least okay.

Or, is she? I head up to her, and see her pants are stained with grass as I try to shake her awake. I hope to fuck she didn't take anything, so I shake her a little harder, hoping she throws some stupid quip at me before I feel my legs give out beneath me.

My head smacks the ground as I hear my sister say my name.

"Geez, Teags. What the fuck?"

"You snuck up on me. What else am I supposed to do? You could've been a stranger."

I guess she's right. Like I said, I knew she could take care of herself, but the bad thoughts still seeped in—like they always do.

"What are you doing here?" she asks me as she sits up, looking around as if she wasn't expecting it to be this late in the day.

I rub my head, a small bump already forming underneath my fingers as I try to figure out a way to phrase why I'm back.

Well, I had this dream about our brother and I, and I think I finally figured out where his clue has sent me! Oh, also, he's been sending me letters posthumously because he timed them all out and left them on the remaining stops of his bucket list! Oh, and I've been getting letters at every stop when you all only got one!

How the fuck am I supposed to say that?

I decide on an easier route—changing the subject. "I could ask you the same thing."

She rolls her very swollen eyes at me, and suddenly, I'm elated to be back. Last I heard, Teags was in Arizona with Gregory, but with that message from Tristan earlier, I can only assume there is a huge chunk of story I'm missing. Yet, I can't wait to hear all about it. I haven't been alone up in Vermont, but I have missed seeing my family as much as I used to. Ever since Tobias, we've all sort of scattered across the country, the three of us trying to make sense of all of this.

"I mean what are you doing back home?"

"I'm looking for something." I don't elaborate because I still haven't figured out the proper words, but maybe she'll think I'm looking for her since she probably has a thousand messages from everyone as to where she is. "Are you okay?"

"No," she tells me, and my eyebrows raise. Teags always was one to beat around the bush about her emotions. She always used to need more space and time to sort through them, even when we were young. Whenever she was in that time, us boys knew to not disturb her. The one time we did, we all paid for it. She hid all of our favorite games in different spots and made us search for them. After that, we never disturbed her. Tobias was mad when she hid one single piece of one of his puzzles from him for weeks, the thing finished except for *one* measly piece until she eventually gave in.

"Your face is all puffy. This is... weird. You never cry. You don't have emotions." At least, the only time I've seen her really cry was at Tobias's funeral, but I was so drunk that day, I barely remember anything else.

"Just because I don't cry doesn't mean I don't feel." I know that, but it's still unsettling seeing her so open with her emotions. "And I do cry. A lot, it seems."

"That's refreshing," I tell her. "I was getting worried when you kept calling me and using that weird voice."

"What voice?"

"The pretend voice. Your tone gets higher when you're acting like you're okay." I push my elbow into her side. I knew she wasn't okay when she called me, but I never asked her about it, knowing it would have gotten me nowhere. "You've done that since you were little. You did it when Dad died too."

I may not remember our father too well, but I do remember how it changed us all when we were young. Tristan became the man of the house, Tobias got quieter, I laughed a lot less, and Teags's voice got eight octaves higher when she was feeling too much. Her music got louder when she was sad too.

That's the worst part about family loss that nobody really talks about. I know how it changed me, but having to watch my siblings and mother change from it, too, is the worst part.

"I didn't know I did that."

"All of us did. We used to call your personal time Teags Time. It was code for when we knew you needed space. Nobody was allowed to disturb you during Teags Time."

"Oh. I didn't think you all noticed I needed my space sometimes."

"You and Tristan. You two are fucking weirdos." They're almost too alike. I'm pretty sure that's why they butt heads so fucking often. They're two sides of the same coin even though Tristan is the oldest and Teags is the youngest.

"Well, you and Tobias were the ones always barging in and trying to get us all to play that stupid game you guys liked."

"Capture the flag?" God, I haven't played that game in years.

She nods, a small smile escaping her features. "That's the one. Except the flag we used was a beach towel. I still think the teams were unfair. Tristan was never fun when we were kids."

"Well, he never really got to be one."

She finally looks at me after all this time of us staring ahead at the headstone in front of us. "Did any of us after Dad passed?"

"Not really."

I finally understand what this is. This is it. This is her breaking point. The point of time when all of this grief consumes her and then finally lets her go. She's no longer growing in her grief, she's growing around it.

Tristan already had his at the cabin. After that, he really got his life together and tried to dig himself out of the hole he was in. Teags is having hers right now. She's breaking down in front of me, tears all over her face and shirt, and I start to wonder if I'll ever get to where they are. Will I ever feel the dam finally break and start to move forward or am I always going to be stuck in the same loop wishing my brother could come back? Did I fully break when I got so drunk I almost died in the grass in Vermont? No, I don't think so. I still feel as stuck as I did before then. I still feel the exact fucking same.

I wonder if I'll ever have this feeling or if I'll always be here—stuck in the quicksand of the sadness crashing down on me.

Her music plays as we take in the weight of the place that surrounds us. She always was the more musical one out of all of us, Tobias included. Teags could name the producer of a song from a million years ago when I didn't even know what the title of it was.

"Do you feel that?" she asks me.

"Yeah, Teags. I do." The soft breeze floats across my face as I smell the rain from earlier. Petrichor, it's called. Tobias used that word when we played scrabble one time, and he spent ten minutes explaining the word to me. Matter of fact, he always used to do that. I stare at the ground where the two family members we've lost lay forever. "I miss them every single day."

"I do too," she whispers. We've never really acknowledged what we've been through, but I'm glad we are now. No longer are we dancing around the topic of death. I guess you can't really do that when you're sitting in the middle of a cemetery. "I'm glad you're home, Theo. We've all been worried about you up in Vermont."

"Don't worry about me. I'm not totally alone up there." The memory of Daisy floats into my head. I should call her in case she comes over to check on me. I could have written her a note and left it in her mailbox or something, but all I was focused on when I woke up was getting back here. Shit, I should call her once I'm home. "Can I hug you or is it not a good time?"

"I could use a hug."

Her voice cracks as I lean in, feeling her arms wrap around me, and I'm reminded of when we were younger as I asked her the same question while they lowered our father into the ground. Tristan and Tobias were busy helping my mother stand up on both her feet while Teags and I stood next to one another, watching as our father slipped away. She sniffled next to me, and I leaned over and asked her the same thing.

"Do you need a hug, Teags?" I know she doesn't like looking weak in public, but I offer it anyway.

"I could use one now, Thee."

She always called me that when we were younger. She always left off the last letter of my name. For longer words when Teags was young, she would shorten them, which included most of our names. Even when we told her that wasn't how the word was said, she just shook her head and continued saying it how she wanted to.

I was Thee, Tobias was Toby, and Tristan was Tris until she was eight or nine.

At our dad's funeral when Teags needed me, I felt like the most powerful big brother on the planet—kind of like now.

"I don't know where to put it all," she says into my ear.

"What do you mean?"

"I've carried it all around with me. All the pain, guilt, and sadness have been my companions for years, along with all of yours, Mom's, and Tristan's. It's like it all trickled down and piled on top of mine, and I don't know how to get it off. I don't know where to put it." She starts to cry again, and all I want to do is take her pain away. I know exactly how she feels. I know what it feels like to be swallowed by grief, but I didn't know she had been carrying all of ours too.

Part of me feels like an asshole for leaving after all this happened, but I had to complete this bucket list. Tobias wanted me to, and they all knew how important it was for me to do this.

But I wish I didn't have to, in a way. I wish I could have been strong enough to stay here and be around for my family when they needed me, but I wasn't. I'm not strong enough, and I don't think I ever will be.

So, I stand up and wipe my pants off even though it's no use. Everything is stained and I'm going to need to use some of that magic stain remover Mom always used on Tristan's white baseball pants to make them look as good as new.

I reach my hand out and she takes it, standing next to me as the breeze starts to pick up. I wipe some of the dirt off of her pants as I offer her my hand again, and she looks at me like I'm insane after I swat her hand away from me.

"What?"

"You give it to me, Teags. Give some of that pain to me and let me help you carry it."

She tilts her head at me, clearly sick of my metaphor. "I don't know how to do that."

"Then we'll figure it out together. Deal?"

She nods. "Deal."

"No matter where I am, call me or text me. Especially, if you're feeling like the world is caving in." We start to walk back toward the road toward my car. I didn't dig for anything today, but part of me thinks I'm in the wrong place. I thought Daisy and I were onto something when the clue he left pointed me here. Stories may surround being the giant clue. How many stories are carried through a cemetery every single fucking day? But I guess I'm back to the drawing board. "You can't just turn your phone off and scare the shit out of all of us like this again."

"What do you mean?"

She seriously doesn't know we would all be freaking out if she didn't answer us for hours on end?

"Dom and Tristan are worried sick. So is Mom. Please fucking call someone before they put out an Amber Alert."

She stops on the gravel, almost as if I stunned her into that spot. "Why didn't you tell them where I was? How did you find me?"

"I wasn't trying to find you." I shrug. "I was already headed back here when I got the message from Tristan, so I came to the first place I would have if I was you." Not technically the truth. I didn't know she was missing until I looked at my phone once I was already here, and she just happened to be asleep in the one place I came back to search. Nobody else knows I'm back, and I'm sure Tristan and my mom are going to be elated to see me.

I'm not back for good, though. I can still feel the house in Vermont calling my fucking name to get back.

"It's my first time here since I've been back."

"Me too. I didn't even come to visit before I left for my trip." Part of me wishes I did, but I couldn't stomach it. Not with all of the memories and feelings I was having before I left. "Also, Dom? Really?" I joke with her. Tristan made it seem like something was going on between them, and I for one, cannot fucking wait to hear that story. I'm sure Tris was pissed, and part of me is annoyed I missed seeing that look on his face, but I'm very curious as to what the hell happened with Gregory.

Teags fooling around with one of Tristan's best friends is something I never saw coming, and I just know he was all pissy and dramatic about it. God, I really have been so fucking far out of the loop while finishing Tobias's list.

That smile on her face tells me everything I need to know. "It's a long story."

"Well, tell it to me on the way home," I say. "Did you fucking walk here?"

"I needed to clear my head. Walks always help."

"Understandable," I tell her as I get into the car, the single bag in my backseat staring at me as I drive her back to Dom's house.

The moment I'm back with these people, my bones start to settle. There's something so calming about this group of people, and the love that encompasses this room brings me back to the good times. Even though I know this feeling isn't going to last, I grasp onto it for as long as I can while I'm here.

Chapter Eighteen

— STUBBORN LOVE BY THE LUMINEERS

I KNOCK ON THE familiar door across the street, my all black attire and suitcases next to me, worry swirling around in my stomach.

I haven't seen Theo in four days. I don't want to seem like a creep, but it's like he just disappeared. I figured when he was going to leave Vermont, he would at least say goodbye rather than disappear.

He's my friend, and I'm worried about him. We made a little progress on the clue Tobias left him, but he told me he wasn't quite done here yet. I know he has to sell the house he's residing in, and since I don't see a for sale sign in the yard, I can only assume he's either hurt somewhere or something worse.

I should stop worrying about him. He's not my boyfriend or anything, we're just friends, but I can't help it. He's still struggling in his grief, and I hope he's not drinking his sorrows away somewhere where nobody might be able to help him.

I sigh heavily, knocking on the door a few more times to no avail. He's not home. He hasn't been home in days. *Fuck.*

Did I do this? I'd like to think I didn't, but part of me wonders if everything I spilled to him made him uncomfortable or something. No.

No, that's ridiculous. Not everything is about me. Maybe he'll come back. Maybe if I send him another message, he'll answer and I can stop worrying about him being passed out drunk in a field, too off his rocker to get help. I've sent one each day he's been gone, and I worry if he doesn't answer this one that I might have to go to the police station and report him missing. I don't even know if I could do that since he technically doesn't live here, but that feels like the only option if he doesn't answer.

I even called Luca and asked him if he's seen him in the emergency room, but he hasn't thankfully.

> Daisy: Hey, just checking in again. Haven't seen you in a while. Just want to know you're okay. Call me or message me back whenever you get a chance.

I'm about to knock again when I hear a horn honking behind me.

"Are you ready for the most awkward wedding in the history of Nettles?"

My best friend pulls into Theo's driveway and parks, hopping out of the convertible her dad and her restored over the years. She rarely drives it, but I guess this warranted dusting the cobwebs off—a wedding nobody is excited for, including the groom.

"I don't think we should be celebrating the downfall of a wedding. Even though Brooks is unhappy, he must have some reason for doing this, right?" I roll my suitcases and toss them in her back seat as she stares at me, about to open the driver's door.

"Still nothing?"

I nod. "He's still not here."

"I'm sorry, babe. I know you two have gotten closer."

"We're friends, Del. I'm looking out for him," I take one last look at the house across the street I've known my entire life. It was once filled with the laughter of a happy family, then it was barren and cold as I grew up, but lately, I've seen some of that magic come back. Now it's gone again, and the sweet guy across the street is gone with it.

"Are you ready to go and mask your emotions for a few hours while you do your favorite thing in the world?"

I can't help but laugh to myself. "Yes, I am."

"Then let's go," she practically screams as she hops in, turning the music on full blast a little too early in the morning as we head for the only church in town.

AFTER SPENDING THE ENTIRE morning faking smiles and laughing at jokes I have no context for, I'm finally done getting the bride and company ready for this day. I can assume most of the people attending did not think this wedding would happen, but it looks like everything is going according to plan.

I've been trying to see how Brooks has been all fucking day, but I was stuck with the bridal party all morning, and I can't seem to find him as I peruse the venue. Though, after I did Jamie's look, she all but disappeared.

"Dais!" I hear Delilah say as she waves me over. "Eloise is here!"

I knew that's who she was talking to. One of the middle Madison siblings hasn't changed a bit, and now that she's back, I can see the resemblance to Elliott, her twin brother. She left Nettles as soon as she graduated and moved somewhere I honestly can't remember at the moment, and when I was younger, I thought she was crazy doing that, but as soon as I left Nettles, I understood.

Sometimes, you just want to be somewhere where nobody knows your name.

"Hey, Eloise," I say as I join the two of them. "How have you been?"

"Oh, you know." She shrugs her shoulders. "I've been as good as I can be."

"That's understandable," I tell her. She's still got the same dimples as the last time I saw her. "Are you just back for the wedding or are you back for good?"

"For good." She smiles, but I can tell she's uncomfortable talking about all this, so I try to change the subject, but Delilah interferes.

"Eloise, I told you that you didn't have to come back. Mom is fine—"

She cuts her sister off. "Del, I need to be here, okay? Just let me be here."

Delilah raises her hands in defeat as Fallon—the other Madison sister—comes over to us.

"God, I'm so glad you all are here." She lifts her hand up to her headpiece as someone talks into her ear, her eyes rolling to the back of her head. "She's gone again?"

The three of us stare at Fallon, unsure of what's going on, but she already has stress lines on her face and the wedding hasn't even started yet.

Fallon is the event coordinator here in town. If there's something going on, there's a chance she has a hand in it. She's not only insanely good at her job, but she's also the one person I would come to if I ever needed someone who was good in a crisis. I swear the bag she carries around is magical. She somehow always has what you need in it.

It's a lot like my makeup kit—if you name it, I probably have it in eight different shades—but she's somehow more prepared than I am.

"Anything we can do to help?" Delilah asks and her sister waves her off, pinning her bangs out of her face.

"Nope." She smiles, but in a stressed out way. Her smile says she's fine, but her bulging eyes are saying she's about to freak out on someone or someone is getting fired. "Just find your seats. The wedding will begin shortly and on time." I swear I hear her mutter *even if it kills me* under her breath as she walks away.

"We should probably sit toward the back," Eloise says as she rubs up and down her arm.

"I'm following you two," I say. "I'm technically just the makeup artist. I don't even know if I'm allowed to sit for the ceremony."

"Oh, please," Delilah says as she hooks her arms through mine and her sisters. "The entire town is here. The prince of one of the founding families is finally tying the knot. *Everyone* was invited besides our parents. The Turners spared no expense."

"Can we just sit down, please?" Eloise says, pulling us to a few chairs in the back. "I'm a little light-headed."

"Let me go grab you some water," I say as I head for the small fridge I saw back near the dressing rooms. I find Fallon opening just about every door in her path, but I have no idea what or who she's looking for. "Everything okay?"

"Peachy," she says as she whisks by me, probably headed for the other side of this place.

Geez, what the hell is going on with everyone lately? Something feels off in Nettles, and I'm not sure if it's just me feeling like this or if it's everyone. I grab two bottles of water as I head back to the seats. My phone buzzes in the small pocket of the dress I changed into. I barely had time to do a full makeup look, so I spread some glitter on my eyelids, and drew some eyeliner on. I tried covering up how exhausted I looked with mascara and some purposefully placed color corrector and concealer, but it didn't really work.

It's not my best work, but my wrist and hand were practically aching by the time I finished with the entire bridal party, so this is the best I could get.

"Are you working yourself too thin again, Eloise? Or is it Mom? You know, you have to stop worrying yourself into oblivion or else you're going to end up in the hospital too," I hear Delilah say to her sister as I hand her a bottle of water.

"Here," I say as I take my seat.

"I'm fine." Her sister takes a sip of water. "Stop worrying about me."

"Never." She swipes her sister's hair back behind her ear. "I'm glad you're home."

I grab my phone from the pocket of my dress, and as soon as I see his name, I can't help but smile at my phone.

> **Theo: Didn't mean to worry you. I'm back home and doing okay.**

> **Theo: I haven't forgotten about you, Dais. That I can promise you. Can I call you in a few?**

I answer immediately, unable to stop my fingers from moving.

> **Daisy: I'm at a wedding right now, but I plan on leaving early and drowning my sorrows in a tub of ice cream.**

> **Theo: Save some for me for when I'm back. I want to hear all about what I missed up there.**

> **Daisy: Will do.**

> **Theo: Atta girl.**

"Who has you smiling like that, Dais?" Delilah pulls me out of the conversation Theo and I are having, and I swear I see a glimmer in her eyes.

"Del, please don't tell me you set her up with Elliott. I've told you he's never going to settle down if you try and force it; he has to do it on his own time." Eloise looks at me, an apologetic frown on her face. "Dais, don't do anything she forces you to. I know she's scarily convincing sometimes, but—"

"She hasn't done anything." I pause because that's not totally true. "Yet."

"I knew it!" Eloise whispers as she points at her sister. "You have to stop."

She only rolls her eyes. "Sometimes I forget where your allegiance lies."

"It's a twin thing." She shrugs, a small laugh bubbling from her body. "Oh, it looks like it's starting."

Music starts to play as Brooks hurries down the aisle, fists are balled, and fuck, if people didn't know he hated this situation he's in before, they definitely do now.

"He's not supposed to walk down the aisle is he?" Delilah asks me as I watch my friend stomp down the aisle.

Everyone stands up, but the music abruptly stops as he waves his hand at the string quartet that was playing.

"Oh no," I hear Eloise whisper underneath her breath.

I hear whispers and murmurs all across the room, but all Delilah and I do is lock eyes, confusion across both of our features as Brooks speaks.

"I'm sorry for any inconvenience, but you all came here for nothing." Shock filters around the room, and the whispers begin to get louder. "The wedding is off. I'd appreciate your privacy during this time. I know how this town works, so it would do you all well to leave me alone."

And with that, he heads back down the aisle, the same way he came as he heads for the doors. I shuffle out of the door, following him in case he needs someone to vent to or something.

"Brooks—"

"Not now, Daisy." He turns to face me, a look on his face I've only seen one other time. "Just go."

I watch him walk through the large entrance to the church and he disappears out of sight, not a single answer as to why the wedding is off. Something must have happened, right? What else could it be? Did he finally come to his senses or what?

"Excuse me," I hear Eloise say as she also bolts out of the church, an odd expression on her face as she heads in the opposite direction Brooks went in.

I spot Fallon hiding behind one of the larger pillars, and Delilah waves to her, the two of us wanting to know what the hell happened. If anyone knows, it's Fallon.

"What the hell is going on?" she asks her sister.

"Is Brooks okay?"

She just shakes her head. "I-I don't know. I couldn't find Jamie for like an hour, and then I found her and told her to stay put. She didn't, and then Brooks found me and said the wedding was off. I have no fucking idea what's going on and all of my beautiful work is going to waste. But hey, it's their money, not mine. I got paid this morning."

"Same," I say, my check handed to me by the bride herself.

And as soon as Delilah and I turn around, Fallon is gone too.

"Well, this definitely takes the cake for the weirdest wedding ever," I whisper as I watch people filter out of the church, Brooks's family nowhere to be found.

"Can we even call it a wedding if it didn't really end up happening? I mean, nobody got married."

"I guess you're right," I tell her, threading her arm through mine. "Ice cream and movies at my house?"

She shakes her head. "I wish, but I might as well open the store up and pretend it's business as usual."

"You were going to take the day off today anyway, Del. Might as well spend it actually relaxing," I remind her. I know I'm practically married to my job, but Delilah *never* takes a day off—even when she's burned out, she pushes through. I honestly don't know how she does it. "Please?"

"Sorry, Dais, but if you need a cup of coffee, the first one is on me." She smirks, knowing I can't ever turn her down.

"Fine, but then I'm going home and turning on all of our favorite movies and watching them without you."

"I'll be over after work, how about that?"

"I'll save our favorites for tonight, then." I smile.

"Just like the old days." She hits her shoulder against mine, and the two of us jump into her car and ride off into the sunny afternoon after the most confusing wedding we've ever seen.

Chapter Nineteen

— SAVE ME BY NOAH KAHAN

I'VE BEEN HOME FOR a few days and all the progress—albeit the small steps—I made in Vermont to handle my grief a little better has been set back. All we've done on the anniversary of his death is talk about him. We told stories, some similar to last year, and my mom pulled out the home videos for us to watch and reminisce.

Every clip that plays feels like a stab to the stomach. Every laugh I hear from him reminds me of what he did. Every smile feels like there's some double meaning to it, I don't care how young we were.

It's officially been three years since my brother died, and I am *still* crumbling. I couldn't even tell anyone how I got here, how I've fed myself, and kept myself alive over the last few years.

Tristan and Teags left hours ago—the two of them headed home to their partners—and I'm stuck here in the same room I grew up in wondering where everything went wrong. I'm happy for them, don't get me wrong, nobody deserves happiness more than my siblings, but sometimes I think I'm not cut out for life like they are. They're both moving forward, both feeling happiness again, and love, and I'm just... here.

I could ask them how they're doing it, how everything looks so easy for them when I know it's not. I know what they feel like. We all shared the same feelings in different ways when we found out Tobias was dead, but they're both headed in the right direction. I'm not. I'm still here, wondering where everything went so catastrophically wrong.

The world changed so much when Tobias died, my life changed, this home, this town, everything changed. It's strange to be moving on without him.

"Knock, knock," my mom says as she walks into my room. I quickly wipe the tears from my face as I sit up a little more. I didn't even bother getting under the blankets on my bed. "How are you doing?"

I shrug, unsure of how to answer that.

"It was wonderful having you all together again. I knew Teags was back, but I didn't know you were. You've been quiet in Vermont. Is everything going okay?"

"Don't worry about me, Mom. I'm doing just fine up there." Another lie because I can't tell her I almost drank myself to death. She doesn't need to worry that another one of her kids might end up not being here much longer. "I didn't know Teags was back here, and with Dom of all people."

She brings her hands up to my face, lightly squeezing my cheeks. "Those two are a whole other story. At least you didn't freak out how your brother did."

"Oh, I bet Tristan had a moment when he found out." I laugh, wishing I could have seen his face. "Vermont is everything I thought it would be and nothing like it was."

"You look different than the last time I saw you," she tells me. "A little lighter."

I don't know if she's telling some sort of joke or what because I definitely don't feel any lighter than I did before. If anything, it all feels heavier, like more weight just keeps piling on top of me, trying to drown me where I stand.

"When do you think you'll be ready to sell?" I ask her, knowing if there's a time limit on my stay up there.

"Whenever you're ready." She smiles at me. "Take your time up there, sweetheart. I know what it meant to you and Tobias. You two were always the ones begging us to go back, but I couldn't do it. Not without your father."

"That's understandable," I tell her. "I'm sorry if we were pushy when we were kids. I know how difficult—"

"Don't do that to your old mother." She laughs, a tear falling from her eyes. "I wish you all got to be kids a little longer."

"You're the best mom ever," I remind her. "I really don't know how you did it for all those years with the four of us."

"You kids got me through it," she tells me, another tear falling. "You were all the reason I got out of bed in the morning. You kept me going, despite how much I missed your father."

Maybe that's why I'm so stuck. I don't have anything to keep me going. My job, sure, but that's just a job. I miss when photography felt like every picture I took was discovering something brand new. I miss when it felt like I was capturing the world through my own specific lens.

"I just wanted to check in on you." She pats the bed as she stands up. "I know how tough today has been. It's hard reliving these memories every year."

She's right. This day will always be heavier than the others. His birthday and holidays are tough, too, but today? The day we found out he was gone? Yeah, nothing will top that.

"Will it be like this forever? This feeling?"

"I don't know," she tells me, a small smile across her face. "It gets easier with time, but it will never be the same again. The day your father died will always be that day. No matter what happens, no matter if we get great news or something wonderful happens, it will still always be the day your father no longer existed on Earth. Same with Tobias. So, I guess no it never gets easier, but it will always get lighter. I like to think that's true, even if sometimes it feels like I'll be stuck in this feeling forever."

"Thanks, Mom."

"Of course." She heads for my door. "I hope you're finding a small piece of your brother up in Vermont, maybe some old friends too. I hate thinking you're all alone up there."

I can't help the smile that spreads across my face as the girl-next-door infiltrates my mind. "I'm not alone, Mom. I promise."

"Good. I'll make pancakes tomorrow morning. What time are you leaving?"

"Probably early afternoon." I still want to head to my father's grave before I leave to see if there's something there, but I doubt I'll find anything, which makes me feel even worse. "Good night, Mom."

"Good night. Sleep tight," she says as she flicks my light off and softly shuts my door.

I try my best to fall asleep, really, I do, but it doesn't come. All that floats through my mind is memories of my brother, how I'm failing him every second, and the fact that he's gone. I try even harder to fall into sleep, knowing tomorrow I'll wake up and feel the exact same weight on my chest.

I can't do this.

I've missed feeling like this—weightless.

This always helps the shitty feelings. Alcohol is not the way to fix all of my problems in the long run, but it's only been an hour or two and the bottle I drank already has me questioning why I thought this was a bad idea. I can't feel fucking *anything*, and that's exactly what I wanted, especially today.

I quietly open Tobias's door, the stale smell of his untouched room infiltrating my nostrils and reminding me that he hasn't lived in this room in years. Even before he was gone, he wasn't home that much, only for holidays and stuff.

I sit in here, and the memories of my brother and I flash through my brain as nothing hurts me. The memories are there, but they don't puncture me, not this time. *Finally.*

My fingers find my phone and I dial my brother's old number, and his voicemail comes up after a few rings.

"This is Tobias West. Not East, North, or South. Leave a message at the—"

I try to leave a message, but his mailbox is full, and that pisses me off, so I swipe off of it and accidentally press another number. Of course she answers immediately.

"Theo?" There's a small pause before I hear her beautiful voice again. "It's late, what are you doing up?"

"I'm sad," comes out before I can shut up. "But I don't feel it. God, it's amazing, Dais."

"Are you drunk?"

"Maybe," I tell her. "That's why I called you, remember?"

"You're supposed to call me before you get this bad," she sighs across the line. I know I disappointed her. It always happens eventually. I befriend someone, they see the real me, and then they run away. I'm a mess. A fuck-up. I'm nothing special. It's no wonder my only friend is someone I work with who I barely have interacted with these past few years.

"I'm sorry, Daisy baby," I slur into the phone, my body no longer able to hold itself up as I collapse against my dead brother's bed. "It just hurts so fucking much."

"What hurts? Did you hit your head? Theo, give me a number I can call to make sure—"

"Don't worry about me," I tell her. "The more attached you get, the more you'll be disappointed."

"Some part of me thinks you're always attached to your childhood friends. Even when you grow up and never see them again, there's still always a part of you that remembers them."

"God, you're so fucking smart. I could listen to you talk all fucking day." I turn the volume up on my phone. "Please keep talking to me, Daisy."

I swear I hear her laugh through the phone. "Why does it hurt?"

"My brother died today. Well, three years ago today is when I found out."

"Oh," she says. "I'm sorry, Theo. That can't be easy. Are your siblings around? Can you maybe try and—"

"They're home with their partners being happy," I blurt out.

"Can you call one of them? I'm worried about you."

"I called you, Dais," I remind her. I think my buzz is starting to wear off.

"You have to stop drinking," she whispers into the phone. "It's not going to make the pain go away. It's a short-term solution, and I know that's easy for me to say, but I have every right to say it, especially after what happened."

"I know." I sit up, her words starting to slowly sober me up. I can't keep involving her in the mess of my life, yet somehow, I keep doing it. God, I'm a piece of shit. "Alcohol seems to be the only thing that works besides talking to you."

"And if I recall, you promised me a practice date." I can hear her smile through the phone. "I can't go on a date if you can barely stand."

"I guess you're right." I chuckle. "I didn't think that was still on the table."

"Well, you are coming back, right? Or is this goodbye again?"

"It's not goodbye, Dais," I tell her. "I came back to deal with some stuff back here."

"I thought you skipped town to never be heard from again until you finally answered my message."

"You didn't think I was just going to leave without saying goodbye again?" She says nothing. "Look, last time I left, I was young. I did what my mom told me. I'd never leave like that again."

"That's not technically true."

She's got me there. I did whip out of town last week with not so much as a note on my door or anything. I didn't even text her that I was leaving. I just left.

Again, I am a piece of shit.

"I'm coming back, Dais. And we can have our practice date and I can annoy the shit out of you until you get tired of me." That sentence slurs more than I'd like it to. "You remind me of plugging in the GPS and having it already know the way home to you."

She doesn't say a word, and I'm starting to think she can't understand me.

"Are you there?"

"Mhm," she whispers and I hear some shuffling in the background. "Sorry, I just—"

"Don't apologize," I remind her. "I should be apologizing to you. I'm sorry I'm such a fucking mess."

"Is the bottle down?"

"It is."

"Good. That's what I wanted to hear."

I'd do anything for you, Daisy girl.

That has to be the drunk thoughts talking, right? I mean, we're friends, and she just got out of a marriage. I shake my head out, needing all of my thoughts to shut up.

"Why do you do this?"

"What?"

"Why do you believe in me? Why do you reach for my hand when I make things worse? I don't know if I'll ever fully put the bottle down, but why do you seem to think I'm worth saving?"

I hear her breathing over the line, so I know she heard me. Sometimes, I wish I could see myself through her eyes. Maybe she sees something in me that I can't.

"All I do is make things worse, Dais. Everything gets harder when I'm around you, and I hate doing that."

"Because you've destroyed yourself enough." She sniffles. "You've served your sentence for whatever you think you've done to deserve what you're feeling." Another pause. "Nobody deserves to walk through the dark alone and afraid. It's better with a friend."

"Is that what we are?"

"I'd like to think so. We've graduated to more than neighbors." She laughs, and suddenly the word friend pisses me off more than it used to. "I'll see you soon?"

"That you will."

"Good night, Theo, not like the flower. Take care of yourself."

"Good night, Daisy like the flower." I smile as I hear a click on the other end.

I ignore the swirling in my stomach as something to do with the alcohol I drank tonight, and as my head hits the pillow, I find myself dreaming of rows and rows of daisies, all of them shining so brightly the only thing dimming them is my shadow.

Chapter Twenty

— **WHO WE ARE BY HOZIER**

"Eloise still hasn't said anything about what happened after the wedding?" I ask, wondering if Delilah has any new information about what's been going on. The entire town has been talking about what might have happened to have it be called off. I haven't seen Brooks since he told me to go away, and apparently nobody else has either. Jamie isn't even in town anymore, according to the rumor mill.

"Not a word," Delilah confirms. Apparently, someone saw Eloise and Brooks talking after the wedding, but everyone was confused as to why. They barely acknowledged each other in high school, so it had Delilah all up in arms when she heard someone talking about her sister at the store. "I'm as in the dark as everyone else is."

I change out of my overalls covered in dirt from the weeding I was doing earlier and throw on a huge T-shirt I ordered a few sizes too big. I throw my phone onto my bed, Delilah now on speakerphone, as I shuffle into the covers with a book I've been reading over the past month and a half. I'm the slowest reader on the planet, and I'm only halfway done with this one, but I've been enjoying it so far. It's a literary fiction book Delilah bought a few months ago because she thought the cover was beautiful, only to find out it's about a family whose patriarch gets diagnosed with a terminal illness.

She didn't want to read it after that, which is understandable given the life she's been living, so she gave it to me. It's raw, and emotional, and I don't know who Henry Hayes is, but someone should check in on him. This book has made me cry since page one.

"Nettles hasn't had true gossip like this in a while," Delilah says. "Most of the time it's small whispers about someone, but when the entire town is together on a topic, that's when it gets *really* insane."

"Yeah, well, I was the topic of discussion for at least two weeks when I came back," I remind her. "It's not fun being on that end of it. I hope Brooks is doing okay."

"Did he look different to you that day or am I seeing something that isn't actually true?"

My eyebrows pinch together. "Uh, no. He seemed like the same Brooks who didn't want to tie the knot. What did you think you saw?"

"Relief," is all she says as I hear her chopping vegetables for dinner. That girl never has a steady eating schedule. I swear she's worse than I am.

"Maybe? I mean, everyone knew he didn't want to get married, but he still looked pissed when he told the entire town it wasn't happening."

"Should I bring him some pastries? Or maybe a lasagna? What food is appropriate to say 'I'm sorry your wedding didn't happen even though I don't think you wanted it to happen anyway?'"

I can't help but laugh. "I think if you brought that over to his house or the Turner family home, you would get yelled off of the porch."

She only scoffs. "I'm just trying to be nice. I don't and never will understand what their problem is with my family. Brooks and Amara don't have this anger towards us, so why do they?"

That has always been the question. The kids of these families get along just fine, but for some reason, their parents don't want them mingling. It's ridiculous.

"I don't think we'll ever know the answer to that."

"Yeah, I doubt it," she tells me. "I have to go or I might accidentally burn my place down. Love you! I'll see you tomorrow?"

"Love you, too, Del, and yes you will." I hang up, getting more snuggled into my gigantic blankets, and just as I open my book, my phone starts to ring again. I pick it up without looking at who it is, assuming she forgot to say something. "Yes, you told me you loved me, and I love you too."

"As much as I enjoyed hearing that out of your mouth, last I checked, I was not your best friend, Delilah." Theo's voice makes my cheeks heat up. *I am such an idiot.* I've only seen him in passing since he got back the other day, and things have been insane at the store. He brought over a puzzle and some flowers to my house as an apology for worrying me, but other than that I've been at the store all hours of the day. I've had so many new bulk shipments I've had to sort through, and I had inventory the other day to keep track of what I have and don't. Basically, life has been a little too busy, and I haven't seen him since he got back.

"Sorry," I say as I sit up. "How are you doing?"

"I'm alright," he says, and I hear shuffling across the line. I can only assume he's moving boxes or something. "Are you home?"

"I am. Why? Did you finally want that debrief of all you missed in Nettles because it's kind of—"

"If you're home, then you must know your front door is open, right?"

"My what?" I ask, confused. "My front door is open?"

"Wide open," he tells me. "Did you—"

A loud bang from downstairs makes me freeze in my bed.

"Dais, go hide."

"W-What?"

"I just saw someone in your downstairs window," he tells me, more shuffling across the line. "Go hide. I'm coming over."

"Theo—"

"Daisy, please," is all he says as his voice gets farther away. "I'm not hanging up, but go."

"Okay." I finally remember how to move and I try as quietly as I can to head for my closet, shoving myself into it as I hear more bangs from below. I have no idea what's happening. I should call the police right? But Theo told me not to hang up. What if he comes over and gets hurt? What if they have weapons? Is there one of them or two? Or three? Or more than that?

Every nightmare scenario races through my mind as tears start to fall. I hate that I'm a crier when I feel any emotion. Even when I'm happy, I feel tears well up and fall from my eyes. I'm not a pretty crier either, or a silent one, but right now, I have to be quiet, so I try to stop my hiccuping sobs in case they come upstairs.

Are they looking for something or are they trying to find me? Is this just a normal robbery or was my house targeted? Every home invasion movie I've ever seen is flashing through my mind, and I wish I could talk back to Theo over the line, but I have the volume turned all the way down.

"Theo?" I whisper as quietly as I can. "I'm scared."

"Hold on for me, Dais." I hear him grunt before I hear what I assume is my front door flying open as he heads inside. I hear a few bangs coming from downstairs and I hate that I can't see what's going on.

"Please be careful," I say even though I doubt he can hear me with how quietly I'm speaking. An image of me driving him to the hospital passed out in my passenger seat flashes through my mind, and more tears come as I put my hand over my mouth to try and quiet my sobs.

Breathe, Dais.

But that's practically impossible with the little amount of air in my closet. I shrink down to the floor, hearing footsteps coming toward me. If I can make myself small, maybe they won't see me and they'll leave with whatever they took.

I hear way too much shuffling for my liking, and I see a light flashing into my room, and just as someone is about to open the door, I try with everything to make myself blend into the clothes hanging up in here.

The doors open, and more sobs come, so I know I'm fucking screwed.

"Daisy?" Theo's voice filters into my ears as he drops a baseball bat from his hands, his arms coming around me in an instant. "I'm here, Daisy girl. I'm here. They're gone."

I burst into tears into his shoulder as his arms envelop me. I can barely speak as he picks me up and carries me out of the house.

"Come here," he says as he wraps me in a blanket, the door shutting softly behind us. I can't stop shivering and I'm not even sure why. Fear, maybe? Or adrenaline? I have no fucking idea. I've never been so scared before. "I'll call the police, okay? And I'll grab you some water."

"T-Thanks," I say, my teeth chattering together. "I'm—"

"Don't," is all he says. "Don't, Dais."

I nod as he stays in my line of sight, the baseball bat he ran over to my house with safely tucked by the front door, the sirens getting closer and closer to my house.

The only thought that filters through my mind is that this has something to do with what my ex-husband called me about, but part of me wants to believe it's not. He couldn't know I'm back in Vermont. I never even told him what town I was from. He doesn't know any specific details about my life here because I wanted to separate myself from here, so there's no way he could have done this.

And he would never go to all of this trouble over some recipes for a business he didn't even have any stake in. There's nothing in it for him except a bunch of money, but he could get that with anything else he stuck his stupid nose in. Why is he so worried about my company that never even got off of the ground and was dead before it existed?

There's no way it's him. Maybe it was a random breaking and entering?

Right?

Right?

— SO LONG, HONEY BY CAAMP

"You're staying here until they find whoever did this," Theo says as he shuts the door, the police officers headed back to the station. This is definitely going to spread around town. A few people on the street were outside of their houses trying to see what was going on with all of the cop cars. The only bright side I can think about is that maybe the attention will be off of Brooks, but I hate that it's back on me.

"It's fine, Theo," I tell him, wrapping the blanket around me even more than it was. "I'll be fine."

"Dais, you might be okay with being in that house all by yourself while your parents are away, but after this, I'm not. I don't want anything to happen to you. What if I had been out of town still? What if they had—" He stops himself from saying whatever he was going to, and my heart skips a beat as I finish his sentence for him.

"What if they had killed me?" Hearing that sentence out loud scares me more than I care to admit.

He rubs a hand across his face as he paces around the living room. "Yeah, Dais. Who fucking knows what they were looking for?"

I can only shrug, unsure of what happened tonight. I'm still all riled up, my body in fight or flight even though it's been hours since I was in my closet. "I don't want to put you out."

"You're not," is all he says, coming over to the couch and grabbing my hands in his. "And maybe this would be better for our arrangement."

"What do you mean?"

"You could keep a better eye on me from my own house, right? You did promise Luca you would look out for me, and this is me promising I'm looking out for you too." His fingers drag through his mustache as his eyes meet mine. My heart is beating out of my chest, the adrenaline still pumping through my veins. "I won't be able to sleep at night if anything happened to you and I was just over here unaware."

A strange conversation from when we were younger floats through my mind as I look at the man in front of me.

"Don't worry, Dais, I'll be your knight in shining armor."

"Sure you will, Theo."

"You don't think I could protect you from anything bad? From all the scary stuff?"

I shake my head.

"Why?"

"You're tiny! They would crush you or something."

I can't help but laugh at the memory. The boy in front of me is still trying to be my knight in shining armor. In a way, he was tonight. If he hadn't looked over at my window, they might have surprised me in my room, and who knows what could have happened.

"What's so funny?" He can sense something is up with me because for some reason I can't stop laughing.

"My knight in shining armor," is all I say and I can sense when he remembers exactly what I'm referencing.

"Always," he smiles back at me. "Now, let me make up the guest bedroom for you."

"Can I come with you?" I blurt out before I can stop it. "I really don't want to be alone at the moment."

He stands, reaches his arm out for me, and as soon as I take it, he whisks me up the stairs, bringing me to the room across from his that I didn't bother cleaning up when I brought him home from the hospital.

He grabs some sheets from inside of the closet while I rip the furniture covers off, moving some of the small boxes to the side as I try to settle down.

"Do you mind?" he asks as he throws the fitted sheet to me on the other side of the bed.

"Not at all," I say as I grab it and fit it around the mattress. "I'm surprised you remembered that conversation from way back when."

"It's hard not to remember everything about you." He only smiles to himself as he fluffs out the comforter. "This house brings up a lot of memories for me."

"That makes sense," I say as I straighten out the bed. "When I left for Boston, it's as if all of my recollections of this place faded the further I got from it. But now, being back where I grew up is bringing up all these things I had forgotten about."

"Like what?" is all he says as he sits down. "Is this okay? I mean, I can leave, I know it's been a long—"

"It's okay," I tell him. "I don't mind the company, especially when it's yours, and I doubt I'll sleep much tonight."

With that, he smiles and gets comfortable on the end of the bed, his undivided attention on me.

"Do you remember that time we sat in your front yard and I talked your ear off about one of my favorite romance movies my mom let me watch with her?"

"I do."

"I remember watching it and thinking to myself that was the kind of love I wanted. I mean, I was young and I didn't even know what love was, but I remember the feeling the movie gave me. It felt warm, inviting, and peaceful. I always remember thinking when I was older I would find that same feeling in someone I loved too. I thought I had that with Derek, but it turns out, I was wrong. All those feelings I felt for him were misguided and for a minute, I lost my faith in love."

I'm still worried I'll never find that again, or maybe I'm worried if I do, then it won't last like the last time. I long for the day I'm confident enough to see the person I love from across the room, our eyes locking and a smile coming to my face just at the thought of looking at them. I want to go grocery shopping with my partner and be grateful I'm perusing the aisles with them. I want to do taxes with them, and all the other mundane things and know for certain that they love me just as much as I do them. I want the simplicity and the mundane with the person I love because even just the small things will always give me butterflies when I know I'm with the right person.

"What he did to you wasn't your fault."

"I know," I lie. I'm not totally sure he's right, at least not yet. "But being divorced at twenty-six is not at all where I thought I would be."

"Having two dead family members isn't where I thought I'd be either. Struggling with alcohol also wasn't on my list for when I looked into my future as a kid."

"This just isn't how I thought my life was going to turn out." I smile, feeling some tears come. "I'm not... good at this. I can't keep doing this."

"Doing what?"

"Trying to see the bright side. It's harder than I care to admit," I say as I pull at the skin on my arms. "Every day I feel like I'm falling further and further into this hole I can't get out of."

"Well, that's what I'm here for, right? Dais, you can lean on me how I'm leaning on you. Let me carry you through some of it how I promised I would when we were kids. Let me be your knight in shining armor."

"Life isn't some fairytale."

"Then let's pretend it is for a little while."

I say nothing as he looks at me. I can't. I can't lean into him and fall like I did last time. I can't keep doing this to myself. I have to figure out how to stand on my own and stop jumping headfirst into all of my emotions. It's not like I love Theo or want to date him, but I worry that's where this could head if I'm not careful enough. I worry I might fall and neither of us could handle that. Theo's still struggling with his grief, and I'm still struggling with everything. The list is too long for me to even share.

"What did he do, Dais?"

He only grabs my hand in his as I try to muster the strength to say out loud everything I'm afraid of. My pulse is still racing from earlier as he pulls me closer, and I let him.

Chapter Twenty-One

— LET IT HAPPEN BY GRACIE ABRAMS

I'M SURPRISED SHE'S NOT pushing me away right now. I envelop her in my arms, the warmth from her skin setting me ablaze.

"He cheated on me," she whispers. I knew that already, still I wait for her to continue. "And he made me feel small."

"Did he put his hands on you?"

"No," she sighs. "But he broke me. He tricked me. Manipulated me. Tore me to shreds in that conference room. I wasn't good enough for him. I wasn't giving him what he needed. I was too big, too ugly, too unperfect for him and his image. He cheated on me and he blamed me for it. The more I heard it, the more I believed it."

I pull back from her, wiping her hair from her face and her tears from her eyes. God, if I ever see this guy in person, I don't know what I'll do to him, but I know I won't hold back.

"I loved him so much. I loved him with every piece of myself, and I fell into him so easily that I lost myself on the way. When I left here, I wanted to become my own person away from this place." She pauses, her breathing getting heavier. "It didn't really work out that way."

"I know who you are, okay?" I tell her, grabbing her hands in mine. "You're Daisy Campbell, the girl next door. You're the brightest flower in the entire garden."

This girl is a field of flowers personified, but even more than that, she's that one singular flower that sticks out over the rest of them. She shines brighter, whistles louder in the wind than everything else, and I don't know how she doesn't realize that even if she's in a funk right now. She's always felt like that to me, even as kids, her light shined brighter than anyone I had ever seen or known.

"Stop," she says as she stands from the bed, the sheets ruffling as she looks at herself in part of the mirror that's uncovered.

I go over to her, standing behind her as she peeks at herself through the small sliver. I grab the cover and rip it off of it, Daisy's face going right to her shoulder as she looks away.

"Look at me," I whisper to her and she shakes her head. "Daisy, please."

"I can't."

I grab her chin in mine and softly turn her head so she's looking at me in the mirror. Her eyes are shining back at me, and I hate that she can't bear to look at herself when all I see in front of me is a beautiful woman, with strength unlike anyone else I know.

"Hey," I say to her as I caress her face. "I can't even begin to describe how angry I am that he made you feel like this."

"Why are *you* angry? Don't be. I'm not worth it."

"He tried to change you," I say to her. "What kind of man does that to someone he's supposed to love? You're just..."

"I'm what?" She scoffs at me.

"You're perfect as you are. How can you not understand that when you're standing right in front of me looking like this?"

"I'm far from perfect." She brushes a tear from her eye. "And you and I are looking at two different things right now. I can almost guarantee that."

"What do you see?" I ask as she finally looks at herself.

"A mess." She laughs, but I can tell she's not joking. "My hair is all over the place. My arms are flabby. I have stretch marks all over my thighs. I'm not… pretty. I-I look nothing like the girls Derek cheated on me with. I'm not paper thin, and I don't have perfect skin. I have bumps and blemishes and hip dips or whatever these are called." She grabs onto her legs and pulls on the skin.

"Look at me." I move her head to look at me. "I need you to listen to me, honey."

"Stop, Theo." She tries to move, but I keep her in place.

I kneel down, my head now where her hands are pulling at the skin on her legs. "May I?"

She nods, still gripping her skin as if she's trying to get rid of it as my hands replace hers, my fingers brushing against the skin showing on her hips as I take her in.

I lightly brush my lips against her. "You are the most beautiful person I've ever seen." I press another kiss right on top of her hand still grabbing at her skin. "I don't know how you don't realize how beautiful you are, inside and out."

"Because I'm not."

"You are," I say, my hands on her hips. "And you're strong," I say as I caress her arms, standing up as I envelop her in a hug. "These arms dragged me into a car on one of the worst nights of my life. You saved me, Dais. These arms and legs saved me. This beautiful, strong fucking body saved me, and I'll remind you of that as long as it takes until you realize everything coming from my mouth is the truth."

"That might take a while," she tells me.

"I'll be here as long as it takes," I promise her. "I'm not going anywhere."

"Do you really mean that?"

"I do." I press another kiss to her shoulder blade.

"I'm sorry." She shakes her head, a single tear falling from her eye. "I-I didn't need you to do that."

"I wanted to. If we could switch gazes for a day and you could see me through your eyes and I could see you through yours, I know you'd like what you see. Because I damn well do like what I see every time I look at you."

Her eyes stare into mine for a few moments before she turns away, her hands covering her arms as if she's shy again.

"I'll leave so you can sleep." Part of me feels like I crossed a line, and maybe I took things too far, but I couldn't keep watching her list off all of the things she dislikes about herself.

She's perfect. Beautiful. She's like if the sun were personified. I ignore the flutter in my chest when I continue to think about her. I ignore the swirling in my stomach as I think about when I touched her skin. I ignore all of that because none of this is about me.

She grabs my hand as I turn to leave, and before I know it, her lips are on mine and she's kissing me.

"I dare you"—she throws a pile of grass at me—*"to kiss me."*

"Kiss you?" I ask. "But kissing is gross."

"It's gross for me too! How do I know where your mouth has been?"

"I have the same question," I joke. "Adults do it and their mouths have probably been everywhere."

"I guess you're right." She pulls a few more blades of grass, fisting them in her hands. "Have you drank out of the hose today?"

"No," I say.

"Okay." She giggles. "So, do you accept my dare or are you skipping your turn?"

"I don't turn down dares, flower girl." I scoot closer to her as she throws more grass on me. *"What do I do?"*

"It's easy." She leans in, her eyes already closed, lips puckered.

And so I lean in too, pressing the swiftest kiss to her lips before we both open our eyes, the two of us giggling until Tristan and Tobias come and drag me home for dinner.

I swear I've had dreams of this before, but nothing really compares to the feeling of her against me, her hands fisting my shirt to pull me closer. I raise my hands, cupping her face as I pull her more firmly against my mouth, hoping this isn't some sort of dream and she's really kissing me.

It's like she can't breathe without me. Her hands are grabbing against my shirt, her chest against mine as I feel her soft lips entangling with mine.

I haven't kissed or been kissed in so long I almost forgot what it felt like, and I don't want this to end. I could spend the rest of my life enveloped in her and I wouldn't give a single fuck about anyone else.

"Theo," she whispers against my lips. "More."

"God, Daisy," I say. "You're perfect. So fucking perfect."

This isn't how I imagined the night to end up, but after the adrenaline rush from earlier and all we've talked about tonight, I don't care. If this is what Daisy needs, then I'll give it to her. Never mind the fact that she never left my mind after the last time I saw her. Never mind the fact that Tobias wanted us to connect again. Never mind any of that. It's just her and I in this room, in this moment, and that's all it needs to be.

The two of us are so enveloped with one another that neither of us realizes we're almost at the bed, and I trip backwards, my back hitting the sheets we just put on as she tumbles on top of me.

"Oh my god," she pants, her hands covering her eyes as she straddles me. "I'm so—"

"Not sorry," I laugh to myself as she smiles, a laugh bubbling out of her too. "That was, um." I can't really find the appropriate words. Amazing.

Surprising. Everything I had dreamed it would be? Yeah. I guess that cuts it.

I move her hands from her eyes, her arms falling to her side as my hands find her hips. I can't help it with the way she's straddling me. I don't want her to fall over anymore than we have tonight.

My thumbs rub circles on her hips, my hands not able to stop grazing against her soft skin. It looks like she feels the same because her hands come to my chest, her fingers grazing against the shirt she was just clutching a few seconds ago. We both know we shouldn't be doing this. We're neighbors. Friends. This isn't what friends do.

But we're doing it anyway, stealing all the small touches we can get from one another.

"Sorry if I caught you off-guard, I just—"

"Stop apologizing," I say underneath her.

"I didn't mean to make things awkward."

"You didn't."

"Are you sure?"

"I'm positive," I say as she gets off of me. I know she's going to keep rambling if I don't stop her, so I press a kiss to her cheek as I get up. "I'll make us breakfast tomorrow."

"Thank you," she says as I turn back to her. "For everything."

"As long as it's you asking me, Dais, you know I'd do anything for you." She smiles at me, and I can't help but smile like a fucking idiot back at her, our gazes lingering for a beat too long, but I can't seem to pull myself away from her. I see her eyes trail down my body as I stand in the doorway. I don't want to tear myself away from her, but I should. "I'll make pancakes tomorrow morning."

She nods, the silence blanketing the room but I can't pull my eyes off of her. I should leave. I should close this door and go to my own room, but I can't, or won't do it. I'm too enamored with her, this beautiful woman staring back at me as if she wants to say something more, but she doesn't. I don't know what to say either, but as soon as I walk out of the door, tonight's over. This will all be a memory, and I don't know if I'll ever have the words to wrap my mind around what happened.

"I can't wait." She smiles, getting comfortable even though she told me she might not sleep tonight.

Then I shut the door, knowing I'm not going to sleep tonight, but part of me doesn't give a single fuck becuase the girl-next-door just kissed me until I couldn't think straight.

And it was everything I imagined it would be, but I doubt it will happen again no matter how much I want it to.

Chapter Twenty-Two

— **IN THE WIND BY LORD HURON**

Autumn has officially reached Nettles, yet I've been frozen in time since Daisy's lips touched mine a few days ago.

There's a chill in the air that only comes when autumn moves in and it doesn't feel like I've been in Nettles for a little over two months already. I guess that makes sense, though. I spent so much of my life only existing here for a few weeks out of the year. Now that I've been here for a longer period of time, I know it's going to be harder to walk away from it.

But I have to—eventually, right? I have a meeting with a realtor soon that my mom recommended and I've made my way through most of our stuff. I have a few boxes to bring back to Pennsylvania with me when I leave since some of the stuff I found has been claimed by my siblings.

I don't want to leave quite yet, so I'm dragging this out as much as I can.

Daisy's at work right now, but the morning after we kissed, she came down, told me she wanted to forget it ever happened, and I reluctantly agreed to never mention it again. Regardless of how many times I've thought of it since it happened, it's for the best.

I guess.

We're friends. Neighbors. She's been inhabiting my house since the break-in. We kissed and now that fact hangs in the air in between us as we dance around one another in the mornings. I've watched her get ready for work this entire week. I've heard her and Delilah chatting when she comes over and has movie night because apparently that tradition can't be stopped even though she's not at home.

I agreed, not only because I love hearing her laugh filter through the vents in the house, but I'd do anything for her.

That night she came over, the two of them updated me on Brooks's wedding that didn't actually happen and all of the drama surrounding that. I haven't seen Brooks since that day in his bar, and part of me wants to talk with him again. I like the guy. He and I seem to be two sides of the same coin, at least I think we are from the conversation we had.

I even went to the hotel to talk to his sister, but she hasn't seen him either, and she's equally in the dark about all this as the rest of the town is. But that's small town life for you, I guess. Gossip spreads like a tornado funneling through Main Street. I'm sure there was some about me when I came back, according to what Delilah said to me when I first saw her.

My phone buzzes as I sit with my arms fully inside of another box—one of the last ones. I grab it, already knowing what's going to greet me on my screen thanks to the ringtone I chose.

> **Lucas: Earth to Theo. Calling Theo West in Vermont.**

> **Lucas: Do I even need to say it?**

> **Theo: Nope.**

> **Lucas:** Well, good to know you're alive, at least.
>
> **Lucas:** Have you not sent any pictures or are we just not receiving the film?
>
> **Theo:** I haven't sent them. I have none.
>
> **Lucas:** Better get to photographing then.
>
> **Theo:** Gee, thanks.
>
> **Lucas:** Call me if you need anything.
>
> **Theo:** Will do.

I know he means well, and I can actually call him if I need anything even if he sounds like an ass over the phone. Lucas would answer in a heartbeat, but I'm not dragging him into my mess. Though, I do need to start to taking some fucking pictures or else I'm going to lose my job and that's not something I can afford to do.

I sigh heavily as I stop what I was doing, grab my camera, and head to my backyard. I haven't found any spots here that have given me my normal urge to grab my camera and take a picture. I haven't been creatively inspired anywhere. Except one place—the bench Daisy and I often find ourselves sitting on. I thought it could be a good picture destination if I maybe tweaked my settings and had a good enough shot, but nothing I've taken over there so far has been magazine cover worthy. If I send any of my shots to Lucas, he would probably say the exact same thing once he developed them.

On the bright side, I haven't had a drink since that night I was home, and I haven't felt the urge to pick up a bottle lately. I could say it's because I've been so busy with other things, but the truth is, the more time I spend around Daisy, the more I want her to see the less fucked up version of me, if it even exists in my body. I would be proud of myself, but I know at some point in the future, I'm going to fuck up again. It's inevitable. I know it will happen. I'm not holding my breath.

By the time I get outside, I already feel the tiny bit of inspiration I had seep from my bones, and instead of trying to get it back, I lay on the grass and stare at the sky. Once again, I've fallen to the last place I can with nowhere further to go.

The wind blows across my face, the sun beaming down on me as I hear the trees blowing, the leaves rustling. All of these beautiful sounds of nature accompany me as I stare up at the clouds, wondering what my place in this dirt is. The sky is a normal shade of blue, the clouds white and puffy as if they were drawn perfectly for a cartoon.

"Do you see that?" I hear in my mind as I continue to lay here. *"Theo, look!"*

I hear my brother's voice as I look up at the sky.

"What?" I whisper into the breeze. "What is it, Tobias?"

"That cloud looks like a puzzle piece."

I move my head from side to side, scanning the sky as a familiar feeling hits me. "I see it."

"Do you remember the last time we did this?" he asks, and I try to see if he's next to me. *"Don't turn your head or I'll disappear."*

"You're already gone."

"Dead doesn't mean gone. Didn't Teags say that a few weeks ago or am I misremembering that beautiful conversation you all had without me?"

I must be going crazy. Here I am, laying in the backyard talking out loud to my dead brother while I try to figure out the puzzle he left behind for me to solve.

"It's not as hard as you think."

"Easy for you to say," I joke. "You are the one who wrote it."

"I thought this one was the easiest," he tells me. *"We did grow up here, after all."*

"We only spent a few weeks here a year."

"Yes, but those were some of the best. At least, in my mind they were. I think about them often. Especially that one time we really did see a puzzle piece floating through the sky. We were laying right in these spots when I pointed it out to you."

"Wha—" I sit up from the grass only to feel nothing. No body of my brother. No ghostly apparition. Nothing. He was all in my head, just like always.

"Shit," is all I say as I grab the dirt in my fingers, the clue he left me filtering through my mind. "Guarded by earth."

He always laid to the right of me when we were back here. I remember the last time we did it. Tristan and Teags were on the swings. He was pushing her and she was yelling back at him that he wasn't doing it fast enough. She wanted to reach the clouds where the music notes floated off into, and he didn't want her to get hurt.

Tobias had pointed out the cloud and I had taken a picture of it. When it printed out of my camera, he made me bury it in the yard where we laid. In fact, I don't know how I forgot about this. All of us had chosen one thing to bury in a box in the backyard the last year we were here. We all figured in ten years or however long, we could come back to it and remember when we were all kids here.

"Fuck," is all I say as I bolt to the shed, knowing there has to be a shovel in here I can use to dig up the dirt beneath my fingertips. I find one buried in the back by the lawnmower and I get to work. It only takes a few minutes of digging until I hit something, that familiar shoebox coming into view. The earth was not as kind to it as we thought it would be as children, but it's still intact, and the moment I rip it open and see a familiar white envelope, I start to cry.

I pull out one of Tristan's baseballs from the box—the one he used to play catch with our father with. The seams are still split. This was his favorite one to throw with because he once threw it so fast that it ripped. My father was so impressed, he would tell anyone who would hear that Tristan was going to be the best player when he was older.

He never got to see him play again, though. He died before the season started, and he never knew Tristan went on to play college baseball for the school we all grew up watching on the sports channel.

I pull out an old pair of earphones Teags put in here so even the worms could hear the music. We tried to explain to her that there was nothing plugged into them, but she just huffed us off and rolled her eyes.

"Music isn't just songs. It's everywhere, you buffoons. Now, put them in the box."

Mom had recently taught her that word—buffoon. She wouldn't stop using it after that, and us boys were often the targets of her new vocabulary.

I pull out the picture of the cloud I took, the photograph worn by time and the dirt, but I can still vaguely make out what it used to be. I flip it over, the scribbles on the back incoherent, but I remember what it says.

Theo and Tobias's final piece of the puzzle.

Our parents always joked that the two of us could find a puzzle in anything, and this cloud proved it.

And now, the envelope. There's a small note taped to it, and I shake some of the dirt off of it as I unfold it.

```
Theo,
The missing piece of the puzzle is yours. I
hope once you see all of them together, it
```

starts to make sense—the reason I sent you on this journey. I hope you found a piece of me you might have been missing, or maybe you found part of yourself you might have forgotten about.

You're a traveler, brother. I always remember the face you made when you discovered something new. You had this certain light about you that I always wished I had. I hope that light hasn't gone out because of what happened. I hope you can still find the light when things get tough because they will. It's inevitable, but with that toughness comes the sun, happiness, and a new puzzle to take on.

Don't try to solve the puzzle of why I'm gone, but try to open up some new ones. Can you feel that light as you read this? Can you see the light you spread to others? Even if you can't, I always could, but now you're on your own, brother.

Take care of yourself and that light you carry. Nourish it. Cherish it. Spread it to someone who needs it. Give some to the family for me, okay? Be the light they need when the darkness gets rough, even if things seem to be turned off.

Forever,
Tobias

And I sit in my backyard, the swings on the swing set rocking back and forth as the wind blows me over, and I cry into the dirt because I miss my brother and the light *he* used to shine on all of us.

At least I didn't let him down how I thought I was, and even though he's gone, I'll carry him with me everywhere I go once I leave here.

For now, I'm going to enjoy every memory that floats through my mind of him since I'm still in this place we inhabited together, and that's enough for me. It will always have to be enough for me.

Chapter Twenty-Three

— HEADLIGHTS BY IN COLOR

"You did what?" Delilah screams as she stops making my coffee.

All I do is nod as I feel my cheeks heat up—from embarrassment at what I did or giddiness. I'm not quite sure which it is. I honestly don't even remember pressing my mouth to his, but when he was saying all of that about me, I just did it. I didn't think twice. It was almost as if it was second nature for my head to move toward his. I've never been so impulsive before. I used to feel so calculated with my actions with Derek, but with Theo, I just went for it.

"Oh my goodness, you have to tell me everything."

I take a look to the right of me and see a line of people waiting to place an order at the counter. One of her employees is taking care of the register, but Delilah is making all of the drinks, and I don't want to distract her.

"Whenever there's a lull," I tell her. I'm on my lunch break from the store, so I only have a little bit, but I've been holding this in for days. Delilah has been staying at her childhood home since Eloise got back. Well, amongst other things. Eloise dropped some pretty insane news on the family the other day, so it's been a little hectic for the Madison family over the past week.

"No," she shakes her head at me. "Now, babe."

"There's not much to tell! I kissed him and then we got so enveloped in one another I fell on top of him and that was it."

"That was it?" her eyes are practically bulging out of her head. "That's like a huge leap in the right direction for you, Dais! I'm so proud of you."

I can't help but laugh as she sets my coffee in front of me, already grabbing the next one and barely sparing a glance at it as she gets to work. I swear this girl makes coffee and scoops ice cream in her sleep with how seamless she makes this all look.

"How was it?"

I tilt my head at her. I don't even know how to answer that question. "It was a kiss."

"You know that's not what I mean."

I really don't know what she wants to hear. Did it sweep me off of my feet? Maybe. Did it make me forget what the ground was for a few seconds? Absolutely. Did it confuse the fuck out of me and make things weird at home? Yes.

I don't do things like this—randomly kiss people. Especially since I'm supposed to be focusing on myself for the time being. I don't even know what came over me, and if he asks me about it, I don't know what I would say. We both agreed to never speak of it again, so that's what I'm going to continue doing. It was a one-off. A one time thing.

"You're thinking about it right now, aren't you?" She smirks at me. "That means it was a good kiss."

"Del, I don't know what to tell you," I say as I sip my coffee. "It meant nothing. It was just a fluke of emotions after the break-in. I was probably just scared and needing comfort like I always do."

She pinches her eyes at me, not buying my excuse. "Sure, babe. Whatever you have to tell yourself is fine with me, but all I'm hearing is that you're maybe ready to get back out there."

"I don't know about that," I tell her. "Dating is a lot different than a kiss. Those are two different leagues, and I'm not sure I—"

"Hey, sis," a familiar voice says and her face lights up as soon as she turns her head. "I'm on my break and I got here as soon as I could. You said one of your sinks in the back isn't working?"

"Oh, is that so?" I say, seeing completely through her. This is very obviously a set up. "This is the first I'm hearing about your broken sink."

"Well, you can't fix my sink, can you?"

"I could have tried," I tell her, my teeth clenched together. "How are you this morning, Elliott?"

"I'm doing well, Daisy. All things considered, you know?"

I nod, knowing what he means. I'm sure their family dinners have been chaotic lately.

"So, how can I help? I know I'm in my bunkers, but I can crawl under the counter and—"

"Actually." She smiles down at her counter as she waits for the espresso to fill the small cup. "The sink is fixed. So, just take a load off and I'll make you a cup before you're headed back for the last part of your shift."

"Del, I really don't have much time."

She simply smiles at her brother and he sits down, knowing he's not going to win this argument.

"She's really hard to say no to," he jokes as he turns to me. "I'm sure you're familiar with that."

"Very." I smile as I take another sip. "Are you finishing up another twenty-four hour shift at the fire station?"

He nods. "I have two days off after this, and I'm going to spend all of it working on my new addition to the house."

"Oh, really?" I don't remember Delilah telling me about that. "What are you doing to the house?"

"Why don't we talk about that over dinner tonight?" He smiles at me as I hear Delilah clear her throat from behind the counter.

"Something to add, Del?"

"What?" She pretends she wasn't listening in on our conversation like I know she does all day long. She is the biggest eavesdropper I know. She always tells me baristas are like bartenders just for people in the daylight.

"I appreciate the offer." I'm not sure what else to say. Do I feel ready for this? Not really, but I've known Elliott my entire life. I don't think it would be awkward, and maybe Delilah is right. Maybe I need to get out more. "I'm sure you know I'm recently divorced, and don't just do this because your sister is meddling."

"That's not why I asked you." He smiles at me. "Delilah actually didn't put me up to anything. I would really like to get to know you better. We've sort of floated around one another our entire lives, and I've always wondered about you, Daisy. I was glad to hear you came back, although it sounds like that's not how you really felt about it."

"That seems like something else we can talk about over dinner." I bite the inside of my cheek, the nerves already flooding my system, but there's also giddiness, I think? Or maybe I'm doing the same thing I did last time and mistaking someone's kindness for something it isn't.

Though, I've known Elliott for a long time, and he's the type of guy Derek couldn't be even if he spent his entire life trying to right all his wrongs. As one of the middle Madison kids, he's a lot like his twin sister, Eloise. They're both caring to a fault. Elliott always had the same friendly disposition as her, and he carried that all the way through his life. He cares about other people—more than most do these days—and there's not a doubt in my mind that someday he's going to be running the firehouse in Nettles.

"Alrighty then." He smiles at me before he looks at his sister. "I assume I'm picking her up from your place?"

"You would assume correctly," Delilah says as she hands him a to-go cup. "Thank you for stopping in even though my sink was already fixed."

"Yeah, yeah. Anything for you, Dels." He heads out, not before taking another glance back at me. "I'll see you later?"

"Mhm," I mumble as he heads out, and before I can even turn back to my best friend, I can already feel what her facial expression is. "You are *way* too obvious."

And with that, she shrugs, continuing to work as I laugh like an idiot.

"I assume you have an outfit ready for me?"

"I'll swing by the boutique later." She smirks at me. "Now, my work here is done, and I took up your entire lunch break but I think it was worth it."

"To be determined," I remind her as she hands me a coffee to-go, and I head for my store, a giddy smile taking up my entire face, but nerves spread through my body like a wave crashing onto the sand.

It's just a date, Dais. It will be fine, I remind myself, but it's been so long since I've been on a date that I know this could go terribly. I'm starting to regret not taking Theo up on his offer for a practice date, but I'm sure that offer is off the table with everything that has happened since we talked about that.

By the time I'm back at the store, my mind is already filling up with different looks I can create tonight depending on what Delilah and I figure out what to wear, and that tiny spark of creativity alone settles my nerves.

My phone buzzes in my hand as I'm stocking the new eyeliner I got in, a number I don't recognize taking up the screen, and my heart drops.

> **Unknown:** I've had enough of this. Come home.

> **Unknown:** I'm not fucking around. Get back here or else.

I block the number from my phone before I get back to work, hoping the messages were just some strange coincidence but knowing in my gut that might not be the case.

Elliott pulls my chair out for me at this adorable restaurant I've walked by a few times as I perused Nettles. I don't remember this place from before I left, and even though I forgot a lot about this place I grew up in, my memories slowly came back once I did.

Elliott looks handsome in his knit sweater paired with simple slacks. His short, sandy blond hair looks freshly buzzed, and his entire outfit comes together with the chain dangling around his neck and the bracelet around his wrist his brother got him for his birthday.

He cleans up nicely, and all of my nerves are swirling in my stomach, but I'm doing my best to ignore them.

"I'm actually pleasantly surprised you said yes," he tells me as he sits down. "But I have to say, you look absolutely stunning tonight, Daisy."

"Thank you," I say as I smooth out my pale yellow dress. It's a slip dress, and it's not the fanciest outfit in the world, but Delilah was right when she showed it to me and said it was totally my style. It's perfect, and I should have known my best friend would never lead me astray.

Sometimes I think the love I've always wanted to find has been right in front of me the whole time in the form of Delilah Madison. Nobody knows me better than she does, and on the days when things get a little dark, she's always there to guide me out of the tunnel back into the light. "You look wonderful this evening too."

"Oh, please." He waves his hand at me. "I had to dig this out of the back of my closet. Fancy clothes besides my Class A dress are hard to come by in my wardrobe."

"And those are your fancy uniforms, right? Or am I making a complete fool of myself?"

He laughs. "You're not a fool, Daisy, and you're right. More often than not I'm in those."

"How long has it been for you?" I assume he knows what I'm talking about. Delilah said it's been a while since he's dated, which is also why she had the brilliant—her words, not mine—idea to set the two of us up. We're both rusty, as she called it, and even if things didn't work out how she wanted it to, at least it was a good step in the right direction for both of us.

"About two years, if I'm counting correctly. I kind of gave up on the whole dating scene in Nettles. It feels easier to throw myself into my job, especially with the hours I work."

"I can understand that," I say as the waiter comes over and takes our drink orders. We decide on an appetizer or two since we both aren't that hungry. I assume he ate at the fire house, but my lack of appetite is from nerves, although, this is already going better than I thought it would. I haven't fallen on my face in these shoes, so I'm counting that as a win.

And I know Elliott, which I think is helping make this all a little less terrifying. I can't imagine I would have said yes or been ready to put myself out there again if it was with a total stranger. Look at what happened last time I dated a stranger who I gave my entire heart too. Not this time. This time, I'm shielding myself, and even though it's Elliott, I still have to protect my heart.

The conversation flows freely as we have some drinks, our appetizers coming out quickly as we dig into those. It almost feels like I'm having dinner with an old friend, even though Elliott and I were never really close when we were younger. He was my friend's brother, and that's basically it. It's easy. Simple. It's light and it's definitely not as terrifying as I built it up to be in my head.

While we're talking, there are a few flashes of the boy across the street, and I can feel the ghost of him on my lips from when we kissed.

I shouldn't be thinking about him while I'm on a date with someone else, but I'm not feeling those anxious jitters with Elliott you feel when it's almost over and you think they might kiss you when you leave. I'm not having the butterflies or the quiet calmness that washes over you when you know you've found someone to care for forever. I almost feel nothing toward him, and I know it's the first date, so maybe I'm putting too many expectations onto it, but I miss feeling those small, intimate moments that are just yours that make you realize the person in front of you could change your life.

Or utterly destroy it. That's the price we pay for falling in love, right? The fact that the person sitting across from you at the table could make or break your entire heart, but you fall anyway because you're a human and you know the reward outweighs the risk. Being loved is *so* much better than being heartbroken. Everyone knows that, and every time we put ourselves out there, we accept the fact that we might get hurt, but we don't care about that in the moment. All you care about is the fact that someday, this person you know nothing about will suddenly know every intricate detail of you. They'll memorize the things you love, and hate, and they'll know the scent of your favorite candle, the movie you can quote from memory. Maybe they'll even listen as you try to explain why the two colors in front of them are indeed *not* the exact same shade, but two different colors, and even though they can't see a difference, they'll agree with you anyway.

Because that's what love is. It's messy, and chaotic, and it's never said to be perfect, but if it's perfect for you and the person you love, then nothing else matters.

I once thought the road I was on for love was running out. After the divorce, I assumed the love I had felt for Derek during that short time was it.

Tonight has proven me wrong, albeit only slightly. Maybe it's not over for me. I know it's a dramatic thing to say at the age of twenty-six. I have so much of my life left to live, but I had this great love—at least in my head and heart—and I didn't think I was going to ever feel like that again.

Tonight has reminded me that there can be love all around, and it's not something you can only feel once. It's in every friendship I've ever felt, every dog I've passed walking around town, in every smile, I am showing love, whether it be to others or myself. Elliott Madison asking me out tonight may have just reminded me that my life is not over even though I'm young and divorced. I may have no romantic feelings for him, but he's helped me in more ways than I can ever thank him for.

The divorce and the chapter of Derek was just one branch of my life, but the good thing is, I can cut that branch off and hop onto another one. One where nothing has grown yet, but one where I am able to find a fresh start, or a new piece of myself that may have been buried underneath all the greenery.

"Daisy? Are you alright?" He chuckles in front of me.

"Yes." I sigh happily. "I'm so sorry. What were we talking about?"

He's about to say something, but my phone buzzes incessantly from the small clutch Delilah lended me, and I try to ignore it, but it doesn't stop.

"Maybe you should get that."

"I'm sorry," I tell him. "It might be my parents. The time difference with them wherever they are now has really messed up our check-in schedule. Normally, I'm home when they call, but—"

"I threw a wrench in your plans." He smiles at me. "It's alright. I'll be here when you're done. Take your time, seriously, I know how important family is to me. I assume it's the same for you."

I nod, a smile overtaking my face. He's a great guy, and someday he will make someone very happy, but I'm ninety-five percent sure that someone is not me. "Thank you. I'll be quick, I promise."

I head to the bathroom, needing a quiet spot to answer my still buzzing phone, but when I take it out to see who it is, my heart drops, and I answer it as soon as I can.

"Theo? Is everything okay?"

"Dais, where have you been? I need to talk to you—"

"I'm on my way home. Don't you dare take a sip."

"Wh—"

I hang up on him before I take a deep breath, collecting myself so Elliott doesn't get worried, but my stomach is bottoming out as I walk out of the bathroom and over to the table.

"I am so sorry, Elliott," I say as I grab my small cardigan from the back of the chair. "I have an emergency at home I have to deal with."

"It's not a problem." He smiles at me. "Is there anything I can help with?"

"Unfortunately no," I tell him. "I swear this wasn't planned, and I really wanted to finish our date tonight."

"You don't have to explain yourself to me," he says. "Things happen that are out of our control all of the time. Do you want me to walk you home?"

"I appreciate it," I tell him, my breathing heavier by the minute. "It's only a few minutes. I'll be fine."

"Take care of yourself, Daisy. I'll see you around."

I assume he feels the same way I do. It was a good step, but we probably won't be doing this again. As soon as I'm out of the restaurant and heading toward Theo, the only thing crossing my mind is what I'm going to find when I get back to him.

Is he going to have a pulse? Am I going to be walking into a future crime scene when the police have to figure out if he purposefully or accidentally overdosed? Is another trip to Luca going to come tonight?

I can barely think by the time I push the front door open to find Theo on the couch, and I can't tell if he's breathing or not, but I don't smell any alcohol, so that has to be a good sign.

"Theo?" I say as I rush over to him. There are papers spread all out on the floor, some of them chalked with dirt which causes me even more confusion. I should have talked to him more these last few days, but with the kiss, things felt awkward. We've just missed each other in the mornings, and I've been staying late at the store to avoid him. "Theo?"

He slowly opens his eyes, and they're puffy and red-rimmed as he looks back at me.

"Fuck," is all I can say as I move my hair to the side. "You fucking scared me. Did you drink anything? Do you feel okay? What's going—"

His hands cup my face to stop my blabbering. "I'm okay," is all he says as he takes in my outfit and the state of me. "Were you on a date?"

"My social life is none of your concern, right now," I say as I don't move a muscle. I can feel my body beating underneath his touch, and I'm afraid if I move, he may feel it too. "What happened? What's the emergency?"

"Emergency?" He sounds as confused as I am. "There wasn't one."

"Then why did you call me?"

"I missed you, and I wanted to talk to you because I've barely seen you. I didn't mean for you to leave whatever has you all dressed up. Maybe I should have clarified over the phone, but you hung up on me."

"I did not," is all I say as I somehow manage to unlatch myself from the couch, my heels clicking around the hardwoods as I feel my legs come back to normal. I swear I was walking on jelly when I was on my way over here. "Shit."

The house is quiet for a few moments, the only sounds I can hear are the two of us breathing as I finally set my clutch down.

"You look absolutely astonishing, Dais," he whispers into the moonlight. There's not a single light on in the house except a small candle crackling in the kitchen. I already know which one it is because it's from my house. Theo grabbed it because I was too scared to go back over there after what happened. He put it on the table and told me I could have a small piece of my home in his, even though our situation is temporary. "I love you in yellow. It matches your smile quite beautifully."

My cheeks heat at his words, spoken so softly I might have missed them over my breathing.

"Thank you." I turn around, and he's already behind me, his puffy eyes looking straight into my soul. Even with my heels on, my head only goes to his chin as I stare back at him, his tortured expression making me want to wipe it off of his face. I'm about to speak but he gets on his knees and starts to fiddle with my shoes.

"Let me," he says, his fingers grazing my ankles as he slips them off one at a time, unlatching the small buckle. "Is that better?"

"Yes, thank you," is all I can say through my dry throat. I may not have felt anything for Elliott earlier, but now all I feel is my body coming alive underneath the touch of the man I kissed a few days ago.

He stands back up, not moving a single inch away from me. "That kiss meant something to me."

Oh, so now we're talking about it. "It was nothing. Just high emotions and adrenaline from what happened."

He smirks at me, and I can tell he doesn't believe a single word from my mouth, and honestly, I don't either. That kiss has snuck into my dreams until I wake up feeling confused about the man across the hall. "Was it not enough romance for you? Because we can most certainly have a redo and I can sweep you off of your feet."

"I kissed you, remember?" I say as I smooth out part of his shirt. "And it won't happen again."

"Why not?" he asks, his face inching closer to mine.

"We're too complicated," I tell him the truth. He has his own grief to sort through, and I'm still figuring out my life that continues to be a mess. "I'm divorced, and—"

"So what, Dais? That doesn't scare me how you think it will." He reaches for my face and I don't pull away; his thumb is against my cheek as he caresses small circles on my skin, his other hand finding my waist. "Let's be complicated together."

"I don't do this."

"Do what? Kiss your neighbor you happen to be living with for the time being?"

"Kiss random people," I say, not elaborating because no other words can come to my head at the moment.

"Did he kiss you tonight?" he whispers. "Did you think of me when his lips touched yours because all I can seem to think about is you against me like the other night." He leans in, just brushing my lips with his as he leaves me wanting more.

Fuck, why do I want more? I'm not like this. I'm not a casual girl. I'm an all or nothing kind of person, and if we dive deeper into this, I'm not sure I'll be able to walk away unscathed when he leaves for good.

But I can't help the buzzing I feel at his touch. I can't help the fact that my heart beats faster when I'm around him.

"Did he?"

"No," I say as I close my eyes. "He didn't. In fact, I ran right back to you in the middle of it, so we never got that far."

"Would you have?"

I shake my head.

"Well then," he says as his head comes to my neck and he softly bites my skin. I try to swallow the moan, but he absolutely hears it as it escapes my lips. "If you need me, you know where to find me."

"You're drunk, Theo."

"Nope," he says against my neck, his eyes meeting mine once again as my stomach drops through the floor. "The only thing I'm drunk off of is you in this fucking outfit standing in my living room."

And with one final caress of my face, he leaves me standing rooted to my spot as he blows out the candle and heads up the stairs, his door shutting softly behind him as I wonder what the hell just happened and why I find myself wanting more of it.

Chapter Twenty-Four

— **COLORFUL BY ASIRIS**

"Thank you so much for coming over," I say to the realtor I hired to help me sell this place. Since my mom didn't want to come all the way up here, it's up to me to get this place ready to sell. Now that I've found the last piece of what Tobias left for me, I can actually start to do that.

But there's still that sinking feeling in my gut about leaving this place for good.

"Thanks for your call." She smiles at me as she comes inside. "Holly Carter."

"Theo West," I say as I return her handshake.

"This is a beautiful property you have here. Why are you thinking of selling it?"

"I'm not totally sold on that quite yet," I tell her. "I think I just wanted more of an estimate of what it would look like and how long it would take if I was to sell. I figured you could help me with that."

"I absolutely can." She takes a look around the first floor, eventually moving upstairs. I tried cleaning this place the best I could, and with Daisy's stuff out of the house, it was a lot easier.

She left a few days ago and took all of her stuff back to her house. I told her she could stay here as long as she wanted to, but since nothing else has happened, she felt safe enough to go back. The officers we dealt with said they had no new updates either, so they figured it was a one time thing.

We haven't really spoken much since the night she came home from whatever date she was on, and I hate that I miss her. I hate that this house feels bare without her in it.

I can't attach myself to her, but it might be too late. It would only end poorly for the both of us. I will say that in the last few years, I've never felt more grounded than when she was around. She makes my head clearer and that alone is terrifying enough for me to stay away from her. I know Tobias sent her a letter asking her to be here for me, but he shouldn't have done that. I'm a lot to put on someone, and I hate that she feels obligated to keep checking in on me.

Maybe I should just sell this place and be done with Nettles, but whenever I think about that, I feel sick. I can't do it. Not yet.

"So, what do you think?" I ask when she comes back downstairs.

"It looks to be in pretty good shape," she says. "If you end up moving forward with all this, I'd have some people come over and inspect everything just to make sure it's still structurally sound. I'd depersonalize it and you would have to get all of these leftover boxes out. I usually advise my clients not to live in the space they're trying to sell, so you'd have to find somewhere to relocate."

"That's not a problem."

"I figured as much. I always recommend the hotel on Main Street. It's a wonderfully cozy space."

"I'm familiar with it," I smile at her.

"Most of Nettles is." Her heels click around the hardwood floor as she sets her small folder down. "I'd then stage the house so my team could come in and get some good photos of it for when you decide you want to list it, and then prospective buyers could come and take a look."

"How long does that process usually take?"

"With the way the market is right now, probably anywhere from three to eight months."

"Oh." I don't know why I expected something a lot longer. A few months isn't as long as I figured it would take to pack up an entire life and all the childhood memories I had in this place.

"Can I ask why you're unsure about selling?"

"I grew up spending a few weeks of my summers here and I'm not totally sure I'm ready to get rid of this place. I'm selling it for my mom. The deed is in her name, but I just don't know if I can part with it quite yet. I might need a little more time," I say as I look at her. "I'm sorry if coming up here felt like a waste. I probably could have just called you and asked all the questions I needed to."

"It's not a waste," she tells me. "I can understand not wanting to leave a place with memories. I have a son—he lives in Virginia now—and I know it's my job to sell houses and help to usher people into a new phase of their life, but I don't think I could ever leave the house me and my late husband raised him in. There's something so beautiful about the way certain spaces hold memories, so I can understand not wanting to part with those."

I nod, knowing she understands the feeling. She did say *late* husband after all, and I know just how strong single parents have to be because my mom is one. "I promise to call you once I figure everything out," I tell her.

"If you have any other questions"—she reaches into her bag and pulls out her business card—"You know where to find me."

"Thank you."

And with that, she leaves. I'm still standing in the living room hearing echoes of the family I used to have surrounding me, and before I think,

I'm grabbing my camera and heading out for a walk, needing to surround myself with anything else.

I'VE OFFICIALLY WALKED TO the highest point of this small mountain, and I didn't bring the right shoes for this endeavor, but I can't really find it in me to care. My feet are going to kill me tomorrow, but for right now, the pain is worth it. Pain anywhere besides the one that's been sitting on my chest for the last three years is always better.

I take a deep breath, the air a little thinner where I'm at, but it's quiet. I can hear the breeze through the trees, the leaves rustling beneath my crappy sneakers. Autumn is in full force around here, and this is the first time I've gone away from the main part of Nettles.

I still can't breathe normally, but as I sit here by myself, I suddenly have the urge to capture everything I see in front of me. The leaves, the mountain ranges, the dirt path my shoes squish on. I see a few animals—deer mostly—and I decide not to take any pictures of them. I just watch them.

There are four of them in front of me, each around the same height and weight. I see them treading along the grass, a few of them running ahead and the others catching up. I follow them for a little bit, trying my best not to make a sound to disturb them.

I know I should take a few pictures of them. Lucas often loves the photos I've taken of different animals, a few of them have been on the cover of the travel magazines my company puts together.

But more often than not, the things I remember most from my travels are the pictures I didn't end up taking. For some reason, those are the memories I can look back on with the slightest bit of joy because they come up whenever I remember where I've been.

Eventually, the tree I'm leaning against starts to sway, and it breaks me out of my haze as I look around for the deer I seem to have lost to the brush. There's not many people on this trail, and I haven't seen another person all day, so I pull my phone out and call my brother.

"Hey, man," Tristan says as he picks up. "Are you okay?"

"As okay as I can be," I tell him, setting my camera on the rock next to me. "I just missed everyone. How's everything in Pennsylvania? Are you still freaking out about Dom and Teags?"

"The fact that you didn't freak out pisses me off," he chuckles through the phone. "I might have been a little dramatic, but it all threw me for a loop."

"That's to be expected. Normally, when things don't go to your plan in your head, you freak out. I'm surprised it was as tame as it was, according to Teags."

"She's happy. That's all that matters."

"True," I say to him. "We all deserve it."

"I never thought I'd hear you say that. Has something changed for the great traveler Theo West? Is he thinking of settling down or something insane?"

I can't help but laugh. Him of all people saying that to me is hilarious knowing his track record of wanting to get the hell out of our hometown. "Don't get too ahead of me, man. I'm still the same guy I was when you last saw me."

"Nah, that's not true. The guy I saw at home was different from the guy who left for Vermont."

"Oh, is that so?"

"You looked better," he whispers. "Less drunk than the last time I saw you."

Yeah, but little did you know what happened up here to get me to be like that. Even after the scariest night of my life I still picked up a bottle when I was home for Tobias's memorial. I'm weak, and I still want to feel nothing. I still ache for that numbness, but I promised someone I would try my best to stop, and I'd hate to let her down again.

"Yeah, well, I can't keep doing this to myself." No matter how much I want to. "I'd hate to keep letting you all down."

"You're not a let down, Theo. You're just struggling like the rest of us are."

"But I'm not as strong as all of you," I say as a tear starts to fall. "Not even close."

"Do you want me to come up there for a long weekend or something and we can just exist in the old house together?"

"No, it's fine. I have... people up here."

"Is that so? Like who?"

"Just some old friends and people I've talked to in passing. Nothing serious." Another lie, but I don't know how to talk about Daisy. Maybe I could talk about her more if I felt anything I could say would do her any justice. No words seem to quite portray how much she means to me, including how terrifying it is that I feel so attached to her.

"Ah, understood," I hear Livvy say something in the background. "Can I call you later? Livvy is trying to set up a new bookshelf all by herself."

"Go help your wife, dude. I'll be fine."

"Call me if you need me. Any time, Theo, you know that."

"Why do you think I called you today?" My brother is the epitome of a broken record. "I love you, man. I'll see you soon."

"You better. I love you," he says before he clicks off of the line and I find myself staring off at the path down the mountain in front of me.

I miss my family, but I'm not quite ready to give this place up yet. It's odd, the feeling I'm having, but it's almost as if this town has sunken into my bones. I'm not even sure when it happened. It could have been back when I was a child or only recently when I came back up here, but something in Nettles has tethered me to the dirt, and I can't walk away yet.

Knowing me, I'd just be pulled back here, so I'm skipping the step where I leave and I'm staying right here until I find what I'm looking for. What once started out as a search for what my brother left for me up here has turned into something more, and I have to find out what I'm missing before I leave or it will eat me alive more than everything else is.

Chapter Twenty-Five

— HOW TO LIVE BY DEL WATER GAP

"This ice cream social is officially beginning," Delilah says as she locks the front door, the rest of us already gathered around the tables we pushed together. "I'm so glad we finally get to do this."

"Me too," Eloise says as she finishes her first cup of ice cream. "I've missed this place, Del."

"You don't get another one until you tell us what's been going on," Delilah says.

"I swear I've heard more whispers about you lately than anything else," Amelie, Luca's wife, says.

"I wish Fallon was here," Eloise sighs. "It feels weird not telling her the full story."

"What did she say she had going on tonight?"

"Some consultation she couldn't cancel. She was being all hush about it at dinner last weekend," Delilah says as she grabs her ice cream and sits. "Now, spill."

"Give her a minute," Amelie says, her long black hair and bangs falling in front of her face as she moves them out of her way. Her voice has always been soft, but right now, it's the quietest I've ever heard her. It's almost as if she doesn't want to be heard in the low light of Delilah's store. Her brown eyes are soft as she rubs her hand up and down Eloise's arm, comforting her as if she knows exactly the situation her sister-in-law is in. "There's been a lot of change lately. Let's not put any pressure on her, especially in this setting."

"This is a no judgement zone, remember?" I remind the group. "What happens in the ice cream shop after dark, stays in the ice cream shop after dark."

"So, do tell us how you managed to come back to town and within a week marry into a family that hates yours, Eloise?" Delilah asks her sister. When Eloise and Brooks were spotted coming out of the courthouse a week or so after his wedding never happened, the entire town wouldn't shut up about it. People were speculating from every street corner that Brooks had been cheating on Jamie with Eloise the entire time. I also heard Brooks got Eloise pregnant, which didn't make any sense since she's been gone for years.

There's nothing romantic about the gossip that spreads through Nettles, no matter what anyone wants to say.

"Go easy on her," Amelie reminds her. "I know it's a lot to process, but this can't be easy for her to talk about either."

"Sorry," she says, shoving a big spoonful of ice cream into her mouth. "It just shocked me, that's all."

"Yeah, me too," Eloise says as her eyes cast down on the table, the ring on her finger sparkling in the low light of the shop. "It still feels like a dream."

"A dream or a nightmare?" Amelie asks her. "Marriage is anything but easy and you all know how much I love Luca and your family, but I knew the way we were headed. It seems like you didn't think this was part of the journey you'd be taking in coming back here."

"I was happy for him," Eloise says, her voice cracking. "I came back here to prove to myself that I was fine watching him marry someone else.

I knew if I saw it on his face, his happiness, that I'd be able to be okay. But he wasn't, and everybody could tell. I'm not going to tell you why the wedding was called off originally. That's for him to speak about."

"It seems like you two have history together then?" I remember in high school the Madisons and the Turners kept their distance from one another. Amara was the common middle ground, and I always thought she was the reason all of the kids stopped this stupid feud, but maybe there was something else.

Eloise only nods.

"What is he to you?" Delilah asks.

"Oh, I don't know," she pauses and takes a breath. "Just... everything."

The three of us look at one another, and it seems none of us knew Eloise and Brooks were even something to talk about beside the fact that Eloise came back here a few weeks ago, and within days, she was married to him.

It seems there's more to this story than we all thought. When the news first spread around town, Delilah marched into my boutique wondering if her parents forced her to do this to spy on their family, but I quickly negated that fact. They would never do that and she agreed. Emotions were high because that same week, Delilah told me her parents sat all of the kids down and told them their mom's cancer had come back.

It was a tough week, and life continues to be unfair to them. I hate it. I wish I could take away all of their pain, but all I can do is be there for them. I've slept at Delilah's house every single day this last week, and even though I moved out of Theo's place I still haven't stepped foot back into my parents' house.

I'm scared to go back. I'm worried that the police are wrong and there is actually something for me to worry about. I don't think this was a random, spur of the moment break-in. I think my ex-husband is behind this, but I have no way to prove it besides the sinking feeling in my gut.

"We dated in secret in high school," she tells us, wiping a tear from her eye. "Do you remember when Mom first was diagnosed?"

Delilah nods her head.

"I was really fucking sad. My grades were slipping because I couldn't focus, and I had cut class one day and went to hide under the bleachers so I could cry where nobody could hear me."

"But someone heard you," Amelie grabs Eloise's hand in hers.

"I knew about our family feud, of course I did. It was all this town ever fucking talked about back then." She shakes her head. "Brooks was running laps during his free period to get ready for whatever sport season had been coming up. He could have left me under there and pretended he never heard me, but instead, he stopped what he was doing, handed me his hoodie, and told me we could leave and ditch for the day if I wanted to."

"Wow," is all Delilah can say under her breath.

"He made me promise if I ever needed to cry again, I'd come find him, but only he found me first. Later that same night, he threw rocks at my window and he took me somewhere we could both just exist together. He was going through some stuff back then albeit a lot different than our shit, but never in my life had someone understood me so easily how he did."

Suddenly, brown eyes are staring back at me as I listen to her talk about Brooks. I haven't talked to Theo in a week, though it feels longer. I've been aching to pick up my phone and call him or send him a message, but I've stopped myself every time. He's leaving soon and he's not coming back. Why would he when nothing is keeping him here?

I can't stop whatever feelings exist between us. I'm not even sure what they are. Nostalgia is my thinking, but even that word doesn't taste appetizing on my tongue when I think about it. It's not right, and I may never have the words to explain what Theo West is to me. Fleeting, maybe. Momentary. Temporary.

"We dated for our entire senior year in high school, and even though it was only a year, it was everything to me."

"But then you left," Delilah reminds her. "Why did you leave?"

Eloise only looks at her sister before we all remember what happened.

"Oh," is all I say.

"His parents announced his arrangement."

"Don't you mean engagement?" Amelie wonders.

"Same thing," Eloise says as Delilah wipes her tears. "Can I please have another cup of ice cream now?"

"You can have anything you want," Delilah sniffles as she throws her arms around her sister. "I wish you had told me."

"There was no point," Eloise looks at the three of us. "I changed all of my plans after I saw that. He tried to talk to me before I left, but I wouldn't let him. I knew a clean break would be best, so instead of going to college half an hour away, I went farther, as far as it would take for me to forget about him."

"Did it work?" Amelie asks her. "Did the distance help you untether yourself?"

"In a way, it did. I met new people. I cut my hair. I changed into a person I thought I needed to be." She sniffles into the new ice cream her sister brought her. "And now I'm back here and everything feels just how it did in high school. It's been years, but I'm back to feeling like that stupid teenager whose mom has cancer and the boy she's in love with doesn't love her back."

I wonder how they ended up married after all she's told us, but I assume that's a story for another time.

The three of us scoot our chairs closer to her as she sighs into her sister's shoulder, the tears flowing freely as we all comfort her. I wish I could somehow take away all of the pain they're all feeling, especially when it comes to their mom. Amelie will always say she married into the Madison family, which she did, but she's as much of a Madison as any of them are. And I wish there was something I could do, but right now, all I can do is comfort them and offer my shoulder, so I do.

"It's going to be okay," I say, knowing my words aren't helping. "I'm here for whatever any of you need, and I mean that."

"Thanks, Dais," Eloise says as she pulls back, all of now teary-eyed and sniffling. "I'd love a subject change off of shitty diseases and marriages that probably won't work out no matter how much you try."

"Excuse me," Amelie says as she sits up and heads for the bathroom, the door closing softly behind her.

"Have you seen Luca lately?" Delilah asks us.

"You mean to tell me you haven't? He's your brother," I remind her.

"He didn't come to dinner. I'm not even sure he knows about Mom."

"If anything, I think he knew before we did," Eloise says as her hands palm her face. "That's why he didn't bother showing up to dinner."

"I'm sure Amelie has seen him then, right?" I'd tell them about the last time I called him when Theo was unconscious, pulse thready as he sat in my passenger seat, but that's not something I want to get into right now.

The two of them just look at me, expressions pinched as she comes back out, her eyes more puffy than they were before.

"Are you okay?" I ask her.

She gives me a smile so trained I can barely tell if it's fake or not. "I'm fine. Just a little tired, is all. I might head home, if that's alright."

"Thanks for coming out," Eloise tells her. "I'll try to pop over soon for some marriage advice."

"I don't know how helpful I'll be, but you're always welcome, El," she says as she gathers her things. "Thank you for the company tonight. It's always wonderful seeing you all."

"You too," I say as she heads for the door. I recognize the look in her eyes before she leaves because it mirrored mine in the past. Loneliness. I make a note in the back of my mind to check in on her more. After what she said tonight, I'm a little worried about her.

"Eloise—"

She cuts her sister off. "I really can't talk about my life any longer. Please tell me one of you has something else to talk about because knowing I have to go home and see Brooks is making me insane. I need a change, even if just for a minute."

Delilah and I look at one another, and I know she hasn't been doing anything social besides working, so my mouth opens and I start speaking before I can stop it.

"I kissed someone for the first time since my divorce and I may have went on a date with your brother and left early to check on the person I kissed because he said he needed me and I'm not really sure how to feel about it."

By the time I'm done blabbering, I'm breathing heavily, but the weight on my shoulders feels lighter.

Eloise turns to her sister. "You set her up with Elliott?"

"Maybe."

"I apologize for her antics," Eloise says to me. "My twin brother is a great guy, but he's not the settling down type, especially with the job and hours he works."

"He's a great guy, don't get me wrong, all of you Madison siblings are wonderful." Delilah's hand goes straight to her heart. "There was just nothing there."

"And you ran away to Theo in the middle of it." Delilah's eyebrows shoot up a few times. "That means something, Dais."

I can only sigh again.

"Theo? Do I know him?" Eloise asks her sister.

"He's Daisy's neighbor, and you might have met him when we were younger, so you probably don't remember him."

"Hm." Eloise searches her head for a recollection. "Nothing."

"Told you."

"Can we focus? Not only have I been divorced for a year, but now I'm the type of person who goes around kissing my neighbor randomly?"

"Is he cute?" Eloise's face lights up for the first time tonight as the three of us gossip. I swear, I've been catapulted back to high school with this conversation.

"He has a mustache," Delilah tells her.

All I can do is put my head against the table.

"Babe? Are you about to have an existential crisis?"

"Well, I already had a mid-life crisis, so what's another one to add to the picture?" I put my hands against my forehead. "I hate that I want to kiss him again."

"Why?" Eloise asks me. "What's so bad about kissing someone? You're single. I assume he's also single. What's wrong with that?"

"For starters, he's my neighbor, and he doesn't even technically live here, so it would be a means to an end, and I've never been able to do short and sweet. Once I'm all in with someone, I'm all in. It's hard to break that without breaking every last fiber of my heart."

"I still say go for it," Delilah says and I throw her a look. "What? Tell me the worst thing that could happen by having hot sex with the even hotter guy next door?"

Eloise only looks at me as she awaits my answer.

"And you can't say anything you just told us. I want an actual answer, Dais. What would be so bad about casual sex for you?"

I take a second to really think about my answer. I can't really think of anything substantial, so I go with the first thing I think of. "Things could get complicated."

"Do you have feelings for him? Would you want to date him first and then have sex?" Eloise asks me.

"All I do is have feelings." I sigh. "But relationship ones? No. I don't know if I'll ever have those ever again after what happened with my last one."

"So, why not go for it then? Why not put yourself out there and have some good sex with someone who is probably also looking for something casual? It's honestly better that he doesn't live here because then you won't have to see him around every corner."

Damn, I hate that they're right. "What you're saying makes sense."

"Of course it does." Delilah smiles at me. "I'm a genius, after all."

"What my sister means to say is, talk to him about it and if you both communicate and keep things casual, you'll be okay. You and that big, beautiful heart of yours will survive as long as there are good boundaries in place."

"But—"

Delilah cuts me off. "Stop feeling guilty about moving on when your ex-husband didn't feel a single ounce of remorse for cheating on you with multiple women."

"Woah, Del," Eloise says.

"No," is all I say. "She's right."

"He didn't deserve you, but someday you'll find someone who does and you'll fall in love again because that's what you do. You choose love even when it feels difficult to, and that is a gift, Dais. A gift that someday someone will choose to keep the wrapping paper for."

"That was beautiful," I tell her. "You're right. I don't know why this has me so wrapped up."

"Because it's terrifying to put yourself out there," Eloise tells me. "Trust me, I'm all too familiar with putting myself out there and being rejected."

"We should do this more often," I chuckle to myself. "It's weirdly therapeutic."

"I told you this was a great idea," Delilah says as she grabs out cups from us. "Now, you go home to your husband," she says to her sister. "And you, head home and stop staying over at my place or perhaps to a certain someone's house."

I couldn't do that, right? It's late, for one, and I can't just show up at his house and blab out this proposal or jump right into his arms.

But as I leave Delilah's store, I find myself drawn to his house as if something is pulling me towards him, and I can't find it in me to grab my keys and change my pathway home.

Chapter Twenty-Six

— OBSESSIVE BY CHASE ATLANTIC

I'M BREAKING DOWN ANOTHER box in the living room as I hear frantic knocking against my door, and I have no idea what I'm going to open this to, but as soon as I see Daisy on my porch, my heart drops to my stomach.

"Are you okay?" I wonder, looking up and down her body to see if she's hurt. *God, I've missed her.* I hate to say that this last week was a lonely one as I gave her some space. I know I came on a little too strong the last time she was over here, and I've been beating myself up about it.

She's breathing heavily, her eyes trained on my mouth. "Can I come in?"

"Of course," I say as I move out of the way. She kicks her shoes off as I close the door. "Is everything okay?"

"Mhm," is all she says as she turns to face me. "Kiss me."

I swear I misheard her as I set the box down. "What?"

"I want you to kiss me because all I've thought about since that night in your bedroom is how badly I wanted to do it again, but I need you to kiss me this time. I need you to want it as much as I do."

It only takes me three steps to close in on her, and by the time my lips are on hers, her bag drops to the floor and her back is against the wall.

"God, you taste so fucking good," I tell her as my hands move all over her body, wanting to feel every inch of her beautiful figure under my touch.

"I had ice cream at Delilah's," she tells me as my lips move to her neck, peppering soft bites to it as she writhes against me. "Theo, please." She grabs my shirt and pulls me back up to her.

I had no idea this is how my night was going to go, but I definitely would have cleaned up in here if I had known. There are not only boxes everywhere, but there's more than one box cutter scattered on the floor, a few pairs of scissors, too, because I couldn't get any of them to cut anything I needed them to.

Her lips are as soft as last time, probably on account of all the chapstick she always carries around with her, and I swear I'll never get enough of this girl. The thought should terrify me, but with her in my hands, I can barely focus on anything else.

"This is just until you leave, okay?" she breathes into my mouth. "A one-time thing."

"Daisy girl, it's not like I'm leaving tomorrow," I say as my tongue threads with hers, giving her just enough to satiate her for a second before I pull away again. "If we're doing this, it's going to be whenever you need me. Does that sound okay?" I bite her ear softly and whisper into it. "Even if it's the middle of the night and you wake up writhing, I'll be over in seconds if you need me to be. I'm at your beck and call."

"Okay." I feel her heart rate speed up as she grabs my face and kisses me again, her teeth grabbing onto my bottom lip.

"So, tell me what you need from me, and I'll happily give it to you." All she does is continue to kiss me, my neck craning down to get as close as I can to her before I pick her up and carry her up the stairs. "Do you need my cock? My fingers? My tongue? What do you *need* from me?"

She throws her head back with a giddy laugh as I kick the door to my bedroom open and softly set her down on my bed.

I grab her chin in my hand, pressing another long, languid kiss to her as I pull back. "I need to hear the words, honey."

"I want you to kiss me." She presses a quick kiss to the palm of my hand. "And I want you to fuck me, Theo. You told me to find you when I needed you, and that's what I did tonight. I *need* you."

"Okay," is all I say before my pants come off, my hands pulling her tiny fucking shorts off. "But you can't hide from me tonight."

"I won't."

"Good because I want to see all of you. Every fucking inch of you is mine until I leave, including these beautiful thighs," I say as I kneel in front of her. "God, look at how beautiful you are."

"You're just saying that, but thank you."

I can only shake my head as I stare at her, not giving her what she needs until she believes me. She is fucking ethereal right now. No, not even just right now. She always is, but somehow when she looks at me like I'm worth something, I can't help the pull I feel to give her everything.

"Come here," I say as I offer my hand to her, and she takes it as I lead her over to the mirror in my bathroom.

"It's okay. I didn't mean—"

"Come here, honey," I bring her in front of me, my hands on her shoulders as I make her look at me in the mirror. "Why can't you see how beautiful you are?"

Her eyes meet mine for a split second before she pulls at the skin on her thighs, her arms lifting up as she pulls on the skin there too. She smooths her hands down the groove of her stomach, then her hips, until they're at her sides again. She didn't say a single word. She didn't need to, but all of the places she touched are reasons why she thinks she's not the most perfect person I've ever seen.

She pinches at the skin at her neck, her eyes cast down at the floor as she threads her arms together, trying to hide more and more of herself from me.

I grab her chin with my hand and make her look at me. "Eyes on me, Daisy girl."

"You don't have to do this."

"Let me show you what I see," I say as I press a kiss to her neck, my hands grazing up and down her arms, goosebumps underneath my touch. "You know what these arms do? They connect to these beautiful hands that paint your face with the art you love to do on yourself and all of your clients. Without them, your art wouldn't exist."

She looks away from me again, but I still continue.

"And these beautiful thighs and the stretch marks that are all over them"—I take a deep breath as I kneel and press a kiss to her legs and hips—"They are driving me insane. They remind me of ocean waves and I want to drown in your body all night long."

Her cheeks get red as soon as I say that, my hands traveling all over her legs as she finally starts to believe me.

"Look at how beautiful you are, inside and out," I tell her. "And when you're with me, you will never hide any single part of you from me or else I'm going to punish you."

"Punish me, huh?" Her lips lift into a smirk as she looks at me in the mirror. "What would that look like?"

"It would look like me bending you over this counter and fucking you until you truly see how stunning you are as you unravel beneath me," I whisper in her ear as I slip one finger under her panties. "I bet if I dipped into your pussy right now, you'd be soaking wet for me."

"Do it," she says, her breath getting heavier by the minute. "Touch me, please."

I turn her around, slide her clothes off of her body, and my cock is aching, but it's not my turn yet. My finger slides right into her pussy, and just how I knew it, she's wet. Fucking soaked, actually.

"How long have you been soaked for me? Did you try to make yourself feel good before you got over here or what?"

She shakes her head.

"Can you handle another one?" I ask, my fingers sliding in and out of her as she nods. My thumb finds her clit, and I see her entire body shiver as I drop to my knees, my face perfectly in line with her pussy. I can smell her arousal, I can feel it on my hand as it drips out of her, and it's not enough. I need to taste her. I need to feel her writhe beneath me. I need to bend her over the counter and watch her ass bounce against me as she takes what she needs.

"Theo," she moans as her hands grip the counter. "This feels so good."

"You're taking it so well, Dais," I coax her, my tongue sliding up and down her pussy as I finally get a taste of her.

So *fucking* sweet just like she is.

I can feel her start to clench around my fingers, her first orgasm of the night begging to come loose, and just as I lightly bite her clit, I feel her unravel around my fingers and onto my face, and shit, the sight of her like this? Fucking everything to me. I've never seen a more beautiful sight, and I know my entire night is going to be spent chasing her moans as I make her unravel for me over and over again.

"You better be ready for another one," I say as I drop my underwear as I make good on my promise and bend her over the counter. "Because I'm just getting started with you."

"Give me all you got." She smiles lazily as I roll a condom on, her eyes practically rolling to the back of her head as I slide my cock through her arousal, getting my cock nice and wet before I slide into her.

I can barely breathe as I inch into her pussy, stretching her nice and wide for me as I make sure I'm not hurting her.

"You good, honey?"

She nods, her eyes meeting mine in the mirror. "I'm so fucking full."

"I'm not even halfway yet, Dais."

Her eyes widen in the mirror, and as soon as she looks back at me, my cock pushes fully inside of her, and I have to steady myself against the counter.

She feels like a fucking *dream*. Her pussy was made for me, and I don't think I'm going to have the patience to hold off my orgasm, but she comes first.

"Shit."

She grinds her hips against me, driving me even more insane and I have to grab her hips to stop her because I could come just from this.

"Take what you need from me," I tell her. "Just a fair warning, I might not last too long if you do. It's been a while."

"That's okay," she says as she rolls her hips, her pussy sliding against my cock as she fucks me. "I'll take control tonight, as long as you're good with not sleeping because I don't think once will be enough for me tonight."

"Do with me as you wish," I moan as she slams into me, her ass bouncing against me as my cock starts to throb inside of her. "Fuck, please keep going, Daisy. Please keep fucking me."

"God, your begging is so hot."

"Please, honey. Please make me come. Please let me fill you up with my cum."

"Do it, Theo. Unravel for me," she whispers, her voice sultry as I let go, my cock throbbing inside of her as I spill into the condom, my fingers digging against her hips as my head falls to her back.

"You are astonishing," is all I can say as she giggles at me, her eyes meeting mine in the mirror.

"That was really fucking hot," she says, her breathing heavy as I think about the fact that she didn't come again.

I pull out of her discarding the condom in the trash before I scoop her into my arms and bring her back over to my bed. I set her down, spread her legs, and devour her.

"You always come first," I say as my tongue fucks her. Her hands are fisting my sheets, but I'm punishing myself for being so fucking selfish. "And I broke that rule, so now, you come twice before I get to again."

"Is that so?"

"That's how it goes, honey," I say as I settle in front of her on my knees. "Think you can handle it?"

She nods, and I swear I have to pinch myself to make sure I'm not dreaming or something because this girl in front of me is my own version of heaven on this earth.

Chapter Twenty-Seven

— NO I'M NOT IN LOVE BY TATE MCRAE

I'M WOKEN UP BY the smell of pancakes, and the bed dips beside me as my eyes open to a small tray of food. Theo's eyes are sparkling above me.

"Good morning, beautiful." He helps me sit up in bed, my back against the wall. "I made a bunch of food for you. I'm not sure if you like breakfast, but—"

"I'm going to stop you right there." I put my hand against his chest. "If I ever decline breakfast food, there's something seriously wrong with me."

He only laughs, his smile different than it's been before. I reach over and fluff his hair as he sets the tray down and cuts part of a pancake, the fork at my mouth as I take a bite. God, this tastes phenomenal.

"Daisy, you've got to stop making those noises or I'm going to fuck you again."

"I'm literally just eating," I say as I giggle. "If you can't control yourself, that seems like a you problem."

"Oh, it's a big problem," he says as he presses a kiss to my ear. "I made you come like five times last night and I want to hear you unravel again."

"Theo..." I say as I take another bite. "You're insatiable."

"Can you fucking blame me?" he says as he turns onto his back, his eyes on the ceiling. "You're sitting here in one of my shirts, only underwear beneath, and moaning around the food I made for us. How am I not supposed to reward you for being so fucking stunning?"

I set the plate on the table, turning to face the man next to me who's staring back at me, eyes full of something I can't place.

"Maybe we should have a code word or something."

"Like a safe word." His head perks up immediately. "Was I too rough last night?"

"No," I say, my hand against his chest. "If I recall, I was the one calling the shots last night and you listened well."

"I told you I'd be good. What kind of word are you thinking?"

"This is temporary between us," I pause, a strange feeling swirling in my gut. "But I have a bad track record of falling way too easily for people. I just worry this is my first time doing something like this. I'm not sure if I have it in me to fall again for someone who's not a permanent figure in my life."

"That's understandable." He sits up on his elbows, his eyes piercing mine. "I've never really done anything like this either, so I think it's a good idea to have a mutual code word."

"So, I figured if one of us says this word, then we call it quits."

"And it's for if one of us starts to fall..." he trails off, not saying the rest of it.

If one of us starts to fall in love with the other. I don't think my heart could handle that again, and if this is what I have to do to protect it, then so be it. I'm not having any romantic feelings for him even though we were together last night, but I still worry.

"Exactly," I tell him. "Do you have an idea for what word we could use?"

He shrugs. "It has to be something neither of us uses on a daily basis."

The two of us think for a moment, and the only things that pop into my mind are different names of fruit.

"What about ghost?" he offers.

"That could work," I smile. "Ghost." I try it out on my lips, the word floating through the air. I hope we never have to use it, but I'm glad we're establishing this now rather than running into feelings down the line and having no idea what to do.

"Do you like it?"

I nod.

"Perfect." He shuffles closer to me. "Now, do you need an actual safeword or do you think you can handle me fucking you again?"

I can't help but giggle. "Oh, honey, I can handle you just fine."

"That's my girl," he says as he grabs my hips and throws me on top of his legs, his dick already pressing against my ass as I feel his hips start to move. "You're so beautiful like this, Dais."

"Is that so?"

"Mhm," he says, a glint in his eye. "I need you to ride my mustache again, honey. I'm already craving another taste."

"You want that?"

"More than anything." His hooded eyes stare into mine.

"Then make me," I say as I lean forward, my hands rubbing up and down his chest before he grabs my wrists, pulls me forward, and pushes my panties to the side. He shifts his body so his head lines up perfectly before he groans underneath me.

"Sit."

I gaze down at him. "Are you—"

"Smother me with this pussy, honey." His tongue darts out and teases my clit, his hands gripping my legs. "Drown me in these fucking thighs."

"If you say so," I say as I lower down onto his face. The hair and stubble grazes against my legs and makes me squirm. His tongue licks and sucks on every sensitive part of me, and I have to grab the headboard to keep myself steady.

He's acting like he didn't spend most of last night on his knees in front of me, as if he's been starved from touching me and feeling my body on his. Less than twelve hours ago, he was making me scream, and he's still as needy as he was last night.

"Grab that headboard, Dais, I'm not even close to being done."

"You've got to be—" A moan interrupts my sentence, his mouth sucking on my clit again. God, I know he knows I love that. Honestly, I didn't even know I liked that, but here we are. "Stroke yourself."

I can feel his mouth turn up. "Yeah?"

"Be a good listener," I say as I stare at him beneath me, my hands still fisting the headboard. "Take your cock out."

"Turn around and spit on it for me," his grip strengthens on my thighs as I feel my pussy clench. God, the way this man talks to me while his tongue is buried inside me should be illegal. My underwear is still in his way, and as soon as I hear the rip of the fabric, I know his patience is wearing thin.

"You know I can take these off, right?"

"I'm impatient, Dais. I can't fucking wait. Please put my cock in your mouth."

I comply, shifting myself to a comfortable position as I watch him take his hard cock out and stroke it a few times.

"Get it nice and wet," he moans, his tongue finding my center again. "Spit on it, honey, please."

"Well, you asked so nicely," I say as my mouth meets his cock. I spit on it, getting it all wet before I take it in my mouth. He lets out a moan as soon as I start to suck, and the only sounds beside what we're doing are the squeaks of the bed frame.

"I need to be inside of you," he says as he flips me over. I'm on my back as I stare at him, my legs going onto his shoulders as he lines his cock up with my pussy. He rolls a condom and then he slides inside of me in one go, my finger holding my underwear to the side as my other hand braces against the headboard.

"Fuck, you're a dream, Daisy girl," he moans, sliding in and out of me at a pace that feels so fucking good. I didn't think sex could be like this, so electric and needy. I've never felt like this before, so rushed and full of want for someone.

I blame the man on top of me and his stupid fucking mouth.

"I didn't get enough last night," he tells me. "You were in charge then, but now it's my turn."

"Tell me what you want," I groan.

"Sit there and let me fuck you, honey." He braces one hand against the wall, his head thrown back from how good my pussy feels. "God, you're clenching."

"Can you blame me?" I say.

"Lift these hips for me," he says as he grabs a pillow, placing it under my lower back. "Yeah, just like that. Let me get as deep as I can. Let me fuck you until you can't walk."

"Please," is all I can say, his cock thrusting into me as his hand finds my clit. He knows I need the friction. I can never come just from penetration and the slow, languid circles he's rubbing on me is making my pussy clench and squeeze his cock inside of me. "Theo, don't stop."

"I'd never dream of it." He smirks just as I feel myself start to let go. "Yeah, that's it. Coat my fucking cock and let me fill you up with my cum."

That only makes my orgasm stronger, his dick still thrusting in and out of me as I scream his name, the only word off of my lips sounding like a prayer to him.

"Shit, Dais," is all he says as his moans take over, his dick throbbing inside of me as I come down, my breathing getting heavier and heavier.

His hand struggles against the wall, and I can feel my legs start to shake as the two of us relax, his body slumping next to mine on the bed as I try to regain control of my breathing.

"I will *never* get enough of that," he sighs. "You're fucking perfect."

For some reason, when he says it, I believe it. "And you seem to know just what I like."

To that, he shrugs.

"And now, I have to walk back over to my house with ripped panties."

He only laughs as he presses a kiss to my nose and starts to get dressed. "Let me walk you home."

"It's like a hundred feet," I tell him. "You can watch me from the window."

"Not good enough," is all he says as he presses a kiss to my forehead. "Ready?"

I nod as he grabs my hand and drags me down the stairs, his kitchen a mess with all of the food preparations he did. God, I can still barely feel my legs.

"I can help—"

"Nope. You're going to go home and get ready for work and I'm going to stop by Delilah's and grab you a coffee because I kept you up all night. Leave the mess to me. I did make it, after all."

"Yes, but you made a mess *for* me." I can tell he's not seeing past my bullshit, but part of me feels weird about this, but what we're doing is what casual is. My heart and brain aren't used to that, but this is all on my terms, Theo said that last night. Whenever I need him, I can call him, just like I told him to do with me. They're two *very* different situations, but with the communication we have with one another, I think it'll be alright. I just have to remind my heart a thousand times that this is temporary, and everything will be fine. And we have our code word in case things get too serious or real, but right now, I'm going to enjoy the beautiful man next to me that has made me come a handful of times in about twelve hours.

Nothing is weird or awkward like I worried it would be either. His hand is in mine and it's like it's the most natural thing in the universe. Things are just how they used to be, and Theo and I will go back to being neighbors with a spicy twist, I guess.

"Dais?"

The tone of his voice breaks me out of my thoughts, and before I can look over at him, my eyes focus on what he's worried about.

My tires are all flat. Every single one.

"What the hell?"

I run to look at them all, Theo close beside me as his hands reach out and graze the hole. It's not a small one, either. It's big, jagged, and it looks like someone took a knife to every single tire on my car.

But I can't understand why. Who in Nettles would do this?

"There's something on your front door," he tells me. I notice a small piece of white paper taped to it, and when I unfold it, my body freezes, goosebumps erupting all over my limbs as Theo comes behind me and steadies me. "What the fuck is this?"

"I-I don't know." My breathing starts to pick up as I read the note over and over again, wondering who could possibly have it out for me this much. The break-in a few weeks ago wasn't an accident. I'm sure of it now because this is far too coincidental to have nothing to do with that night.

```
Come back or suffer the consequences.
```

"I'm calling the police," Theo says as he dials, and my stomach sinks as he explains what happened, and within minutes there are cops at my house *again*. Minutes before all this happened, I was smiling, laughing, enjoying the life I've been living since my divorce.

All it took was thirty seconds to unravel that.

I have no idea who could have done this, but that sinking feeling in my body is reminding me of what my ex-husband could pull off. He has all the fucking money in the world, and if he really thought he owned me, he'd stop at nothing to get me back with him. No piece of paper stating we're divorced could stop him, and that's the scariest part.

He might know where I am if this is him, which means I'm not as safe as I thought I was. He never seemed like the type to be like this—violent, cryptic, malicious—but I always thought any amount of money could turn him into someone I didn't recognize.

This just proves it.

Chapter Twenty-Eight

— **POOL BY SAMIA**

"You're staying with me," I say as we all gather at Delilah's shop. What happened has already made its way around town, and Delilah offered to open a little later so we could figure out the best plan going forward.

"I don't know if that's the best idea," Delilah says. "I mean, you do live right across the street. What if this person knows about you too?"

"Then my tires would have been stabbed out," I say as I pace around the shop. Daisy has barely said two words since we left the police station, and by the look on her face, she isn't doing well. I know that look. I've been in that look. She's retreating into herself, and I need to get her out of it before she falls in completely. "I will keep her safe."

Delilah takes one look at me before turning to her brother, the firefighter Daisy went out with before she came to my place. "I would feel a lot better if she was with you."

"I agree with him."

Oh, maybe I do like this fucker. "Really?"

He nods. "I'd do it, really, I would, but I'm barely home. You know that, sis. I'd feel a lot better knowing she was safe with someone who's actually around all the time."

"Well, she can still stay with me," Delilah says. "We work down the road from one another and—"

"How about asking her what she wants?" I wonder as I grab her hand in mine. "How are you feeling about all this?"

She opens her mouth and nothing comes out but tears. "I'm sorry," she says in between sobs.

Delilah wraps her in her arms, her hand caressing her hair as she cries into her best friend's arms. "Cry it out, babe. It's okay."

"I'm just exhausted," is all she says.

"You've had a lot going on these past few weeks," Delilah reassures her.

Daisy's cries turn into laughs as she pulls back from her friend. Elliott and I can only stare at the two of them as I take a sip of my coffee.

"Not even just these past few weeks. These past two years or however long, all I've been doing is treading water, and I think everyone around me can tell I'm falling behind. I tried to swim back to shore—that's what coming back here has felt like—but somewhere along the way, the swim lessons I paid for failed me. I'm moving forward at what seems like a snail's pace, and now there seems to be someone after me."

The three of us sit and let her continue. None of us have lived what she has, so we let her get it all out and we'll help to pick her back up when she needs it.

"I tried drowning. I tried letting myself go and it didn't work. Somehow, I always float back to the surface."

"Because you're resilient, Dais," Delilah reminds her.

"I'm not. At least I don't feel like it at the moment. Other people make it out of the water just fine, but for some reason, I am *stuck* in the water, in these feelings, in *everything*, and I cannot seem to make my way out of it. This is just another rock in the gigantic ocean of my life that I am stuck in, and again, I'm not going to be able to make it out."

A quiet silence covers the ice cream shop, only the sounds of Delilah and Daisy sniffling through the tears. I never thought today was going to go like this. After the magic that occurred last night, I thought nothing could stop the feelings I was having in my chest.

But seeing her cry and share feelings that have mimicked my own before has pushed me back down. I'd do anything to make her tears stop. I'd do anything to tell her that even just treading water on the days where things feel impossible is good enough, and even if treading is all you can do, you're still doing *something*.

"The water gets calmer," slips out of my mouth before I can stop it.

"What?"

"I know the exact feeling you're talking about," I tell her. "It's how I've felt since my brother died."

Delilah probably knows about Tobias, but I'm guessing her brother doesn't, and although I don't like going around town telling everybody what I've been through, I trust the people in this room. If Daisy trusts them, then I do too.

"It used to feel like I was white-water rafting at first. I could barely keep myself afloat, but lately," I pause, trying to articulate what I'm trying to say. "Lately, the water has been a lot calmer than it has in years, and for the first time in a while, I can see the shore. I'm not quite sure if I'll ever get to it, but even just the thought of it being there comforts me in a weird way. It's because of you that I can see the shore, I think."

Daisy's eyes lock onto mine, and I can't find it in me to look away from her eyes that have never looked so fucking blue. She nods just for me, and I'd have forgotten if Delilah and Elliott were still here until they speak.

"I want daily check-ins," Delilah says. "And if anything suspicious happens, I don't care how small it is, you better call the police. No walking anywhere by yourself. One of us can drive you until your car is fixed. It's the top priority in the shop right now."

"Del, your family has enough going on. I should be the least of your worries."

"Don't worry about it, Dais," Elliott says.

"I hate that you all are doting on me like this. I don't want to pull any of you down with me. What's the use if we all drown? Then what's left?"

"Let us help you to shore, honey," is all I can say to her. "Or at least let us try."

"You're not a burden," Delilah tells her. "I know that's where your mind went, but let us help you because we love you, not because we feel like we have to. You are my best friend. I'd fucking drown right with you if I knew you were going down."

"I mean, I can't condone drowning," Elliott says, and we all laugh. "But I'll do anything I can to help."

"Thank you all so much," her eyes linger on me for a beat longer than everyone else. "I should get to work so you can open."

"I'll walk you," I say before we head out, leaving two of the five Madison siblings in Delilah's place. A few people eye us outside of the shop. I should have known Delilah's place would have a line, but I don't really care. What we were discussing is far more important, and thankfully, it looked like most of them had patience.

I've never been so alert in my entire life. What if one of those people lining up was the one to slash her tires? What if they're watching her right now? Part of me wants to stick by her all fucking day, but I know I can't.

"I appreciate all you've done for me," she whispers to me as we walk.

"I could say the exact same thing to you. I mean, shit, you literally saved my life."

"I know, but—"

"No buts," I say as I open the door to her boutique for her. "Let me be here for you how you've been for me since I've been in Nettles. It's the least I can do, and you better show me a picture of this ex-husband of yours in case you're right and he really has found you and wants something from you."

She shows me a social media profile on her phone. "That's him."

"Thank you," I whisper, committing his face to memory. I saw the look on her face when she read that note. She thinks it's him, and with everything she's told me about him, I wouldn't be surprised if he was the one behind all of this.

She flips her closed sign to open before she sighs heavily, trudging over to the iPad so she can start to play music. "What are we doing, Theo?"

My brows furrow as the question comes from her mouth.

"I appreciate everything you're doing for me by letting me crash at your house, but all I've done for the last month is hop between your house and mine. What happens when you're gone and this is all still happening?"

"I'm not leaving until this is done."

"Don't say that," she shakes her head. "You can't stay here for me. You have a whole life back in Pennsylvania. I don't want to keep you from it."

I can only laugh because the life I have back home is not even close to anything. The only time I've felt that I had something to come back to was her up here. Sure, my family is back home, but that's about it. I travel for my job. I don't settle down. That's how it has always been.

Nettles is starting to slowly change that for me. I could see myself settling down here. I could see myself staying in this place with these people, but I have to get myself together first. I have to learn how to stop leaning on alcohol so fucking much. The people around me deserve better, and I'm starting to think I do too.

One day, I'll get to the place where I'm leaning on myself instead of a bottle, but that day might be way in the future. I officially have nothing left to discover about my brother. No new notes. No new adventures with him guiding me. Nothing. It hasn't really hit me fully, and when it does, I worry about what I might do while under the influence of something that almost killed me.

Matter of fact, whenever I'm in a room by myself, I'm with the person who almost killed me. It's scary thinking of it like that, but it's true.

"Why were you laughing?"

"Because I don't have a life," I tell her. "My life has basically been on pause for the last three years. It's been filled with traveling and distractions and drinking away my pain because I couldn't bear anything."

"Well, you have a life here, don't you? With me?" she pauses before she realizes what she said. "And everyone else in Nettles. Sometimes this town reminds me of a huge, messy, kind of fucked up family with how gossip spreads through it."

"This place is definitely the closest feeling I've had to wanting to settle down." Her eyebrows shoot up at me. "What?"

"Nothing."

"Daisy girl," I say as I walk over to the checkout counter, leaning against it. "Tell me what you're thinking."

"You had a realtor at your house the other day."

"I did," I tell her. "I told you my mother wanted to sell it. That is still the plan unless something changes. She's leaving it all up to me."

"Ah," is all she says as a customer comes in. "I'm sorry for assuming, but—"

"I know what it looks like," I say. "I have no idea what the future holds for me. I'm truly taking things one agonizing week at a time."

"Me too," she smiles, trying to hide the tears that almost fall. "But to be honest, the water has felt calmer with you around. More bearable to tread in."

Hearing her say that hits me in the chest. I don't think anyone would ever describe me as a calming presence, or someone that they can lean on when things get tough. It's always the opposite. I'm always the one taking things from other people, but I like how she makes me feel. I like being in the garden of her life and getting to watch her grow and change in front of me. She's not the same girl she was when we were kids, and I'm not even close to being the same person I was either.

If I was to give my heart to someone when I knew I could do it fully and without consequence, it would be her. I've never been so sure of anything before, but I feel it in my bones. Daisy Campbell, the girl next door, the one who believes in me when she has no reason to, would be *it* for me.

If only I had anything to give. It would be hers in an instant, but I'll take her however I can while I'm up here. I'll take bits and pieces and I'll carry them with me until the current somehow drags me back to her, if I get so lucky to be around her a third time.

"It's funny."

"What is?" she asks me.

"That's exactly how you make me feel too."

She smiles a real smile for the first time since we got back to her house before we're interrupted by someone in her store.

"Excuse me? Can you help me with a shade match, please?"

"Of course I can," she says as she brushes past me, her hand grazing mine, and I have to stop myself from latching on to it. "I'll see you at home?"

"Call me when you're closing and I'll come get you, okay?"

"I will."

"You promise?"

Her cheeks get red as soon as my whispery tone comes out of my mouth. "I promise."

"Good girl, honey," I say as I head out of her store. This day has been the biggest whiplash ever, but even in the small moments with her, I've still found little bits of joy to cling onto.

And fuck, am I clinging to those with all my heart because I know she deserves better than me. She deserves a whole goddamn forest full of flowers, not the one wilting away in the shade like I am now.

Chapter Twenty-Nine

— LOVESICK BY PAIGE FISH

> **Lucas:** Anything yet or are you just going to leave me hanging and get fired?

> **Theo:** I'm headed out today. I'll get something I deem worthy enough, I promise.

> **Lucas:** I need something, dude. Anything. I'll even take a shot of your feet.

> **Theo:** I didn't know you were into that.

> **Lucas:** Asshole. Just get me something, please.

> **Theo:** Will do.

I LIGHTLY TAP ON Daisy's door, unsure if she's awake this early. After this whirlwind of a week, I was going to let her sleep. She's had a lot going on, but maybe getting her out of the house would be good for her. Like me, she hasn't been sleeping well. Last night we stayed up and worked on a puzzle, and the entire night was filled with us talking and I crave more of that, but right now, I have to shoot.

I'm hoping she's up and willing to go on a tiny adventure with me away from town because if I don't get something to Lucas, my time as a traveling photographer is going to come to an end. Then, I'll be a washed up alcoholic with a dead brother and no job. I'll truly have nothing left, and I don't even want to think about what would happen to my mental health if that were to happen.

"Theo?" she says, rubbing her eyes as I open the door. "What's up?"

She must have just woken up—her hair is a mess and her face free of makeup. I don't think I've ever seen a prettier sight than the girl in front of me right now. Her eyes are droopy, her smile soft, and the sunshine from the window frames her face beautifully.

"Good morning, honey," I can't help the nickname that slips out. She's golden like honey, especially in the early light of the morning.

"Good morning, neighbor," she laughs to herself. "I guess I can't call you that anymore since I'm sitting in your bed."

"You can call me whatever you'd like," I say as I lean against the doorframe. "Are you working at the hotel this weekend?"

She shakes her head.

"Thank goodness," I say as I show her my camera bag. "Want to go on an adventure with me?"

"Where do you have in mind?"

"You're my tour guide around here, Dais. Anywhere you take me that you think I could capture with my camera is good enough for me."

She thinks to herself for a few moments, the sheets of the bed sticking to her skin where she's sitting, and I can't help but want to photograph this moment to remember forever.

"I have a place. It's not too far from here."

"Great." I smile as she moves to get up. "Take your time getting ready and I'll pack the car with some water and snacks."

"Sounds good."

I grab the small cooler I brought with me and fill it with ice, throwing a couple of water bottles inside of it before I make some sandwiches and throw those in there too. Daisy comes down while I'm packing some snacks in my bag, and she tries to start loading the car, but I'm faster than she is.

"Nope," is all I say to her. "You're not carrying a thing."

"I can at least help."

"You are helping."

"How?"

"You're my tour guide and that's all I need you to be." I grab everything I need in my hands as she opens the door for me. "Thank you."

"Did you pack a bathing suit by any chance?"

"No, why?" I ask as I open the trunk. "I know it's warm out for it, but I didn't even think about going in the water."

"Just wondering." She smiles. "Ready?"

It only takes about twenty minutes to get to wherever Daisy is taking us, and as soon as I park in the small lot, I still have no idea where we are. It sort of looks like the beginning of some horror movie where everyone dies because in front of me is a bunch of trees and that's all I can see.

"Oh good, there are no other cars here."

"That's a good thing?" I wonder.

"Mhm," she smiles at me as she gets out of the car. "God, it's been so long since I've been here."

"How long?" I ask as I grab all of my stuff.

"Not since high school." By the way her eyes are taking in our surroundings, I can tell she has memories here that she's fond of. "It's as overgrown as I remembered it."

"I'll follow you, honey," I say as I adjust all the bags I'm holding. She leads the way and as we make our way through what feels like thousands of fucking trees and bushes, I see a small clearing after a few minutes of walking. "Wow."

That's the only word that comes to my mind as she pulls the branches to the side and in front of me is a small beach, a lake in front of us but the real thing blowing my mind is the mountain ranges in the distance. I never would have known this was here if it wasn't for her, but I can already feel my creative juices flowing as I rush to set everything down and grab my camera.

"I take it this is a good sign?"

"It's beautiful," I say as I point and click in a few different directions. I put a whole new roll of film in my camera this morning, and with the way I'm feeling, I might go through all of it today.

"The last time I was here was right after high school graduation," she tells me as she sets some blankets down on the sand and gets comfortable with a book she's reading. "This place really hasn't changed a bit. Is this what you were looking for?"

"Yes," I say as I smile behind my camera. "This is the perfect slice of Vermont."

"So, where are these pictures going to be used?"

I pull my camera away from my face and join her on the blanket for a second. "The developer at the magazine I work for has been hounding me for pictures for one of their new spreads. It's all about Vermont and the scenes of this place way up North in the United States. One of these photos will be used as the cover, the rest will be throughout the spread, along with a piece from me about Tobias in the end."

"Wow." She smiles at me. "That's really cool. You must be excited."

"Sort of."

Her eyebrows pinch at me as she waits for further explanation.

"This is my last stop on the journey Tobias wanted me to go on. I wish it could go on forever and I know it can't, but part of me thought if I stalled on work stuff, I could stay longer. Unfortunately, the real world always comes crawling back."

"That's how I felt when I left Nettles," she tells me. "I felt brand new in Boston because nobody knew me or my family. I was just Daisy Campbell. Nobody had any preconceived notions about me or knew all the gossip that had swirled about me in town. It was freeing to be in a place where I could figure out who I wanted to be while discovering new things about myself." Her smile turns down as she thinks about her life back in Boston. There's no doubt in my mind that she's thinking about her ex-husband, and I wish I could erase every bad thing he ever said to her. "What is that face for?"

"I don't know," I say as I look down at my camera. "I wish I could make Boston and that period of your life easier. I hate knowing there are bad thoughts swirling through your head when you think about the past."

"That's just life, unfortunately. There will always be things that make my face pinch how remembering him does. Sometimes I think I was wired this way."

"Why?"

"Do you know the way daisies grow?" she asks me.

"I can't say I do. That's more of a question for my mom." Her and Tristan have only recently started to really get into gardening. Over the summer, my mom kept sending me photos of the plants all over the yard, and though they were beautiful, I don't understand planting them if they're just going to die when the snow comes and the ground freezes. Why bother, you know?

"At first, they're beautiful. They grow to the perfect size and for a few days or longer, they're picturesque and perfect, but when they get too tall, the stems can't bear the weight of the flower anymore, so they sort of flop over. They're more of a burden than anything." She pauses, embarrassment covering her features as if she didn't mean to say so much. "That's how I've felt for my whole life."

I turn to face her, grabbing her hand in mine. "Why do you feel like that, honey?"

"Because I'm sensitive. I can't take a joke. I cry whenever I feel any emotion even if I'm not sad. The tears always come and I've spent my entire life like this, just feeling *everything* to an absurd degree. I have good days where I'm upright and smiling feeling like nothing can hurt me, but the days where my emotions and my heart get the best of me is when I finally fall over. It's a cycle I can't really get out of no matter how hard I try. My mother named me after a flower and I don't think she meant for me to relate so heavily to it, but I do."

"What are you feeling like today?"

"I don't really know."

"Can I show you what I see?" I've been dying to shoot Daisy on film. She's got the perfect fucking aura for my camera, and the selfish fucker in me wants to have some small pieces of her for when I leave.

"Don't you have other work to do?" she smirks at me.

"I can do it after," I scooch closer to her. "Let me capture you how I see you. You'll look beautiful on film."

"Oh, really?"

"I promise." I smile back at her, already getting my camera ready. "Let me show you how you shine."

"You get a few shots and then I'm going to read my book, listen to the water move, and enjoy myself, okay?"

"Deal," I say as I get up and test out some angles. I want the small sliver of sunlight on her face to look exactly how it is in person, so after messing with a few settings, I put my camera to my face.

"What do I do with my hands?" She giggles as I take a shot of her. "That's not fair."

"What? It's a candid," I smile behind my lens. "Just act natural."

She only rolls her eyes at me as she lays back on the blanket, stretching her arms above her head as she giggles, clearly feeling the stare of my camera at her. She took her coverup off, so she only has her jean shorts and pale yellow bikini top on. When she took it off earlier, I swear my mouth started watering, but we haven't had sex since the morning her tires were stabbed out.

I wasn't sure if she wanted to keep it going with all she had going on, so I've left it up to her when it comes to that part of what we are to one another, but seeing her unfiltered like this and being able to shoot this memory is making it really fucking hard to be calm.

I can already feel my dick twitching under my shorts and she's not even doing anything. She's just laying on the blanket looking like a fucking dream.

"You're beautiful, Dais," I tell her as I shoot as many pictures as I can, the light on the beach making her eyes sparkle as she smiles at me.

"You get one more shot, so you better make it count."

"Oh, just one?" I say as I lower my camera. "Call me crazy, but I have an idea for my last shot."

"How do you want me?" She must understand the face I'm making because her voice turns to a whisper as her pupils dilate. "We are on a very public beach."

"I haven't seen anyone, and I can make it quick."

"What does that mean?"

"It means I make you come and we both go home happy."

She scoffs at me, but I can tell she likes my idea. Her cheeks are flushed and she can't look me in the eye anymore.

"Too shy or too scared?"

"Might be a little bit of both. What if someone comes down here?" She looks down the beach, but there's not a single soul besides us here. There's not even anybody on the water today.

"Then I'll stop."

"Theo..." She doesn't say anything else before she pulls her shorts down her long legs, throwing them to the side. "Okay."

"Pull your bikini to the side," I say as I kneel in front of her, my camera on the side as I get her ready for me. My fingers snake up to her mouth. "Get them nice and wet for me."

"I've missed this," she tells me as she takes my fingers in her mouth and sucks on them. This might have been a horrible idea because now all I can think about is her mouth around my cock.

"Have you?" I ask. "I've been right across the hall from you."

My fingers pop out of her mouth. "I know. It felt weird to just knock on your door and ask."

"Do it next time," I say as I tease her clit, my wet fingers rubbing against her as she starts to squirm. "I know you're a screamer, but you might want to be quiet this time around."

"Shut up." She lets out a breathy moan as I slip one finger inside of her. "Shit."

"Does that feel good, honey?"

She manages a nod as she covers her mouth, a few moans threatening to come out.

"Can you handle another one?" I ask as her pussy strangles my finger. I hear a few leaves rustling, and I turn my head, but I don't see anyone there.

"Yes."

"I know you can, Daisy girl," I say as I slip another one in. I can't help myself, she looks so goddamn ethereal as she comes undone underneath me, so I bury my face in her pussy as she grinds all over my face.

"Theo." The way she moans my name only makes me want to go faster, harder, longer, but I know I have to make this semi-quick. No matter how much I want to worship her all day on this beach. "Oh, fuck."

"You better soak my fucking mustache," I tell her as my tongue swirls around her center, my fingers still pumping inside of her as I hit a spot she fucking loves. Her back arches off of the towel, her pussy tasting as sweet as she is. "God, I'll never get enough of you and this beautiful pussy."

"Don't stop."

The only thing I'm focused on is making her come, and as soon as she covers her mouth, I know she's right on the edge. I replace both of my fingers with my tongue, my fingers finding her clit, rubbing small circles in the lightest of touches, and as she finally unravels, I find myself in a fucking dream as she soaks my fucking face.

"Theo," she moans into her hand as I watch her shake and unravel in my hands. The moment she comes down, she looks at me still licking up her sweet cum as I press two kisses to the inside of her thighs, leaving the smallest of marks so every time she looks at them, she'll remember this.

"Territorial much?"

"Maybe a little bit." I smirk as I move her bikini back to the right spot and hand her shorts back to her. "And look, nobody else showed up."

She smiles lazily at me as she looks at my camera off to the side. "You didn't take anything?"

"Oh, honey, I'll remember this. Trust me." I lick the remnants of her off of my fingers, drying them off with the edge of the towel.

"You're such an asshole," she says as she puts herself back together, a laugh coming off of her lips. "And maybe tonight I'll sneak into your room and take care of your problem."

I look down at my dick. I felt it straining against my pants while my tongue was buried inside of her, but I didn't care about me. I still don't. "I'd make you come about four more times before I even spare a thought about myself, Dais. Don't worry about it."

"Well, where's the fun in that?" she asks as she picks her book back up.

"I guess you're right," I say as I grab my camera. "I only need a few more shots and then we can head back home."

"I don't mind staying for longer than that," she tells me. "It would give me time to finally finish this book I've been reading for ages."

"Noted," I say as I head a little down the beach in search of a good shot, but my mind keeps straying to the girl on the towel I can't seem to get out of my head.

Chapter Thirty

— **NETTLES BY ETHEL CAIN**

For the first time in a while, I woke up early to do my makeup before I head to work. Granted, it's a Sunday and I'm headed to Amara's. She texted me yesterday when Theo and I were on the way home from our excursion and asked if I wanted to pick up a shift because one of her employees is sick. I said yes because not only could I use the extra money after shelling over a bunch for new tires, but it's not a bad gig Amara runs at her place.

I can have breakfast there, and I'll be done right after the checkout rush, so it won't be a terrible morning.

"You ready?" Theo pokes his head into my room, his fists rubbing circles around his eyes. I kept him up a little later than I should have, and I slept in his bed the whole night, only sneaking into my room this morning to get ready.

"Mhm," I say as I set my makeup with my favorite spray. "Is there—"

He holds his hand up, a to-go cup of coffee already ready for me as I take it from him.

"I tasted it and I think I used the perfect amount of your favorite creamer."

I take a sip and it's just the way I like it. "Thank you." I notice he has his camera bag with him. "Are you going to shoot the sunrise this morning?"

"I'm certainly going to try."

And then we're in his car and headed into town, the radio on a low volume as we both try to fully wake up. It's still dark out by the time he pulls into a spot on Main Street, practically sprinting out of the car to get my door for me.

"After you." He waves in front of him, and I can't help but laugh. He walks me all the way to the front desk, pressing a small kiss to my cheek as he waves goodbye to me and heads out of here. It feels so weird how far we've come in only a few months. The first time I saw him again was in this lobby. He looked so different, and I still don't understand how he recognized me after all the years lost between us.

Now he's making coffee for me, I'm living in his house, and I know what it feels like for him to be inside of me.

I think Daisy from a few months ago would have a heart attack if she knew what the future was going to bring her, but weirdly enough, I feel okay about it. So much has changed within a few months, and I'm glad it has. Never again do I want to be the girl I was when I first came back here—heartbroken, depressed, and silent. I lost so much of myself because of what happened, but with a little help from my friends and distance from what happened, I'm starting to leave those memories where they belong—in the past.

I head into the buffet, a few early risers in here with me as I grab a plate, throwing some eggs, toast, and hashbrowns onto it, and my mouth starts to water as soon as I'm back at the desk. My phone buzzes as soon as I take a bite, and I already know who it is.

> **Amara:** How's everything?
>
> **Daisy:** I've been here for about ten minutes. Everything is fine.
>
> **Amara:** Shirley told me there were a few problem check-ins yesterday and people were being really rude to her, so if anything like that happens today, call me and I'll be over in five minutes.
>
> **Daisy:** Don't you live like twenty minutes from here?
>
> **Amara:** So? I will not have any of my guests being rude to my staff. It's unacceptable.
>
> **Daisy:** That's why you're the best, but don't worry about this place.
>
> **Amara:** I'll try not to. My bigger worry comes in the form of my brother.
>
> **Daisy:** Best of luck.
>
> **Amara:** Thanks. Back at ya.

Huh, I wonder what's going on with Brooks. He's back in town, well, he never left, he did disappear for a little while though. All of my updates about Brooks have come from Amara, Eloise, and sometimes Delilah. I swear sometimes I can't keep track of everything going on in this town.

There really isn't much to do around here like there is in a bustling big city, which is why I prefer it here. In Boston, there was always somewhere to be. Everyone was constantly rushing around trying to beat the traffic, or trying to do it all, and I liked the change of pace at first, but I quickly backtracked. The soft, quiet town of Nettles is where I'm meant to be, and I'm so glad I found my way back here though it wasn't through the best circumstances.

I love going to sleep and not hearing horns honking. I love the crackling of the fireplace with no sirens in the background every four minutes. I love hearing the rain against my roof rather than footsteps from the apartment above mine. I love the birds chirping in the mornings and saying hello to people as they walk down Main Street. It's peaceful and serene and *perfect* for me. I don't know why I thought I was a city girl. There's too much I love about this place.

My phone buzzes next to me again, and I expect Amara's name, but an unknown number comes up instead.

> **Unknown: Does he give you everything?**
>
> **Unknown: *One attachment***
>
> **Unknown: Don't forget who you really belong to.**
>
> **Unknown: Give me what I want and this all stops.**

My stomach bottoms out as I assume whoever this is has the wrong number, but the goosebumps all over my skin have me thinking this is the same person who left that note on my door. There's a picture of Theo attached with the messages, and I know for certain this is the same person that texted me before, which means it's probably the same person who broke into my house and slashed my tires.

I lean down for my water bottle in my bag, needing something to coat my dry throat, when I hear a familiar voice. My hands are shaking as I reach for my bag, and I can barely breathe as I try my best to sound coherent even though these messages are making my stomach swirl with nausea.

"Daisy?"

I bang my head on the front desk as I try to get up quickly. "Ow."

"Are you okay?" Eloise asks me as she leans over the desk, my hand rubbing the spot on my head that I whacked.

"Peachy," I say in the sternest tone possible.

"You sound like I have for the past few weeks," she chuckles, gripping the mug tighter in her hands.

"What are you doing here? I thought you were living with Brooks?"

"I am," she takes a sip of her coffee, the ring on her left hand dazzling in the low light of the lobby. "It's been a little weird in the house lately, so I decided to take a little break."

"That's understandable." I can tell she doesn't want to talk about her relationship, so I change the subject to something that everyone loves to talk about. "It's getting a lot colder out there, isn't it?"

She smiles at me, knowing what I'm doing. "Yeah. I'm sure it'll snow soon. I'm hoping this coffee will warm me from the inside out."

"Amara keeps the good creamer on the shelf underneath the pot," I tell her, my voice still shaking with nerves. "Unless you like drinking your coffee straight up, then by all means."

"Noted," she laughs. "I'll keep that in mind for tomorrow if I'm still here."

My phone starts to buzz again, and my heart stops beating. I lift it up, expecting to see an unknown number attached to the call, but Luca's name flashes on my screen.

"Luca? What's wrong?"

Eloise is still standing at the desk, and her brows pinch as she mouths her brother's name to me. I shrug my shoulders as I hear a bunch of clanging in the background. Is he making breakfast or something?

"Is there a reason your boy is unconscious in my emergency room?"

"What?" My heart rate starts to pick up immediately.

"You should get here, Daisy. He'll need you."

"I'm on my way," I say as I start to grab my stuff, knowing I don't have a fucking car because Theo drove me to work and he took his keys with him.

"Is everything okay?" Eloise asks me as I'm halfway around the desk.

"Do you have a car here?" She nods. "I need you to take me to the hospital. It's Theo."

"Fuck," she says as she rifles through the pockets of her hoodie. "Let's go."

"Thank you," is all I can manage to say as I text Amara to update her about what's going on.

> **Daisy: Please don't fire me, but Theo is in the ER right now.**

> **Amara: Oh, go babe. Is he okay?**

> **Daisy: I have no idea.**

> **Amara: Keep me updated and don't worry about the front desk.**

> **Daisy liked a message.**

Eloise and I head into the emergency room, my heart beating out of my chest as I look around for her brother.

"There." She points to the same fucking room as last time I was here, and we head over. Luca is typing on the computer outside of Theo's room.

"How is he?" I say through the knot in my throat. "Is he okay? Is he fucking alive?"

"Why don't you ask him yourself?" Luca smirks at me as I look into the room. Theo is leaning against the bed, his face black and blue, and there are bruises all over the rest of his body.

"You're such an ass," Eloise says to her brother. "She was worried the entire way over here."

"Missed you, sis. How's the husband doing?"

She smacks him on the arm as I open the door into the room, tears already welling up in my eyes as I look at the state of him.

"It looks a lot worse than it is."

"Don't you lie to me," I say as I sit down on the end of his bed. "What the hell happened?"

"He doesn't remember," Luca says as he pulls a chair up. "A moderate concussion, one broken rib, and minor internal injuries will do that to a person. We did some scans to confirm all of that, but all in all, he's going to be fine."

"Can you not be an ass for like five minutes?" Eloise asks her brother. "He's your patient."

"For the second time, which reminds me that I told you I didn't want to see you in here again. Were you drinking again?"

It takes him a few seconds to put together a sentence. "I already told you I wasn't. Didn't you do a blood test?"

"Still waiting on the results," Luca says. "If you want my expert medical opinion, it looks like you were in some sort of fight."

His hand goes right to his head, his eyes swollen and bruised as he tries to remember what happened. "I-I had my camera in my hands, and I was looking at the film strips of the photos I had taken to see if I could see anything, when all of a sudden, this guy came out of nowhere and just started pummeling me. It was the weirdest thing. I barely had time to defend myself before I was knocked out. I honestly don't even know how I got here."

"A passerby called it in. They waited for the ambulance before they left, but now I'm going to call the police to report this because what happened to you was a crime."

My mind goes right to the texts I got this morning. Those must have been around the same time Theo was attacked, right? They sent me that picture of him too. This was intentional, and now it's not just me being targeted.

"When can he go home?" I ask Luca.

Luca looks between the two of us before he answers. "As soon as I get his results back. I'll write a few prescriptions for some pain meds—"

"I don't want them. Over-the-counter stuff will work just fine."

"Right." Luca nods. "And you'll need someone to monitor you for at least forty-eight hours, and you'll have to come in two weeks from now for another scan to make sure you won't sustain any long term brain injuries."

"I'll keep an eye on him," I tell Luca. "And I'll bring him back in for his next scan. Just tell me when you need him in here and we'll be back."

"Perfect," Luca says as he gets up. "I have other patients. A nurse will draw-up the discharge paperwork after the cops talk to you and take your statement."

"Thank you," Theo says, and Luca nods as he looks at me.

"Eloise, can I speak with you?"

"Sure," she says as she follows her brother out. "I'll drive you two home."

"You're the best," I tell her and she smiles.

"Be back in a minute," she says as she disappears around the corner.

"I didn't mean to worry you," Theo says. "I-I don't even know what happened, but I wasn't drinking."

"I know that," I say as I grab his hand in mine. I don't squeeze too hard on account of the scrapes and cuts on both of his hands and knuckles. "I know."

"It's important to me that you know that."

"I trust you."

"Do you know if my camera is in here?"

"Uhh," I say as I look around and find a small blue bag. I dig through it and find his camera, thankfully not smashed to pieces, and I set it on the bed for him. "Can you see it? Does it look okay?"

"Kind of." He moves his head back and forth. "It's still a little too bright in here, but the lights are down all the way according to Luca."

"I'll keep all of the lights off at home, okay? And you're not going to lift a finger for the next two weeks if I have anything to say about it."

"Daisy, please—"

"Don't. Let me take care of you. Do you want me to call your family?" I ask as I grab my phone from my pocket.

"No. I don't want them to worry. There's a reason Luca only called you."

"Why?"

"I put you down as my emergency contact the last time I was here. I had hoped I wouldn't need to use it, but I'm glad you're here."

"I'm going to find whoever did this and punch them in the face," I say as I caress his cheek, wishing I could erase the bruises underneath my touch.

Even if that person is my ex-husband.

"Oh, really?" Theo tries to smile at me, but his face pinches in pain. "Don't make me laugh, Dais."

"Sorry," I say as I lay down next to him in bed, my hand automatically finding his. "Is this okay?"

He leans his head against where mine rests against his shoulder. "I'm feeling better already."

Chapter Thirty-One

Theo

— CARRY YOU BY NOVO AMOR

"Thank you so much," Daisy says to whoever just left the porch. Ever since we got home from the hospital, there have been people knocking on our door all day long to drop off food or something else.

I have to say, it is nice to see so many people care about a guy who isn't a permanent resident here. Most of the people dropping things off are saying that the town won't rest until they figure out who beat me to a pulp. Some have even said that Nettles isn't used to this kind of violence—tires being stabbed, threatening notes, beatings in public—and they're worried about it escalating.

Most everyone has been kind, but some of those throwaway comments are a little weird. I appreciate the food and well wishes, but something is very off. I can feel it in my bones that I'm missing something about all this. It seems very focused on the girl in front of me, and I'm worried. I don't have an official link between all these things, but maybe I could give Nico a call and have him look into it so he can ease my fears. Nico is not only Vince's business partner, but he also runs the top security firm in the country. He can find anything about anyone, even if you have nothing to go on. Honestly, he scares me a little, but he's damn good at what he does.

The police have no leads into who beat me up last week. Not a single camera from the local businesses at the end of Main Street caught anything. It's the weirdest fucking thing, but I can't do anything about it because I can't remember what the guy looked like. I hate that my mind is betraying me, and it pisses me off that Daisy hasn't gone to work all fucking week because of my condition.

I hate that she's stopped her life to take care of me. This is exactly why I knew we wouldn't work in a relationship while I am the way that I am. Sure, I've been sober for a few months, but even without alcohol, I've still managed to fuck something up and need someone to lean on.

"Wow," she says as she closes the front door. "I thought that conversation was never-ending." She sets the dish down on the counter as more knocking comes.

"We need to get a sign made or something," I say as I put the ice pack on my head. "This is getting out of hand. The counter is already full, and so is the fridge. Where am I going to put all of this stuff?"

"I'll figure out a place for everything, just don't get up."

"Whatever you say, honey." I press the ice pack into my head, hoping it will help the pain on the inside and the outside.

"Oh, thank goodness," Delilah's voice filters through my ears. "I've missed you."

"You too," Daisy says as I watch them hug. A few other voices come into my house as I close my eyes, wanting the thumping of my head to stop.

"It's dark in here," someone says.

"I always wondered what the inside of this place looked like," Elliott says. "How are you feeling, man?"

"Shitty," is all I can manage to say. "But better than yesterday."

"I'll kill the fucker who did this to you," Brooks says to me as I open my eyes at the people standing in my living room. Delilah, Eloise, and Elliott Madison all stand next to one another, and this is the first time I can truly see the resemblance of the twins. It's uncanny, actually. Brooks is here too, his face matching the tone of his voice. He's as pissed off as I am about all this.

"Calm down," Daisy says. "Can I offer any of you anything to eat? Also try not to talk too loudly; Theo still has a minor concussion."

"That's a downgrade from a moderate one," Eloise says as she reaches her fist out to me. "Hell yeah."

I bump her fist because I am glad I'm finally healing. I had another scan yesterday, and I have to go back for another one next week because Luca is the most anal doctor ever and wants to make sure my brain is clear of injuries before I, in his words, leave Vermont and never come back to his emergency room again.

He *really* needs to work on his bedside manners, but he is a ridiculously good doctor. He fucking better be with the amount of hours he works, according to every Madison sibling.

"Please help me get rid of some of this food." I really do appreciate everyone's kindness, but there is no way in hell I'm going to be able to eat all of this. "Aren't you all supposed to be at work?"

"I don't have a job." Eloise smiles as she sits on the other couch. "And it only took a thousand hours to convince Delilah to leave the store in the very capable hands of her employees to come over here."

It looks like she's about to have a panic attack when I look over at her. "I've already called the store four times today, but this was important, so I am relinquishing control for one single workday."

"I'm proud of you, Del," Elliott says to his sister. "I'm not working until tomorrow, and spending one of my days off whooping all of you at board games sounded awesome."

"Is that what you all are doing over here?" A small smirk forms on my lips. Did they all really play hooky today just to come and see me? Is this what it feels like to have friends? "You really didn't have to do that."

"We wanted to," Brooks says as he sits next to his wife. "You both have had a tough few weeks and we thought this was a good way to cheer you up."

My eyes flit to Daisy, and her bright smile lights up the entire room. It's true. We've had a rough few weeks—months, really—but to be honest, with her around me, it hasn't felt so bad. I have a literal concussion, but waking up to her face every morning has brought me more joy than I ever felt. Her soft, warm hands are always wrapped around my torso, and this morning, I spent the entire time kissing every inch of her hands that I could. After I was finished, I counted the freckles on her face and when I got to twenty-five, she had woken up.

"Well, then by all means"—I sit up a little more—"Let's get this going."

"I'll grab some of the overflowing food from the fridge," Daisy says as the girls all hop up to help her. It's just Elliott and Brooks left, and with all of the gossip I heard about their families hating one another, all of them look surprisingly comfortable near one another.

"How has married life been treating you?" I ask him and he just stares at me, but I swear I see a small smile lift the corner of his lips.

"A little bit rocky." He shakes his head. "But it's been good."

"So, was she the one that got away you told me about all those weeks ago?"

"Oh, do tell," Elliott says as he leans back on the floor. "How long have you loved my sister, Brooks?"

He only rolls his eyes at the two of us and I laugh, the lukewarm ice pack going to my head even though it really hasn't been helping.

"As long as I can remember," he whispers as the girls come out.

"So, what are we playing first?" Delilah asks as Daisy sits next to me, handing me another ice pack for my head. "I'm quite partial to anything to do with cards."

"Preferably something I don't have to think too hard at." I laugh as I take a few chips and dip them in the salsa someone made. "God, that's really fucking good."

"Is that from the Masons? I swear they make fucking everything from scratch and it tastes like I've never had food before," Elliott says as he grabs a few chips, a spoonful of dip on the plate his sister handed him.

"What about this?" Daisy asks as she holds up a board game I haven't played since I was young. "Since there are more than four of us, we could do teams?"

"Sounds good to me," Eloise says, a smile on her face as she looks at Brooks. "Want to be on my team?"

"Always, darling," he presses a small kiss to their joined hands, and my head finds Daisy's shoulder.

"Partners?" I ask her.

"Of course." She smiles at me. "Put the ice pack back on your head."

"Yes, ma'am."

"Do you need more medication?"

I shake my head, the pain more bearable with these people around me.

"So, I guess that leaves you and I, Elliott. Three teams then?" Delilah asks and we all nod.

"Right, then let's get to it," Elliott says, and I can already see his competitive side coming out. This is not how I saw this afternoon going, but I can't complain because for the first time in a long time, I don't feel pulled between two versions of myself in two different places.

This place feels like home around these people, yet the future still looms, but I push that away while they're here. For now, I'm going to enjoy this feeling of community while I still have it.

"Let's get you to bed." Daisy guides me up the stairs, and even though I don't really need her to do this, I let her. "How are you feeling?"

"My head still hurts, but I feel great, Dais. Was it your idea to have them all over?"

"Yes." She smiles. "I hope it was okay. I know this is your house, but—"

"You live here too," I remind her. "And that was the best afternoon I've had, well, ever."

"Really?"

"Really." I look over at her as she opens the door to my—our—room, and she leads me right over to bed as I get comfortable and watch her peruse around the room. A lot of her clothes are in here. All of her makeup is sitting on the desk, and all her face products have infiltrated the sink in the bathroom.

I wish she could infiltrate my entire life like this, but I know that's not what she wants—yet or ever. I'll cherish these little moments of Daisy for the rest of my life.

"I used to have a crush on you when we were kids, you know."

She turns to face me, a makeup wipe against her face, and I can tell she doesn't believe me.

"The last summer I was here, I remember wanting to spend every second with you. Sure, at the time, I didn't realize it was a crush, not until I got back to school that year and everyone was talking about who had a crush on who."

"No way."

"It's the truth, and now here we are years later. I can't help but feel lucky to have you like this."

"Like what?"

"I don't know. You sort of feel like mine. We just had a bunch of friends over. I held your hand in front of them, and you let me. I guess I just really liked being able to do that, and I know we're teetering towards a relationship and we promised to keep this casual, so I can stop. Just say the word."

She knows what word I'm talking about too.

Her face pinches as she comes over to me, sitting on the end of my bed how she always does, and I love feeling the mattress dip because I always know it's her. Every hand against my face, every brush against my wrist, every time I find remnants of shimmery powder, I know it's her.

The other night, she was playing around with a makeup look while I rested, and when I woke up, she was talking to herself about whatever she was doing. I asked her to explain it to me instead, and she spent two hours going over every small and intricate detail of her process.

I wanted to ask her to explain everything to me in the future because hearing anything come from her lips when it's pointed toward me is my own version of heaven.

That's when I knew I was fucked. That's when I knew walking away from her was going to be difficult. Not only would I be leaving this house and all my childhood memories here, but I would be leaving her too. It's just a matter of when that happens.

"I wish we could stay frozen in time here," she whispers. "Because I would choose to do that with you, Theo. Every single time."

"Even after everything I've done?" The word everything feels like too little to describe what my life up here has been like. Not only did I almost die because I drank too much, but Daisy has been letting me lean on her since that night. She deserves better. She deserves me being better for her, no matter how long it takes.

"Just because you're a little broken, doesn't mean you don't deserve love. You've been through a lot, which is the understatement of the century, but you still deserve love."

"So have you, and yet here you are, still soft and open to love even though it hurt you before."

"I think you learn more about love from the people who don't love you," she scoffs as she starts to smile. "Because love didn't hurt me, he did. He weaponized my love for him, and that's not really love. It's ownership, and never again will I allow myself to be owned by someone just to try and make them love me."

"You deserve to be loved with no compromise. After all the tears and hard days, you are the most-deserving person I know to have a happy ever after."

"You're deserving of it too."

Neither of us are saying the true thing we want to say, but it hangs in the air as it stabs me in the chest.

You deserve to be loved by me forever, but that can't happen.

"Um, I'm going to shower and then I'll get into bed." She grabs her robe and heads for the bathroom. I hear the water turn on as I close my eyes. A little while later, I feel her arms wrap around me as I pretend to sleep. "Somehow, someday, things might work out for you, Theo West. And I better be the first person you call when that happens."

"You will be," I whisper back to her.

Chapter Thirty-Two

— BAD OMENS BY 5 SECONDS OF SUMMER

I'VE ONLY BEEN OPEN for half the day, and part of me didn't even want to come to work today because knowing Theo is home all by himself with a mild concussion still makes me nervous. What if he falls over and his phone isn't near him? What if he needs me and I'm not there?

I've probably checked in with him more times than I can count in the last five hours, but I'm finally closing up. Brooks is picking me up today. He also drove me into work after his lunch break because he's way too fucking nice. Theo practically begged me to go into the store today because he felt bad for putting my job on hold for him, and the only reason I agreed to a partial day here was because we had a shipment coming in this afternoon and I wasn't going to ask anyone to come and cover it for me.

Theo can't drive, and he didn't want me driving into town all by myself, so this is the best we came up with. Though, it has been a bit since something weird has happened. I've gotten no new texts, no notes, nothing that has made my stomach drop. It's been radio silence since Theo got hurt. I would like to think all this weird shit is behind me, but I know not to get my hopes up yet.

I told my parents about everything that has been going on. They finally had good enough service to call for more than ten minutes, and I practically sobbed into the phone about everything going on. They almost cancelled the rest of the trip to come home, but by the end of it, I had told them I was fine and the Madison family was here for me if I needed it.

My parents are already planning a cookout for them when they're back to thank them for all they've done and continue to do for us and the town.

I'm sorting through the last box, and Brooks already texted me he was on his way over, so when I hear the bell ring and someone comes into my shop, I assume it's him.

I was wrong. So fucking wrong.

Because the man who just walked in is not even close to how wonderful of a human Brooks is. In fact, he's quite the opposite. His three-piece gray suit, somewhat graying hair, and asshole-like smile reminds me of the first time I saw him. Except that time, I had stars in my eyes because I had never seen anyone like him before. Now, the stars have faded, and all I have left in my heart for him is hatred and sadness. Hatred because of what he did to me and the fact that I would have *never* done that to him. Sadness because I believed everything he said about me, everything he said to me. The sadness is more for me, though. I am sad for the girl who tried to love him into being faithful. I am sad for the version of myself who believed leaving Nettles would make me find the place I belonged. Sad for the girl who thought every word from his mouth was the truth, even when he was calling me names and telling me I was worthless.

How worthless can I be if he's come crawling back? How worthless am I if he spent all this time trying to find me?

"Hi, Daisy," my ex says as he walks into my boutique, his head moving from side-to-side as he surveys my store. "I love what you've done with the place."

I drop the makeup brush I had in my hand right back into the box I was sorting because all of a sudden, I can no longer feel the nerves attached to any part of my body. My breathing picks up. My heart rate thumps in my chest, and I cannot believe he's here. How is he here? Why is he here?

"Huh, you look a little bigger than you did last time I saw you," he snickers at me. "Maybe the lights of the conference room made you look thinner."

I will not cry in front of this man. I will not let him see that he gets this under my skin because he thrives off of that, and he has no power here. He's in my store. In my hometown. He doesn't get to have the upper hand.

"You still look like the same asshole I divorced."

"Ouch." His hand goes right to his chest. "Now where did that fire come from? You sound a lot different than you used to when you belonged to me."

When I belonged to him? Oh, yeah, he's definitely the one who has been messing with me. I have no proof besides that one sentence, but I can almost guarantee it was him.

"What the hell are you doing here?" I'm not going to entertain him any longer than I have to.

"Straight to the point, okay. Forgive me for wanting to catch up a little bit."

"You don't deserve to know anything about my life after you took everything from me." I shake my head and grab my phone from the table in case I need to call someone. Elliott is on call right now. He'd come running, I'm sure. "What are you doing here? You have about three seconds to answer before I throw you out of here and call the cops."

"Call the police?" He tilts his head at me. "I haven't even done anything. For all anyone knows, I am a paying customer here."

Well, that was a lot more than three seconds. "Get the hell out of my store."

The bell rings again, and in walks Brooks, his eyes focused on me as he looks between the two of us. "Daisy? You okay?"

I shake my head, my eyes still trained on my ex-husband and the space he's taking up. "You need to leave."

"I'm not leaving until we talk. We have some business matters to discuss."

"Get. Out." I'm actually really proud of myself. My voice hasn't started to shake yet. "I don't want to talk to you without my lawyer present."

"Daisy—"

Brooks interrupts him. "She told you to leave."

"If that's how it's going to be." He sets his business card on the counter. "I have a room at the hotel down the street. I'll be there until you agree to talk with me."

"That's not happening," I tell him.

"You can bring your lawyer if it will make you feel better."

God, he's such an ass. Always acting like he's the one taking the high road and he's done nothing wrong. I can't believe he's staying in town. Why now? Why is this the perfect time for whatever he wants to discuss?

"Okay, you've said what you needed to," Brooks says as he opens the door for Derek. "Time to go."

"You'd be smart to talk to me, Daisy. Don't make another mistake now."

"Oh, is that what you're calling our divorce?"

He only smiles as he leaves, the heavy stench of whatever cologne he's wearing now filling up the air in my boutique. My mask falls as soon as he leaves, and I can't breathe as Brooks comes up to me, his eyes searching my face.

"Breathe," he tells me. "Let's get you home."

I can only nod as he leads me to his car. The entire ride home is filled with a ringing in my ears and my heavy breathing, and Brooks doesn't bother asking me about anything I said to Derek. He just gets me home because he knows Theo will be able to help me more than he can.

Chapter Thirty-Three

— SOMETHING, SOMEHOW, SOMEDAY BY ROLE MODEL

I'M RELAXING IN THE living room when Daisy bursts into the house, tears streaming down her face as Brooks walks in behind her. It takes my three strides to reach her, enveloping her in my arms as she cries.

"Did something happen?" I ask, running my hands all over my girl to check she's okay. "What's wrong?"

"I'll leave you two," Brooks says to us. "I'm going to call Amara on my way home."

Daisy nods as her arms come around me, her head in my chest as Brooks takes one look at us before he leaves.

"Why is he calling his sister?" I look down at the girl in my arms, and instead of continuing to bombard her with questions, I just let her exist in my embrace. Physically she's okay, and that's all I need to know right now. The rest will come in time.

I scoop her legs into my arms, carrying her over to the couch, and when we sit down she nuzzles further into my chest, her hands fisting my shirt as if she can't bear to let me go.

"Ghost."

My heart sinks with one word. I always thought it took a lot more than something as simple as one word to break me, but after Tobias died, I learned it doesn't take much. That one word uttered from her lips makes my chest cave in, and I swear my heart stops beating.

"Really?"

She nods against my chest. "My ex-husband is in town."

"What?" I feel like I didn't hear her correctly, but I'd be lying if I hadn't memorized every word that comes out of her mouth. "He's here?"

Another nod.

"Did he fucking hurt you?"

"He doesn't have that power anymore," she says as she sits up and wipes a few tears from her face. "He wants to talk to me. He isn't leaving town until he does."

"Do you know what he wants?"

"With him, it could be anything, but he's been in town longer than he's made himself known. I think he's the one behind all of the weird stuff happening."

"How do you know?"

"I don't," she tells me. "I wish there was a way I could know for sure."

That gives me an idea. I know someone who is a little too good at getting information from places it feels impossible to do so. I guess I should give Nico a call. I swear he could find someone who doesn't want to be found. Suffice it to say he's in the right career.

I won't call him yet. Right now, all I care about is the girl in front of me.

I grab the box of tissues from the coffee table and set it on my chest between us.

"When he walked in, the first person I wanted to walk in after him was you. Towards the end of our relationship and into our divorce settlements, Derek always had this habit of making me feel unsafe. I was always cautious around him and every time I left those awful settlement meetings, I was always looking over my shoulder, waiting for him to corner me and say something to me without our lawyers present."

"I hate that he made you feel like that."

"You don't. You never have. Even when we were kids, the only time I remember looking over my shoulder at you was when you'd chase me around the yard and the two of us were laughing. I laugh a lot around you, and I feel good about myself around you. I don't know when it happened, but over the past few months you've been here, you've become a safe space for me."

"Don't give me all of the credit." I run my hand through her hair. "You put yourself first. You did that. I was just here for you and whatever you needed from me."

"I did it again," she whispers as I wipe another tear off of her face. "I fell hard and fast, and I didn't even try not to because it felt so easy being with you."

"Don't do that. Don't blame yourself because I fell just as in love with you as you did with me."

She sniffles as she shakes her head. "You're being serious?"

I nod. "Ghost."

"Well, it looks like we're on the same page."

"It seems so," I agree with her, neither of us wanting to say anything else. The morning has come on our never-ending evening together. It always comes. The sun will always rise. It's one of the only guarantees on the planet, and yet, I found myself hoping it would choose to never come just so I could spend eternity with this girl in front of me. "I finally realized why that practice date never happened between us."

"Why?"

"Because I never wanted to practice anything with you," I tell her. "I wanted the real thing. I didn't want a smoke screen between us. Part of me must have known that would have never been enough."

No amount of anything from her will ever be enough for me. I'm sure of that now. I've been chasing her ever since we were kids, and now that I've found her again, I know I'm going to have to let her go and find her a third time.

I *have* to get better, not even just for her, but for me.

"I don't want to watch you leave," she cries. "Not after all we've been through."

"This was always the plan, Daisy girl," I remind her, no matter how much my heart is being crushed. "I have to go back home to what's left of my family, and you have to deal with your ex-husband."

"I wish love was enough," she tells me. "But it never is, is it? Love is the base of everything, but as much as we want to think it can conquer all, it can't. It's not strong enough on its own."

"I don't want to love you like this," I whisper to her. "Who I am now is not even close to being good enough for what you deserve."

"Don't say that."

"It's true. I'm a drunk mess who can barely stay sober, and even though these last few months have been some of the best of my entire life, I want to be enough for you. I want to be able to handle myself better than I do now because I will never put you through anything like the night you drove me to the hospital again."

"And maybe some time by myself will do me some good. Maybe that's exactly what I need—some family and friend time while I fix whatever mess Derek brought with him."

"Right now just isn't our time for forever."

"Will it be like this forever or will another decade or two pass before things work out for us?"

I grab her neck with my hand and bring her forehead to mine. "It won't be forever. It won't."

She shakes her head at me. "You don't know that."

"I do," I beg. "Because I'm going to wait for you. Will you wait for me to become someone you deserve?"

Her sparkling eyes meet mine, more tears falling onto my shirt as this beautiful girl looks at me and nods. "I've waited for what feels like a lifetime for you, Theo. What's a little longer?"

She laughs through her tears and I can't help but smile. She believes in me enough to wait for me to come back to her, and that alone is going to carry me through the next few months or however long I'm away from her and this place.

"I promise it won't be total radio silence either." My hands cup her face and I run my thumb against her skin. "But I need to get better. Sober. For you."

"For yourself first," she reminds me. "And then you come back or I'll come to you and I will love you so loudly that all of these tears will turn into laughter as we look back on this in the future."

"I never meant to hurt you like this. If I could give you all of my love right now, I would, but I can't."

"I know," she smiles at me. "This is what has to happen for now."

"For now, not forever," I remind her.

The silence is deafening in this room as the two of us sit with our fate. I can't bear to look at her because if I do, I'm going to fall fully apart, and I can't or else I'll never be able to walk away.

"Can you do me a favor?" she whispers to me.

"Anything," I say as I grab her hand. "I'd do anything for you."

"Can you hold me until I fall asleep tonight? And can we have one last night with dinner, and do a puzzle? When tomorrow comes, Delilah can pick me up while you're still sleeping so you don't have to watch me leave and I don't have to watch you drive away. Is that okay?"

The thought of her not being in my arms when I wake up tomorrow kills me, but if this is how she wants it to be, then so be it. "You'll come back for all of your things after I'm gone?"

She nods. "Delilah can help me grab everything, and I'll stay with her until my parents are back in town and Derek is gone."

"Good." I tuck a piece of hair behind her ear. "I'm glad you have the people around you that you do. I can leave at least knowing you'll be safe."

"So, one last night?"

I press a kiss to her lips, wanting to savor the way she feels. My forehead falls against hers as the five words off of my lips break my heart into pieces. "One last night, Daisy girl."

Chapter Thirty-Four

— IN THE LIGHT BY THE LUMINEERS

My swollen eyes somehow make it open as I feel strong arms wrapped around me how they've been every night since I moved over here.

I know I should get up. I know I can't wake him because we promised last night that this is how it was going to be, but the selfish part of me wins as I take a few extra minutes and look at the man next to me in bed.

Never in my life have I felt so entranced by someone sleeping next to me, but as I sit here and think about Theo West and how drastically my life changed when I first knocked on his door, part of me wants to stay here forever.

I met him when we were kids, and then he left, only to come back decades later. He's the boy who pushed me on the swing set, and also the man who I could tell every terrifying thing to without fear of being laughed at. He's the boy who rode bikes with me when I was still figuring out training wheels, and he's the man who drove me to work when my car was out of commission.

Every minute I spend watching him sleep is the selfish part of my heart trying to memorize every part of him so I don't forget about the crook of his neck while he's gone, or the way his mustache flows on his face.

I can't lay here forever. We promised we would only have one more night, and Delilah is going to be here any minute because I texted her last night and told her to pick me up at exactly five thirty this morning. I don't know how long I've been laying here. It feels like it has only been seconds that I've been awake watching him breathe.

As soon as my phone buzzes on the side table, I know Delilah is here and I'm going to have to grab some of my things before I leave.

I allow myself three more seconds to be in his bed, in his house, in this place he'll no longer inhabit after I walk out of the door.

Three.

Two.

One.

I sigh as I slide out of bed, doing my best to not wake him up. I grab some random clothes and shove them into one of my small duffel bags. I grab my makeup bag and my hairbrush and all the other day-to-day things I might need before I take one last look at him.

I spot his camera, and before I can help it, I snap a quick photo of me as I scribble a note down and leave it on the pillow my head was lying on.

I wish it didn't have to be like this. I wish we could just move forward together, but we both need some time to figure ourselves out.

When I got back to Nettles, I swore I was going to focus on myself and not jump into another relationship where I fall too easily and everything goes to shit. That could still happen. I could be waiting forever for Theo. I won't know until he comes back but it feels different this time.

He'll get better. I'll spend some time by myself and learn more about who I am, and maybe when the timing is right one day, we'll make things work. Or maybe it will only work for a little and we'll go our separate ways again. I have no idea what could happen, but I'm starting to love that feeling. I can drive my own path because I have *nothing* holding me back.

I'm back home. I'm back in the place I love with friends that love me as much as I do them.

No matter how often I find myself grieving who I once was or the life I once lived with a person who was *so* wrong for me, love always shows up. I lost faith in love at one point in time, but it always came back. It always showed up when I needed it most. Every single time, without fail. I know it'll show up this time. I know it will always carry me through.

It comes in the form of Delilah bringing me coffee, or picking me up at the start of the morning and not asking why. It comes in the form of my parents playing my favorite songs that filter through the house. It comes in the form of the Madisons yelling at me whenever I ring the doorbell at their house because they consider me a part of their family, and family doesn't ring the doorbell, they just walk in.

And it comes in the form of walking away from someone you've fallen for because you both need some time to figure some things out. That's love—knowing when to walk away from someone no matter how much it might hurt. How did I ever give up on that? Why did I ever give up on it when it's been around me all of this time?

My phone buzzes again.

> **Delilah: Take your time. I'm out here when you're ready.**

With one final look around the room, I see the rise and fall of Theo's chest as I study him one final time, a single tear falling from my eyes as I think about the last few months he's inhibited my life here in Nettles.

"I'll wait for you, Theo. I promise. I've waited over a decade for you before, so whatever this next stint is has nothing on that."

And then I'm gone. The next thing I feel is Delilah's arm against my back, rubbing it as she leads me to the passenger side of her car, grabbing my bags from my hands as I regulate my emotions and cry it out. She drives me to her shop, doesn't even bother turning on the lights as she scoops some ice cream into a bowl, douses it in sprinkles, and hands it to me.

Neither of us says a word as I eat it, Delilah drinking coffee in front of me as she watches me for any signs of breaking, but I don't. I stay strong despite the tears I've already shed. This is for the better. This is what had to happen, and I know in my bones that our story isn't over yet.

Love is sitting and eating ice cream way too early in the day. Love is a cup of coffee split two ways. It's someone saying they've been where you are when you can't seem to find the words. It's my best friend smiling at me because she always knows just what I need.

I'll lose it again, I'm sure, but it will always exist in so many forms.

I ALREADY KNOW SHE'S gone before I open my eyes. I start to think maybe if I lay here forever and don't move that she'll come back and it will all have just been a terrible nightmare.

It's for the better, I remind myself. I need to get better. I need to get better for myself and for her because I need to come back and prove to her that she's worth fucking everything to me, even conquering my biggest fears.

I will not keep leaning on things that aren't healthy for me. I will not lean on her when things get too hard. I need to learn how to stand on my own two feet, even if it hurts leaving Nettles, this place I was lucky enough to call my home for a few months.

I open my eyes, the ghost of where she once laid still there in the form of a small note on the pillow, a piece of film right next to it.

```
I'm proud of you for finding another way to
climb the tree. Take care of yourself. Don't
        be a stranger, neighbor.
```

I take a deep breath, knowing there's no alcohol in the house for me to drink these feelings away and I'm not going to stop somewhere and buy any.

Because while I came here looking for a reason about why my brother sent me on this goose chase around the country, I happened to have found another reason in the form of a girl across the street. I want to make her proud. I want to be someone who is worthy of every single atom in her body.

She is the reason I want to find something else to lean on, and I never knew coming back here would bring me all of this, but as I start to pack up all of my things, I find myself already missing the community I had here, but knowing I can get it back one day when I'm better.

I've officially run out of road here in Vermont, and I thought that was going to terrify me, but I've discovered a brand new opening up ahead of me. Thankfully, I'm smart enough to take it.

Chapter Thirty-Five

— CHEMTRAILS BY LIZZY MCALPINE

THE SOUNDS OF HER laughter filter through my head as I think about what I left behind in Vermont. Since I got back home last week, I haven't stopped thinking about her, about how I want to get better for her, about how I don't deserve her yet, but someday I will. I miss her so much, but what we're doing is for the best. I repeat that to myself every time I want to rip my hair out.

I stare at the six envelopes in front of me, the last one still in the box I dug up from the yard, some dirt on my hands as I wonder what's in it.

I'll find out soon enough. I called Teags and Tristan back home today, and after spending a few days with my mom, I think my head is clear as it'll get. I think I'm ready to find out what waits for us all inside of these envelopes I've been hiding from them since I started on this journey.

Part of me will never understand how Tobias had the energy to do all of this and still take his own life at the end of it, but I'm going to have to live with that question unanswered. It made sense to him when he left these breadcrumbs for me, but I have to go through the rest of my life confused as to why he didn't mention he was struggling but felt the need to leave these for me.

I hear the front door open and I grab all the envelopes as I head downstairs. I'm surprised to see Teags and Tristan standing at the front door, but as soon as they see me, their faces light up. The last time I saw them both was when Dom hosted dinner for us all and those few days I was back here for Tobias's memorial. It's been longer than I intended, but now I'm back home until I figure out what's best for me.

Though, I already know what my future holds, and I might be terrified to take this next step, but I know it has to be done.

"It's been too long, brother," Tristan says as he brings me in for a hug.

"Sorry for staying in Vermont a little longer than I thought I would," I say to them.

"Well, it seems like you found what you were looking for," Teags says as she bumps me with her elbow. She's not much of a hugger, although, when I was back here before, she let me hug her. I think Dom is softening her up, or maybe her grief had a hand in that. I know my grief has changed me in ways I never thought it could, so it wouldn't surprise me if it happened to these two as well.

"In a way, I did," I tell them. "Can we head to the living room?"

"Oh, I've missed having you all home." My mother smiles as she leads us all over to the couch. I take a seat on the ottoman, the rest of them sit in front of me because they know I have a whole spiel to make. "Whenever you're ready, darling."

"You're making me nervous," is all Teags says as she gets comfortable. "Calling a family meeting at random is kind of terrifying, you know."

"I'm more curious about the envelopes," Tristan says, no doubt recognizing the familiarity of them.

"Let's hear what your brother has to say." Mom smiles as she gestures for me to speak.

"Thanks, Mom," I say as I poke at one of the envelopes. I don't know why this is so difficult for me. Part of me feels guilty for lying to them about my travels, but this was also *my* journey to go on. I think they'll understand that. I *hope* they will. "Um, so, obviously you all know Tobias sent me on the rest of his bucket list stops as he said in my first letter."

"First?" Tristan asks, his eyebrows pinched on his face.

I nod. "He led me around each stop. I got a new letter at each destination, either from a courier or hidden somewhere he knew I would find it. It sort of felt like he was leading me around each stop, and in every note he left a clue for me to find some other thing he had hidden."

"What?" my sister says as she leans forward, her elbows on her legs.

"And you kept this from us?" my brother wonders.

"He told me to," I say, taking a deep breath. "I was under strict instructions not to open any of the things he led me to at each stop until I found them all and was back home with you three."

"So, you waited for all of us to open these?" my mother asks, picking up the first envelope with a one marked on it. "I wouldn't have had the patience you did. These would have all been ripped to shreds if he had done this for me."

We all laugh because it's true. Our mother is brilliant at many things, but opening packages properly is not one of them. One of my favorite memories was one Christmas morning when my father wrapped this giant box and stuck it under the tree. It was for my mom. It turns out he had wrapped a pair of slippers in about fifteen different boxes, each decreasing in size as she opened the gift. It took her *so* long to get to the actual present, and the rest of us were laughing so hard at how ripped the boxes ended up being. I remember Tobias even spit out his chocolate milk because he was laughing so hard.

"What's this first one from?"

I hand it to my brother. "Pittsburgh. I found it outside of the baseball field he used to take us to."

"Can I?" he whispers as I nod, letting him open this one. He clearly left a piece for each of our family members, even our father. This has to be the one for Dad. He loved baseball just about as much as Tristan does.

He tears the envelope open, and out falls a small puzzle piece. The rest of us lean forward and look at it.

"It's your father," my mom says as she grabs it, holding it in her finger as she smiles. The picture looks familiar, but I can't quite place it.

"Where did you go next?"

I hand this one to my mother. "New York City."

"Where was this one hiding?" Teags asks me.

"The box office of a play on Broadway." I laugh under my breath. I remember that part of the trip fondly. I had to go up to a very specific person and say the stupid riddle Tobias left me. It felt like I was a spy in an action-thriller movie when they slid the envelope to me and smiled, not another word uttered as I left.

My mom rips the envelope open, and out falls another puzzle piece, this time a picture of her on it.

"Here." I hand Tristan the third one. Out falls a puzzle piece with his face on it. "This one was in the dugout at Summit. Well, buried a little behind it."

"I owe a lot to that field." Tristan smiles as a tear falls from his eye. "Wow, I was young in this photo."

"It looks so familiar," my sister utters the same thing I've been thinking. We've definitely seen this photo before.

"This one was in the basement," I say as I tear open the fourth one. Out falls a puzzle piece with Tobias's face on it.

"If I'm counting correctly, then yours is next," Teags points to me, and I also saw the order she mentioned. Oldest to youngest. Mine should be next, but when we rip open the next envelope, out falls a picture of my sister.

"Vermont was the last stop," I remind her. "I think he saved the best for last."

I dodge a swipe from my sister's hand as she smirks at me, her eyes rolling to the back of her head as she inspects her puzzle piece.

"Where did he take you for mine?" she wonders. I forgot she was in Arizona for the first parts of my adventure around the country, so she missed out on me coming home, staying for a few days, and then leaving again. Poor Tristan. He had to deal with the mess that was my life over these past three years.

"Charleston."

Her eyes sparkle with recognition as she takes the piece and holds it up to her chest. "My favorite record store."

"It was buried in an old record. One that you probably already have," I tell her. "I was going to buy it for you, but I figured if Tobias put it in there, it was probably one you two loved."

"You'd probably be right about that." She smiles at me, sniffling into the puzzle piece in her hands. "My collection is quite impressive, if I do say so myself."

"Open the last one," Tristan says as he leans against my mom's shoulder. "Tell us all about it."

"This clue had me stumped for a long time," I say, reminiscing about my time in Vermont. God, I spent so many sleepless and drunk nights trying to figure out what it fucking meant, only for a memory to float into my mind and make me realize. "It was buried in the backyard. I had been struggling with the clue he left me for a while, and being back at that house was harder than I anticipated."

"That's understandable," my mom says, her voice tight with emotion.

"But I remembered this memory of Tobias and I and it all fell into place," I rip the envelope open and out falls a piece with my face on it and another folded up paper. "We were all just kids in that house. It's all we had to be."

The four of us put all of the pieces together, and it all clicks into place once we see them all together. It's a family photo from our last summer in the Vermont house. I remembered the pieces of it because it's in a frame in the basement. My mom had it hanging up for the longest time after we left that summer, and once my father died, she took it down and stashed it in the basement with the rest of his things.

"Our last summer," my mom says. "Wow."

"I don't remember much about that summer," Teags says, her eyes welling up with tears as she looks at us.

"I have plenty of stories for you." Mom grabs her hand. "Come over and I'll tell you as many as you want to hear. That goes for all of you."

"What does the letter say?" Tristan wonders as I pick it up.

"I can read it out loud," I say as I unfold it.

Dear everyone,

I can almost see the look on all of your faces as you match the puzzle pieces together. I know how confused you must be, so let me explain.

This trip I sent our dear brother on was one final trip down memory lane, not just for him, but for all of us, me included. I know you probably have a lot of unanswered questions about why I did what I did, but I don't really have an answer for you either. My brain has always been so... loud. That's the best word I can use to describe it, and I've been searching for ways to quiet it, but nothing has really worked. I'm sorry it ended up this way. It wasn't the fault of any of you. I hope you know that.

All I wanted to remember a piece of you all as I wandered around the places I went, and yes, even the basement. Right under your noses, and I bet you all are mad at me for that, and that's your right. I thought driving down memory lane might even help me. Maybe it would remind me of some of the things I'd be missing, but it didn't. I didn't feel any different after taking this journey myself.

But I wanted you all to have a piece of me even though I'm gone. I know a puzzle piece is nothing close to having me, and fuck, maybe I could fight this a little longer? Maybe I could, right? I mean, I've tried. I've done all that I can. This trip was the one thing I thought might actually help, and fuck, it hasn't. It hasn't helped and I'm sorry. I'm sorry it had to end this way because I tried. Really, I tried to get better. I tried to remind myself of why I shouldn't do this, but it hasn't worked. I thought it would. I thought it might fix me, or give me a reason why I should tell you all what I'm feeling, but I don't see how that could help. I don't see how anything could help, and fuck, I wish I did. I'd do anything to feel that, but I don't.

Dad, I'll see you soon.

Mom, I'll say hi to Dad for you. I'll tell him how much you miss him.

Tristan, I'll always look up to you and all you taught me growing up.

Theo, I'll always let you lean on me when you need it.

Teags, I'll always play the music for you to hear.

I love you all, and I'm sorry. Fuck, I am so sorry. I wish there was something I could do, or have done, I guess. I tried. Let it be known to you all that I tried to get better. To be better. To feel better, but I can't feel like this forever. I can't.

I couldn't find a reason, and I'm sorry. I hope you all can forgive me someday.

Forever,

Tobias

P.S. The back of the puzzle is heat sensitive...

My eyes pinch together as I look around blurrily at my family.

I hear the *click* of something as Teags puts her lighter up to the puzzle.

"We didn't even flip it yet," I say to her.

"Okay, so do it!" she yells at me, her tears falling from her eyes as she picks at the end of her hair.

Tristan is shaking his head, his fingers wiping his eyes. "We should not have an open flame this close to furniture."

"Just be careful," my mom says as she laughs through her sobs.

"I will." Teags puts her lighter closer to the pieces, and just as she waves it around, another picture starts to appear. Suddenly, the four of us at Tristan's high school graduation appear, and I feel more tears start to come.

It looks like there's a four drawn on whatever picture he must have uploaded.

"I need a minute," our mom says as she heads for the half-bathroom near our living room.

"Four," Tristan says as he breaks the silence of us all sitting here. "Four of us. No matter what."

"In every life," Teags whispers.

"I'm sorry I kept this all from all of you."

They both shake their heads at me.

"It's okay. God knows I've kept worse things from you." Teags cracks a laugh. "I can't believe he was struggling so much and I didn't see it."

"None of us did," I echo her sentiments. This last letter really showed it. He was torn between himself. There are tear stains on the paper, and a few places are even scribbled out from him misspelling certain words or trying to figure out what he wanted to say. It was hard reading it, but I can't imagine living in that. I can't imagine him reaching the final road of his journey only to have lost hope in himself and his life. In a way, he sent me on this journey and we were both looking for the same thing—a reason. Except I was looking for the reason he did what he did, and he was looking for a reason not to.

"Yeah, I'll say," Tristan smirks as he wipes a stray tear. "I can't believe it's been over three years now."

"It feels like it was yesterday I got the call," Teags says. "How have you all been doing since the memorial?"

"I almost died," comes out of my mouth before I can stop it. This isn't how I wanted to tell them about my difficulties, but they're here now. I might as well.

"What?"

"You're kidding, right?" Teags asks me.

"No," I say as I feel more emotions bubbling up. "Do you remember the first time I came home after you called us?"

"Yeah," my sister says. "You were drunk off of your mind."

"I thought you had it under control after all this time," my brother asks me, his eyes piercing mine.

I shake my head. "I got better at hiding it. I almost died in Vermont, and if it wasn't for Daisy, I might not be here right now."

"Daisy? The girl across the street you used to chase around the yard? That Daisy?"

"Mhm."

"What happened?" Teags asks, steering the conversation back on track. I can see her hands find the ends of her hair, her leg starting to shake as she thinks about attending another funeral. She told us months ago that she didn't want to sit in the front row again, and I just told her that might have happened again.

"I almost drank myself to death. I knew it was bad when I saw Tobias standing in front of me before I passed out. She found me in the yard and drove me to the hospital." I can't help the tears that keep coming. "When I struggled before, Tobias was my crutch. He was the person I called when I was having a hard time figuring things out. After he died, I kind of spun out of control. I had nothing to lean on, nothing to hold me up, so I found something that did the trick."

"Why didn't you lean on me?" my brother asks, his tone sharper than it was before as he stands and paces in the living room. "Fuck, why didn't either of you! I know I've been overbearing and acting like a total fucking helicopter of a brother, but you could have come to me."

"Can I be honest?" He nods. "Alcohol was easier. It was easier drowning out my emotions than living in them. I've learned better. I've been trying to do better, but the itch to drink is still there." Another few tears fall. "I have a really bad problem, and I need you to help me fix it."

"Anything for you," Tristan says to me as he pulls me in for a hug.

"What do you need from us?" my sister asks me.

"I was hoping you would ask me that." I smile at them. I explain all of the research I've been doing the past few days, and by the time our mom comes out from the bathroom, we've found a better path forward for me. No longer am I running out of road, but now, I've found a new one all together, and I can't see the end of it yet, but I can see the beginning.

And that's enough for me.

Chapter Thirty-Six

— **PENTHOUSE BY KELSEA BALLERINI**

"Wow, you really weren't kidding when you said—"

"Sit down," I say to my ex-husband as he waltzes into the conference room at the Nettles town hall late, like always. "This conversation is going to be short and to the point. You have about fifteen minutes before I get up and walk out of here."

My lawyer starts the countdown, and Derek looks at me as if this is the first time he's met me and he's ready to put on a show. It reminds me of the beginning of us. He would always look at me as if I was the only person on the planet, and only later did I realize he was flattering me so he could lure me in and trap me how he did.

"Oh, so that's how it's going to be?" He sits down, a snarky smile on his face, as his lawyer sits next to him. I'm having flashbacks to that very first discussion after I served him with divorce papers and he tried to sue me. I didn't say a word the entire first meeting we had. He just fought with my lawyer, his lawyer intervening when things got heated, and I cried silently as I barely looked the man I still loved in the eye.

By the end of all of it, I had maybe said a total of two-hundred words. Not this time. He came to me, and I won't let him silence me anymore.

"Clock is ticking," I remind him and he falters into speaking.

"I want you back," is all he says as he lays his hands on the table.

I swear I misheard him. "You what?"

"I want to try again." He smiles at me, but I'm seeing straight through him.

"No."

"Oh, come on, Dais." He rolls his eyes at me. "Don't you miss what we had?"

"What we had? Are you talking about the part where you manipulated me into signing a pre-nup so you could take half of my livelihood when I found out you were cheating on me? Or what about the part where I walked in on you in *our* bed fucking other women I had worked with? Which part specifically do you miss?"

"Don't do that." He shakes his head at me.

"The only thing you miss is being able to control someone. Well guess what, I'm not letting you do that to me anymore. I got out. I escaped, so I guess I should thank you for being the worst husband on the planet because you saved me a lot of years of my life by showing your cards earlier than you planned."

The clock keeps ticking, only a few minutes left on it as I try to steady my breathing. I've never been so vocal in front of him before, but shit, it feels really fucking good.

"I need the recipes."

And there it is. "Need is a very strong word. You *want* them."

"Fuck, Daisy," he says as he stands, pacing around the conference room. "Of course I do. Do you realize how much money we could have made together? Then you had to go and ruin it."

"You did that when you cheated on me," I remind him. "And you will *never* get them."

"I swear to—"

"Sit down," is all my lawyer says as Derek points his finger at me. "That is her intellectual property, and she has ownership of it. So, don't even try to argue over that or perhaps we should show certain camera footage to a judge and get Daisy an order of protection against you."

His face turns white, all of the color draining as he realizes I have proof that he fucked with my house, my car, and everything else that happened in Nettles. I got a letter a few weeks ago with a small package. I knew it came from Theo, but the letter was signed from some guy named Nico who owns a security company. He said Theo asked for a favor and he tracked down the footage we needed and traced a conversation from Derek to a few guys—the ones who were hired to break into my house and beat up Theo. He said he had a lot of fun doing it, and he would be in touch to install a new security system for me at some point.

I have no idea who this guy is, but if Theo knows him, then I trust him.

"You've got to be kidding me." He slumps in his chair as my lawyer turns his computer to me, showing me an article that just broke.

"Oh my gosh," I say as I start to laugh. "This is why you're trying to get me back?"

His face pinches since this story just broke and he hasn't seen it yet.

"You got two models pregnant? Congrats, you're on the front page like you always wanted." I turn the laptop and he immediately looks away from it. "Yet again, you run from the vows and responsibilities you have because you're a coward, Derek. A coward who runs from person to person with no genuine relationships. All you look for in a person is how you can exploit them, and I'm glad I never understood that about you."

"You fucking bitch," he says under his breath.

"What was that?"

"You're a bitch."

"You're the one running back to me and tracking me down because you can't handle the responsibilities of becoming a father. What does that make you? Maybe the smallest man on the fucking planet?"

He looks at his lawyer. "We're out of here."

"Good." I smile as I stand up. "And if you ever come back here again, I will file a restraining order against you." My lawyer slides a folder over to them as they stand. "And Derek?"

"Hm?" He turns back, his smile wiped off of his face.

"I truly hope you do the right thing."

He scoffs as he leaves, his shitty cologne following with him, and I sigh heavily as I slump into the chair.

"Wow, fifteen minutes on the dot," my lawyer says to me.

"Impressive," I agree.

"Honey, I'm home," I say as I open the door to Delilah's apartment and all of the lights are off. "Del?"

"Surprise!" a bunch of voices say to me as I drop my purse to the ground.

"Oh my," I say as I catch my breath. Delilah, Eloise, and Brooks stand in front of me, a giant cake with candles on it as I get further into the apartment. "It's not my birthday for another month, so what is this for?"

"We heard Derek left town," Delilah shrieks with excitement. "Good riddance to him and yay for new beginnings!"

"Word really travels fast." I smile as I hug them all. "God, I feel so much lighter now. I'm so glad it's over."

"I swear it felt like ages that he was looming around here, but I'm glad you took some time for yourself. That bastard could wait, and that's exactly what he did."

I can't help but laugh. After Theo left, I gave myself some time to get my head on straight. Even though that meant delaying the conversation with Derek, I knew it was what I needed. Delilah and I went full sleepover mode since my parents are still gone, and even though I feel like a nuisance, it's been really fun living with her for the last few months.

"I'm proud of you," Brooks says as he brings me in for a hug. "It was hard seeing you mope around here all sad."

"Oh, I'm sorry," I say as I tilt my head at him. "Next time I get divorced, I'll make sure to bounce back a lot quicker!"

"Ignore him," Eloise says. "If I recall, before I came back, you were doing lots of similar moping."

He just shrugs as Delilah shoves the cake in my face.

"Blow out the candles and make a wish!"

I smile as I take a deep breath, filling my lungs with the warm air hitting my face as I think about my wish.

Brown eyes that remind me of the leaves falling from a tree. A smile that could rip my chest to pieces.

Then I blow them out.

"What did you wish for?" Eloise asks me as Delilah cuts the cake.

"I can't tell you." I kick off my shoes as I get comfortable on the chairs around Delilah's table. "Then my wish wouldn't come true."

"She obviously wished for her boy to come back," Brooks says before Delilah smacks him.

"You all know you can talk about him, right? It's not some do-not-mention topic around me." *No matter how much I worry about him forgetting about me.*

"Have you heard from him since he left?" Eloise asks me as I bite into the cake Delilah cut for me.

I shake my head.

"Nothing?" Brooks asks me.

"Nothing besides that favor from his friend," I tell them. "But I'm not worrying about that right now. The next few months are dedicated to me getting my spark back."

"We will get it back, girl," my best friend says. "I see bright things ahead."

"Did you decide on the first step of your plan yet?"

I can only laugh. The other day we were all at Delilah's eating ice cream and I made this grand declaration that I was going to create a list of things to do to get my spark back. I haven't even made the list yet, but maybe I should actually do that. At the time, I was joking, but now it feels like a good idea.

"I haven't, but I don't think it will be too exhaustive of a list."

"You could change your hairstyle up, get a tattoo, or maybe get *really* into yoga." Delilah smiles as she starts to list out all these things.

"I could." I laugh with her, and after the anxiety I felt this morning walking into the conference room, the end of the day has made it all worth it. Because being surrounded by good people, good food, and even better energy than this morning has already started to recharge my batteries. In fact, my ultimate form of self-care is spending time with people who feel like a balm to my soul.

When I came back here, I never imagined it would be like this. Sure, I'm still struggling with a lot of internal things, and my life is still a mess in more ways than one, but for a few hours tonight, I feel warmth seeping into this apartment and surrounding us all.

And for these few hours, that is enough for me.

Chapter Thirty-Seven

— **WORDS BY GREGORY ALAN ISAKOV**

My dearest Daisy,

I'm not even sure how to start this. I want to update you about all of the things I've been doing and going through, but that almost feels too personal for a note. But then again, this is the only way I can communicate in and out of here. No phones are allowed in rehab during the detox stage, and probably for the rest of the time I'm in here since it feels good to not be attached to it, so this is all you'll get for a bit. I'm finally doing the steps to get better, and honestly, this was the best decision I've made since I came back to Pennsylvania. This won't fix me overnight, but it will help me in the long run. I'm hopeful of that.

I'm sort of nervous, I guess you could say? Writing all of my thoughts down and sending them off to you feels like I'm cutting a piece of myself open and dripping it onto the paper. I don't know how to do this. I'm not sure if I'm going to make any sense, but here goes nothing.

I opened the envelopes from Tobias. It was... emotional. I did it with my family as we sat around the couch of the home I grew up in and we all cried as we read the final note Tobias buried in the yard. He left us all a puzzle piece. You knew Tobias. You knew puzzles were sort of his thing, I guess, and he left us all a piece, including one for himself and my father. Six pieces for the six of us that once existed. His last letter was brutal, if I can be honest. We could all feel his inner turmoil, the back and forth of him wishing he could get better but knowing nothing he had done had worked. After that moment, I told my siblings about what happened to me in Nettles. I told them everything and they agreed that I needed help.

Now, I'm here at this fancy place hours away from home. Tristan paid for it. I was going to check myself in somewhere, but of course, he looked over my research and chose the best one possible. I love my brother, but this is just another thing I'm going to have to pay him back for. He told me the only thing he wanted to be paid back with was me being healthy and learning to cope with better ways. I told him I would do what I can.

There's this one thing my sister said to me when she dropped me off that has stuck with me. She gave me a hug and she whispered to me, "You do this and bring my brother back." I didn't really understand what she had meant, but the more I think about it, the more I'm reminded of the last little note you left me on our last night together.

I'm learning different ways to climb this tree of life I've been given. I mean, shit, after all of the alcohol was purged from my system, things started to feel more clear to me. I feel better, I guess. I'm learning to lean with others toward recovery, not on others or other things that are unhealthy for me. I guess you could say I'm on step four of this process. It's a slow and steady climb, at least for me. I'm taking a fearless and moral inventory of myself, and it's helped me realize a lot of things.

One being how I cannot believe you stayed by my side after everything I put you through in Vermont. You kissed me, fell for me, and even though I'm the worst person on earth, you still saw something in me that I didn't see in myself.

See every time I chose to drink rather than anything else, I was giving up everything I had for this one thing—alcohol. I still can't for the life of me figure out why I kept choosing that one thing over everything else. I still can't figure out why I have this issue of standing on my own two feet, but at least now, I'm trying to figure out a different way to climb the tree. I used to think in order to love me, you also had to suffer me and the drinking problem I had. I thought those two things went together, but now I'm sure they don't. You loved me while you accepted all my imperfections and flaws, something I never thought was possible. You proved me wrong.

But I hate that I chose drinking over you. I hate that I chose it over grieving my brother properly. I hate that I chose it over talking to my family about why I feel how I do, but I'm learning. I'm growing. I'm trying to do better, and I guess all I really wanted you to know is that I'm trying to do better so I can see you again. It's all I think about really, is you. I remember your laughter and the freckles on your face. I remember your touch in the mornings and the way you smirked when I kissed that spot on your collarbone that you loved so much. All of these things about you have kept me going these last few weeks, so I guess I owe you a thanks.

Thanks for being my reason, Daisy girl.

Feel free to write to me at this address. It'll get to me after a bunch of screening and people looking through my mail, but I'll see it. If it's too soon, or you don't want to talk to me quite yet, that's fine too. I told you to wait for me, and I can do the same for you whenever you choose to write back.

Theo

PS. I hope Nico was able to help you. I gave him the information and he said he would get it all over to you before I left. He's a friend of mine, and I figured it might move things along for you in Nettles. Sorry if I overstepped.

THEO,

I have to say, seeing your name on an envelope has been the highlight of my week.

Nettles has been quiet without you, and I've hated not speaking with you, but I know you're doing everything you can to get better. I'm really proud of you, you know. I wasn't sure if I had said that. In fact, it kept me up those first few nights because I couldn't remember if I had said it or not. Delilah kept telling me I probably had, but I was so unsure of myself. So, here's me correcting my mistake. I am so proud of you for trying your best.

I don't really have many updates for you besides everything wrapping up with my ex-husband. He officially left town and I no longer have to deal with him anymore. I stood up to him in front of our lawyers. I wish you could have seen me. Sure, I was still terrified and my voice was a little shaky at first, but I stood my ground and honestly? It felt really freaking good.

Besides that, I don't really have much for you. Typical small town gossip. Eloise and Brooks seem to be really hitting their stride as a married couple. Delilah is still married to her job, and my parents come home tomorrow, so I'm excited to see them. I'm currently in the middle of crocheting some coasters for them, but they haven't really turned out how I wanted them to. They're a little lopsided, but I think they can still be functional? I guess I'll just have to try them out before they get home.

I've been watching way too many movies at Delilah's. We keep watching our favorites, mostly Hello, Goodbye on repeat. That's one of our favorites. I swear it gets better every time. I'm sure you haven't seen that one, but in the future, I can't wait to watch all of my favorite movies with you. I wonder what yours are. I hate that I don't know. I hate that I didn't ever ask you.

I'm really proud of you.

I know how difficult all of this must be for you. I can't imagine going through any of what you did, but I never thought you leaned on me. I always thought it was us against your addiction, not you alone fighting that. It was always two versus one. I will always be on your side, Theo, at least as long as you'll let me be. I know I'm still working through some things, but that will never change. And honestly? I haven't felt this good in a long time. Being with you sort of felt colorful. The past few years, everything had dimmed, as if a cloud was covering every aspect of my life. I knew that, too, that's the sad thing. I knew what I had felt like and how I looked to the people around me.

When you filtered back into my life that day you saw me at the hotel, it had felt like some color had seeped back in. Seeing you again, this boy from my childhood in front of me, felt like I had connected back with the joy I once had as a kid. It's as if—now stay with me here—all of the saturation in my eyes had been turned up. (I figured you would like that. I'm not even sure I used that right, but you're into cameras and stuff, so I figured I would try to make a joke? Did it work? Are you laughing? I'm going to imagine you're laughing, and I'm going to imagine you're clutching your chest how you do when you laugh so hard you can't breathe.)

That's all I have for this letter, I guess. I miss feeling your arms around me. I miss you so very much, but this time will be good for the both of us. If I have to miss you for a few months or however long, it will be worth it. I know it will be. This time away is just how it has to be, and I can live with that no matter how much I miss you right now.

(Sorry for the tear drops. I promise these are proud tears on this paper for you. I may be learning how to love myself and how to be alone but not really alone right now, but the one thing that will never change about me is how emotional I am.)

I'll split my coffee into three cups tomorrow. One for me, one for you, and one for Tobias. Do you guys like cream or sugar or do you do it straight? I guess I'll just do whatever feels right.

Keep doing your best, Theo. Keep climbing this tree.

Love,

Daisy-like-the-flower.

PS. Yes I got the stuff from Nico. You didn't overstep. You helped a lot. Even from afar you're still looking out for me. Thank you.

November

Happy Thanksgiving, Daisy girl.

This letter will probably get to you a few days after Thanksgiving, but I wanted you to know I was thinking about you on a day like today. My family has this tradition where we go around the table and say one thing we're thankful for before we eat. It's something we've always done, even after my Dad died. Then it sort of spread as our family grew when Tristan brought Livvy home for the first time. Now, Liv and her sister, Bree, are involved in our tradition. I have a feeling we're going to need a bigger table at some point with all of the partners and family we've grown into.

You'll love Liv and Bree. Liv is married to Tristan, and Bree has a partner named Vince, who is a little scary at first, but once you get to know him, he's sweet. They have an adorable dog named Nellie that I can't wait to introduce you to. She will lick your entire face and bring you her favorite toy, though. I hope that's okay.

And of course, my sister is now dating one of Tristan's friends. That was a big surprise to me when I went home, but everything seemed okay, at least when I saw everyone at home when I left Nettles the first time.

I'm really excited to introduce you to the people I'm lucky to call my family. It felt like I had seen a small glimpse into yours up in Vermont, and once we've figured everything out, I know you'll fit right in. My sister and the other girls will absolutely adore you. They're a close bunch, but don't let that deter you. They're some of the kindest people I've ever met, and you obviously know Teags already a little bit from way back when.

I guess part of me is nervous to write all of this down in case something has changed with you up in Vermont. How are things going? Are you enjoying your newfound self? Are you still thinking about me as much as I am you? I guess I'm just a little scared you won't like the new me. I still don't understand how you liked the old me, but in a way, I'm still me, just learning healthier coping methods. I don't really know what I'm saying. Maybe I should stop writing and just leave you be?

Or maybe I just need to go to sleep. It is pretty late, and this place has been kicking my butt. I've been working out every single day this week, and part of me hates that it's helping to make me feel better.

The whole point of this letter was really to say that even though I'm not around the table this year, I still have something to be thankful for. You.

I'm thankful that despite everything we've been through, you still seem to tolerate me and want to have a life with me.

I hope you've found some things to be thankful for this year despite everything.

Love,
Theo

Theo,

Well, you're right. It is way past Thanksgiving by the time I'm writing this, but in the spirit of staying on theme, I am also thankful for you this year. I'm thankful for you and for new experiences and for walks around the pond in Nettles. I'm thankful for all the little things you and I did together this year. The walks, the adventures where I would watch you take pictures, amongst other things.

That tradition sounds beautiful. I can't wait to be around that table with you and your family one day, and I'll admit, I'm really excited to meet your siblings again and everyone you've talked about. I loved showing you a piece of my family life here, and all I've been doing lately besides working at the store and hanging out with Delilah is trying out new makeup looks. I have my artistic spark back, thanks to you and the people around me. A few months ago, all I felt was stagnant and I had no energy to even attempt creating new looks like I used to in the middle of the night or after work.

Lately, all I've done is play around with colors and patterns. I can send you some photos, if you want to see them. It's hard to explain them through words, and I know I taught you some things, but I don't think they would make a lick of sense written down.

I'm glad you're doing better. That's all I really wanted for you, and yes, to answer your question, I am enjoying my newfound self, though she's pretty similar to my old self.

Delilah and Fallon are helping me feel more assured in my decisions and emotions. I've also funneled a lot of energy into makeup looks and trying to express myself that way. It helped more than I hoped. I got a little more into crocheting and I've started to slowly master it. I'm really leaning into my grandma hobbies, *if you can't tell. Crocheting, going on walks, coloring books, the whole nine yards, but the one thing that hasn't changed is you and how you fit into my life. I can't wait to see you again, and however much time you need is fine by me. Like I said before, I'll be ready whenever you are. Nothing about us has changed, I promise.*

I hope the holidays treat you well. I'll be spending mine with my parents, and all of us are going to do a secret Santa sort of thing. I have Brooks, and I really don't know what to get a guy who has everything he's ever wanted. Seriously, you should see his face most of the time. I've never seen him smiling so much, but the guy is whipped for his wife. It's adorable, but it makes shopping for a gift for him nearly impossible. If you have any suggestions, I'm open to them.

I know I've said it a thousand times, but I really am so proud of you. You should be proud of yourself too.

Love,
Dais

Chapter Thirty-Eight

— WHITE WINTER HYMNAL BY FLEET FOXES

As I BREATHE IN the cold morning air, I find myself at peace for the first time in a while.

My camera goes up to my face as I spot a few animals on the same branch of a tree I'm near, and my lens captures it in a moment, the next, they're gone, all dispersed into the forest I'm standing in.

It's hard to believe this place is only a short drive away from my house, and I rub my hands together to try and gain the tiniest bit of warmth during this chill in the air. Winter is in full swing around here, and the holidays have mostly passed. I'm grateful I was able to spend at least one holiday this year with my family, but unfortunately, it wasn't the one I wanted.

Thanksgiving is a West family staple holiday. We prefer it over Christmas with all of the traditions we have now, and I missed it because I was in rehab. And now, it's Christmas Eve and I'm out taking photos for work. Thankfully, I still *have* a job after everything I've been through this year. I thought at one point I was going to get fired or fucked over because I was drinking so much. I don't know why Lucas hasn't turned me in or let me go by this point, but he must see something in me and my photos, even though my process is so weird.

I take another breath, the cloud of fog in front of my face as I spot a small, half-dead nettles plant in front of me. I didn't even know they survived the winter. Before I can stop myself, I snag a few pictures of it.

I can't help it reminds me of the girl with platinum hair; her smile filters into my brain as I stare at it. Nettles, a plant that can sting and gets defensive, but also a plant that survives. It reminds me of myself, of Daisy, of people, really.

We survive. We do what we have to, but we also lay softly on the ground when we have no further place to fall. Humans hurt, and sting when we're angry or upset. Some of us are painfully existing on the planet, doing whatever we can to get through the day without stinging someone, yet sometimes, we're still and we get to exist. I've stung people who have drifted too close to me. It's a fact of life. It will happen no matter how hard you try it not to. You will hurt people, and others will hurt you, but you also have to choose to let people in. You have to choose who you let lie next to you on the ground when you can't bear to get up, and thankfully, I have people in my life that will do that for me.

I take a few more pictures of it, quietly traipsing around the path I'm on and snagging a few more shots before my fingers and hands start to go numb. I head back to my car, my childhood home not too far from here as I see cars lining the driveway.

Did everyone else come over early or am I late coming back?

I look down at my watch and it is a little after lunch, but I thought we were all doing dinner. I grab my camera bag and head inside, a strong cranberry scent hitting my nose as I walk in, the warmth already helping my circulation to come back.

I drop my keys into the small table by the door, a half-dozen or so copies of the magazine's latest issue on the shelf beneath it. I grab one. I can't help it. No matter how many times I swiped through the digital copy Lucas sent me, I'll still always love holding my work in my hands. There's a ton of pictures from Vermont that I took and he developed into something astonishing. There's even a forward from me in the beginning that Livvy helped me write. It was so hard for me to articulate what Vermont means to me, and she kindly helped me get all of my thoughts down without me sounding like an idiot.

I flip to the last page of the magazine, two cups of coffee staring back at me as I reread the small note on this final page.

One for you and one for me. Just like always, brother.

"That picture is my favorite." Livvy's voice startles me as I smack it closed. "I'm sorry. I thought you heard me say hi."

"I didn't, but it's good to see you, sis." I wrap her in a hug as she steals the magazine from me.

"You too." She looks at me, her eyes shining as a smile blooms from her face. "You look a lot better. We're really proud of you, Tristan and I. Well, and everyone, of course."

"Thanks." I chuckle as I think about what I put everyone through these past few months. Every single person in my family and surrounding life got letters from me while I was in rehab. It was part of the steps to getting better—I can't remember which one—and it was the most honest I've ever been to the people around me. It was terrifying and vulnerable, but it helped get it all out there. Nothing was hidden anymore, and that helped my slate to wipe clean for the actual work to begin.

"I find myself flipping through this a lot." She smiles as she opens it. "Tristan keeps one on our side table and sometimes while I wait for him to wake up, I flip through it. I love all the photos you chose. They're all very intentional."

"It's my favorite project I've ever worked on," I say as I slide in next to her, looking at all of the pictures of the place that still feels like home.

Since Tobias died, I've had a really complicated relationship with home. Pennsylvania felt like this trap knowing he wasn't here when I got back from traveling or doing whatever I was doing after college. Everywhere I went, I was a stranger passing through, waiting for somewhere to feel like a place I could relax and make my own. Vermont was the first place I felt that way, and it's all because of my brother that I went back to Nettles. I got to relive moments of my childhood that I had forgotten about. I got to see people I had forgotten. I got to unearth things that were buried, feelings and physical items alike.

For him, the end of the line was in Vermont. For Tobias, Vermont was the last place he couldn't find a reason.

But for me, it's where I found mine. It's where I first felt like I belonged. For me, Vermont is the place that I loved as a kid and rediscovered as an adult.

"I miss that place a lot," I whisper to Liv.

"I know you do," she smiles at me. "You know how I know that?"

"Hm?"

She flips a few pages before she points at a small picture of a daisy in one of the corners of the page, right next to the pond I walked around almost every morning in Nettles. The biggest photo on that page is of a tree, one that looks like it has multiple avenues to climb. That page was for her and I knew it the moment I sent my film to Lucas and told him negatives thirty-three through thirty-six had to be on the same page.

Nettles may feel like home to me, but so does she.

"Tristan told me about her from when you all were kids."

"Of course he did," I say as I set my camera bag down and head for the living room, feeling Liv following me. I was going to talk to her about this later, but I guess now is as good of a time as any. "Can you two psychos join me on the stairs?"

My sister looks at me, rolls her eyes, and grabs her best friend, the two of them heading for Liv and I as I move to the stairs.

I wave to the rest of my family since I just got home, and my mom steals a hug from me as she goes back to cooking with Vince in the kitchen. I tip my head at Tristan and Dom in the living room, and I'll make a proper hello to those two once I'm done having this chat with the girls. Nellie, Vince's dog, should be around here somewhere, but she could be outside chasing the squirrels.

"I feel like I should be nervous," my sister says as she sits below me on the stairs.

"I'm excited," Bree says as she takes a sip from her mug. "I've been *waiting* for this conversation to happen."

"Don't scare him away," Livvy whispers to her.

"Okay, what is going on?" I wonder. There's no way they know what I'm about to say, is there?

"We're just a little excited," Liv says.

"Oh, come on, brother," Teags rolls her eyes at me. "You're about as see through as a window."

I throw my hands up. "What the hell does that mean?"

"It means that this is obviously the conversation where you ask us, the women of the family, to help you get your girl." Bree pats her hands together as she smiles at me.

I can only stare at them. How in the world did they guess what I was going to say?

"We already have a few ideas." Livvy smiles at me as she pulls out a post-it note.

"Are you kidding me?" I run a hand through my hair. "Am I that obvious?"

"Have you maybe seen yourself since you've been out of rehab?" Teags tilts her head at me. "Well, allow me to elaborate. It looks a lot like this."

My sister attempts some extravagant scene, to what looks like her writing very aggressively on or in something as she fluffs her hair and proceeds to take pictures of everything.

"Okay, that's enough," I say as I steal her fake pen and camera from her. "You're an ass."

"Yeah, but I'm your sister, and you love me."

"Is that really what I look like?" I ask Liv and Bree, and when I'm met with kind eyes and silence, I have my answer. "Okay, maybe I have been a little sad and mopey, but at least I'm not drinking anymore."

"And we're very proud of you," Bree smiles at me.

"How many days has it been now?" Liv asks.

"One hundred and fifteen." I smile, a proud feeling washing over me. I haven't even had the urge to drink. I know it will be back when things get tough again, but this time, I know a better way out than the bottom of a bottle.

"Hell yeah," my sister says.

"Thanks." I smile, but my head floats back to my girl. "But what do I do about Daisy? I told her to wait for me, and we've talked a little bit, but I'm so fucking bad at this. What if I didn't let her move on? What if—"

"I'm going to stop you right there," Bree says. "When was the last time you talked?"

"Right before I left rehab. I didn't have my phone in there, so I wrote her a letter and that's how we talked."

"How very Tristan and Liv of you two," Teags says and Liv lightly hits her on the arm. "Oh, what? That was like your thing in college, wasn't it?"

"Yes, but she doesn't like talking about it because of our stupid parents," Bree says as she looks at her sister. "But that was your thing."

"I know," Liv agrees, a soft smile on her face. "Have you called or texted her since you got out?"

I shake my head.

"Not at all?" Teags asks, and I stare blankly at her. "What is wrong with you?"

"What?" I defend myself. "I had a lot to work on and so did she. I wanted to give her some space. It's been a few months, and I don't want to pressure her or anything if she's not ready."

"I think a little distance is okay." Livvy calms my racing heart with just a few words. "It seems like you both had some personal stuff to work on, and distance is needed to feel like you can do that."

"Exactly," Bree agrees. "But if you do start communicating again, I would maybe take it at her pace."

"That's a good idea," my sister agrees.

"That I can do," I tell them. "But how do I keep the romance alive?"

Livvy shakes her Post-it note in the air. "That's where we come in."

"Wow," is all I say as I try to peek at the list they made, only for Liv to tuck it into her chest.

"Oh, come on," Bree says to me. "You have a romance writer and two romance readers in front of you. Of course we have a list."

I guess I can't argue with that. "Let's hear it."

"Well, you've already written letters," Liv says as her eyes move down the list.

"Make her a mixtape," Teags offers and I shake my head.

"That seems like a you kind of thing," I tell her. "I need something specific that will work for her."

"What about flowers? Those are easy to send long distances with and you can usually send little notes with them," Bree suggests, and I remember a conversation I had with her about her namesake.

"That could actually work." The plan starts to form in my head and I can't get it out as soon as I think about it. Once a week. One bouquet for her home and another for her store. Her two favorite places always have flowers in bloom for her to look at and smell. It's a good start, but I'll definitely need something bigger for when the time is right. Maybe I'll continue our letters after a few weeks of flowers. "Thank you. I owe a lot to you three if this ends up working out how I want it to."

"I'd like my thank you at your wedding," my sister says as she gets up, no doubt heading to steal some food from Vince and our mom as they cook.

"No need to thank us," Bree says. "I was happy to help when Livvy told me about your girl."

My girl. I love the sound of that.

"It's nice seeing you happy, Theo. It's nice seeing all of us happy and together. Almost whole even though nothing really ever will be." Livvy's eyes shimmer in the low light over here and I lean into her, offering my shoulder how we all do when we're struggling.

"But we have one another," I remind them.

"That we do." Bree smiles as she holds her hand out to me. "Do you want some hot chocolate?"

"I would *love* some." I smile as I head into another holiday, still missing the ones we've lost, but thankful to be surrounded by people who understand what I'm feeling.

Chapter Thirty-Nine

— HOPE UR OKAY BY OLIVIA RODRIGO

My phone buzzes as soon as I sit down on the bench Theo and I used to inhabit, and when I pull it out and look at it, a name I haven't seen in a long time pops up.

> **Grant:** Are the rumors true? Did the house across the street from you finally sell?

> **Daisy:** The rumors are true. Did your mom tell you she closed the sale?

> **Grant:** Yes! She was elated. Nobody had been able to get the owners to list. What the hell happened?

> **Daisy:** That seems like a story for another time.

> **Grant:** I miss Nettles. Maybe I'll bring my girl up soon for a visit.
>
> **Daisy:** I'm sure your mom would love that.
>
> **Grant:** How have you been doing? Still the same Daisy I grew up with or what?
>
> **Daisy:** Not quite, but when you come back, we should get together. I'd love to meet the girl who floods your social media photos. You two look perfect together.
>
> **Grant:** It wasn't always like that. We have a lot to catch up on.
>
> **Daisy:** That we do. Let me know when you're back in town.
>
> **Grant:** I'm sure you'll hear me before you even see me.
>
> **Daisy:** That is true. See you, loser.
>
> **Grant:** Bye, flowers.

I can't help but laugh at that old nickname Grant gave me when we were kids. He sat next to me in third grade when we were assigned seats, and the rest is history. He was one of my best friends up until we graduated and I never really saw him again, but we still kept in touch. He was the hotshot hockey player everyone knew as we grew up. Nettles even won the state championship during our senior year because of him, and hockey was his everything, alongside his mom.

And I'm still trying to come to terms with the fact that the house sold. I didn't believe it when the sign went up, but my heart sank as I realized what it might mean.

Until the flowers started coming.

Every week, a bouquet with a note from Theo came. The first one that showed up at my house had me confused, until I read the note.

A bouquet of daisies for my Daisy girl. One for home and one for your safe space. You'll find the other one delivered right to the store. I miss you. I'm always thinking of you.

I was smiling ear-to-ear that entire day, and when I saw the roses at my boutique, I cried. I kept crying when they kept showing up, week after week, bouquets filled my room and the desk behind the cash register at work. He always mixed one of the bouquets up every week, but the one thing that never stopped showing up was the daisies.

We haven't called or texted in months. It's been so long since I heard his voice, but the flowers kept on coming, and now this note floated into my mailbox, his handwriting all over the front of the envelope, a small heart sticker on the back of it where I'm supposed to open it.

I can't wait any longer as I carefully tear open the envelope, folded pages of paper falling into my lap as I pick them up, the stale wind hitting my face as I adjust the mittens on my hands.

Winter in Nettles hasn't been too bad yet. Snow has barely been falling, but the cold has been the worst part. The ground is frozen, as is the pond I sit next to, but this was where I wanted to open this. It feels right. It feels as if he's sitting right next to me as my eyes float through the words he wrote down and sent to me.

Dear Daisy,

I know it's been a while, but I really hope you enjoyed the flowers I sent. I've missed talking to you like this, but I wanted to give you some space in case you were still figuring things out. I've been through a lot in these past few months, lots of changes and mindset shifts, and I know how difficult it can be to do that with something tethered to you, so I hope I made the right decision for you, for us, I guess.

If that still exists, us, I would love to hear from you, but all of this is up to you. Whenever you are ready is how long I'll wait for a letter or a text back. I have my phone again since I'm out of rehab and home, so you can call me if that's something you're interested in. I've been sober for over a hundred days. I forget exactly how long it's been, but the app I have helps me to keep track. I've been going to meetings once a week since I got out, and I'll tell you, talking to people who understand what I've been going through is actually helpful. Nobody is judging me because they've all had similar thoughts and done similar things, and it's a true safe space for me. Journaling has also been crucial for my recovery. It helps my thoughts seem a lot less scary if I'm simply writing the words down and physically seeing them on the page. Bree gifted it to me at Christmas and I've already filled a ton of the pages.

> All that is to say I've learned a few different ways to climb the tree, and I'm hoping when I get down, you'll be at the bottom, if you still want that.
>
> I have the same number I've always had, and I can't wait to hopefully hear all about what you've been up to back in Nettles. I miss it up there, and you can even tell Delilah I've had dreams about her maple ice cream. I don't know why it doesn't taste the same down here, but I'm starting to think she has some sort of magic touch.
>
> I look forward to seeing your handwriting, or seeing your name pop up on my phone, or hearing your voice. I'll take any part of yourself you want to give me, honey.
>
> I hope you liked the daisies too. I know you once told me daisies grow tall and can't hold themselves up when they wilt, but all I see when I look at you is the strongest, most beautiful flower in the bunch. I hope you see yourself like that, or are on the way to, because in every garden, or every field, I'll always choose you.
>
> Love,
> Theo

God, I've missed him. I've tried not to think about him, really, I have, but it hasn't really worked. It doesn't help that every inch of Nettles reminds me of him or something we did, but I've also taken a lot of time for myself.

I've started a new routine and it has helped me come back to myself, or at least come back to the version I want to be. A healthy one. One that isn't afraid of looking at herself in the mirror in fear of what she might see, or what her brain might trick her into seeing.

I'm going for more walks, spending more time in nature and feeling the sun on my skin, at least when it's out. Now that it's winter, I've moved inside and have been starting every morning with stretches and mindful meditation. The thing that has helped the most has been reframing my thoughts. Delilah actually recommended it. She told me to start talking to myself as if I was talking to a friend, and that has done wonders. I would *never* talk to my friends the way I talked to myself, and something as simple as that has helped to reframe my mind. No longer am I going right to something negative when I think about myself.

Sometimes, it is still hard to look in the mirror, but lately I've started leaving Post-it notes all over my house with small phrases and affirmations to remind myself I'm doing the best I can. Even just those notes I leave for myself—sometimes Delilah sneaks a few all over my new apartment—have helped my thoughts immensely. I love myself as much as I can, and on the days I'm struggling, the reminders on my mirror help to bring me back to better thoughts.

I'm not perfect with it. I still have thoughts that can overwhelm me and set me back in my journey, but now, I've found an easier way out of them. I've found my own way to tread water and get back to shore easier than I used to. I'm not always at the shore, though. I've come to think about my journey in waves. I used to be drowning and nobody could see it. Some days, I got to shore on my own, and then waded back out to sea where the current would take me. Now, most of the time, I can feel my feet on the ocean floor, and I can stay here for a while, knowing I can feel what's beneath my feet.

It seems like that's what Theo has been doing, too, and I'm really proud of us both for doing what we said we would. It seems like it's helped him, and my time alone has surely helped me through some of the things I thought would drown me.

I grab my phone, ripping a mitten off and swiping to his contact, pressing the button to call him as fast as I can. He answers almost immediately.

"Hi," is all I say when he picks up.

"God, I've missed your sweet voice," he groans over the phone. "Hi there, honey."

I can't help the smile that bursts from my face as I hear his voice over the phone. "You sound good."

"Happy New Year," he says, and I can tell he's feeling a little shy. It has been a while since we spoke to one another.

"You know that was weeks ago, right?" I cross my legs, getting more comfortable on the bench as I watch people go in and out of stores on Main Street. "But Happy New Year to you too. Here's to new beginnings."

"What's your mantra for this year? Mine is 'I am strong and I am capable.'"

I smile to myself. "You absolutely are."

"Thanks," he whispers. "Do you have one?"

I sit and think to myself, really wondering what I want to bring into this year so it's different than the last. "What is done with love is done well."

"Oh." Surprise laces his voice. "Did you just quote Van Gogh?"

"I did. It felt fitting, you know?" I laugh to myself. I *knew* he would know that quote. "Delilah wanted me to watch a documentary with her about him the other day. It was really cool."

"That sounds fun."

"It was."

The silence is comfortable for a few moments, the words we aren't saying hang in the air, and I'm not sure if he's going to bring it up or if I am. He did say it was up to me in his letter.

"I have your letter here," I say before I can stop it. "And thank you for the flowers. They're beautiful and my store smells wonderful."

"Nothing is as gorgeous as you, but I wanted you to know that even from afar, I'm still thinking of you. I could *never* forget about you."

"Likewise," I tell him. "Do you think you need more time?"

"Do you?"

"I asked you first."

"That you did, honey." He laughs. "But I told you the ball was in your court. Whatever happens is all up to you. I'm not going to rush this if we're both not ready."

"Nothing is ever going to be perfect," I remind him. "I'm better, really, I am. I feel more like myself and I've taken a lot of good steps these past few months we've been apart. But I worry if we wait for things to be perfect, we'll always be stuck waiting."

"I'd wait forever for you, but if I don't have to, then I'll see you soon."

"Are you serious?" I sit up, my heart starting to beat faster as I feel my eyes start to water. "You're coming back? Where are you going to stay? I mean, you sold the house, so—"

"I'll stay at Amara's or something. You saw that I sold it?"

"The sign was up and everything. The realtor you used was my friend's mom."

"Oh," he says as I hear more shuffling. "We'll figure something out. I have a few things to wrap up here, and then I'll be back, okay?"

"Okay." I can't help the excitement coursing through my veins. Theo's coming back. He's *really* coming back. "I guess I'll see you soon."

"Damn right," he chuckles through the phone. "And Daisy girl?"

"Yeah?"

"Call me later?"

I smile up at the sky as I answer him. "Of course I will."

Chapter Forty

— **PACKING IT UP BY GRACIE ABRAMS**

"Dais, someone is moving all of the benches around the pond!" Brooks runs into my shop, and I don't even take a second to think before I'm throwing my snow boots, coat, and mittens on as I run after him on this warm winter day.

Warm being in the low forties, yet the wind is biting against my face as it hits me. I cannot believe someone would try to take the benches. Some of them even have plaques on them with dedications, and whoever it is, I'm going to be going straight to the mayor if this is really true.

The Madison family would never let this happen, so it has to be some sort of outside company or person trying to do this. But as Brooks starts to slow down, I pass him, wondering if the cold is getting to him, but when I see a familiar figure slouched against the bench, a camera against his face as he points it in my direction, I can't help but smile.

I look back at Brooks, Eloise settling into his side as he waves at me.

"You little liar," I shout at him.

"Got you out of the store, didn't I?" He shrugs as Eloise leads him back to the bar.

I can't help but smile as I see Theo, his camera still against his face as I hear a few clicks, my cheeks hurting from the cold wind and the smile on my face.

He's back. He came back for me, for us.

We talked last night, and he said nothing about when he was coming back. All he told me was that he was almost done wrapping up everything in Pennsylvania and he would see me soon. Soon to me is a few days or weeks, not the next day, so this is a surprise I never saw coming.

"Are you going to come and kiss me or what, Daisy girl?" he shouts as I start running again, this time toward him, and he takes a few photos before he sets his camera down on the bench, his arms open wide for me as I crash into him.

"I missed you," I say into his jacket. "Eek! I didn't know you were coming today."

"It was a surprise." He laughs. "And I hope it was a good one."

"The best one," I say as I look up at him, my lips connecting with his as soon as they can. My nose is cold against his face, but his kiss spreads a warmth all through my body as he embraces me, his arms getting tighter around me as if he's worried this may be a dream he'll soon wake up from. "I'm so glad you're back."

"Me too." His hold tightens on me again. "God, I can't believe I'm feeling you beneath my hands."

The two of us laugh into one another, and as I stare into his eyes, I don't see anything dark anymore. No longer is there blue behind those brown eyes of his. I only see him. Just Theo and the boy I used to know.

"I missed you, and you look amazing."

"I'm better now that I'm holding you." He scoops me up and sets us on the bench we always sat on, another kiss against my nose, cheeks, forehead, and lips. "My Daisy girl."

I can't help but smile as I nestle into his chest.

"I don't even know what to talk about or where to start."

He laughs at me, my hands going right to his cheeks. "I have one."

"Go ahead, baby," I tell him as he hands me a small jar with a paper bouquet in it. My heart beats out of my chest as I graze the beautiful gift he made for me. "Were the thousands of other real flowers not enough for you?"

"Not even close," he tells me. "And while I love real flowers, those die. These never will. Just like my love for you."

My hands stop as soon as I hear that word.

"I love you, Dais. So much that it feels like my heart might explode when I'm without you."

Tears start to flow as I think about how I was so close to giving up on love way back when, and then he came out of nowhere when I was supposed to be focusing on myself. It didn't start as love, not even close. He was a childhood friend, one I hadn't seen in so long. Then we got intertwined, and maybe became friends—with some benefits. Neighbors with benefits, one might say? But love was there all along, hiding as a thousand different things like breakfast in the morning. Pictures sneakily taken when he thought I didn't notice. Puzzles and candles at night before bed. Letters sent back and forth because we couldn't bear not to talk. Every time he asked me to explain my makeup routine in the morning because he just wanted to hear me talk. Riddles trying to be solved over ice cream at Delilah's. Chases through the grass when we were kids. Laughing on the swing set as we each tried to get higher than the other. Playing hopscotch on the sidewalk.

All of that was love hiding in plain sight.

"I love you too," I whisper to him as if it was floating in the wind. "I'd love to hold you every morning forever."

"Sounds good to me, honey." He presses another kiss to my lips, this kiss sweet and leaving me wanting more. "I love you *so* much. Thank you for being my reason when I wake up every morning. Thank you for waiting for me."

"Thank you for everything," I tell him because everything encompasses all of the things he's done for me. He helped me through the worst feelings about myself. He knew when to leave when we both needed a minute to sort through our shit. He knew when to come back. He's everything to me, and I'm thanking every star in the sky that I knocked on the door when I was a kid and introduced myself to the new family across the street. "I can't believe you're here."

"I'll never leave you again."

"Promise?"

His forehead connects with mine. "I promise."

My eye catches on the new, shiny gold plaque on the back of the bench. "What's that?"

"Oh, you know," he shrugs his shoulders. "Consider it another promise."

My eyes water as I read the plaque, Theo's cold hands coming to my face as he wipes my tears away.

For Daisy.
For all of our chats here—past, present, and future. May we water the flowers our life brings us.
I love you.

"You did all of this for me?"

"I'd do anything for you, Dais. This is just a fraction of what you deserve." He adjusts me on his lap. "Do you know what I've been struggling with?"

"What?"

"An answer to what happens at the end of all this." He gestures to the world around us. "Since Tobias died, it's all I've wanted to know."

"What have you discovered in your time away?" I ask, knowing he's not telling me something.

"There is no answer," he smirks at me. "But there is you, and that's the best answer I could ask for."

"What do you mean?"

"I realized there will always be so many things I'll wonder about. I'll always wonder why my brother died. I'll always wonder what space looks like, and what happens when you die, but I realized for all I don't know, there is something I'll always know, and that something is you. You will always be the answer for me. You will always be the person who knows me and who I know completely because you are a cool breeze on a warm day. You'll always be the first fall of snow, and every time I run out of road, you will always be at the end of it, telling me there's another way we can go together. I love you, and I'll always have all I need or want when I hold you in my arms."

I can barely breathe through my tears. "I love you so much." I burrow into his chest again, and he holds me as I squeeze him tightly, loving the feel of him and not caring if we look insane to anyone walking by.

"What should we do now?" he asks me.

"I want to stay like this forever."

He only laughs, and that sound brings me right back to when we were kids, the echoes of who we were surrounding us. It's as if I can hear my younger self knocking on the door of his house. "We can stay like this as long as you want. Eloise is covering the store for you."

"You really thought of everything, didn't you?"

"Of course I did."

"Can we go for a walk?" I ask him, his eyes gaze into mine with some shine.

"I was hoping you would say that." He picks me up, sets me down, and his hand slips into mine as he grabs his bag and the two of us walk around Nettles how we used to. The path in front of us never-ending as I smile at the man whose hand is in mine.

We're home. I'm home.

Forever sounds heavenly with Theo walking next to me.

"Was today better than yesterday?" he asks as I nuzzle into his side.

"Every day is better than yesterday now that my hand is in yours."

Chapter Forty-One

— I'VE SEEN IT BY OLIVIA DEAN

"This is terrifying," I say as we walk up the small path to the front door. "Am I overdressed? Did I overdo it on the makeup? God, why did I choose to do a smoky eye—"

"Honey." Theo grabs my hand and turns me to face him. "You look as beautiful as you always do, and don't be scared. They're all going to love you because you love me. That's about the only criteria we have here."

"Really?"

"And they know how much I adore you and worship the ground you walk on. I think they're mostly excited to see what you see in me."

I adjust the cardigan on my shoulders as he takes my other hand in his. "You're not just saying this to make me feel better?"

"No." He smiles at me. "All they know about you is that I love you. No specifics. You can share however much or little about your life and your past that you want to. It's all on your terms."

Hearing that makes my heart beat faster in my chest. I love how thoughtful my man is, and he always knows exactly what to say to calm me down.

I take a deep breath before he raises his fist to the door, knocking twice before he opens it, a warm gust of air enveloping me as I slip my shoes off. I thought we were going to get swarmed by the door, but it looks like that isn't the case. I hear whispers and voices further inside the house, but just for these few seconds, it's the two of us. He slides my coat off of my shoulders and puts it in the small closet by the front door before he takes my hand and leads me into the house.

"Well, it's about damn time," someone says as they bring him in for a hug. I think that's his brother. The two of them have the same exact facial features—same face shape, same eyes, the only stark difference I see is Theo's mustache. Someone taps me on the arm as I stop staring at them like a creep.

"Hi," she says, a bright smile on her face. "I'm Olivia, Tristan's wife, but all of my friends call me Livvy."

"It's nice to meet you, Livvy," I say as I hold my arms open and we hug.

"Theo has told us absolutely nothing about you. I'm excited to get to know the girl he's been swooning about since he came back."

"Swooning is the nice way of saying it." Theo smirks. "It was more mopey."

"Sorry if we come on a little strong," a blonde woman says as she slides next to her. "We're just a little excited Theo has finally found someone. I'm Bree."

"Oh, you're her sister." I smile, remembering them from the letters Theo sent me while we were apart.

She leans her head on her sister's shoulder. "That I am."

"Angel." Another man comes up to her. "Are you feeling okay?"

"Vince, she's fine. You're hovering. Stop hovering," a familiar face from childhood pops into my head. This has to be his sister. Her hair is darker than I remember, and I don't think she had glasses when we were little, but those eyes are telling me all I need to know. "I know we're about twenty years older than the last time I saw you, but hi. Teagen."

"I remember you." I smile, loving the familiar faces even though it's been a while. "Are you still carrying around headphones and a CD player?"

"That she is," another man says from next to the boys. There are *so* many people here, but for some reason, I don't feel nervous or crowded. It feels warm, inviting, and safe. This group is safe, and you can tell that's how they all feel when they're together. "I'm Dominic, her boyfriend and Tristan's best friend. It's nice to meet you."

"You too," I say as I wonder how *that* story played out. "It smells wonderful. Can I help with anything?"

"Absolutely not," Teagen says as she grabs my hand, pulling me over to the couch. "In fact, all of the boys are going to help Mom with dinner while we sit and talk with some wine. Does that sound okay to you?"

Theo looks at me, a smile on his face I've never seen before, and I already know which smile of his it is.

He's home. He's with his family even though there are less people than there should be, but he's okay. This space he has with these people is enough for him, and it's enough for me.

"That sounds perfect." I smile as I take a seat, one of the boys handing us all a glass.

"Thanks, baby," Bree says, and I assume that's her husband. Theo told me Bree is a huge influencer and she married her bodyguard. When he said that I literally thought of about ten different movies and books I've read. I've never heard of her, but I have read one of her sister's books. I didn't know Theo was technically related to her until he saw me packing it in one of our moving boxes. His face got all giddy as he explained that he knew her and he even told me the story about why she wrote it. It was adorable, and I love how involved they all are in one another's lives. They remind me a lot of the people I love back home.

"So, Daisy." Teagen crosses her legs as she gets comfortable. "My brother tells me you're a makeup artist."

"No way!" Bree's eyes light up as she looks at me. "I've worked with a few makeup artists on shoots and stuff. The magic you all create always astonishes me."

I can't help but smile. "I am. I don't have a very extensive client list besides some people back home, but I am. I used to work on photoshoots and featurettes and stuff in Boston, but when I moved back to Nettles, I downsized a lot."

I thought I was going to be a lot more nervous, but I'm not. Even though Theo's watching the four of us intently from the kitchen, this space with these women feels safe, and I'm really excited to get to know them better.

"Nettles sounds beautiful." Bree's face lights up. "I'd love to come and visit you two up there."

"I always knew he'd end up back there," Teagen says. "He was always begging Mom to go back."

"What made you move back home? I'm not a city girl myself, so I can understand leaving a big one like Boston for a more quiet town." Livvy smiles as she sips her glass.

"I got divorced," I say, and after a few quiet beats of silence, I think I might have made things *really* weird, until Teagen speaks up.

"Was he a piece of shit?"

"The biggest." I can't help but laugh. "He stole my company from me."

"Shut up." Bree's eyes widen. "No he did not!"

"He did." I run a hand through my hair. "But it's fine. All's well that ends well, right?"

Livvy turns to the two of them. "We should have Nico or Dom bankrupt him or something."

"Oh, Dommy would be all for that. We all know how much he fucking enjoys it," Teagen says, rolling her eyes into her glass.

"I think Nico has already helped me where my ex is concerned," I can't help but giggle. "You all are funny. Theo neglected to mention that."

"Well, that's rude of him," his sister says. "I think we're hilarious."

"Especially when there's wine involved," Livvy says. "Well, it's his loss and our gain."

Bree raises her glass between the bunch of us. "To new friends."

We all raise them together, a loud clink echoing through the living room as Theo's eyes pierce mine.

"Are you okay?" he mouths to me.

I can only nod back at him. I'm more than okay. I'm *perfect*. This place reminds me of home, and I can't believe Theo's leaving this all behind to start a life with me in Nettles, but I know for certain we're going to be taking lots of trips back down here.

I can already feel this place sinking into my bones, and I never want that feeling to leave.

Dinner comes and goes with delightful conversation, bunches of stories traded back and forth, and I've officially been added to the group chat the girls have. We're all huddled in the living room, Theo's Mom already upstairs in bed, and I can't help but feel like all eyes are on Theo and I.

The fire is crackling as we all enjoy one another's company. It's quiet and peaceful, and I can't help but get emotional thinking about Theo leaving this group of people and moving to Nettles with me.

"So, have you two closed on the house yet?" Tristan asks us, his arm comfortably around his wife.

"Not yet," Theo says as I try to hide my emotions. I *just* met these people, most of them for the first time. I cannot cry in front of them already. "We're still waiting to hear if our offer was accepted, but I think we have a really good chance."

"Those pictures you sent us were perfect." Bree sighs. "A house in the mountains away from everything is my ideal living situation."

"I'll get right on that, angel," Vince says, the rest of them laughing at how willing he is to do that for her. Their adorable dog is sleeping on the floor next to them, her tongue sticking out as she snuggles up to Bree's legs. "If you need any security cameras, Nico and I wouldn't mind coming up there and setting a system up for you."

"Actually, that would be awesome. I've been meaning to ask you about that, but I haven't seen Nico in a while. Is he doing okay or just busy?" Theo asks.

"He's been pretty busy. I haven't seen him in a few weeks, but we have a meeting scheduled for next week. As soon as you close, let me know your address and the property specs and I'll get something ready for you."

"Thank you," I tell him. "With my ex-husband, you really never know. I'll sleep better at night knowing we have a good system set up."

"If you need me to station someone in Nettles, let me know. I have plenty of guys ready and willing."

"Oh, wow." I can't help the laughter that bubbles up. "That's so fancy."

"Pardon my husband," Bree says. "He can't ever quit the work talk."

"I can't wait to come and visit you all up there," Teagen says. "Maybe we could get a place up there. Oh! Or maybe we could franchise the store up there!"

"Easy, girl," Dominic says to her. "Let's take a look at the numbers after the first year before we jump the gun."

"I know," she says, taking a sip of her wine. "It would be fun, though."

"Of course it would be." He presses a kiss to her forehead. "And if it would make you happy, I'd do it in a heartbeat."

Tristan and Theo both groan at the same time.

"Something to say, idiots?" she asks her brothers.

"Nope." Theo clears his throat before he looks over at me. "Nothing at all."

"Be nice," I remind him.

"Listen to your girl," Teagen says as she flips him off. "You too, asshole."

"I'll never be used to it," Tristan shivers.

"Daisy, are you okay?" Bree asks me, and I turn to her, not able to stop the stray tear from falling from my eye.

"I'm perfect," I say as Theo wipes it away. "I just hate that Theo's coming back with me and won't be surrounded by all of you."

"Oh, you won't have to worry about that," Livvy says to us. "We bought the house in Nettles."

"Are you serious?" her sister says, pummeling Liv in a hug. "Oh my goodness! Family trips up to Vermont are *so* going to be a new tradition for us."

"You were the ones who bought it?" Theo is as surprised as I am. "I guess this is what happens when I don't want to know who I'm selling to."

"Congratulations," I say as my heart starts to beat faster. "You're going to love it up there."

"And consider us your tour guides for all the best spots," Theo says. "My girl is an expert."

"Thank you," I say. "I cannot wait to introduce you to my family up there. Oh, especially Delilah. She's going to *love* you all. You'll get free ice cream and coffee anytime you go in, and don't even try to pay her."

"Ice cream?" Dominic asks. "She has an ice cream shop?"

I nod.

"Oh, fuck yes. There is *nothing* better than free ice cream."

"I second that." I smile at him. "This is so exciting."

"And you don't have to worry about Theo leaving us," Tristan says to me. "I'm actually surprised the fucker is settling down somewhere after floating around the country with no specific home to come back to. It seems like he's found that in you and in Nettles. I couldn't be happier for the both of you."

"I appreciate that more than you'll ever know," I say as my throat closes up.

"Take it from us." Liv grabs her sister's hand. "Home isn't always a place. More often than not, it's the people in your life that make the word home have meaning. Bree and I learned that when we intertwined with the West family."

"And thank goodness for that," Teagen says. "I can't imagine a life without you all."

"I have an idea." Bree sits up on her knees, Nellie adjusting with her, and she looks to her husband. "Vince, what's your idea of home?"

I see where she's going with this already.

"Cutting strawberries in the kitchen." He smiles at her, and I wish I had the context to that. It sounds so simple coming out of his mouth, but I know there's meaning underneath. "What about you, angel?"

"Throwing eggs at the tree with my sister." She starts to get emotional, but grabs her sister's hand to steady her. "And now all of you who have done that with us since we snuggled into this family."

"What about you, Liv?" Vince asks her.

"Watching the sunsets every night."

"You stole mine, pretty girl," he tells her as he searches his head for another answer. "Home is the table we all just sat around, no matter where it may be."

"And you, Teags?" Bree asks her best friend.

"Wherever the music is." She looks to her boyfriend.

"Home is in your arms, baby," he tells her as he looks at Tristan. "And it's also in our last college apartment."

"Damn right it is," he agrees.

"What about you, Theo?" his sister asks him. "Where's home for you?"

"Nettles, obviously." Everyone laughs a little. "But that feels like cheating, so home is everywhere for me, I think. It's in the clouds I used to stare at with Tobias, and the puzzles we used to do. It's here in this house where we all grew up. It's the backyard I'm staring at where we used to run around when Dad was still around. Home is everywhere, and I think that's why I never wanted to settle down. I always thought I was stuck between two places, here and Vermont, but lately I've come to realize home has been everywhere with me, and I carry it in my heart and through the pictures I take with my camera."

"That's beautiful," I say, more tears coming.

"Where's home for you, Dais? Can I call you that?" Livvy asks me, her eyes glistening with tears as well.

"Of course you can." I giggle, my cardigan sleeve wiping my tears. "Home is the place I feel most like myself. Lately, it's been with you," I gaze at Theo. "But right now? Home is here, if I can jump the gun a little and say that. Never in my life have I felt more welcomed in a space than tonight, so thank you for allowing me to have a glimpse into your home life for even just a little bit."

"There's plenty more of this in the future, Daisy," Teagen tells me.

"Oh, absolutely," Liv and Bree agree with her.

I don't know how I ever thought love had disappeared. Maybe it was just waiting a moment to get back to me, but how can something like love disappear when I've seen it everywhere. In people, in things, in gestures, it always exists, and tonight is the perfect example of that. I should have known love has been inside of me all along, and even when I didn't feel it, it was still there. I didn't have to search for it or worry about it disappearing completely because it never will. Not with people like this around me. Not with the home Theo and I are going to create. Not with the ones we've already created.

I hope when I grow old, I don't forget these moments—the ones with new beginnings. I want to remember them, cherish them, water them so they bloom into beautiful things because life can hurt and love can bring out the absolute worst, but it can also do the opposite. It can help, and bring out the best. It can survive months apart and the worst things imaginable.

When I went back to my hometown, I thought that was it for me. I thought the one true love of my life was all I was going to get. I should have known life had more in store for me than someone who spent so much time making me feel small and unappreciative of what I have to offer.

Because this man next to me with these people around me have already made my heart grow about ten sizes just in a few hours. That's what love is, despite it all, and I'm lucky enough to have found it again.

My road has not run out, in fact, it's just beginning, and isn't that the best thing about roads?

There will always be another one that pops up when you least expect it, waiting for you to drive down it and see what it has to offer. It won't all be perfect. There will be bumps and potholes and unmarked signs that lead you astray, but you'll always get where you're meant to go.

I'm sure of that now.

Chapter Forty-Two

Theo

— EVERY SIDE OF YOU BY VANCE JOY

"It's perfect," my girl says as she steps into our new house, her smile lighting up the spacious living room.

Since I sold the house across the street from her—to my brother of all fucking people—the two of us decided to start anew in a lovely, quaint house on the edge of Nettles. It's not too far away from town, so Dais can still get to the boutique in a decent time, but it's away from all the hustle and bustle.

It's perfect for us. We have our own little secluded area for us to grow and live in, and we could not be more excited. We were worried we weren't going to get it, but as soon as we got back from Pennsylvania, the call came in. Daisy said it was perfect timing, and I attributed it to this place officially welcoming me home.

Either way, I am so glad this worked out for us. I can see us here for a long time. The first time we toured this place, I could almost see me carrying her through the door, a white dress on as she kissed me. I could see our lives playing out so fucking beautifully, and I have to remind myself to savor the now and not think too far ahead.

One day at a time has been my mantra since I started going to meetings and it's helped me more than I thought it ever would.

"It's even more beautiful with you in it," I tell her. Dais has been packing up all of her things from home, and even some stuff she left at Delilah's during their many sleepovers. "I'm so excited for this next chapter, honey."

"Me too." She sets the box down and comes over to me, throwing her arms around me as she presses a kiss to my neck. "What time did everyone say they were coming over?"

"Sometime in the afternoon," I say as I pick her up, carrying her to the counter in our kitchen, needing her in my space even more than she is. I can't get enough of her. Ever since I came back to Nettles, we haven't spent a night apart. I was staying at the hotel for a little while until Elliott offered his spare space for me to stay in, for a decent price. It was the perfect space I needed while we looked for a house, and luckily, this one came on the market only a few weeks after.

I'd describe this house as like a cottage, a small house at the edge of town with a stunning view of the mountains around us. Though, I'm more focused on the view of her in front of me. Every day, I wake up sighing with how stunning she feels against me, wrapped in my arms and wearing my shirt as a dress, her fuzzy socks still on her feet from the night before.

"We really have to get our stuff in here so they can help us unpack," she reminds me, but I'm not fully listening to her.

"I can't enjoy my astonishing girlfriend in our new house? What happened to christening every corner of it?"

"I meant that." She glides her hand across the back of my neck and down my collarbone. "But not when we're about to have a bunch of our friends in our house helping us get settled when they could be spending their time doing anything else."

"Oh, come on, honey," I say as I tease her through her shorts. "I can make it quick."

"What about you?"

"Don't worry about me," I say. "Seeing you unravel and moan my name on this counter is going to be perfect."

"Well, I can't say no to that," she says as she leans back on her elbows and I slide her shorts and underwear off, needing a taste of her. "But if anyone shows up, you better stop. You know I'm not good at hiding my..."

"Your screams? Sounds? Moans and groans?"

"Yes," she says as my tongue licks up and down her center, her clit needing attention as I bite and suck on her, her legs squirming against my face. "God, feeling your mustache never gets old."

"I love feeling you soak it," I tell her, biting her savory thighs, leaving small marks on them that drive me fucking insane. "Can you take my fingers?"

"Please," is all she says as I thrust two of them inside of her. "Just like that."

"Does my girl need more? Tell me what you want me to do to you."

She throws her head back, another loud moan coming from her lips. "Make me come, Theo."

"God, the way you say my name, honey," I say as I take her clit in my mouth. "Dripping with lust and making me want to go even harder."

"I can handle it." She smirks, my fingers driving harder into her, her cum already starting to drip out. "Shit, please don't stop."

Fuck, I feel my dick getting harder by the second. It's barely been five minutes and I can feel it start to throb against my jeans. Daisy always drives me fucking crazy with her teasing and her newfound confidence in the bedroom, but now all she does is make me insatiable. All I want is her. Sometimes, all I want to do is lock the two of us in a room and make her feel good all day long, not giving a single fuck about my release.

But now, it's different. She's going to be mine forever, and for some reason, it takes way less to get me off.

"Theo! Please," she begs me to get her off, her moans echoing off of the walls of our new home.

"Keep screaming for me, honey," I say as I feel my own release coming, and as soon as her pussy clenches around my fingers, I'm falling over the edge, too, my cum spilling into my underwear as her sweet voice chants my name over and over again. "Fuck, you taste so fucking sweet. Please keep coming."

"Yes, Theo, yes," more chants and groans before she finally relaxes against the counter, and I lick up the remains of her orgasm, loving how my face and fingers smell like her. I lick my fingers clean before I offer her a hand up. She looks fucking divine, her hair a mess, her clothes sprawled all over the floor.

"I've never seen a prettier sight," I say as I breathe heavily. "You did so good for me, Daisy girl."

"Seems like you did too." She smirks, knowing I came too. "That was hot, you know."

"What? The fact that I can't fucking control myself around you?"

"Mhm, and hearing you moan into me is something I fucking love." She hops off of the counter, pressing a long kiss to my lips. "You taste like me."

"You're driving me mad. I came in my fucking pants without you touching me," I groan as she giggles up the stairs. "I need new fucking pants and underwear."

"I'll hand wash those later since we don't have a washer or dryer until tomorrow."

"Thanks, honey," I say as I head to our bedroom, boxes everywhere just like the bottom part of the house.

As soon as I change, I can't help but sit on our mattress, our bed frame in one of these boxes still waiting to be set up. I look out of the window, the view of the mountains and the sun streaming into the room, and I'm so excited to wake up to this every morning. I'm excited to wake up to her in my arms. For the first time ever, I don't feel torn between two places. In my bones, I can feel that I'm meant to be exactly here, in this place, in this bed, with the girl of my fucking dreams in the next room.

She's seen me as a kid running around the yard, growing up and making a fool of myself, and even injured from the scooters and bikes we used to ride around town, to an adult in the pit of my grief. She's been there for me through all of it, and even though we spent a decade and a few months apart, she's still by my side, and I'm trying my hardest to be the man she deserves, to be the man she seems to think I already am.

I first came back to Nettles with baggage the size of a small fucking truck. I was grieving. I was angry, sad, fucking terrible to be around. I was not a good person. I was struggling and I couldn't really seem to find a way out of that. I didn't have a reason good enough to get out of it.

And then she came into my view. Daisy might have described herself as a little broken in the past, but I think her broken pieces matched mine, and together the two of us created a whole person, or maybe a whole feeling in one another that we didn't think we could mend ourselves.

Now, through a lot of fucking work and time away from one another, we're two whole people loving every part of one another. I'm no longer leaning on alcohol, and she's learning to love herself every single day while I try my hardest to prove to her that she's enough for me simply by existing.

I leave her Post-it notes everywhere. I write notes on the mirror while she's showering so she sees it when she gets out. She tries to walk with me in the mornings and talk about our day, and I still call her when I feel the urge to drink. It has been far and few between lately since I've been talking about my grief during meetings, and both of us are happy we've found a different way to climb the tree of life that we're creating together.

A new branch has come onto it, one that we can climb together. No longer is she waiting for me at the bottom, watching me struggle and waiting for me to fall so she can catch me. We're climbing it together, hands intertwined and smiling as we figure out the best way to break through the leaves and meet the sunlight.

"You okay?"

There she is. My sunlight. My reason. My Daisy. My girl forever, if she'll have me for that long.

"I'm more than okay."

"I heard a car door shut," she tells me, sitting next to me on our bed, her head on my shoulder. "Are you ready for the chaos?"

"I'm ready for anything now that you're by my side."

"Anything?" she questions.

"Anything," I remind her. "I love you, Daisy like-the-flower."

"I love you, too, Theo-not-like-the-flower." She stands holding her hand out to me. "Are you ready for this next chapter?"

"It's going to be the best one yet," I assure her. "And do you want to know why?"

"Why?" she smirks.

"Because today was better than yesterday, and all of my days will be better because you're in them." I press a kiss to her forehead. "I finally have an answer." Her eyebrows pinch. "One hundred and forty three."

She continues to stare at me.

"You have one hundred and forty three freckles on your face." I press a kiss to each of her cheeks.

"Are you watching me sleep?" she grabs my hand as I twirl her around.

"Of course I am because I can't believe you exist when you're wrapped in my arms, and I'll spend my entire life counting your freckles if it means you're waking up next to me every"—I press a kiss to her lips—"single"—another kiss—"morning."

"I wouldn't dream of anything else."

"Neither would I, honey. Now, let's go make this house our home."

"It already is a home because it has you," she reminds me. "Because home is wherever you are for me, Theo."

"And I'm never letting you go again."

"Promise?"

I press a kiss to her knuckles as I hear our friends walk through the door. "I promise."

Epilogue

The Future

— DOG DAYS ARE OVER BY FLORENCE + THE MACHINE

"What do I do now?" my daughter, Hayden, asks me, an egg in her hand as she stares at it.

"Throw it, baby," my sister says as she comes over to us. "Here, watch me, okay?"

"Okay, Auntie Teags." She watches as my sister throws it at the tree, the egg splattering against the giant tree in Bree's yard. This is one of the West family's new traditions. Every Easter—or really, whenever the eggs go bad—we save them up and chuck them at the tree. The tradition may have started between the two Hart sisters, but it's filtered into our giant extended family now.

"Wow," my daughter says as Daisy walks up to me, holding our newest little member.

"Hi, honey," I say, pressing a kiss to her and our daughter's head. "How's my little Lana doing?"

"She's fussing for her daddy," she hands her to me, our little one bundled up since it's still a bit cold out.

"Daddy, look!" My son comes over, egg all over his hands as he shows them to me. "I picked one up to hand it to Tobias and it exploded!"

"Wow, that's cool, buddy." I can't help but laugh.

"I wanted to eat it, but he told me it's not cooked so it would give me a tummy ache."

"And he would be right." My brother comes over, a few eggs in his hands as he looks at his son. "Tobias has a special egg hunt planned for you all, so why don't you head on over to him and make sure your listening ears are on."

"Okay, Uncle Tris," Cameron says as he heads for his cousins, and I swear, it gets harder and harder to keep track of all of us as we keep growing. I thought I knew chaos when it was just one kid, but three kids later for Daisy and I has been the most fun and rewarding thing of my life.

When Cameron was born, I freaked out. I was the world's craziest helicopter parent because what do you mean I'm in charge of this tiny human who has the smallest toes and fingers I've ever seen? I'm still like that, always worried I'm doing the wrong thing and fucking everything up, but Tristan and my wife have helped to ease that for me. All of us boys, besides Dom, have had the parent freak out. It's different for each of us, but we're all here to help one another through it. Dom still has his pet fish, but every time one of us freaks about doing the wrong thing, he's always cheering us on from the sidelines. The other day, I freaked about Hayden scraping her knee when I was watching her. I took my eye off of her for two seconds as I tried to load my film into my camera, wanting to capture everything I can about their childhoods, and she fell.

I freaked out at our poker night we have every Friday. Vince and Tris know how fucking hard it is, but the reassurance from Dom always makes me feel better. He may not have kids, but he watches us with ours, and he's the perfect outside presence to calm my anxiety.

I always thought the phrase saying it takes a village was full of shit, but it really does, and I'm glad to have the village around me that I do. Not only the one back here in Pennsylvania, but the one we have in Nettles too.

The group of us stands from afar, watching the next generation we've created sit in a circle and listen to Tristan's oldest, Tobias, lay out the rules for the egg hunt, his twin sister, Tahlia, right beside him. Every Easter before dinner, we throw the colored eggs at the tree and then the egg hunt begins. In some of the eggs—in true Tobias fashion—we've hidden pieces of a small puzzle. Whoever gets the most pieces, wins the golden egg.

It's our way of trying to keep Tobias's memory alive, and we want all of the kids to know who their uncle was when he was still here. I know Tristan talks a lot about him to his kids, and I've even heard Teags doing the same when I take my family to her store to walk around. Teags kept pointing out his favorite records to listen to, and I watched in awe as Cameron asked her a bunch of questions about what Uncle Tobias was like.

I wish he was here to see the giant family we've created. He would have loved the chaos and the children running around with Vince and Bree's dogs. It's days like these where I miss him so much because he never got to see us all grow up. We're all older now than he'll ever be, but I know we're all going to make sure he's never forgotten. It's our job as his siblings to keep his memory alive, and we've tried our best to do so.

I know he'd be proud of us. I know wherever he is, he's smiling and probably telling our father how one of Tristan's kids was named after him. Hell, I'm sure he's bragging up a storm.

"How are you feeling?" my wife asks me as she taps our newborn on the nose.

"I'm okay," I tell her. "Haven't felt the urge."

"That's good, honey," she says. I had a few slip-ups with alcohol after Daisy and I figured things out, but when we got married and had kids, I made a vow to her that I would never touch a drop again, and I've kept my promise. Grief and addiction is never a linear thing, and she knew that, but I hated feeling like I let her down.

Never again is what I told her the night before we got married, and I've kept that vow since our first kiss as a married couple.

"God, they grow up way too fucking fast," Tristan says as he slides up next to me. "Tucker is about to fucking lap me around the bases."

"Well, you are getting old, Tris." Teags comes over to us. "A little too old to still be running around the bases."

"Oh, come on." He pokes us with his elbows. "What kind of coach would I be if I didn't run the bases?"

"You would still be a great one," Livvy says as she hands him a glass of water. "But maybe slow down on the running. You already have arthritis in both of your knees."

"See?" Dom says with a smirk. "We're all getting really fucking old."

"Speak for yourself," Vince says as he and Bree join us. "I told you all to workout with me every morning, but none of you wanted to."

"Forgive me if I enjoy the very little sleep I get," I tell him.

"Even you've had to cut it down a little," Bree reminds him. "And let's stop using that word to describe ourselves. We're timeless, remember?"

"I like that," Teags thinks to herself. "Timeless."

"What do you say while Tabitha watches the kids do the hunt, we keep throwing eggs?" Daisy says.

"Oh, you read my mind," Livvy says, already handing us all an egg from the remaining cartons. "I want to switch it up this time."

We're all confused, but Tristan laughs as soon as she pulls out a marker from her pocket.

"Remember this?" she asks him, knowing he already does. "Everyone take an egg and write something on it that you want to solidify forever, and even after the egg is crushed, whatever you write will forever be remembered because this tree will stand tall long after we're gone."

"This is a little different than last time you handed me a marker for this tradition," Tristan laughs.

She writes hers down and hands it to Tristan, the rest of us following suit as we hand the marker around the circle we're created. We take turns showing each other what we wrote.

Livvy wrote sunsets.

Tristan wrote oranges.

Bree wrote peace.

Vince wrote family.

Teags wrote music.

Dom wrote Teags's name.

Daisy wrote love.

And me? I wrote Tobias's name with the world puzzle underneath it.

"Are you ready?" Liv asks. "Let's throw them at the same time."

"Wait," is all I say before we throw. "Can I say something first?"

"The grass is yours," Dom jokes with me.

"Without you all, I wouldn't be here. I'm sure of that, and I know every Thanksgiving we sit around a table and say what we're thankful for, but today, I wanted you to know that I'm grateful we're all still here. We've had some tough moments, more than anyone can really count, and I've struggled my entire life trying to stand on my own two feet." I look down at my daughter, wondering if Tobias hadn't led me back to Nettles all those years ago if I would be here now. I don't think I would. "I just want to thank you for sticking by me, us, all of you." My eyes find Daisy's, Dom's, Vince's, and Livvy's. "From the West family to all of you, I can confidently say that you four saved our lives after what happened."

"I second that," Teags says, grabbing Dom's hand in hers.

"Me too," Tristan's eyes fill with tears. "I don't know where we would be without you."

"We were all drowning at some point in our lives," Bree sniffles. "And you all pulled us to shore."

"You treaded water enough for us to be able to get to you," Daisy reminds us. "That's a feat in itself."

"We're always proud of you," Livvy reminds us. "So fucking proud."

"I just want to say thank you for everything one more time," I tell them. "I wouldn't be here without you all in some capacity. I wouldn't be holding my daughter if I kept down the road I was on before everything changed. I once thought I was running out of the road ahead of me, but shit, look at all the things I've seen since that moment of uncertainty."

"I thought I ruined my life when I was grieving," Teags says. "But sometimes it takes a little fucking up to realize the road to ruin was actually the right one you had to head down, and yes, I will put a five in the swear jar."

We all laugh, we can't help it. Dom and Teags are the ones who are constantly filling that jar up.

"You ruined me, baby," Dom tells her. "And I never want to go back to who I was before you came into my life."

She only smirks at him, the two of them telepathically communicating with one another or whatever they do.

"I thought I had it all figured out," Bree says. "And then I realized the road I was traveling down was one I had never taken before." Her eyes turn to Vince. "With you, that road was less scary than it could have been."

"I only accompanied you, angel. You're the strongest person I know."

"I love you," she says as he presses a kiss to her forehead.

"And us, pretty girl," Tristan wipes a tear away. "Fuck you, Theo, for making us take a walk down memory lane."

Well, that's another ten to the swear jar. "I'm not even close to feeling sorry," I laugh.

"You grabbed me off of the road I was on, grieving and full of anger, and pulled me onto a road I had never taken before. A brighter one. One full of color like I had never seen before. Thank you will never feel like enough."

"It's been my honor walking alongside life with you, Tris." She smiles, and he looks at her as if she hung the moon especially for him. "Now, can we get to throwing or are we going to keep standing here crying?"

"Sorry," I say as we all spread out. "Ready?"

"Ready," everyone murmurs, and as soon as the eggs crack against the tree, we barely have time to spare before our kids come over, all of them showing us what they got.

I can't breathe with the amount of love that blankets this family we've created. I'm lucky to be living this life with these people, and I can't believe I get to watch my siblings and my best friends grow into this beautiful village we've fought hard to create.

We all may have lost people along the way, but never will they be forgotten. Tomorrow, I'm going to take my kids to see their uncle and grandpa, and we're going to say goodbye before we go back home to Nettles.

This is the life I fought for. No longer am I torn between two places, unsure of where I belong. Now, I have two homes, and so many more that I can't count. When Daisy is in my arms, that's home. When she smiles at me, our daughter in her hands, that's home. When I see my brother and sister thriving and living the life they fought for, that's home. When I see my mother laughing and playing with her grandchildren, that's home too. When I push my kids on the swing set in our yard, that's home.

I'm feeling everything I used to run from, and when I think about who I used to be, there are so many things I want to say to myself.

The one thing I repeat to myself every morning is that I survived. The feelings I once thought would drown me? The ones I was worried I'd never get out of? I survived them, and I'll spend every day thanking Daisy and the rest of my family for that because I couldn't have done it without them.

In every life, I know I'll find my way back home, in whatever form it decides to come in, but the one I'm living in now is by far my favorite.

The End.

Acknowledgements

Being an author would not be possible without the amazing people I have around me!

Lexi—For being the best PA and friend around. Your talent never ceases to amaze me every single day! My words would not shine the same without you. Thank you so much for your knowledge on Daisy and all the makeup things I asked you about. Daisy would literally not be the same if not for you. I love you so much. To the moon and Saturn, babe!

Hannah—For my beautiful covers. Your talent is out of this world. I truly don't know how you take my poorly drawn stick figure drawings and turn them into such beauty how you have for nine books—not even counting the signing exclusives you've created! I love you the mostest.

My Beta readers—Sara, Shannon, Samantha, Maggie, & Marina. You guys truly made my words shine in this one. I am so utterly grateful you took the time to dive into this story in all of its imperfect glory. This book would not be what it is today without you! This book was a feat, full of grief and mental health, and I so appreciated all of the insight you gave me on Theo and Daisy's journey. Thank you times a million.

Josh—For proving once again, I am marrying the right guy. Through all the scary feelings and doubt about myself, you're always there for me to tell me how insane I am, but also how much the world needs stories. I love you forever.

Alyssa, Taylor, Abbie, Loretta, & Sarah—For being hilarious at work, and for keeping me sane. You have no idea how much I love you. Alyssa, sorry for the playlist, and thank you for eating ice cream with me even when we're sad. Taylor, just because you would rage bait me until I put you in one of these. Abbie, for making me laugh when all I want to do is yell. Loretta & Sarah, thank you for helping to name one of the side characters, and for the laughs. I love being weird with all of you.

Kristen—My editor. Thank you for making this story shine and for reminding me how commas work. I'm so grateful for everything you did to make this one shine as much as the last one did.

E. Salvador—For everything. For the laughs, the rants, the screaming when we send character art back and forth. It is the honor of my entire life that I get to call you my friend. Your light shines so brightly that it dims out every aspect of when I feel like a failure. I love you to pieces, babe.

My therapist—Because none of these books would get written without you. You'll never see this, but thanks for moving up our sessions when I feel like an absolute failure. Being in my twenties has been a feat, yet I am thankful to have you to walk me through it and remind me that I'm a good person, even when I don't feel like it.

My agent—For believing in my stories! I can't wait to see where the future takes us! Thank you for making my dreams feel like they could be a reality in the future.

Pat—For the firefighter knowledge. When I texted you all those questions and you called me wondering why, it was funny trying to explain to you what I was doing. I appreciate every piece of knowledge you gave me about Elliott and his job, and you better believe that I'l be back asking you about a thousand more questions, LOL.

To my Smallest Man Who Ever Lived—For nothing. I hope you realize one day what a *horrible* person you are, and I hope maybe, if you ever find yourself in a bookstore, you happen to see my name on the cover of a book, and I hope you regret every single thing. I hope you realize I have become what I am in spite of you, not because of you. I know you'll never realize a thing, but just know that every horrible character I write has a piece of you in them.

To my readers—Without you, I would have nothing. Thank you for championing my stories and loving these characters so much that I decided to continue them. This duet would not exist without you all wondering about Tristan's siblings, and this entire duet was all for you. I am deeply upset that we have to say goodbye to this universe, but just know, this world and cast of characters changed my life. They carried me through my twenties and the grief of the unknown, and I'm so happy knowing they will be safe in the hands of you all. Thank you for everything, though that word never cuts it.

I hope these characters found you when you needed it because that's what they did for me. In every life, we're all watching the sunset with music playing in the background and flowers everywhere.

Also by Emily Tudor

The Grand Mountain Series:
Replaying the Game
Redefining the Rules
Reconsidering the Facts
Reconciling With the Rival
Rewriting the Story

The Hart Sisters:
The Road Not Taken
The Road Less Traveled By

The West Siblings:
On the Road to Ruin
Running Out of Road

About the author

Emily Tudor creates characters and stories about platonic and romantic love for anyone and everyone. She lives in the state of New York and loves listening to music and creating stories. She loves Marvel movies, the song *mirrorball* by Taylor Swift and buying too many books when she already has many to be read at home.

You can find her on social media at:
@authoremilytudor
www.authoremilytudor.com

www.ingramcontent.com/pod-product-compliance
Lightning Source LLC
LaVergne TN
LVHW091659070526
838199LV00050B/2214